Chapter 1

Constantly griping concerning the sweltering heat, a small handful of folk relentlessly clambered along the sturdy edge of a rugged mountain trail; knocking their way by passing clumps of fast rolling tumble weeds, they methodically plodded by Samantha Webb, leaving her almost dumbfounded. Pausing beneath the partial shade from one of the sycamore trees, she set down her cumbersome, overstuffed rucksack. Craning her neck, she marvelled towards the complex and diverse group. In awe, Samantha, invariably known as Sam, mindlessly tucked an errant strand of auburn hair behind her ear; her piercing green eyes with dancing golden flecks widened as she observed, wondering, trying to figure out who the men were, to where they were travelling. They clearing a pathway for themselves, it was perceived how a number tramped barefoot; she suppressed a giggle from behind her hand for they sported only the brief of loincloths. At the far extreme, the apparent superiors wore white cotton shirts which gleamed with a bleached splendour, their immaculate hems scarcely below their tanned knees. Those better clad likewise wore light brown sandals, similar to her own, doubtlessly crafted from calves' leather.

For ten killer miles both teams humped their own master's accumulated paraphernalia. Formerly, they valued such lucrative pilgrimages to and from the ancient city of Shiloh, yet several demonstrated those tale tell signs of advancing years; jaded, they began to hurt as would light into their dark eyes when staring directly into the sun. They, with raised volumes, speculated how their masters should, in future, employ only the youthfully robust. Even the overladen donkeys became weary under foot, their caring owners anxious to graze the beasts in green and pleasant pasture.

Hardly reticent in their protestations, the penny-a-day workers scrambled over rocky trails, frequently grabbing at either the branch of a tree or a trailing vine, just to steady themselves as their loads swayed precariously.

When the narrow route widened into a roadway, a designated silver-haired elder, the oldest son of an aged priest, paused. In a lethargic, quivering voice, he first encountered the tall, tougher master before pleading with the second; as an advocate, he required those priestly brothers' unanimous approvals, to okay some much deserved respite, merely for a while.

Threads of guilt wove themselves through Sam's conscience as she struggled to eavesdrop, trying not to miss the brothers' transient confab. The senior responded; signalling an agreement, he nodded the go-ahead. Turning, waiting for the weighty burdens to be heaved down, to be deposited upon the ground, they too dismounted, patting their stallions' necks. They settled beside a knee-deep trickling stream; running crystal clear, it became ideal for drinking, for watering their thirsty animals. Following, Sam winced at the

WAY BEYOND THE MIRAGE

A Romantic Fantasy
a novel

by

J S Lockwood

Grosvenor House
Publishing Limited

This book is published by
Grosvenor House Publishing Ltd
Link House
140 The Broadway, Tolworth, Surrey, KT6 7HT.
www.grosvenorhousepublishing.co.uk

A CIP record for this book
is available from the British Library

ISBN 978-1-78623-081-2

This book is a work of fiction. Names, characters, places and incidents are either a product of the author's imagination or are fictitiously. Any resemblance to actual people, living or dead, events or locations is entirely coincidental.

DEDICATED

to my

WONDERFUL

SONS

suddenness of the shock, it almost taking her breath away; even with her Jesus style sandals, paddling through the water under a cloudless blue sky, it became ice cold between her toes.

Resembling his big brother, the younger master possessed a darkened chin, presumably covered in a few days' rugged stubble. Slipping a little way from the older men, Sam watched him remove his tea-towel type of head gear before running his long fingers through his black wavy hair. She heard him drawing a breath before exhaling a long, lingering sigh; he declared to anyone who may listen, how he was relishing going home, to returning to some sort of daily normality.

A few of the other fellows stretched out, they, shoulder to shoulder, elbowing for shade from either an oak tree or from the dense foliages of the Eucalyptus. Those who brought along their wives, women who carried wicker laundry type baskets upon their heads, located situations within the bowels of a nearby dank cave; they tastelessly chuckled, using the ineffective excuse how the cavern's interior was cool, well away from the stinker of summer's heat. Every few yards, positioned along the irregular crags of its rocky walls and, relentlessly unable to suppress themselves, each witnessed the rigmarole of his woman hurriedly disrobing, only enough for exploration, to repossess her; none bothered a fig concerning the next couple, they boasting their performances. Their throaty sounds and gasps echoed throughout the interior, yet, indiscreet, they cared less. They simply needed to grapple with their immediate overwhelming frustrations. The younger master, anxious to spy upon them, strolled across with his own special brand of silky smoothness. Scintillating, he found it merciless to avert his eyes. The more vigorous the couples, the more agitated he became.

The senior master, having filled his cheeks with somebody else's fresh bread, planted his fists upon his own hips, throwing back his head to chuckle at him. 'Easy, son. Easy!' he exclaimed, almost as if it was a good joke.

Nevertheless, to see men's muscles rippling, to view various couples moving in unison, the younger appeared to quiver throughout his body, to imagine himself with them. For him, the torrid flirtations became the highlights of the return trips until one chunky female heard a hissing, a rattling, obviously in the tail of a venomous viper; she opened her large ember dark eyes, directing her attention to a rattlesnake slithering her way. Terrified from being bitten, everyone discontinued once they heard. For a split second or two, all remained motionless until her uncontrollably hysterical screams became thunderously deafening. The snake rattled closer. Vacating the rocky cave post-haste, the couples, first seizing their simple belongings, shot forward. Accidentally bumping into some as they dashed, they frantically raced to be first out. Samantha, sauntering around as a solitary pedestrian, became eager to procure shade; all the trees' shadows were at a premium. She, bewilderment showing in her eyes, found herself in the way of the advancing mini stampede; with her feet apart, she shifted, prancing first one way before dodging the other. One burly big bloke, he then as raw as the day he was born, snorted, impeding her pathway, clipping discomfort to one of her shoulders as he sped; for her, it became unnerving. With the chase in full swing, she previously stretched out a hand in an attempt to regain her balance; despite all, she fell prostrate, sprawling across the shingle nearing the water's edge.

Getting to her feet and swinging around, Sam heard a deep masculine voice; he, the younger of the two masters, sounded eager to discover she was all right. Previously cutting across, he rushed to help her regain a foothold to safety. Composing, she, allowing herself the weakest of smiles, made a quick introduction. 'Thanks. I'll be okay.' Sam lifted her eyes to ask: 'So, what's your name then?'

'It's Eable.'

Offering him a polite acknowledgement, Sam most of the while stared, preoccupied with the sore palm of her hand, at its slight graze near to the fleshy base of her thumb. Quickly, she moved to bend over by the clear water's edge, performing her best to rinse the hand before patting it dry against the side of her long, wrap around skirt. She hunched her left shoulder before circling it; it did not seem half as bad as she first thought. Lifting the skirt's hem with one hand, enough to peek below, she gave her knees a bit of a rub, along with a brief dusting down. She felt vulnerable with him standing too near to stare; Sam offered him an embarrassed smile, trivialising the moment of her fall.

As a kind gesture, he stretched out a hand to her, but she ignored it. 'Is there nothing I can do to help you, lovely lady?'

Screwing up her freckled nose, Sam thought. Glancing up and a little shaken from the happenings, she shook her head.

'Sam?' He stared before grinning in a disbelief. 'Isn't it a boy's name, short for Samuel?' Before she had a chance to answer, he was eyeing the gentle curvatures of her feminine frame, jesting how she was nothing like a guy. With an unusual name such as his, Sam felt he had no right to smile at hers.

Experiencing some qualms, she surmised him watching. Folding her arms across the front of her tight T-shirt, it was if she somehow became psychologically protecting her womanhood; with the slightest of affected smiles, she informed him how 'Sam' became shortened for Samantha. 'Pretty obvious, eh?'

Better than being distracted about her first name, he was wishing he could sneak a peek beneath the oddity of her westernised form of clothing, it supposing being utterly foreign to local men and women alike. 'Anyway, Sam,' Eable began, 'where have you been? Where are you off to?'

Stern, she frowned for, in her own opinion, she ought to have known from him where she was, about the immediate situation; nothing much more. To delight her dad Henry Webb, upon the conclusion of her and Paula's vacation, she ought to be able to tell him all concerning the previously planned fifteen-minute camel ride, yet Sam's time up on the beast took longer than a quarter of an hour. The trip, albeit slow, smelly and dusty was, however, an excursion he long coveted; but, Sam became uncertain concerning her then strange destination. Nevertheless, she heard tall, dark Eable prompt: 'Well, like us, are you also on your way to ancient Ramah?'

Sam stared, breathlessly repeating: 'Ancient Ramah?' After a quick chat, she understood he held the whole area in a high esteem, he informing how it was a picturesque Samaritan market town, with its main virtue being friendly folk.

'It's where my noble and high priestly family live,' he declared. 'Me, too.'

With the hint of a nod, she moved, seating herself upon a smooth flat rock, not too near to where he suddenly perched himself. 'Hmm. Perhaps, I should be on my way there?' Sam responded as she removed a facial tissue, unable to no longer resist the urge to mop the beads of perspiration from her brow. 'Phew! It's baking hot here; it's a bit like being in an oven, isn't it?'

'Probably.'

Jealous of those shading beneath the various foliages, Sam fanned herself with her floppy cotton sun hat, but, thinking better of it, she folded it, replacing it into one of the luggage's pocket. She rummaged to fish out an atomiser; she sprayed its gentle fragrance around her neck and beneath the thin fabric of her T-shirt ... anything to keep cool.

Nevertheless, the problem with her fragrance, it appeared to captivate him, causing him to verge nearer and, whatever else filled his senses, he twice sniffed the air, enveloping the moment before inhaling: 'Ooh, your perfume smells divine ...'

A lengthy sigh slid from her lips. Sam, edging away another few inches, grinned, wondering how the divine smelled. As her perfume maybe?

He, emanating a kindness, questioned: 'Have you actually travelled around these parts by yourself?'

Sam, obviously quite alone, lifted a wry smile from the corners of her mouth; it was pretty obvious to all and sundry she was unaccompanied.

Eable lifted his dark brows. 'Oh, how brave you are, to travel all around on your own?' He stated: 'I actually wouldn't dream of it and I reckon I'm no whimper ...'

Squeezing her eyes shut, just momentarily, Sam inwardly wondered: Brave or foolhardy? With the intensity of the humidity, it felt almost too hot and sticky to even think rationally, to act sensibly, she half longing for the chill of London; instead of a usually pale porcelain complexion, her cheeks felt hot, presumably with a ruddiness? Sam experienced a mild panic; the heat became laborious. Oh, to be able, she thought, to simply turn tail, to return to the security of the Alexandrian hotel, yet how? With a woefulness, there seemed a no turning back from where she seemed stranded.

Her much longed for holiday to Egypt, the special birthday gift from her parents, became half surreal. Sam, almost dreamlike, could not recollect how long, how far she travelled; but, surely, as the proverbial crow flew, she must have clocked up a minimum of fifteen hundred miles. They were bizarre distances, she having motored by a Mercedes taxi, it complete with blacked out windows, a camel and through a stone arch where an overladen donkey stood. How, she speculated, could the young owner of the ass, know to be waiting for her? Examining the time with a nearby sundial, Sam remembered her own wristwatch's date window jamming, it ticking through the annals of time; she noticed this while checking through the Egyptian-cum-Israeli border's passport control. Having viewed her unusual route stretching before her, it frantically became urging her to travel way beyond the mirage. She tried fiddling with the timepiece's tiny dial, yet, winding it remained useless, almost as if already over-wound. Mesmerised, Eable stood, bending at his waist to reach, to hold her wristwatch, he became speechless by viewing it; throughout his life, he declared he never saw such an object.

Inwardly telling herself not to become fearful, nevertheless Sam involuntarily shuddered. Within her spirit she was experiencing a great sense of unease, becoming bewildered concerning her current environment; even so, she declared to Eable: 'My friend Paula and I are on our holidays. In Egypt, you know?'

'I didn't; but, it sounds like being a fantastic vacation?'

'Yes. I believe this year of 1969 shall definitely be one we'll never forget.'

Stroking his unshaven chin, he reflected. Unable to avoid Sam's worried eyes, of her immediate anxiety, he, nevertheless, told her how she must be muddled. Eable, shaking his head, stated with a grin: 'This year isn't anywhere near 1969.'

'Yes.' Sam reassured him. 'Of course it is.'

He pressed on. 'Please, Sam, I don't mean to argue, but here we are bang in the middle of our summer of 1106.'

'1106 BC? What are you talking about?' Sam raised an index finger, asking Eable to wait a tad. She turned around to her her backpack where she pulled out her small diary, showing him proof. 'See? Look at the date on its cover; it is definitely 1969. Fact. Okay?'

He stared at its bright red leather cover before briefly flicking through the small diary where, at the top of most pages, 1969 was printed; he, nonplussed, returned it to her. 'Whatever, here, way beyond the mirage, I'm utterly convinced our year is 1106.'

With the sudden shock, Sam nearly hyperventilated, only briefly; before staring hard, she half rendered herself speechless. Resilient, rarely one to usually panic, she nevertheless breathlessly urged: 'What is it you're telling me, I've somehow been energised into the year 1106 before the birth of Christ?'

'Exactly.'

Sam shrugged. She, not having inadvertently ingested any strange cheese, pinched herself, to discover if she was either dead, alive or sort of dreaming a weird lot of nonsense. She even began to consider the possibility concerning an out of body experience? 'You're surely teasing? Right?' she quizzed. Yeah, that's it, she thought, this fellow must surely be having a laugh? But, no. Definitely, he seemed, to her, serious.

'Why are you so desperately scared about being way beyond the mirage?'

'Way beyond the mirage? Is that where I really am?' Sam's usually bright green eyes widened. Despite the suffocating heat, it was as if something icy cold touched the nape of her neck before slithering down the length of her spine; again anxious, she wondered why she, of all women everywhere, should become energised way beyond the mirage. 'This actual place, Eable?' she quizzed on. 'You must tell me about it ...'

'All I know is. our wise astrologers who constantly study the movements of the celestial bodies, interpret it to be 1106; therefore, I suppose it is.' With a sympathetic kindness, he changed tack, informing Sam she again appeared pale, which, considering all she came through, it was no surprise the colour drained from her cheeks. 'You aren't from ancient Shiloh, are you?'

'Me? Ooh, I'm from the south of England, raised by good Irish parents.'

'England? Where's that?'

Sam saw little point in telling him her parents resided near Wimbledon Common. What difference, she thought, could the annual lawn tennis tournaments make to Eable in his era? Preposterous, she may well have spoken geographic gobbledegook to Martians, for all she knew.

'Well, Sam, even when my big brother Elkanah and I were school kids up in the hill country of Ephraim, we weren't au fait with such far away places,' he stated before continuing: 'Whatever, I welcome you, sweet lady, to our ancient land of Ramathaim Zuphim, it simply known as old Ramah?'

Perplexed, had she really been energised into the spectacle of an Old Testament land? Yet, why her? Sam wondered.

Samantha Webb recalled the start of her North African vacation, the awesome trip planned over months; finally, the splendour of the day arrived. Flying from London's Heathrow Airport, she and Paula Taylor, they nursing friends, became destined for Egypt's Alexandria. To say they were monumentally excited was probably a gross understatement.

It began all in an April evening, at around eight; as a group of four, they were just enjoying a pleasant dinner at Sam and Paula's Earls Court apartment. The first Friday in the month became Paula Taylor's off duty, it happily coinciding with Sam's free weekend - a welcome opportunity to entertain. Promising themselves not to talk shop, about their own hospital work, but making it to hopefully become a relaxing evening, Paula suggested Sam should invite her own parents to join them. It became preferable to eating out in a busy fish restaurant, especially as they prided themselves as dab hands in their kitchen.

Henry Webb, Sam's ex-Army father, nevertheless spoke of his wartime experiences, when, as a young army officer, serving in the second World War's North African campaign, fighting in the Libyan and Egyptian deserts, he enthused about a fifteen-minute camel ride. He added how he would have loved to have visited Egypt in peace time, when he would have no German enemies, such as Rommel's lot.

She, slicing her scrumptious home-made apple pie while Paula offered each a glass of a sweet sauterne, a liquid gold of a smooth wine her own father often sipped with deserts: 'So, dad,' Sam, looking puzzled, asked, 'why don't you simply do it?'

He deeply frowned, shaking his head, but it was his wife Daisy who unexpectedly piped up, declaring how he would never travel there all alone. There became a note of distress in her voice, even as she spoke. She glanced sideways towards Paula, wishing she was not listening, yet she was. 'The truth is, girls, I'm, for some reason, too frightened to fly abroad ... I became scared stiff of 'planes when my twin brother was shot down during the war, so perhaps that's why? Now, my hubby won't go off again without me.' Daisy confessed she was therefore ruining any chance of his Egyptian holidays.

Henry reached forward, patting the back of her hand, calming Daisy to shush, not to distress herself. 'We can still enjoy nice holidays here in Britain, can't we?'

Sam half twigged as much concerning her mother's phobia. Even so, Samantha concluded: 'I would fly absolutely anywhere - and in a heart beat.'

'Me, too,' added Paula.

Detecting the tears welling up in her mother's Irish eyes, Sam believed it more kind to quickly change the subject. Nothing else needed to be said, or so she thought.

Jenkins, the daily who did for Daisy, often cleaned for Sam, too. It was a late Tuesday morning when the same cockney cleaner stopped polishing the legs of a dinner table, just to overhear a quiet conversation between Henry and Daisy. Bursting with the new gossip, it was Jenkins who quickly turned to face Sam: 'You and that posh nursing friend of yours are going to be given tickets. Keep it under wraps.'

'Tickets? What tickets?'

Jenkins shook her head; 'I never said a dickey bird ... all right?' She started up the noisy vacuum cleaner, moving it only across that section of the blue bedroom carpet facing the ceiling.

'Oh, but, Mrs Jenkins, you did.' Unable to reach her parents on the 'phone because of a presumed faulty signal, Sam grabbed her handbag in which were her bunch of keys, she reminding Jenkins to reset the sophisticated burglar alarm before leaving.

Jumping into her car, Sam drove over to the district of Wimbledon where gracious, large old homes lined leafy areas. Leaving her own motor in front of her dad's garage, she tried to let herself in the back door; it was still bolted from the inside. She finally nipped around to the front, ringing the door bell with its sounds of an annoying jingle; it was Daisy who, wiping her hands on the edge of her pinafore, unlocked, she being surprised to have her daughter's visit.

'You, Samantha dear, normally only drop in on us during a Sunday ... nothing wrong, is there?' There was the tempting whiff of baking bread, a delicious aroma. Sam kissed Daisy with a peck before following her along the dour hallway and into their bright living room where her dad's ample body distributed itself onto the comfy sofa.

Daisy remained standing to ask: 'Do you want something to eat or drink, Samantha?'

'I ate a little earlier.'

'Next to nothing, I'll bet!'

Sam exchanged a smile with her mother, for Daisy was always anxious how her daughter appeared pale and too slender. 'Fancy some of my home-made bread?'

'All right; thanks, but a little later?' Sam agreed. She, sitting herself beside Henry, patted the vacant seat for her mum; ever the inquisitive, she came straight to the point. Flanked by her parents, she asked them what on earth Jenkins was talking about?

Henry barked, half cursing the woman. 'The honest truth is, Samantha, I'd like to buy some tickets, but nosey Parker Jenkins, as per usual, only heard half the tale ... '

'What? Theatre tickets, to see a West End show?'

'Maybe?'

Daisy leaned across their daughter, smiling towards Henry: 'Tell Samantha the truth, Henry, dear.'

'Okay.' He sighed, informing Samantha how he would like to purchase airline tickets. 'I'm off, in a day or so, to see a travel agent, to enquire about Middle Eastern trips ...'

'Ooh, daddy,' Sam interrupted, 'does that mean you're off to Egypt, after all?'

Henry squeezed one of his daughter's hands, raising his Irish eyes heavenwards before shaking his head. 'Not for me, silly girl; the Egyptian holiday will be a birthday gift for you, a nice surprise from mummy and me.'

'Egypt?' Sam's mouth almost fell open, she queried with a breathy gasp; releasing her father's hands before hugging around his neck, prior to turning, to kiss her mother again. Egypt was a place she never considered for herself, but why not?

Sam's mother who cursed no-one, added, with a mark of devotedness towards Samantha: 'Daddy and I certainly don't want you to travel alone, so, we said we'd pay for Paula, too ... we presumed you'd want to travel together?' When Paula's parents heard of the trip, the Taylors insisted of forking out for their own daughter.

Before Sam, cock a hoop, could utter a sensible word of thanks, her father added: 'All I ask of you, Samantha, is that you take one of those fifteen-minute camel rides, perhaps also to see the Pyramids? Take my Polaroid camera, to photograph it all.'

With whoops of joy, hope blossoming in Sam's mind, she and Paula used much of their off duty times to plan, to finalise the exciting peace time trip. Waiting for the awesome holiday to arrive seemed to drag on forever. Along with Paula, Sam received all the regulation vaccinations. Both the Taylors and Henry bluntly made sure their daughters possessed enough local currency, enough Egyptian pounds, along with everything to do with their adult girls' holiday.

An apprehensive Daisy Webb made the girls faithfully promise, once they touched down in Egypt, to 'phone home, only to reassure both sets of parents they were all right ...

'Relax. We'll both be absolutely fine, mum,' Sam declared. 'Do, please, stop worrying about us. Nothing shall happen to the likes of us, not for a split moment; anyway, Paula and I are not emigrating ... it's simply only a couple of weeks as a special holiday.'

With bags packed and repacked to make sure they really had everything necessary, the two eventually left the drab grey of the London weather where a drizzling rain chilled their faces; they flew from Heathrow Airport.

A cheerful beauty in a neat blue uniform sat Sam and Paula by what she declared was the correct Gate number. They waited so long, Sam became concerned; their boarding passes showed no Gate numbers. She collared an equally smart young man who discovered they were waiting by the wrong Gate; their flight was being called for the final time. They ran like their lives depended! Seeing the sardine packed craft, Sam was relieved the Taylors forked out for them to fly club class. Paula recently finished her seven nights' shifts, leaving her almost over tired; finally, with her almost zombie-like, they landed, with their 'plane touching down in the Egyptian Alexandria.

A toppers and tailed, purple dressed man, whose duty it was to stand near the entrance of the hotel, welcomed guests as they stepped from their taxis; he, filled with his own self importance, removed his right white glove to click his fingers, summoning a young porter to carry the girls' bags. Shown to their adjoining rooms, they, after so much previous planning, arrived. Sam smiled towards the teenager who humped up both sets of their luggage; he beamed back, chuffed to receive their monetary tips.

Stifling a yawn from behind the back of her hand before flopping upon her sumptuous bed, Paula declared her room preference. After showers and changing their clothes before tucking into the fabulous hotel's predictably awesome lunch, it was again Paula who declared: 'Before I do another thing, Sam, I really must catch up on sleep. I hope you'll understand?'

She, keen to take some African air, did, telling her

not to worry about it. 'We did, however, promise we'd 'phone home.'

Having worked like a Trojan before feeling dead on her feet, Paula frowned, hardly seeing the point, stating: 'The parents forget we're adults.'

'I know. Anyway, you go off to get some shut eye. I'll make a quick call to home, to say we're fine. Okay?' Sam checked the brief time differences with her wrist-watch. From a small telephone table in her own room, Sam sat to 'phone.

Despite loathing the telephone, calling it a wretched contraption, Henry, hurrying in from his garden, breath-lessly wheezed to answer.

'Hello, dad. It's me. I'm ringing, as promised, to say we're actually here ... can you hear me all right?'

'Definitely.' He found it amazing he could hear her all the way from Egypt. 'But here's your mother,' he told her. 'Talk with her, then she can tell me all about it?'

With it being long distance, Sam inwardly groaned, anxious Daisy may chat too long.

'Hi, mum. This must only to be a quick call, simply to assure you we're actually here, in Egypt and all is well.' She knew the call to her mother would bring a parental relief; Sam added how she and Paula eventu-ally had a good flight.

Daisy, half ignoring Samantha's expenses, asked several predictable questions, including: 'Is the hotel nice, Samantha?' and 'What about all the foreign food?' to which she informed Daisy everything was glorious. Sam told her how her own room enjoyed views over the blue Mediterranean sea; she mentioned how fresh blooms, they almost with an explosion of colour, were placed in both their rooms. 'I wish you could smell my vase of flowers?'

She heard the next obvious question: 'What are you going to do today, dear?'

'Today? Oh, tell dad I'm going to try to take one of those fifteen-minute camel rides?' She heard her mother repeating it all back to Henry who was trying hard to listen in. 'I'll have his camera with me.'

'All right. You and Paula ... you're going on a camel ride together?'

'No. She's still asleep.'

'Still? Oh, dear. Is she not feeling too well?'

Sam sighed, informing her mother Paula was fine, too. 'It's just she did a long stretch on night duty. 'Phone Paula's parents, please, but she'll probably ring when she finally surfaces?'

Daisy promised she would do it straight away.

'Must go, mum, as it's quite expensive to ring from here.'

'I understand. Oh, and by the way, Samantha, when shall you ring again?'

Sam told her when they touched back down into Heathrow. 'Paula's father is meeting us there, at the end of our trip. Tell dad it's all arranged.' She sent her sentimental love before replacing the 'phone into its cradle. After she hung up, she organised a coffee for herself before leaving the hotel.

The guy in the purple gear became far too busy clicking his fingers, bowing and scraping to two shipping magnates, to concerning himself with her.

Samantha previously changed into a cool, cotton top, a long wrap around skirt and Jesus style sandals. Reading the 'Do Not Disturb' notice upon Paula's door, she left a note in the hotel's reception for her, to say she was off for a camel ride and how she, Sam, would meet her later; she left her tired buddy to snooze away all the weariness. With her impeccable neatness and her backpack, Sam strode across the lobby and out into the Egyptian brightness of the day. She hailed a taxi. From old Cairo, a white Mercedes with blacked out windows was already for hire; seeing it directly parked outside, Sam requested its driver to take her across to the cameleers. 'Where,' she asked, 'are all the camels?'

The enigmatic cab driver sniggered, stating: 'This is Africa, my pet, with camels to spare.'

Loathing being regarding as either his or anybody's pet, Sam paid him the correct fare, yet after arriving at her allotted destination. It was there she planned to undertake one of those fifteen-minute camel rides until it felt as though she was half existing upon a different planet; reassuring herself, she could hardly believe her own eyes. Not knowing how to react, whether to laugh or cry, she became awe struck by a strange phenomenon. Sam spied an unusual mirage; it became nothing as she either saw in a book or that which her dad presumably noticed when he was a young soldier. The particular mirage demonstrated itself as a lengthy metallic strip, a silver sea of shimmering water; it rapidly spread itself across the desert's horizon, almost as if it beckoned. Well covered up from any impending sand storms, the toothless cameleer attempted to take her on and way beyond the same mirage. Nevertheless, with his camel too wide, due to its heavy load, the growling beast could not squeeze through an arch known in ancient Samaria as their old Needle's Eye. The caramel-coloured camel turned to spit at its master, but he managed to dodge its saliva. Slightly saddle sore between her thighs, Sam dismounted. She reckoned it preferable to trudge her way through the arch where, at its brightened outcome, she noticed a brown and grey donkey, it available for her to ride. However, having seen it also weighted down by saleable goods, it would not have been comfortable for travel. Before Sam made any further decisions, a woolly, greyish green dessert plant, it being a gigantic circular tumble-weed, belted across at a speed, presumably by a freak wind; it first clouted her hard in the small of her back, pushing her on before racing away to wherever, she had no idea. Spooked, Sam's nerves almost stood on end, she half wishing she aroused Paula from her deep sleep; Sam would not have felt alone, so full of a fear, with the threat of stinging tears from behind her eyelids, they about to spill down her warm cheeks. Always an animal lover, she allowed the ass to pass her by. Alone and not a little lonely, she had no alternative but to foot slog it, following a previously well trodden trail.

Noticing the younger of the two masters, Sam faked a loud cough, she hoping to grab his attention: 'Listen, Eable ...' She observed him promptly glancing around to where there might be an unusual sound.

'Whatever am I supposed to be listening for?'

Sam's tone became petulant; she groaned, wondering if he was acting the fool. Was she expected to laugh with him? Hot, moderately saddle sore and her feet ached, she inwardly wanted to temperamentally flip, but, instead, she, having values of integrity and compassion, offered the indication of a smile, declaring: 'Oh, to me, of course. It's only, Eable, that I don't wish to barge into your camp, but may I travel with you to Ramah?'

Scarcely needed convincing and, lucky for him, he,

enormously impressed by her, told her she was most welcome to ride with him on his stallion. 'Hunter is a big strong horse, seventeen hands high, yet he's oh, so gentle.' The fellow, however, half biting his bottom lip, became hesitant. 'There's only one real problem ...'

'Oh, gosh, not another! What ever is it?'

He defensively lowered his dark eyes. 'It's just that, Sam, I don't yet own a saddle; for me, I always ride Hunter bareback.'

She turned to face him: 'Ah, is that all which is troubling you?'

He nodded. 'So, what do you reckon? Are you okay with riding bareback?'

Sore from her lengthy camel ride, Sam, nevertheless, would have preferred riding side saddle. Even so, she quickly explained how, having long won a series of red, white and blue rosettes, she became regarded as a fine horsewoman.

Impressed, his mind, dazzled by her appearance, wandered; he was struck by how beautiful her hair was. 'All the young women in these parts have locks as jet black as ravens' wings, but your red hair ... ooh!' He instinctively reached to finger the ends of her long curls; sharply, Sam frowned, edging from him. The curly ends were almost reaching over her shoulders, to her breasts; for all she knew, he might inadvertently touch where she believed he ought not venture.

'Auburn.'

'What is?'

'The colour of my hair, of course.' Sam ran her slender fingers through the curls while she corrected: 'It's neither ginger nor red. Okay?' She felt him edging too close.

'Whatever, I think your hair is lovely for, you know, it actually gleams like copper under the sun ...' he, a self confessed ladies' man, began. He inwardly wondered how it would feel to press his moistened lips to the silkiness of hers, but he, sensibly and rarely a mug, was not likely going to chance his luck. Not then.

Sam's ears pricked up. She became distracted by one of the group quarrelling with the Master Elkanah. She heard the group leader grumbling about his sore feet. Feeling shattered, the man, unkempt, contorted his face to show the pain and his exhaustion; he claimed it hurt to even weight bear. Sam, inquisitive, strode away from her chatty admirer, introducing herself to Elkanah. Stating a little of her personal information, she became polite in telling him: 'I am a British nurse ...'

Elkanah, also quite a charmer, knew a little about nurses, but nothing of being British.

Sam gave a nod, trying to keep calm, levelling voice as she anxiously explained: 'I've travelled all the way from London to Egypt's Alexandria – now shocked, I've just discovered from Eable I am now way beyond the mirage.' Trying to curve her lips into a broad smile and seeing him through her large Hollywood film star type of shades, she offered her hand.

He, surprised by a woman rendering this, became unsure if he should either kiss or shake it. He decided to welcome her with a handshake, to bury her cool, white hand deep into the warmth of his own. That also known womaniser, savouring her perfume in his nostrils, felt the gentle touch of her soft skin; he experienced a quick sensual tug within the depths of his loins, to hopefully sample only the imaginable. This female, he thought, could do a whole lot more than make me weak at the knees. 'Well, Samantha ...' he began to speak up.

She interrupted. 'Sure enough, my name is Samantha, Samantha Anne Webb. However, almost everybody, with the exception of my parents, calls me "Sam".' Before he could utter another word in edgeways, she continued: 'Now, Master Elkanah, I'd like, with your permission, to check your employee's feet. Will that all right with you?'

A muscle tensed in his strong jaw as he observed this confident, slightly haughty young woman, five feet six, in a long, wrap around skirt and a tight white, scoop-neck T-shirt, all caressing her slender frame. Intrigued, he never saw anyone as her, let alone wearing such attire. He heaved a sigh, folding his muscular arms. 'Oh, you please yourself, Sam, but listen! Simply a word to the wise ...'

'Which is what?'

'Well, you need to realise this snivelling fellow is simply a lazy good for nothing ...'

'So, it's your impression of this poor fellow, eh?' Po-faced, Sam frowned, informing Elkanah, she, with a justice and compassion, was capable of deciding such issues for herself; she pushed her sun-glasses on the top of her head, almost losing them in her mop of curly hair. Keeping her cool and drawing upon every ounce of her poise and professionalism, she squatted down, she bothered by the complainer's disgraceful situation. Following a quick examination, she shook her head, informing him he should keep his feet more clean. 'Haven't you any shoes or socks?' she asked.

For him, she realised her question became quite ridiculous. He declared he possessed next to nothing more than a few loincloths.

She scowled up at his master Elkanah, stating how he really should be providing his men with adequate footwear, near enough to his own.

Elkanah, even more strong-willed, shook his head, confirming he would not. Nevertheless, with her fixed stare, he half backed down; yet, he would do nothing until the next trip to Shiloh when he again attended its temple.

Turning and promptly searching deep down in her rucksack, she produced a tube of ointment. She knew it was stupid applying the lotion straight upon the guy's dusty feet. 'Listen to me, please, fellow?'

With Elkanah, overseeing and his arms folded, the guy nodded towards her.

'Right. Go across to that water's edge, to thoroughly wash your feet.' Sam instructed him to return to her once he was clean. She, in the meantime, noticed some free shade beneath one of the trees; she grabbed it while she waited for him.

He, having obeyed, watched Sam's stern face change into a warm, sympathetic smile which probably offered much comfort as she gently squeezed the tube, smoothing on the cool cream. Simply the gentleness from her touch became sufficient to cause him to be delighted. He, impressed, raised his hands, clapped and, declaring with a loud shout, how Sam owned a magic potion ... a peculiar worm wiggled out from a silvery tube; the salve then all disappeared into his feet, replacing stars for his scars.

Elkanah's olive-skinned face broke from the firm, polite mask he first worn. 'Well, Sam,' he smiled, 'I do thank you for your exceptional kindness to this good-for-nothing bloke. I confess how I'm more than a little impressed by all your magic.' He asked to be shown how she did it.

'Another time, huh?' Smiling, Sam's green eyes sparkled with amusement. After she retained some of the remainder of the cream for her own tired feet, she searched for her own small coin purse. 'Here, man, are just a few shekels. Promise me faithfully, you'll only spend it on socks and nothing else, such as alcohol?'

'Sure. I swear. Thank you, lady.'

Within next to no time, several other bare-footed, scrawny men wailed strangling sounds, deciding they, too, possessed sore feet.

Sam's thoughts, momentarily, wafted back to the large hospital in London. Care, way beyond the mirage, she presumed, became a far cry from where she was a career-driven, workaholic, always anxious to become one of the finest of its nurses, of its midwives. Nevertheless, right there and then, she simply observed a foot fatigued man to whom she performed an empathy, the very basics of first aid.

'Okay now, Sam. All my men have rested long enough; they really need to be loading up.'

'I'm really sorry, Elkanah, if I've kept you.'

'No problem. I shall then offer you my fond farewells. Perhaps we'll meet again one day, eh? Who knows?'

Sam shook her head, explaining how the younger master, who she understood was his brother, said how it would be all right if she travelled with them. 'Eable can take me as far as your ancient Ramah.'

Elkanah shrugged, consenting his okay.

Sam leaving him, she hurried back to where Eable was resounding a roar at the top of his voice, he regrouping his servile folk. Noticing Sam out of the corner of his eye, he staged an about turn. Full of softer, quieter tones, he presented his hand, urging: 'Please, permit me to take you across to my stallion?'

As the only foreigner in their midst, Sam, having already shown a complexity, with fears one moment and an authoritarian assertiveness the next, she was attempting to remain quietly reserved; politely, she promptly pulled her hand from his. Touching, threading through each others' fingers, she reckoned it may have become enough for her to relight an old buzzing sensation within.

'My Hunter's tethered way over there, beside the water,' he stated, adding: 'See?'

Within a proximity, they heard the animal whinny.

Even with her sunglasses, Sam held her hand over her brow, shading her eyes from the overhead sun. She saw a young stable lad preparing to calm the horse for its master. 'Of course, I can see. Hunter is a very fine looking stallion, if ever I saw one,' she declared, asking if he ever used him as a stud.

Eable's dark eyes shone at her compliment concerning his beloved Hunter. Carrying Sam's backpack for her, he so wished to be able to link his arm in hers, yet she firmly informed him she preferred to walk independently.

Sam remembered the 'phone call she made from Egypt to her parents. She knew they, along with Paula who would not be able to find her, must surely be worrying; nevertheless, she knew she could do nothing about it. Not then. They would probably not understand what was happening, where she found herself.

Placing his large hand onto the back of her waist, Sam, with a foreboding, felt it gradually dropping down to cover her neat backside. Promptly, he was somewhat surprised when Sam naively hoisted her long skirt between her knees, causing the garment with its designer label to appear as baggy culottes; strongly refusing Eable's assistance, she asked his stable lad to help her onto Hunter's apparently strong back. Taking her possessions again, Sam steadied the backpack by laying it across her lap.

With a strength in his own muscular thighs, Eable mounted behind her, she feeling him too forthcoming, as if it became impossible to insert a sheet of parchment between them. Sliding his hand through, he reached beneath her right arm, grabbing for the leather reins. His olive skinned face nuzzled into the sensitivity of the nape of her neck, in between locks of her loosed hair … auburn hair which still fell free in soft long curls. Her so-called divine perfume could not fail to tempt him. He did not speak, but with a kick and two clucks with his tongue, he urged the stallion to instinctively make for home; while still gripping the reins in his right hand, his other tightened around her slender waist, making her to blush as she experienced his thumb creeping beneath the hem of her T-shirt; he caressed, bringing to her a dreamlike quality, arousing within an old overwhelming urgency. Grabbing his freed wrist, she prevented him from any more. Hearing her free express breathing, she felt the occasional palpitation within her own heart; with her head tilted, she permitted his moistened lips against the side of her neck. Not being with a man since her broken engagement the previous year, she, perhaps on the rebound, tried to ignore the warmth from his breath. Eable's enforced close proximity caused within her a quick and rising fizz of excitement, bringing back all those special moments with her Irishman from Balygar. With low moans and gasps, Sam, despite her initial resolve, was leading this comparative stranger to the edge of no control, giving herself up to his embrace until she snapped herself back into the reality of the moment, she elbowing him away.

Elkanah, with a sideways glance, rode his own stallion close to them; no fool, he knew his young brother became affected by the activities in the cave, even prior to his encountering Sam. At the sight of feminine white flesh from beneath her T-shirt, it became as if he needed a woman, too, he eager to reach home, to either his wife or into the house of his mistress; he cared not. With base amusement, he brought his own horse close enough, allowing his right thigh to nearly touch her garment, causing himself to inwardly chuckle.

In reverse, Sam could not fail to become attracted by such handsome young men. However, she, feisty, planned neither should not rob away her heart. Never?

Dusk had fallen when Sam entered the ancient town of Ramah and, interspersed with its tall palm trees, the scent of wood smoke drifted upward from the homes where meals cooked. Thirsty, she half closed her eyes, for she could hear nearby water gurgling in a covered cistern; throughout the streets, women were sending their slave girls to the well for more water. Wondering where she, Sam, might check in, to stay for the night, she wanted to quiz her horseman, yet he was nowhere to be located, not even in the stables with his beloved stallion.

Undaunted, in every home along her route, lamps glowed in the windows facing the street; she planned to run after Elkanah. Surely, she thought, with him being a local man, he may be able to recommend an hotel where she might stay.

Although old Ramah was small, with less than six thousand people living up in the mountains of Ephrain, the brothers Elkanah and Eable resided in the immense grandeur their forefathers cultivated for generations. Elkanah, hurrying through the fading light, was eagerly where, as a twice married man, he lived. He knew his young wife Hannah would be waiting indoors; hardly able to restrain himself, within his psyche he was pursuing her. Knowing she was such a beautiful nineteen year old girl, he beamed, his footsteps quickening. Without thinking, he drew back his broad shoulders, walking with a firmer step, his back straight and his rough unshaven chin proudly lifted.

Sam was about to summon him, but resisted for, irate, he heard a familiar sound, a shout; he sidetracked to see old Elihu frantically waving, coming towards him as fast as his tired old legs would carry his obesity, relieved Elkanah returned safely from a temple in Shiloh. Sam stayed aside, noticing Elihu had an ageing skin like an old cream parchment; he was breathless from catching up with his favourite grandson. 'Oh, my beloved boy, there's trouble on every side.' He signalled to Elkanah, to sit on a wide flat rock nearing by the edge of an uneven pathway. 'I think you've heaped up more troubles than you are prepared to accept.'

'Go on then, grandfather,' he sighed, 'tell me exactly what's up.'

'Not what, my lad, but who ...' he chastised.

Sam became intrigued, straining her so-called rabbit ears to struggle strenuously, to eavesdrop into their chat.

Elihu, single-minded, with dark, wide-set eyes, was determined to have his say. 'In a word, Peninnah. She's a devil woman and you, Elkanah, jolly well know it is so, don't you, eh?'

Briefly knowing Elkanah, Sam was itching, wondering who Peninnah might be.

Elkanah pursed his tight lips; his dark eyes narrowed as Sam continued to listen hard into his private conversation, she staring severely at the old man. 'I was on my way home, to see Hannah,' he informed him. 'She'll be waiting for me indoors, and, oh, I'll be in the dog house if I'm late.'

Elihu puckered a deep furrow across his aged brow. 'So you should be, Elkanah. My boy, you shouldn't be anywhere near that nasty Peninnah woman; disgraceful, she's obnoxious to your new, young wife.'

He deeply sighed, raising his dark eyes heavenwards. 'Oh, goodness gracious me! What's Peninnah supposed to have done now?' he pumped.

'I'll tell you what. She has once again publicly mocked your Hannah, leaving the poor dear in floods of tears ... and it's all simply because she hasn't had any babes of her own.'

Sam, stunned, immediately knew the answer to her mystery. Fancy, she thought, how could anyone be so horrid to someone, only because they hadn't conceived?

'Mark my words, though, one day the worm will turn,' prophesied the old man. 'Your wife Hannah shall have her day, and then may the God of our fathers, of Abraham, Isaac and Jacob help your wicked mistress?'

'Aye, but you only know half the tale, grandfather.'

'Which is what, Elkanah? Go on ... inform me.'

Samantha wished to goodness he would get on with the story; she was absolutely itching to know the news.

He sighed, 'I've pleaded with Hannah, ooh, at least a dozen and one times, if I'm surely better to her than all of ten children?'

Sam watched the old man cupping his ears to listen. 'And what did Hannah say to that then, eh?'

Elkanah shook his head. 'No deal! She still hankers after having a baby of our own.' He noticed a nearby sundial, how time was knocking on. 'Now, I really have to go or she'll never get pregnant,' Elkanah grinned, raising himself to his feet, he thinking of his beautiful Hannah in his bed.

Elihu did noticed Sam's imposed presence, yet his one time thoughts remained elsewhere; having offered his twopenny worth, he inwardly groaned before puffing his way back along the cobbled pathway to his little cottage on the far edge of the town.

Samantha delayed to watch the old grandfather take his leave, he slowly disappearing from their sight. Turning back the other way towards Elkanah, it became her one and only chance to speak with him, but where, she wondered, was he?

Feeling again desperately alone, lonely and homesick for London with its bright street lighting, black cabs and everyday red buses, she walked up and around where there were undistinguishable landmarks. Nothing was westernised or, indeed, with a single, solitary place beckoning as did the the odd mirage. Frantically, she searched along a few unlit streets; she rapidly lost her bearings. No longer could she trace either Elihu's pathway or that to Elkanah. Not a little unnerved, tearfully, she tried to suck in a deep calming breath; all she

could do was to search for a bed and breakfast establishment, a place with hopefully clean blankets and
sheets, a shelter from the elements with fresh running
water.

Pursuing a rotund dimpled landlady in the middle of
her years, Sam trailed up twelve steep stairs, onto a
small landing; she was promptly shown into the vacancy
of a shared attic room where she set her backpack upon
a black seated dining chair which partly lost its veneer;
it was preferable to the grey flagstone floor with its
clumps of dust bunnies, they appearing from beneath
the bed with its one floral cotton sheet. Instead of a
pillow, there was a moth eaten folded woollen blanket.
Pulling open wide the wonky wardrobe door, she was
overtaken by the most obnoxious stench. Deuteronomy
6:4 was scribed in white chalk upon the inside of one of
its precarious doors; she thought better of hanging up
any of her clothes. She crossed to the spare single bed
where, over the bed's headboard, there was a fixed iron
ring affair from which anyone, suffering from a physical
disability, maybe independently raised up. She sniffed at
the lumpy mattress, abandoning testing it for a bounce.
Parting the short hanging green curtains which, like
their owner, obviously saw better days, she opened the
window, hoping for some fresh air. The flying midges,
along with bugs which sounded a buzzing racket, saw
the flickering candle light and decided to join her. Her
quick task was to annihilate them before she became
their dinner. 'Is this really it?' Sam queried with a deep
frown. 'Are there no alternative rooms which are a sight
cleaner than this?'

The insufferably loud mouthed, starchy and crabby
landlady, with folded arms the size of any beefy bloke's,

leaned her ample body against the door jam. 'You either take this room, Miss Hoi Polloi Lady Muck, to pay me up front, or you can clear off elsewhere. Frankly, I couldn't care a rat's tail.'

Her loud words half stunned Sam. 'That's definitely no way for a woman to speak; I reckon you really ought to be quite ashamed of yourself, you know?' she pointedly chastened.

The woman raucously laughed it all off without humour.

Sam wistfully pondered within herself: was this really the ancient town of Ramah, the self same pleasant whereabouts of which Eable spoke?

Chapter 2

With a stirring of resentment, Sam, unprepared to withstand another moment in those two-bit digs, tried to calm herself. Nevertheless, after a night from spasmodic sleep, she remained determined in finding somewhere pleasant.

Walking slowly, Sam became unsure of her whereabouts until she encountered a well. Peering down its shaft, she was surprised it was square. Believing they were mostly all wishing wells and round, its surrounding area, cobbled, she saw an overturned terracotta jar. The chipped earthenware vessel was probably capable of holding about five to six pints of water; with her ability to stop fighting a smile, Sam met a sun-parched raisin of a young lass, she arriving to draw water; the scrawny, long legged kid, hoisted up a small container of cold water. She, an expert, was competent with a ladle, to provide Sam a drink. Promptly, she gulped down every last sloshing drop, thirsting for more.

'Hey, let me try to get some water?' Sam urged: 'I'm still needing extra.'

The kid giggled, demonstrating how to drop a leather bag for drawing water, before yanking it from the darkened depths.

Satisfied and, before attempting to depart, Sam enquired if the youngster, a local, knew how to reach Elkanah's. 'I'm searching for his house. Do you know where it is?'

Beckoning, she did.

'Your water jar now seems too heavy. Let me carry it for you?'

The child nearly refused, saying it was her special assignment, but Sam insisted. The sprightly kid was speedy, but Sam, with a dogged determination, traipsed, following along the higgledy-piggledy, steep and narrow cobbled streets; she, for any subsequent times, tried hard to remember all the left and right turns, she scoffing herself for not meticulously visualising the route. Finally, with a sense of relief, happier and more relaxed within her mind, Sam spied his country house.

The lass, needing to leave, pointed towards Elkanah's ample front porch with its swing for two. Before Sam set down the stone jar and offered her any sense of a monetary gratitude, the youngster lifted her task; it was upon her shoulder and she was off like a Jack rabbit.

Sam hoped Elkanah, at least, would be able to offer a quick solution to her dungeon of despair - her homelessness. His place was located in the picturesque setting of then a men's world, with rich farmland, with a dream of vineyards and fig orchards; hesitating a short moment beneath his porch, she sucked through her teeth a deep breath of air, wondering if she ought to have visited quite so early. The additional notion struck her, how perhaps he and his present wife may still be in bed, in the private world they thrived, engaging in which couples regularly enjoy. Whatever, mentally calming herself by inhaling a few long breath, she ultimately summoned enough courage to tap on his front door. She waited, hearing from within the frenzy of a large barking dog. An elderly gentleman, dressed as a butler, shuffled due to bad feet; he unlocked the front door. With a somewhat superior air, he questioned: 'Is my lady, the mistress of this house, expecting you?'

Sam, briefly glancing at her wristwatch, stated: 'Err, no, sir. Not exactly.'

'What do you mean by "not exactly"?' The guy's face became firmly set as he waited for a reply. 'Quickly, girl, for my time is at a premium.'

Maybe so, but was he was speaking of her? Sam refused to recognise herself as just being a 'girl'. She rightly inflated herself as a professional young woman; she, nevertheless, bone tired, nearly put him straight, yet, she was not up for a fracas. 'Um, the honest truth is, next to no-one knows I'm here, but ...' She half remembered the kid at the well; she knew.

Grim, he raised an index finger, as if instructing her to wait. Momentarily, he hobbled his way back to snap a stern guttural command, trying in vain to suppress his master's dog before again facing Sam. 'So, carry on then, miss. State your business.' Before she could utter another word, the supposition swiftly hit him she must either be selling door-to-door or flogging an odd religious sect. He stretched his neck from his stiff white collar, to glance over her shoulder, to notice her rucksack. 'Ah, but whatever merchandise is in that backpack of yours, we neither need it nor want it. So, have a nice morning, now ...' He was about to close the door.

Samantha shook her head, ready to plead: 'Oh, sir, no. Please, whatever else you do, don't shut me out?' The pupils of her green eyes widened with a fearful anxiety, making them seem darker. She tearfully implored: 'Listen! I'm now a stranger here in old Ramah and, oh, I've absolutely nowhere to live ...'

Sam, to him, appeared nothing like the usual homeless. 'Oh, dear me, my pet. So, why ever has this happened?' He wondered if she left another town, following some sort of a domestic hoo-ha, but no.

Forgiving him for referring to her as his pet, she sorrowfully declared: 'Frankly, sir, I feel as if I'm at the end of my tether.'

He arched one quizzical eyebrow. 'Now, would it help if you told me all about it?'

She agreed, introducing herself as Samantha Anne Webb. Her worried features changed with a sigh of relief. 'Well, you see, sir, I arrived in old Ramah, only to stay somewhere horrid; truly, last night was purgatory for me ...'

'Really? That bad?'

She psychologically scratched an imaginary itch as she recalled the ghastly place. 'You know, sir, I really ought to speak with your Master Elkanah; he's the one who may be able to help me with the matter of ... of some accommodation.'

Dashing down a white marble staircase and padding across the hallway, Elkanah overheard the southern tones of Sam's English voice; for him, it was as attractive as she was beautiful. In addition, he eavesdropped, his name being referenced. With a paranoia, it hit him how she must have arrived, primarily to complain; convinced, it had to be concerning Sam's ride on Hunter. Increasing the length of his strides and, with erratic breathing, he knew his wife would soon show up. He panicked. As if in a flash of forked lightening, he became aware he needed to quieten her before she spilled the beans. He thought the old butler, devoted to his wife, would be off like a cork on a fast moving river, to be a talebearer. Elkanah, promptly interrupting the doorstep conversation, instructed the butler to quietly show Sam into his study, well away from Hannah's listening ears; deliberately or not, the ageing fellow misheard, believing Elkanah instructed not to go into his study. Half grinning to reveal two missing teeth, the fellow led Sam along the hallway and into a bright family room. Too late for contradiction, Elkanah heard his wife making her appearance.

Noticing him barefoot, Sam presumed outdoor shoes were forbidden inside, therefore she had slipped her feet from hers.

He, offering Sam a seat, sat immediately opposite. She tried averting her eyes from his nether region; legs akimbo, he was clad only in a loincloth beneath his long cotton shirt. He, sporting so few garments, she could not help but wonder if she interrupted his bedroom time with his present wife. Not so.

Almost instantaneously, Hannah appeared, waltzing around the room, yet alone. She, bejewelled, glistening with diamonds in her hair, hair as black as ravens' wings. With a strong Egyptian influence, she, heavily made up around her dark eyes, became dressed in long blue finery. Sam could do nothing but watch, reminding herself of the Shakespearean misquote: 'Vanity, thy name is "woman"!'

With her hands upon her slender hips, her chin in defiance, Hannah shook her head; tutting, she glared down at Elkanah's bare feet. 'You really are silly,' she began. 'Honestly, how on earth could you manage to lose a brand new pair of sandals?' She added how foot-wear did not simply disappear into thin air.

With Sam listening on, Elkanah was mountainously embarrassed at being domineered by his nagging wife. He had more than enough with Peninnah, his first wife, a woman he retained as a mistress; was it a case of 'out of the fat into the fire'?

Hannah continued on until, with a double take and an about turn, she stopped dead in her tracks; she mind-lessly sat herself upon a chair next to his own before coming face to face with Sam. Discourteously pointing while directing her words towards to Elkanah, she sus-piciously queried: 'And who, may I ask, Elkanah, is this? Now, I suggest you spit out the truth; it'll be quicker in the long run?'

Before he, supposedly the master in his own domain, had any chance to stammer out his reply, a weak smile tugged at the corners of Sam's mouth; courteously, she quietly corrected the young woman never to point, for it came across as impolite. 'Now, my lady,' she added, 'but, as your husband already knows from an encounter yesterday, I'm Samantha Anne Webb.'

'Really?'

'Yes. Really and truly.' She continued with the brief introduction. 'Anyway, just as with Eable, I'd asked your Elkanah to simply call me Sam.'

'How chummy?'

'Chummy?' Sam scowled how she was in a fix. 'All which really happened was that Elkanah's brother helped me yesterday, to travel on here into old Ramah.'

Hannah asked why Sam was in a fix.

'All right. Well you see, I'm actually here in old Ramah, because I journeyed first from England, then into Egypt; both of which are literally ages from way beyond the mirage ...'

'I know a little of Egypt because of its various foods and, of course, its fashions.' She stood to convey a quick twirl, asking Sam: 'Do you like my frock? It's brand new today.'

'Yes. It's very pretty.'

She, sitting again, stated she would eventually give it to the poor, unless of course Sam, with a face devoid from make-up, wanted it? Sam believed it was a darn cheek, but said nothing. 'Anyway, sadly, I haven't heard about your England.' Hannah, having switched to sprawl out across her own comfy chaise lounge, was busily rearranging her long skirt. Notwithstanding, she urged: 'Ooh, Samantha, do, please, go on with your story? I'm still listening.'

'Okay. It all began yesterday ... well, a white Mercedes cab with blacked out windows, motored from ancient Cairo, to park outside the Alexandrian hotel where my friend Paula and I were staying.'

Hannah glanced across at Elkanah and then gazed back at Sam, urging her to continue.

Sam stated how its rather strange driver took her to where she might have a fifteen-minute camel ride, 'but, I was eventually left bang outside the old Needle's Eye stone building.' With a deep seated loneliness, Sam breathed, wondering what to do?

'Whatever, Samantha, did you eventually do?'

Half tearfully and with an anxious look in her eyes, she moved to the very edge of her seat as she explained: 'I obviously had no choice. I foot-slogged my way through where a brown and grey donkey should have brought me up here to old Ramah, but, ah, the poor thing was already overladen with kitchen wares for a teenage entrepreneur to sell.' Sam, so pitying the animal, allowed it to pass by.

'Weren't you, as a young woman, all on your own, quite scared?'

'Quite scared?' "Quite scared" became to Sam as a gross understatement; it was as if, much of her lonesome time in a strange, bright and hot land, she was darkly terror-stricken. Sam replied with a faked laugh: 'Frankly, I was just about petrified!' She pushed her fingers through her own loose auburn curls, again sighing: 'Nevertheless, I forced myself to manage on foot, only to find I'd travelled to way beyond the mirage.'

For once, Hannah, with a sad smile to her, towards Elkanah, remained mostly silent.

'Well, I suppose it's a bit like "Que Sera Sera" for whatever will be, will be. What's happened has happened.' Sam stated how, by meeting up with Elkanah's brother, she was, at least, able to get a lift up on Hunter.

'And?'

'And, now I am well and truly stranded. Err, you see, Hannah, I initially came here today, to contact your Elkanah … '

Disparagingly, Hannah felt she could not resist: 'Hmm. I am wondering, why ever did you want him, of all people?' It was as if, to Sam, this nineteen year old was rarely happy unless she was throwing out snide remarks.

'Why? It's actually because right now I'm desperately in need of somewhere to stay.'

'Ah, you minx; so, that's it?' The woman's brow knitted together as she declared: 'You're hankering to stay with us newly weds, in this house of ours?' Hannah was immediately regarding Sam as a somewhat crafty flirt, wheedling her way into their home. 'That's what you're really after, becoming our long time visitor, to become a cuckoo in our love nest?'

'Oh, no. How shocking of you to even think that of me?' Sam almost shot forward in her chair, exclaiming she was no minx: 'I truly swear, I never gave a thought about staying here; nothing was further from my mind.'

'Ha, I bet!'

Sam stared straight into the woman's dark eyes, folding her own arms, telling her she could bet all she liked, yet, with an intensity filling her voice, she was definitely no liar. 'Honestly, all I want to be told is, where I can rent a small pad, clean and comfortable, which isn't a stinking woodpile! Is it too much for me to ask?'

'And that's the absolute truth? It was the only reason you came here?'

She, exasperated, was having a terrible job convincing Hannah; she almost tearfully screeched the words to her: 'Blimey, O'Reilly, it is!' Sam exhaled a breath as a long drawn out sigh.   Sam so wished she was not being trapped way beyond the mirage, like a caged rat, and with no means of communications. She felt shockingly lonesome; despite her adult years, she needed her parents, of Paula's friendship, too. Thinking of the comfortable life Sam left behind, what if she could never return to see them?

For a long moment, trying not to permit herself either welling tears or panic, Sam took a long inhalation before declaring: 'Ask the gentleman who is your butler? He's not dumb. He'd tell you why I came here in the first place.' She, irate at the way Hannah treated her, pumped on. 'Why else should I be nuts enough to visit at this hour, huh? Oh, Hannah, think!'

She was thinking, reflecting hard. Normally puce with jealousy, Hannah quietened herself, she seemingly pushing any envious resentments onto the back burner of her mind; satisfied, she solicited for pardon regarding any wretched mistakes. She, after a moment or two, hung her head in shame. 'Samantha, I'm sorry I doubted your words.'

'All right. Anyway, yesterday evening,' Sam added, her voice softening, 'after I couldn't find Eable any-where, I needed your husband to recommend a nice hotel where I may stay, but, after he'd chatted with an old gentleman, he seemed to disappear; I suppose he came straight here to you?'

'I did.' Elkanah, elbows on his knees and an unshaven chin cupped in his hands, felt it his turn to exhale a long, drawn out sigh. He briefly glanced up, informing Hannah he chatted with old Elihu. 'Granddad caught up with me, to have a bit of a chat. You know what he's like once he gets talking?'

Sam piped up again, speaking with them both: 'Where I stayed last night … ooh, I cannot even begin to tell you … it was absolutely obnoxious.' She rolled her Irish green eyes heavenwards. 'It's like a sty!'

The woman asked about the whereabouts of the sty-like digs.

Sam screwed up her eyes, trying to think; she did her best to remember the place.

Hannah had a rough idea. 'Samantha, tell me, what-ever made you go over into that area?' Before Sam had another chance to speak up, the woman shook her head, staring across at her husband. 'That's the ghastly red light district, isn't it, dear?'

Elkanah gripped the polished mahogany arms of his own chair, he concealing a cracking wide grin, relieved Sam had not visited to complain. He turned sideways to face his wife: 'Hannah, my sweet, it's true, I did bump into Sam yesterday. It simply slipped my mind.'

'What? A bit like your forgetting where you left your sandals?'

'Oh, if you like. Any way, it was when we were travelling home from the Shiloh Temple.' He added how Sam helped one of his good-for-nothing leaders who complained of sore feet. 'She, having travelled from those faraway places, Eable gave her a ride upon his stallion.' He stared towards her: 'Isn't that right, Sammy?'

Sam agreed.

'Fancy. Samantha, dear, have you eaten yet?'

'Goodness, no. I didn't dare where I stayed.' Her top lip curled. 'It wasn't exactly the most hygienic of places.'

'I'm sure. And you obviously didn't think about dropping in at the early farmers' market?'

'Farmers' market?' She cocked her head. 'Where's that?'

Elkanah, scratching the dark stubble on his chin, interrupted. He told Sam it was held most mornings. 'It's situated here in the centre of old Ramah town.' He informed her how she could have acquired some good takeaway foods. 'The chicken soup is always really tasty.'

Blankly staring, she thanked him for the advice.

'So, obviously you don't yet know your way around.' Hannah changed tack, smiling to add: 'Would you like to breakfast with the two of us?'

Overwhelmed by such generosity, she declared:

'Ooh, thank you, but I don't wish to be a burden; simply a cup of coffee would be most welcome. Black with no sugar.' Sam believed this may revive her after her lack of sleep.

'Coffee? Sugar?' Hannah seemed baffled, turning to glance at her husband with some concern. Again facing their English guest, she looked regretfully: 'I'm sorry, Samantha, but those you mention neither of us have heard of such items.'

Sam discovered, way beyond the mirage, folk only drank mostly lemon tea, otherwise it was either beer or, from the vineyards, locally made wines. Only water from the well became safe to drink.

'And understand, dear, you're definitely no burden to me.' Full of her own self-importance, Hannah simply barked her orders, trusting every servant slaved to her total satisfaction, to her high standard.

With a growing tiredness, Sam mindlessly played with a stray lock of her long hair, twisting it around a finger into a single ringlet. She last enjoyed a coffee when she was in the Egyptian hotel, where she knew Paula surely had to be hunting high and low for her. However, there was nothing she could do. Not then. With a nod, with an engaging smile, Sam remarked: 'A lemon tea might be nice. Thanks.'

Hannah stared pityingly at Sam. 'By the looks of you, Samantha, I think you'll need more than lemon tea. I don't wish to hurt your feelings all over again,' although she supposedly did not worry about those of her husband's, 'but frankly, Samantha, you're looking so pale.'

'I am?'

'Clearly. When did you last tuck into a thoroughly hearty meal?'

At the Egyptian hotel. Not since.

Hannah, becoming like a commanding general, slightly raised her arms and twice clapped her hands. Within next to no time, the skinny young servant girl, the one Sam met at the well, came leaping in for her military type of instructions; she acknowledged with a nod and, after a few minutes, returned with a large dish of steaming hot lemon tea, it sweetened by a fragrant lavender honey made from the local bees. The child nipped back for an ornate silver platter filled with goats' cheese, a small bunch of black seedless grapes from Elkanah's own maturing vineyard, juicy orange segments, all overpowered by chunks of freshly baked bread, the aroma of which filled where they sat. The kid, wearing a white pinafore, frowned as she carefully set it on a low breakfast table, beamed because nothing either slid on the tray or fell from it; she gave a practised curtsy towards her mistress. As she swiftly disappeared back to the kitchen, she was heard to squeal with a delight.

Sam's face lightened with a sudden radiance, she pulling up a chair closer, her Irish green eyes widening. 'Surely, Hannah, all this food can't be only for me?' she stated, almost with a whoop in her voice.

It was.

'Ooh, wow! This is truly fantastic, but what about the two of you?'

Hannah urged her to tuck in, she stating how their own breakfasts would shortly be brought through to them. 'Once we've all eaten and the dishes are cleared, my household staff have their own meals.' She explained to Sam that, by feeding them up and paying them extra well, it helped stop pilfering.

Shifting in an attempt to become more comfortable in the chair and then trying to keep the atmosphere light, Sam stated how she reckoned she was not in the area simply to either holiday or to seek a life of adventure; although Elkanah already knew from the day before, she offered to Hannah brief details of her nursing and midwifery qualifications, along with postgraduate experiences. She quizzed Hannah if she believed in providence, to which the young woman replied how she credited herself with a godly faith.

'And you, Samantha?'

'Well, right now, Hannah, my Catholic parents virtually believe similar.'

'But, no, I asked about you?'

'Me? I'm personally wondering if some twist of fate brought me to Ramah. Perhaps, first and foremost, for me to help you.'

The young woman became astonished.

Sam turned, flicking a sideways glance towards Elkanah, as if she should not have listened into the conversation between him and Elihu, when they discussed Hannah's childlessness. 'Perhaps another time, Hannah, we'll have an all girls' together chat. Okay?'

'So, what's wrong with now? I mean, once we've finished our breakfasts?'

'No.' Sheer exhaustion was new to her; it was seriously kicking in. 'Frankly, I didn't sleep hardly a wink last night; I'm so tired, I can hardly think straight.'

Hannah claimed she understood. She did not.

Not anxious for a night beneath the stars, Sam revealed: 'I still haven't found a decent place for tonight; it really is my number one task.'

Elkanah and Hannah unanimously displayed an annoyance, how Sam previously dossed down in such a rough house. 'We here in old Ramah pride ourselves in making visitors to the town most welcome,' she stated, before adding: 'It's also one of Eable's jobs, to care for any new guests.'

'Ah, perhaps it simply slipped his mind. At least Eable was kind enough to give me a lift on Hunter, bringing me as far as old Ramah.'

'Slipped his mind? He knew full well he should have given you the door key to our guest annexe.' Hannah declared she would see to it in quick sticks. 'One of my senior servants will later check as to whether it's all spotlessly clean; she'll also stock up the kitchen with basic provisions.' Her mouth twisted in disgust: 'Ooh, just wait … wait until I see that lazy Eable? He certainly won't fail again, not after I've chatted with him.'

Elkanah exhaled another lengthy sigh, thankful he was not in his young brother's shoes. His mind switched to closely watching Sam's fine table manners as she took small bites instead of filling her cheeks, eating quietly, slowly and not speaking with a mouthful. 'You're enjoying your breakfast, Sammy?'

She acknowledged him with a brief nod. 'It's delicious.'

'Well, once we've all finished eating, I'll walk you over to our guest annexe.' He informed her it was a really nice little place and not too far. 'I can show you where we keep the door key, where to get the candles and so on?'

'My word! This is all most kind; you know, I simply don't know how to show my thanks.'

Elkanah inwardly smiled, possessing his own ideas concerning any gratitude she may wish to offer. 'You haven't seen the guest annexe yet. What if you don't like it?'

Sam was positive she would.

Hannah raised an index finger, almost as if she forgot something. 'Ah, yes, Samantha, there's also a large bolt; it's a bit rusty. It's long been fastened to the inside of its front door,' she added, it allowing her to be quite safe. 'No-one at all will be able to let themselves in, to bother you during times when you need your privacy.' She scowled towards Elkanah to ask: 'Isn't that right, dear?'

Elkanah winked at Sam, she guessing he probably had quite a history when it came to the ladies.

Eventually, his own manservant, the uncle of the skinny kid, located the mislaid footwear, those new sandals which squeaked with every step. He turned to face his wife: 'I shouldn't be too long, Hannah. I promise.'

Hannah threw back her head, offering a laugh without humour. 'I know all about your so-called promises. They rarely hold water, do they?'

'You seriously misjudge me.'

PART 2:

Away from his house and being the centre of servants' interests, speculation and attention, Sam felt Elkanah sidling so close; his arm brushed against her side until it crept around her waist. They, beneath a cloudless sky, amidst the heady scent from wild flowers, briskly stepped out along an unmade road until they bumped into one of the stable lads.

'Good morning, Master,' he stated. 'I was just on my way up to the vineyard, to find your brother.'

'If you do locate Eable, warn him how my wife, Hannah, is hunting for him.'

The lad nodded with a knowing grin; he well remembered Sam from the previous day, when he helped her up on Hunter's strong back, but, as a servant, it was not his place to be chummy.

Elkanah and Sam soon reached the guest annexe – a dwelling with one bedroom. Seeing it half covered in variegated ivy, it was not unlike her late grandfather's retirement place.

Stopping beneath the guest annexe's porch, Elkanah squatted to half lift a loosened flag stone where he removed a door key. She turned to face him, watching as he opened up. Full of a superficial charm, he stepped back, shrinking against the wall, allowing for her to hesitate before entering, to viewing its interior; for once, she experienced herself blushing as she followed him into the bedroom where she noticed the large, but sumptuous bed.

Still bone tired, Sam told him how she wished she could have had that bed, sinking into it sooner, particularly during the previous night. 'Frankly, if I was on there, I'd most probably sleep for a week.' She remembered her friend Paula Taylor saying something similar after they checked into the Egyptian hotel.

He informed her how he sometimes slept there, too, when he was in Hannah's bad books. 'You see, Sammy, my wife nags so much, it's as if I'm always in the "dog house", even when I've actually done nothing wrong.'

Sam believed him, she having heard a sample of the nagging.

As a result, he kept some spare shaving equipment in the annexe. 'Anyway, later, I'll shift my toiletries back to the house; but, while I'm here, would you mind awfully if I have a quick shave?'

Quite taken aback, Sam blinked. 'What do you mean? Now?'

He nodded, continuing: 'Later on Hannah and I are going out for drinks; I don't wish to appear like the village scruff.'

Sam frowned, wondering why he did not nip back home to shave, but she, simply grateful for the fine accommodation, thought it best to keep tight-lipped. She realised he probably had his reasons, only known to him; if she argued, she thought she may lose the opportunity to have such an awesome place. About to pull open the zip, to unpack some of her own items, she shrugged. 'Frankly, I don't care, but did you know there's no mirror?'

'What do you mean? There's always one.' He nipped back, staring at the empty wall space where it was, wondering what happened.

She made a hurried search through all the drawers and in the cupboard. 'There isn't one anywhere. So, how are you going to see to shave?'

He, in sheer disbelief, added how there was definitely a mirror prior to his recent trip to the Shiloh Temple: 'You know, all I can think, it must've been one of the servants who broke it.' He declared how the woman would not have confessed as Hannah may have docked its cost from her wages.

At first, Sam considered Hannah harsh. Nevertheless, she remembered how if nurses broke any thermometers, the Deputy Matron stopped the cost of it from the girls' already meagre salaries. It only happened once with Sam; she retained one in the breast pocket of her uniform - a cocky young pharmacist chanced his luck one Christmas eve, hugging her tight to his own chest before passionately kissing her beneath the mistletoe. The unexpected clinch left Sam with a top pocket full from tiny glass fragments, along with globules of silver mercury.

Sam grinned towards Elkanah. 'If Hannah's servant did break the bathroom mirror, then, like it or lump it, she'll have seven years of bad luck!'

He raised one quizzical eyebrow and stared. He had never heard of such a wacky old wives' tale. 'You don't believe that mumbo-jumbo nonsense, do you?'

Sam shook her head before perching herself on the edge of the bed. 'Hey, I'll tell you what, Elkanah ...'

'What?'

'Well, if you really need to shave here, why don't you feel all around your face, to brush the soap on exactly where you reckon it needs to be, then I could shave it off?'

Tall and broad shouldered, she saw him standing between the bedroom and the bathroom, he throwing his head back, laughing loudly at her idea. 'It amuses me no end to think you, a mere woman, should shave me. Women aren't barbers. Ooh, wait until I tell my chums? They'll never believe me.'

'Usually, in the general hospital where I trained, the male nurses dealt with the guys, but I also shaved a few.'

'You're kidding, eh?'

Holding his gaze, she shook her head.

' You actually shaved men?'

'Yeah.'

'Were they nuts allowing you?'

'No.' Her expression changed to a broad grin: 'I'm certainly no Sweeney Todd; they weren't made into meat pies - the guys I shaved all lived for another day.'

Having stripped to the waist, he frowned, not having a clue about Sweeney Todd – the old demon barber. Pausing to consider Sam's offer of a shave, he reluctantly nodded in an agreement. Sitting at the kitchen table with a small bowl of hot water, with a soapy lather, he promptly brushed where he thought it needed attention. Swinging around to face Sam, he gingerly passed the razor to her, he ready to wail through the excruciating pain. She, smiling, bent towards him; he was immediately confronted by the same wonderful torture, from her exquisite perfume – tantalising his senses, he could detect it from around her neck; he remembered the same glorious scent from the previous day when they first met. He had not forgotten. As she brought the razor towards his face, he clenched his white teeth, almost hyperventilating; she needed to steady herself, to balance as she scraped away the dark stubble. Unlike most professional barbers who work from behind their clients, she stood astride one of his parted thighs. Sam gave not a thought concerning her pose, yet it became pleasing for him. It took less than moments to confirm within himself how Sam was breathtaking.

Eventually telling him she finally completed the shave the best she could, he exhaled a long sigh of relief; he grabbed a hand towel to wipe himself clean and dry during while she removed the water, along with his shaving gear. Returning, Sam paused somewhat proudly; staring closely into his face, she admired her awesome handiwork, she not even drawing blood. Reaching out to stroke his face, she told him how it felt almost as soft as a baby's bottom. 'You'll look jolly fine when you and your wife go out for drinks.' The corners of her mouth lifted into a smile as she sat herself down upon the edge of the bed, confessing how it was the first time she handled such a razor. 'In the hospital we used safety razors, never a cut throat.'

Elkanah appeared shocked, but contorting his face, he felt around the smoothness from the shave; while they were on the tack of confessing, he cheekily told her how, when needs must, men manage just fine without a mirror; he rapidly moved to seat himself beside her. Sam gave him an elbowing shove. 'Ooh, I didn't know. So, Elkanah, why did you let me go ahead to shave you?'

He saw it as a way to keep her close. He stopped to stare with his dark eyes, they glazed with a masculine passion; remembering her time on Hunter, he became positive Sam may permit more. Promptly, he hugged her tight to himself. Meeting no resistance, he pulled back, his forehead resting gently against hers. She heard him speaking quietly, urging her: 'Kiss me, Sammy.'

However, she felt her heart's palpitations in anticipation of all which may happen, but, curt, Sam frowned. 'We really must not, you know?'

Elkanah steadied his gaze. 'Hey, I only asked for a kiss.'

'Yes. And what if Hannah discovered?' Sam, shaking her head, knew it would not cease at simply a kiss; neither would be able to call a halt. She, nevertheless, felt his hand slowly creeping beneath the back of her T-shirt. 'Come on, Sammy. Please?'

'Do you really not know the meaning of the word "no", Elkanah?'

It was almost as if he refused to listen. 'Hey, Sammy. You know full well you want me, just as much as I you. Admit it. Say it!'

Sam's mind demanded the right, but her heart declared otherwise; she dare not even breathe her innermost feelings, she wondering if there became a frighteningly chemistry between them; yet, she hardly knew this twice married philanderer, he residing way beyond the mirage. Whatever, she was experiencing that same fizz of a quick excitement, as during the previous day. Elkanah, he making her heart sing, caused her to be physically and emotionally alive. Desperately, she inwardly longed for him. Dare she permit him, with such an intensity, to join with her in an oblivion? She was trying hard to inwardly fight it, she invariably being the strong-minded, tenacious woman.

Falling gently back, her long auburn hair spilling against the soft feather pillow, Sam needed him, noticing the perspiration beads touching his brow; he, without any more protestations from her, became available for each other. With an added surge of a feisty strength, she believed she ought, with the injustice, to have fought him away; yet, too late, she cherished every touch, every movement; as with a blindfold, blocking out the truth from the light, she gave up her freedom to him. 'Elkanah.' Compromising, daring to even breath his name, she knew, as with her perfume, it would prolong her own torture. His, too.

In next to no time, they both lay totally spent, he, breathlessly dropping down beside her.

'Your wife shall be wondering where on earth you are,' Sam declared, seeing him still in all his masculinity. 'We need to get dressed.'

He turned over on his side to crack a wide grin. 'In a tick. It's just good remaining here, being with you.'

Sitting up and edging herself away from the reach of his touch, she, having quickly dressed, gave a sudden jerk, her hair still in a disarray; the front door rattled but, thankfully, the old rusty inner bolt held. The rapid banging continued with a woman's voice yelling loudly to Sam through the letterbox.

Elkanah cursed with a great annoyance, at the immediate intrusion.

Sam turned to stare towards the doorway before back at him, she keeping her voice down to a whisper: 'Who do you think it is?' She wondered if it may be Hannah, hunting him down.

He shook his head, stating she would never dare. 'I'll bet you any shekels, it'll be one of her servants.'

'Already?'

'Of course. My wife said she'd send around one of her women to clean, to fix you up with provisions.'

Sam's usual pale face flushed a high pink, she feeling anxious. 'Keep your voice down, Elkanah.'

He glanced at himself. 'If the servant sees me like this, she'll not only gossip all around the town, but,' he frantically quaked, 'if it comes to my Hannah's ears, she'd just about kill the pair of us. I kid you not.'

Sam raised an index finger up to her own lips, to quieten him. 'Shush!' She, in a bell like clarity, instructed him to hide.

Grabbing his clothing before crouching down in the bathroom, he remained as quiet as any mouse.

As oblivious to three outside stray goats, they chomping their way along the hedgerows, so the servant hireling was to her and Elkanah's movements. Hannah previously trained the servants to twice bow low before stepping in and out of the guest annexe's kitchen; she, with an imaginary speed, supplied a heavy basket filled with a half flagon of white wine, some crushed grape juice, along with various root vegetables, a cucumber and one fine cut from buffalo meat. Gratified, Sam asked her to pass on thanks to her mistress. She nodded, requesting from Sam if she might return later to clean through the guest annexe; she was also a kettle-seller with other sales to finalise.

Sam, running her fingers through her own dishevelled auburn hair, tried to conceal her huge sigh of relief, expressing it would become a preferable arrangement; the cleaner declared how she appreciated Samantha's understanding before turning tail to bow again; she left as fast as she arrived.

'All right. She's gone; you can come out now, Elkanah.' Sam giggled at her own brand of humour: 'Forgive the diabolical pun, but that really was a close shave, wasn't it, eh?'

Looking through the basket of provisions, Sam told him: 'I shall enjoy tucking into this lot.'

'Yes,' he said with a glance at the goodies, 'but, watch out concerning the wine Hannah sent for you.'

Sam appeared worried, she staring at the half flagon. 'Something wrong with it?'

'Not really, but, go easy; the next morning, you may be anxious to choose to go on the wagon.' She, thanking him for the advice, reminded him: 'You did promise your wife you wouldn't be long, you know? You must not dilly-dally any longer; you have to go on your way.'

'Yeah, I shall, Sammy, but you have to admit, there's something extra special between us, huh?'

She flatly refused to admit anything except to confirm how she was unprepared to become a cuckoo in his and Hannah's nest. 'I am not like that nasty Peninnah woman, you know?'

He knew that day was only Sam's second, way beyond the mirage, so, he wondered, how could she have discovered about his previous wife, then his mistress, the mother of his six children?He simply grinned towards her, he asking, with some obvious jealousy, about how she felt concerning Eable, her time with him upon Hunter?

'You're not silly. You knew full well Eable was eyeing all those couples in the cave; he was, I reckon, watching them too closely for his own good, seeing exactly all they were doing - it's why, I believe, he became affected by me.'

'Oh, that!'

'Exactly. All of it fired him up; hey, but once we were actually riding, well, Elkanah, you know the rest, don't you?'

'And I reckon you, Sammy, secretly, enjoyed your time upon Hunter ... with me, too, just now, what?'

She remained unprepared to confess anything.

He ignored her standoffishness.'Whatever you might have had with Eable, it won't have compared with me.'

Sam scowled towards him; she declared: 'I have told you, Elkanah, I am definitely not going to join forces with that Peninnah woman, becoming another one of your mistresses. All right?'

'I am so sorry, Sammy,' he started, almost as if he was backing down. 'Maybe you and I should get to know each other better in future?' He frowned, thinking for a moment or two before a devious glint showed up in his dark eyes. 'How much?'

'Oh, I reckon we should only become good buddies; nothing more.'

Elkanah was not planning for a platonic relationship; even so, he knew he needed to watch his step with someone as sharp as Sam, to understand her way of thinking when it came to romance. Crafty to the core, Elkanah was scheming to get her on his side, asking her to tell him about her western way of life.

Sam, close, sat beside him, stroking again his smooth cheek with the back of her hand. 'Where would I even begin to start?' she asked with a lengthy sigh. 'It is hard for me to tell you; it's a bit like explaining colours to the blind.' The thoughts, the words were causing her a sudden homesickness.

He very gently moved to grip her hand, threading her fingers through his. 'So, go on, sweet lady. Try me?'

Silent for a long moment, she eventually began to tell him how she became previously engaged to be married. 'Anyway, the entire relationship finished a year ago, for it simply didn't work out.' She supposed there was no real harm in telling him about Mick. 'Well, although I loved his company and he was great fun, the dreams and goals, the plans and excitements I saw ahead for myself became more important.' Sam persuaded herself to believe Mick, an Irishman whose family hailed from a dairy farm near Ireland's Balygar, strove towards different horizons. Emotionally, Sam remained hurt, still licking her wounds by it all.

'Ooh poor you, eh?'

She thought long and hard about those romantic feelings.

Sam's mother Daisy, who did not understand her daughter's ideas, stated how it was better to have loved and lost, than never to have loved at all. So passionate, Sam almost became obsessive about her career, channelling midwifery to become her immediate life.

Whatever, to Elkanah in his culture, in his country, in his time frame, it was tough for him to comprehend her Western way of life, with her differing customs, to air and space travel, automatic washing machines, fast cars and telephones with international calls, yet she was suddenly a foreigner in his ancient Ramah.

'Oh, Sammy, what I wouldn't give to ...'

'No.' Before he uttered another fanatically passionate word, Sam, with a dogged defiance, spoke quintessentially firm: 'Listen, to me, Elkanah. Although I'm single and free, you are anything but.' She had not arrived there to break up a marriage. Precisely the opposite. 'We both know you belong with Hannah. Not me. Okay?'

'So, what when I'm in the "dog house" with her?'

Sam paused to think.

'Remember, I told you, it's a fairly regular occurrence?' Before Sam arrived on the spot, the annexe invariably became a place of refuge for him; hence, the reason for his toiletries in the bathroom. 'May I then continue coming here, into this guest annexe?'

Sam shook her head, promptly intervening: 'I'm a single young woman, lodging here all alone; therefore, this guest annexe must become out of bounds to you.'

She had no wish to be seen by all and sundry as Elkanah's other lady, for whenever the fancy took him.

He, however, was still trying to speak up for himself, but Sam became more firm in her resolve, she saying how they needed to really nip their present feelings in the bud, to cease anything more between the two of them, before it became way out of control.

Elkanah slapped his own thigh, he beaming before bursting into laughter: 'Oh, Sammy, they're already way out of control, as well you know.'

Chapter 3

During her first night, she sustained nothing less than a harrowing time. Then, with a benevolence far beyond any neighbourliness, Samantha experienced such an elation; as if floating upon cloud nine. she was waking up in the guest annexe. She cogitated in her own mind about opening up the wooden shutters, to greet in, perhaps, a glorious new morning? Yet, Sam was still remaining familiar with the oppressive burden of fatigue, from journeying to way beyond the mirage. Softly groaning, she uncharacteristically mused how long the tiredness, after time travelling, may last. She just had at least eight hours sleep, from eleven the previous night when the temperature was still in the nineties and with no air conditioning, but Sam was hankering for five more minutes beneath the crisp white sheet. She frowned, peeping over it, unsure if she heard either somebody or something directly outside; intrigued, maybe it was either her fertile imagination conjuring up all kinds of weird tricks upon her mind or the results of some left over cheese? She, in two minds, became uncertain.

Failing to smother a yawn, she rose to stretch; with the tiled floor being too cold, she quickly slipped her feet into her Jesus-style sandals before finally moving across to sink into the comfy couch, she emitting a lengthy sigh of contentment.

Involuntarily, she suddenly sat bolt upright upon its edge; she caught her breath, for, oh, there it was again? Sam clasped her own hands, wringing them tight, instructing herself, as a single woman, not to be lily-livered; pooh-poohing, she toned down again, dismissing it as probably a stray nanny goat chomping away at the hedges. She noticed a couple the morning before. Yes, that was it. She, usually a London town dweller, told herself to stop fussing concerning unusual country sounds.

Nipping into the small kitchen to make herself a bowl of lemon tea, a sharp beverage her palate would need to become accustomed if she should remain in ancient Ramah, she sipped at it before setting it aside on a small table. Leaning to blow into the bowl, to cool the lemony beverage, Sam mindfully pondered concerning Hannah's infertility problem, but, hey, there was that wretched noise again? It was indeed worrying her.

She, with her eyes widening, almost jumped out of her skin as she definitely heard someone lingering upon the guest annexe's cobbled courtyard; they even tried the door handle. It definitely could not be Elkanah so early. Hannah would, no doubt, be overseeing his present incarceration. Who, then, might be hanging around at such an hour? She dare not open up, for her wise father always warned her to watch out; it may be a prize fruit and nut case of a bloke? Unless, of course, it was an early bird servant coming to do for her? No. Surely, not before breakfast? Well, there could only be one way to root it out. Sam gingerly walked across to open one of the shutters only to see a big guy's unshaven face; he stepped back only a little as Sam moved forward. She could see him pointing towards the door, he first mouthing a "Shalom".

'What?'

'Shalom,' he loudly repeated. 'Peace be with you.'

Sam thought: Well, it was gloriously peaceful until then. She rapidly grabbed the sheet from the unmade bed, quickly wrapping it tightly around herself before walking to open the door, yet only by a fraction; she kept her body in the doorway, giving him no chance from barging in. Her voice still sounded as croaky as she reckoned it might; she needed that cooling tea to clear her dry throat. She breathlessly exclaimed an indeed: 'Blimey! You actually scared the living daylights out of me.'

He, fully repentant, stated he did not intend to startle her. With a broad, beaming smile, he pleaded to be let in.

'No.' Sam levelled her eyes before grinning. 'You, whoever you are, have to be joking?' She blinked. Her tired green eyes focused, travelling over his unshaven face, saw him as someone familiar.. Then, it was as if the bright light switched on in her brain; she twigged. He, Elkanah's kid brother Eable, the bareback horseman she encountered upon the day before last. Not unlike his older brother, he was tall, yet maybe broader across his shoulders. Masculine, there was, to Sam, a childlike softness about him.

'May I come in?' he asked all over again.

Aghast, she informed him yet a second time, no. 'You see, it's quite improper for you to be here,' Sam stated: 'Anyway, I've only just this moment woken up.'

Disparagingly, he scorned: 'What? This late?'

Sam gave a brief nod.

He, normally up as the local cock crowed, had returned from having exercised Hunter; she could locate the odour of the stables from his near position.

Hannah, during the previous evening, gave Eable quite a tongue-lashing for neglecting Samantha; upon her first arrival to old Ramah, he knew he should have brought her straight to the guest annexe, yet he failed. Young Hannah loudly demanded to know his then whereabouts when Sam came to the town, but, no longer a child, he left her none the wiser.

Better my silence, he thought, than lying. Making no bones about it, he basically came to apologise.

'Apology accepted.' She, still gripping tight to the lone sheet, gave a small wave. 'Anyway, I'll perhaps see you around town sometime?'

'Awe, don't be so rotten. Let me come in ...'

She was becoming bored from echoing her explanations, for the reasons were becoming as plain as the nose on his unshaven face.

'I'm famished; all I need is a bite of breakfast.'

'I'm really sorry about all that, but, frankly, I couldn't be more explicit. You must not, while I am lodging here alone, set one foot over the threshold.' She was usually soft-hearted when it came to anyone in real need and, sentimental, she would help out willingly. She did not like the idea of him going hungry, but, from his fine physique, he was hardly skin and bone. She reckoned, if he was famished, he should either call in at his brother's or eat at the farmers' market; she heard of the market from Elkanah who recommended the chicken soup. 'This guest annexe needs to be out of bounds to both you and your brother. Gosh! Only yesterday morning, didn't I tell him exactly the same?'

'But Samantha?'

' "But Samantha" nothing! Anyway, have a heart, for I'm needing my rest. Okay?' She was about to slowly close the door when she folded her arms, stating: 'I could maybe see you outside, nearer to late morning; definitely not before. Any good?'

Morosely and with his stomach growling, Eable begrudgingly agreed.

Hours passed.

Sam wondered about Eable after her coolness, if he would still take her up on her offer, to meet her outside the guest annexe?

When he eventually did show up, shaved, showered and no longer wreaking from his horse, she kept him outside; she listened as he questioned concerning her comforts in the annexe for he needed to report back to Hannah, his sister-in-law. Sam asked him to inform her: 'Everything here in this guest annexe is simply lovely. I am highly pleased with it.'

His unconcealed delight at Sam's coming to old Ramah became evident; even so, unbeknown to him, she was retaining her future hopes and plans strictly under wraps.

Despite being a growing connoisseur in the tasting of local wines, Eable, nevertheless, spent most of his working days over on the rocky, south facing limestone vineyards; Sam was later told by an older employee how, when the vineyards were in full leaf, there became a great aroma no-one could quite identify. She would look forward to such a lovely scent. However, Eable declared how his first love, apart from his horse, became his artwork, so much so that Elkanah's senior manager ticked him off for neglecting the vines.

'What is it you were proposing to do today, Sam?' Eable quizzed.

Sam was curious concerning the local medical work, although, with the long rigmarole of the journey to way beyond the mirage, she felt it preferable to remain outside upon the shaded veranda where a swing for two was long erected. She wanted to relax quietly with some much needed 'me' space.

He quickly grumbled: 'Oh, don't let's stay in and around this boring guest annexe, with you moping?'

She half bit a curt reply, how she was unaware of being someone who moped.

'So then, change your mind? Ride with me today? Please, say you will?'

'No. Not today, chum.' Sam, but not in defeat, tried not to notice how he was the spit image of his brother. Not unlike Elkanah during the previous morning, he wore a long stripy knee-length shirt. He declared he could stay and wait, until she, firm in her resolve, decided what to do. When he realised he was still not likely to scrounge there and there, he said he would skedaddle; 'I'll be back.'

Two hours and a bit later, Eable returned with a full stomach, thanks to his granddad's larder.

She, somewhat refreshed, Sam changed her mind, deciding later, she wanted to see old Ramah after all, to wander around, getting her bearings in that ancient market town, to also discover the whereabouts of the farmers' market. To protect herself from the blazing August sun, she would wear her sun hat; he stared, wishing she had left her auburn hair long and loose, to see it afresh beneath the sunlight, causing it, as he previously declared, to shimmer like copper.

'Why should someone like you, Sam, want to come out sightseeing?' he asked. 'Surely, where you come from, well, it must be much more exciting than this old place?'

'I won't know unless I see for myself.' Exhaling a deep breath, Sam previously dressed, hoping to please him; although she would be escorted by Eable, a tiny smile played across her lips as she remembered her half morning with Elkanah. One thing she believed following her first day, her times with those two priestly brothers may never become dull. She had brushed her long hair, pulling it up into a knot on top, although she knew the long curls may quickly fall loose if the only elastic band did not hold for long. She ran her finger tips over the soft fabric of her favourite vest top, with its kitten soft duck egg hue, her favourite colour; broadly smiling, she wore her pale denim shorts, completing the outfit with her small pearl earrings and sprays from her designer perfume.

Back upon his arrival, Sam told Eable she was ready, doing a quick twirl, asking if she would do? Although he greatly admired her lovely appearance, he seemed to her, a bit miffed.

'The main town is only a stone's throw from this guest annexe,' Eable told her; rather than sitting for a time on the swing, they could stroll, arm in arm, around the town.

'Are you all right?' she pressed. 'You seem heaps quieter than before.'

He pushed his fingers through his own black wavy hair; he, frustrated, admitted in a sulky way, how it was nothing as he planned for their first date. 'And, everything I've suggested, you've simply scotched.'

'First date?' She, with a voice like a soft cream, became amazed; not wanting to offend, she needed to make their immediate romantic situation abundantly clear, how they could be nothing more than simply good friends. Sam pleaded with Eable to stay back in the shade of the guest annexe's veranda. 'I do also have plenty of food here ... Hannah sent it.'

He, full up, eventually, ate a late breakfast at granddad Elihu's house. Eable shook his head, informing her she did not need to prepare a meal. 'Boy! I nearly forgot. It almost slipped my mind; we've actually been invited out to a big lunchtime buffet party.'

'What?' She, all over again, inwardly groaned: 'Oh, I am really so sorry, but I think you'll have to go alone, Eable. I really wouldn't know a soul; anyway, I don't want ...'

'Why, what is wrong now? Whatever is the matter with you this time?' Eable appeared dejected, like a whining spoilt kid who just had his candy removed. 'Oh, holy Moses! Don't you even like parties either?' He lowered his voice, but spoke only loud enough for her to hear him exclaim: 'What a drag!'

Of course, Samantha enjoyed parties as much as the next one, yet, there and then, she remained still tired, with a type of a jet lag; it would maybe leave her in a few days?

'But,' he interrupted, 'granddad said almost everyone whose anyone in old Ramah shall turn up for drinks and nibbles. If we perhaps simply stay only for a very short while? Would that actually suit you, eh?'

Throughout the mid afternoon Sam and Eable quickly became surrounded by some he knew; beautiful children tore around, weaving in and out, they playing tag with their best friends. Contented women hummed, rocking their gorgeous newborns. Locals naturally became somewhat fascinated by Sam's sudden visit to way beyond the mirage. She, finding a seat next to one of Elkanah and Peninnah's teenage daughters; the lass informed Sam how she hated school, although she secretly had a crush on one of the teachers.

Sam, remembering her own far off school days, chuckled with her, asking if he was nice. 'A real dish of a guy, huh?'

The pretty teen, with hair as black as ravens' wings, half sulked, confiding in Sam how she was at the luncheon party under protest; Sam gave her a gentle nudge, whispering: 'Ooh, me, too!' Samantha, removing her wide-brimmed, floppy sun hat to fan herself, was offered some wine; remembering Elkanah's warning about the local brew, she stayed nursing only lemon tea while picking at some cheeses, green pistachio nuts and apricot nibbles, but the majority of other guests were all taking turns to drink a local fire water from stone jars. Throbbing music from drums, cymbals and lutes filled the stifling air.

Elkanah and his then mistress Peninnah, were reported being together, shading under one of the eucalyptus trees, laughing and joking together. He had sampled the local fire water; to him, everything appeared quite hazy. He was heard shouting personal issues only Hannah should have heard. Humiliated and yet again publicly mocked by his mistress, Peninnah giggled because his present wife remained childless. Hannah, in floods of tears, stomped back home ... alone.

Sam, refusing to become party to such nonsense, tactfully informed Eable: 'Come on. I think it's high time you walked me back to the guest annexe; I'm definitely in need of a siesta.'

'It's actually the wrong time for a siesta.'

She would soon discover the correct siesta times; it was mostly Sam's way of trying to influence Eable, to nudge him to leave the party, to stop listening to Peninnah's piffle.

Reaching the guest annexe, her home, new to her, she told Eable: 'I really don't mean to be a killjoy. Be patient with me and I'll, hopefully, be soon back to my normal self.' Sam was planning for a nap.

Smelling her divine perfume, Eable asked, on the off chance, if he could join her.

Sam protested, believing it would not then be anything like a rest; inwardly, she sort of liked him and, mustering a smile, she shook her head. Strong in her resolve, she, nevertheless, offered him nothing but a simple, friendly kiss.

Elkanah had other plans, to return to his mistress' home, but Peninnah gave him the cold shoulder; she did not want their vulnerable children, especially the teens, to see him inebriated. He pleaded to the point of begging, yet, when he was flanked by her two big beefy brothers who strongly advised him, for his own health's sake, to go on his way, he thought better of it. After seeing the fury of Hannah, he was convinced he would not be welcome at home. The only places left were either the smelly stables or Sam's pad. Not fancying stinking from horses' manure, he tried his own key into the guest annexe, but Sam, upon Hannah's previous advice, bolted the door from the inside; not finding

Eable any place, he presumed he would still be with Sam. Not so. Yelling through the letterbox, he asked Sam to open up.

Blinking open her tired eyes, she was none too pleased at being disturbed. She again grabbed her white sheet, and, wrapping it around herself, opened the door, no more than a few inches. 'Whatever do you want now, Elkanah? Remember yesterday morning? Didn't I make myself abundantly clear?'

'Yeah, yeah, Sammy. I know about all that malarkey stuff, but, please, let me in?'

'This isn't fair, you know?'

'Listen? By the morning, I'll go off to sort out matters with my Hannah. I swear to you as a kingly Ephrathite, the older son of the late Jeroham, I shall honestly be not a dot of trouble to you. All right?'

'No. It isn't convenient, Elkanah.' Her usual calm veneer almost snapped. 'I'm tired out; clear off home now to your wife.' Sam recommended he should say he was sorry to her. 'Tell Hannah you love her. You do, don't you?'

'Don't be such a crack pot, Sammy, my pet! How can I? She'll have locked me out.'

'And you mean to tell me, you've no door key to your own home? I just cannot believe it!'

'Yeah, but she'll have bolted both doors from the inside.' He declared how she usually did.

'You've a quick answer for everything …'

He loudly chuckled, knowing he had. 'I definitely won't come any where near your bedroom. I'll promise you faithfully.'

Sam shook her head, she wondering if he would keep his word.

'I'll kip on the living room's sofa; by morning, I shall be gone. I'll be out of your red hair. Okay?'

'Auburn,' she corrected. She mostly possessed her mother's gentle softness, with an inbuilt ability to charm the birds from the trees, but, at such a moment in time, Sam became her father's Irish child, becoming tough, rarely giving in for the sake of peace and quiet; she would not relent. 'Heaven help you, Elkanah, if you dare to break your word ...'

Elkanah's dark eyes raised heavenwards, he hoping for its angelic help.

She squared herself, warning: 'If you think your wife Hannah has a quick temper, boy, Elkanah, you haven't heard anything as yet.'

He half grinned, although the quick sharpness in Sam's southern English tone seemed to have made the big fellow sit to obey, to nod with a recognition.

Sam, believing this situation was plain ridiculous, raked her fingers through her untidy hair; giving him one of her own pillows and pumping it to one end of the comfy sofa, she left him to settle down, by which time he became as sober as a judge.

Chapter 4

With hours feeling like days, Sam left Elkanah to snooze.

A voice resonated inside her, telling her to brace herself, to copy the old nursing sisters when they were nothing but prim and proper; yet, in the presence of the big man, Sam switched to a gently kind smile. Climbing back upon her big king-sized bed, she dived beneath the only sheet, pulling it right over herself. She was doing her uttermost to sleep, but, with the combination of the stifling humidity and his close proximity, he, with the status of being a notorious philanderer in and around old Ramah, Sam became unsettled.

Elkanah dreamed how he may again win Sam for himself, yet this beautiful foreigner was proving herself far too clever, to be manipulated; she was becoming no easy push over. Hannah, despite all her incessant nagging, adored him. Peninnah, with their six children, did, too. Sam, however, was becoming similar; she, he knew, was a woman previously wounded by a broken heart. He decided he may be able, with a kid glove care, to replace her Irish Mick. Elkanah was constantly scheming. He knew she had just once lost control concerning a passion for him. Maybe, she might fall even in love with him? Sam, though, with an implacable seriousness, impressed upon him, for her own reputation, for Hannah's sake, too, never to venture into her domain.

'Hmm,' he lay whispering to himself, 'this isn't going to be as easy as I thought?'

Elkanah's young wife longed for a baby, she hoping first for a son. Months passed with her remaining as barren as the vines in the depths of winter. Ironically, it was to be Hannah's twentieth birthday, yet sorrowfully, all she received was a heavy weight of grief.

However, during the previous day's street party, Elkanah, seemingly with an indifference to Hannah's forever misery, was up to no good, laughing and joking, boldly cherishing most of his partying time with his mistress.

Throughout the early hours of the night he needed the bathroom. Sam, finally sleeping, neither heard him, nor did she stir when he tiptoed by; the sultry night, being forever hot and sticky, caused her to inadvertently partly push aside even the cotton sheet's covering. Returning from the bathroom, Elkanah took a few long strides before stopping dead in his tracks; with a double take, he remained almost motionless by the foot of the bed. Within the obscurity of the night's light, he quietly manoeuvred his way to the side where she slept, he feasting his ember dark eyes upon her white flesh. Unawares, with a deep sigh, Sam turned over into the foetal position she usually comfortably slept. The female form he so savoured, became mostly hidden from him by her folded arms, her sheet; yet, with all his heart, with every fibre of his masculinity, he alone yearned for her.

If only? he pondered.

Delusional, his present wish was to be next to her. For a few brief moments he was happily close to Sam where he inwardly swore he could see the rise and fall of her chest wall as she breathed; instead of immediately returning to the living room's couch, he sat in a nearby rocking chair, simply to cherish she whom he claimed he loved with all his heart.

Beginning to stir, she half wondered if she saw Elkanah's silhouette, she speculating the unfamiliar; illumination was maybe playing a deceptive dream with the blur from her sleepy eyes. Remembering their clandestine lovemaking during her first morning in the guest annexe, Sam inwardly knew it should never happen ever again, with him yearning for her; she secretly desperately desired him, too, but those secret desires of hers began worryingly disturbing.

At such moments in time, there became nobody Sam desired more than Elkanah; nevertheless, she stubbornly made him out of bounds, for her to become his forbidden fruit. Simply, to prevent her from catching him spying upon her privacy, he bent way down low, half crawling upon all fours back to his promised couch. Maybe, he thought, if I play my cards right, she'll relent, to be longing again for me?

Their old grandfather Elihu sometimes needed physical help and the task fell upon young and single grandson Eable. Throughout such a particular night he remained with the wheezing, chesty old fellow. At around six in the morning, Eable quietly called into the guest annexe; his unexpected visit shocked Sam. She promptly grabbed the remains of her white sheet, to cover herself up to her chin. Propping herself up on one elbow to face him, she deeply frowned, questioning what on earth he was doing, as to why he dropped in there. She reached across to her bedside table where she left her wristwatch. 'Eable! It's so early that I betcha the cockerel hasn't even opened his eyes yet.'

'He probably has.' Eable told her how he always left for the stables around about that time.

'Whatever for?'

'Well, to exercise Hunter, of course.' He profusely apologised for simply letting himself in, explaining how, prior to her unexpected arrival, way beyond the mirage, the annexe became his pad. Inadvertently, he left behind some of Hunter's special lubricating liniment. 'This is only why I am here. Sorry to have disturbed you.'

She frowned, looking tense from being again disturbed, but declared: 'No worries.'

'My brother Elkanah is sound asleep on the couch, so I'll do my best to be extra quiet ...'

'Yeah. You didn't worry about disturbing me, though, did you?' Sam flopped back, her auburn tangled curls spilling again over her own pillow.

'Sam ... Samantha, just one other thing -.'

She inwardly groaned.

'Are you actually listening to me?'

'Hmm?' She nodded, wondering if she had a choice. 'Yes, Eable, I've heard you. So, what is it now?'

'I'm simply asking if I could have breakfast with you?'

'When?'

'This morning. In perhaps a couple of hours?'

'This morning?' She hesitated. 'Ah, I suppose so ... but, only if I'm up in time?'

He leaned across, pressing a warm kiss on her forehead before hurriedly emerging into the dawn, heading en route for the main stables. He, slowly and quietly passing by Elkanah, noticed his brother's head was laying back, his dark brown eyes tightly squeezed closed; he was faking the occasional snore.

During the short time Sam became energised into the old Samaritan area, she realised how vital it was to keep their working animals in good shape, especially their horses for, apart from camels and Shank's pony, they were the only means of transport in such ancient times way beyond the mirage.

A waiting and patient Elkanah saw the exit of his brother as his golden opportunity. He stretched and deliberately yawned loud enough for Sam to hear, pretending to her he had only there and then woken up. Swinging his long legs around from the couch and placing his bare feet flat to the cold tiled floor, he hurried across to tap on her bedroom door.

Hearing him, she sighed.

'Sammy, are you up and decent?'

Sam lapsed into a silence for a lengthy moment, wondering what he was scheming. 'Why?' she called back. 'What do you now want?'

'May I come through to the bathroom? I'll need a shower and a shave ... can't go home to my pretty Hannah looking like an old tramp ...'

She thought, if he told Hannah he bedded down on a couple of bales of straw in the smelly stable, and he appeared showered and clean shaven, she may smell a rat, convinced he was again in Peninnah's bed. Sam once more grabbed hold of her bed sheet, she pulling it over herself. 'Come on then. You can nip through.' Sam stopped to ask him: 'Why don't you become completely up front with your wife, for the truth will always come out?'

He stopped to glance back. 'Hannah never believes me, even when I do tell her the truth.'

'Turn your back then, please, Elkanah?' Sam quickly abandoning the white cotton sheet for a long floral silk robe, on loan to her from Hannah.

By heck or high water, he was still scheming, determined to take her again for himself.

He, emerging fresh from the warmth of the shower, enquired if she would hold up a mirror for him while he shaved. 'I'll definitely have this new mirror fixed up on the wall sometime today, Sammy,' he promised all over yet again. 'In the meantime ...'

'Wait up. You crafty man! Didn't you, on my first morning, tell me you could shave without a mirror?'

'Yeah.' He smiled, saying how it was absolutely true; nevertheless, it was still easier to shave with one. 'You'll also need a mirror for yourself, to see to your hair and all the other things you women do for yourselves ...'

'You don't want me to shave you again, then?'

Elkanah, unsure if she really was jesting, took a backward step before quickly shaking his head.

'Wait a minute.' She bent to grab her brown sandals, for her feet became chilly on the tiled floor; before she helped him with the mirror, she flicked back her curly, unkempt hair and, in some way, the silk tie around the waist of her robe loosened, causing the garment to discretely open.

In a happy disbelief, Elkanah smiled mischievously, he exclaiming a wow, He cast aside his mirror, leaving it propped precariously on the floor by the side of her bedside table, but, before she could rearrange her silk robe, it ridiculously slipped with a life of its own; anxious to grab it, to surround herself, it was too late to shield herself from his prying eyes. She swallowed, gulping hard as his dark eyes continued to hold. Feeling her mood swing, Sam did not believe she felt such an instant attraction to any other man, never even with her previous betrothed, not with Eable. She stopped to clear a huskiness from her throat: her face felt hot and she was aware her cheeks must have flushed a high pink, but she forced her words to become frankly brusque. 'Oh, go on your way ... go home to Hannah,' she implored. 'Remember, it's your wife's special day today?'

He frowned, speculating how Sam knew about Hannah; had she inadvertently overheard at the previous day's party? He threw his head back and laughed loudly. 'I shall be on my way, Sammy, my pet; but, frankly, I believe you're secretly enjoying every solitary bit of being with me ... you boss me about honesty, yet, now I reckon it's your turn to stop telling porkies.'

Bold and defiant, Sam tried to dismiss him, to know she would try to get on with her life without him.

' Tell me the truth now, sweet heart, Do you actually want me as much as I need you?'

Sam, tired from the early morning's wake up, scowled, shaking her head, not feeling she owed anyone a 'show and tell', especially those two brothers. 'Elkanah, I'm under no obligation to answer to you.' She, nevertheless, was sure he knew precisely how she felt concerning him; yet, she was convinced it would be madness to encourage him by spelling it out. Sam was trying with all her might not to permit her feelings to get in the way of her self control. 'You're becoming the proverbial thorn in my flesh!' she exclaimed.

The bright daylight was beginning to flood the bedroom. He rapidly moved across, to again close the wooden shutters, he preventing any inquisitive passers-by from peering through the window. 'I'm truly begging you, Sammy, only this once,' Elkanah reasoned, his large, gentle hands moved aside the softness of the robe, causing her to gasp; yet he remained a twice married man. Like a pleasing, yet a tantalising dream, they held each other and, stunned, she knew she could no longer deny the chemistry between them. As he slightly bent to caress her, she half pleaded with him to stop, although, in truth, Sam begged for more.

'I love you,' Elkanah breathed out, he prophesying the most precious of all sentiments. 'No. I adore you, my sweetheart; one fine day we'll be together as one.'

Hearing those three little words, her mind twirled in a turmoil, Sam knew it was wrong and, with 'more things in heaven and earth than are ever dreamt of ', she, nevertheless, succumbing, knew she should have become a tower of strength; this new relationship was becoming stronger than them both. 'No, no, Elkanah. You only think you love me?' Listening to his rhetoric, she declared: 'All you do is to simply lust after me.'

'You're the one who's mistaken. From the bottom of my entire being, I really love you, Sammy.'

'No.' Sam was adamant. 'You know next to nothing about me.'

'I know enough.' Not listening, he was about to ease her gently back into his arms when they heard Eable's voice; he, loudly laughing, chatted just outside the porch with a passer-by, someone he obviously knew. In quick sticks, Sam yanked herself away from an irate Elkanah who grabbed hold of his mirror, moving back to the bathroom where he carefully propped it up on the window sill. She, forcing herself to revert to being a feisty female, knew she needed to give a friendship to Hannah, how Elkanah should no longer become encouraged outside his present marriage.

'Adieu, adieu, Elkanah!' Sam exclaimed towards him, with a cheeky grin.

She, leaving the big jealous man, quickly glancing at her watch before turning towards the door, facing Eable as he let himself in: 'Gosh! You're back earlier than I expected,' she remarked. 'I haven't even started to make breakfast ...'

A little off cue, he deeply frowned towards her; indignantly, he piped up: 'Well, woman, you've had more than enough time, so why didn't you get out of bed, to move your lazy self? Quickly now. I'm famished, needing my food.'

Elkanah's jaw involuntarily dropped. Blinking, he stared in a shocked disbelief, he listening to his Eable's words. Watching Sam's normally full lips pressed tight, he reckoned it was more than time to rapidly clear off home, as if a small still voice was echoing around in his head: 'Don't wait around here!' it exclaimed. 'Sam's about to explode.' He thought their new visitor from England may well kill him; if it was said to either Peninnah or Hannah, Eable's young life would be hanging by a single thread; Elkanah believed he would be a fool to hang around any longer. Sam jumped as she heard him slam the door, he making a rapid retreat.

Her Irish green eyes blazed; she, with tight lips, angrily thought: I am not being instructed what and when to be doing young Eable's breakfasts, as if she, a mere shackled slave, became at his beck and call. 'You want breakfast bang on the dot, then you either eat at the farmers' market or try moving in with Hannah? You can join with her, clapping hands and watching the poor servants come running.' Sam took a deep breath in before exhaling. She wagged an index finger at his face before poking him in the middle of his chest. 'You listen to me, Eable? Are you hearing me?'

He, along with maybe any passers by, heard, loud and clear.

'Okay. Right then. So, get it straight into your thick skull … I am not, buddy boy, your woman, your servant, your slave. And I never shall be either those or your "bit on the side", not yours, nobody's. Do you understand plain English, Eable? Go on. Flaming well answer me?' Sam was near boiling point.

Eable took a few strides, across to a bedroom chair, sitting himself down, his hands in his lap, he staring up at her. A contrition whipped through him as he began to declare: 'It's just that …'

In what she saw as a righteous indignation, Sam straightened her silk gown, tying it too tight around her slender waist. Dragging in a deep breath before slowly exhaling, she completed his sentence for him: '… I'm hungry?'

'Yeah.'

'Tough.' Sam, patting his unshaven face a little firmer than she intended, made him stand upon his two feet, she ushering him towards the familiar kitchen. 'Ah, then, so, leach, tuck into my food, my provisions Hannah sent me, but you prepare it for yourself? Understand, chum?'

With his hands protecting his ear drums, he claimed he did.

Chapter 5

Subsequently, one Sunday, perhaps a little after eleven, she walked the short distance to meet with Hannah; Elkanah, from the previous sundown when their own Sabbath was over, went out. He, polygamous, was content to do which became right in his own eyes; he, therefore, hurried off. Sam could only speculate as to his whereabouts.

Having passed the heady vineyards, mostly worked by Eable, he as the overseer, Sam became keen to arrive for the promised chicken and salad brunch, she hoping there should be more to drink than either lemon tea or cold water from the local well.

She became aware how Hannah regularly visited the Shiloh Temple; it was a twenty mile round horse trip from old Ramah. In ancient Shiloh, Eli, the old priest who sat on a seat by the doorpost of the tabernacle, could not miss Hannah's inner bitterness, how desperately upset she was; even Elkanah made offerings, he giving her the double portion from the animal sacrifices, for, in his own way, he loved her, despite the irritating nagging. Hannah yearned for a baby boy. Sadly, back in Ramah, the only voice she heard was not from above, but the harsh, jesting one from Peninnah; her bullying sport was to make Hannah utterly miserable. Peninnah, being Elkanah's first wife, remained as his nearby mistress. She had sons and daughters, six offspring in all by him; she and Elkanah were still counting.

Jethro, the aged butler, still shuffling due to his bad feet, welcomed Samantha. With a weak smile, he informed her how his lady Hannah was waiting in the family room. He added: 'Follow me, please?'

Thanking him, Sam remembered the way. Elkanah's unruly, large dog obviously remembered her, too. It came noisily bounding down the marble staircase; Jethro rapidly shooed it off to elsewhere before it jumped up, spoiling her clean clothing.

Sam, invariably devoid of cosmetics, rediscovered an overly made up, bejewelled Hannah. The lady of the house was perched bolt upright on the edge of a chaise-lounge, rather like a naughty child being informed to behave herself, instead of the twenty year old she recently became.

'Hi, there. May I come in?' Sam asked in a sing song type of voice, she first tapping upon the room's door, calling through with a smile.

'Of course, Samantha. Come on in. I am expecting you.' She stood to hug Sam, almost squashing the colourful sweet peas she previously picked. The large room was as before; she saw it neat with its two large framed wedding paintings, of her and Elkanah, showing them both smiling and happy. Maybe they were painted by the talented Eable? All the furniture and showy furnishings, along with what her own mother Daisy would state as 'darn knick-knacks', were probably quite valuable.

Hannah greeted Sam in the self same way one of her more mature relatives might, she half forgetting how she was still only an immature twenty year old. When Sam was her age, she was approaching the end of her second year as a student nurse.

Jethro, clearing his throat, interrupted the liaison, reminding Hannah how he was soon to go off duty; he, a little like an overprotective granddad, wondered if there was anything else she required before he left. With a good natured tone towards him, she shook her head; there was nothing.

'By the way, Jethro,' Sam piped up, 'if your mistress wouldn't object, come along to the guest annexe sometime and I'll sort out those sore feet of yours.'

'Most kind, Miss Samantha. I shall definitely take you up on your kind offer.'

'Tomorrow?'

'All right.'

After the usual pleasantries between the two women, Sam politely refused a lemon tea. 'Is there nothing else?' She inwardly longed for a coffee which she knew was out of the question; homesickness felt as if it was suddenly assaulting her, she wondering concerning those left behind? Against her better judgement, she asked for a small white wine, hoping it would not be the fire-water, as it hit Elkanah during the street party.

Hannah was about to twice clap, to attract her servants, but Sam began suggesting they left them be, that they both went into the kitchen, to make their own salad lunch, pouring out enough booze for themselves? Hannah's dark, overly made up eyes widened; she was somewhat shocked to the core. 'If my servants saw us working, well, Samantha, oh, no ... it'd never do. Not within this household.' She said it may remove her own credibility.

'Sorry. It was only a thought.' Being perfectly at ease, Sam chatted with her hostess, seeing Hannah as trying to be content rather than blissfully happy; sunshine and laughter seemed remote, as if it became unwelcome at the big country house.

During the mealtime, Hannah wondered, asking with a serious expression: 'Would you like to be married, Samantha?'

Sam, somewhat taken aback, blinked, to inwardly think for a moment or two, of the amorous Elkanah; he secretly became her forbidden fruit. 'Perhaps, one day, if I meet the right guy?'

'Isn't that a rather obvious statement?'

She sighed to the point of inwardly groaning; there seemed little point in frittering away precious time of what might have been. Looking into her half empty wine glass, Sam gave a light hearted hint of a nod. 'I've still to meet my "Mr. Right".' She sometimes wondered if she would ever remedy the issue, for her biological clock was definitely ticking. A once colleague informed her how, if she did not marry by the age of thirty something, it was pretty unlikely she would ever become a wife and mother.

'And you haven't as yet, not even in your own far off land of England?'

She was unprepared to speak to this woman, this perhaps local chatter box, concerning Mick; she could hardly say: 'I very nearly became a cuckoo in your nest.' How shocking it would be, huh? Sam thought, Had I been in her shoes, I'd have kicked me out.

'I suppose, Samantha, you're aware Eable is potty about you?'

Sam's bright green eyes widened before pushing the remark aside, she hoping it would rapidly fade into oblivion.

There was a slight accusation in Hannah's tone. 'If you return to wherever it is you actually belong, Eable shall be left heart broken.'

She held out her small glass. 'Sorry to ask, Hannah, but is there any chance of a refill, please?'

Nodding, she, as ever, twice clapped, openly reprimanding the poor servant for the neglect. However, as the hostess, the neglect became hers, not that of the poor servant

Despite all, Sam became still convinced she was only energised into 1106 to help Hannah concerning conception and motherhood; it was surely a primal part of her birthright as a woman. Hannah longed for a son, one who would become a profound landmark in the whole of history.

She informed Sam: 'Every time I go out shopping in the Ramah market place, I seem to bump into that wicked Peninnah.'

'And she is nasty to you?'

'Horrid.'

'Hmm. I heard half as much.'

'Yes. In such a close knit area of ancient Ramah, I expect you did.'

'And it's all because ..?'

' ... because I haven't any babies; she points and makes fun of me.'

Sam found it unbelievably cruel, how any person could be so very unkind to another. It was outside her own comprehension.

Almost with her tears, she added: 'When I show I'm upset, Samantha, she laughs at me even more, calling me a cry baby ... even singing: "Cry baby, Hannah; cry baby!". '

Sam was shocked, wondering about Elkanah. 'Surely, if he sees you so upset, doesn't he correct the woman?'

Her frown reappeared as she shook her head.

If anyone ever dared to upset Sam's own mother, Henry Webb would rapidly rise up from his chair and state: ''That is my wife you are hurting. Watch your step, chum ...''

'And, phew, they jolly well did as they were told.'

'Elkanah stated I shouldn't be quite so intense; he simply allows it to happen. It's really not fair, is it?'

Sam stared towards her; she experienced her own heart softening as she heard such woes. 'Hannah, although I respect your going all the way to the Shiloh Temple, to pray for a child, it's actually your husband who'll get you pregnant.' Surely, Sam thought, Hannah understands that much?

Young for her years, the woman seemed confused. She listened intently to Sam who recommended how she, Hannah, should cherish her man instead of nagging.

'Me? Nagging? Do you, Samantha, honestly think I'm a nag?'

Sam, almost spluttering on the remains of her drink, nodded a quick yes. 'Hannah. I'm afraid you appeared to me how you're quite a shocker.'

'Really? When?'

She, reminding her about Elkanah's mislaid footwear, informing her how no man likes a nag, stating how a nagging wife was apparently likened to a dripping tap. 'It jangles on the poor guy's nerves, invariably driving him away, often into the arms of another ... someone like Peninnah?'

Hannah became tearful; Sam was sorry to be quite so blunt, yet, however, she knew it needed to be said: 'I'm advising you to make Elkanah happy, to please him and ...'

'But how? '

Shifting in her seat, Sam, as if she was in a difficult fix, declared: 'I suggest you talk everything over with Elkanah. He's obviously your man, when all said and done ...'

'When?'

'How do you mean "When?" ?' Sam chuckled, for Hannah sounded like a young kid: 'I dunno. Any time; Be a sweetie, instead of humiliating him by nagging; I'll bet my bottom shekel he'll eventually not bother then with anyone else, such as his mistress?'

The woman began to grin concerning Sam's words: 'And you think I may then become pregnant?'

Sam thought for a brief moment. 'I hope so.'

Hannah's dark eyes sparkled at the thought of nursing a child.

Sam, having nursed yet another empty glass and chatted at length, the spit roasted chicken and the green salad, followed by two large slices of peach pie, were awesome. She had one more worry. Almost jumping the gun, Sam stated: 'Once, if you do become pregnant, I'd like to become your own midwife, to care for you right up until your baby is born; oh, and then also through-out your postnatal time.'

It became a lovely afternoon. They moved onto the decking where there was a double swing. Sitting together, gently swinging back and forth, Sam stated:

'Hannah, do you understand? I, alone, wish to be your midwife.'

'But, there are older women who ...'

Sam immediately interrupted: 'No. No-one else.' She heard the most horrific tales about locals claiming to be so-called midwives, they working throughout old Ramah. 'Those women must never be called in by you. No-one at all.' She asked Hannah if that was the deal. 'Okay?'

'Okay.'

PART 2:

Expensive perfume wafted from Hannah where Elkanah investigated; she flirted after special candle-lit meals, intimate times between themselves, without their servants' prying eyes and gossiping tongues. They rapidly became a good balance for each other, she matching his own volcanic intensity. No matter how unpleasant things became regarding Peninnah, Hannah remained cool, quiet and elegant; she even danced with her bemused husband. Day in, day out, night after night, she, with a glow to her complexion, lived and breathed his all consuming passions until he became utterly zonked out. Spent, a breathlessly weary Elkanah soon begged for a thoroughly good night's sleep.

Eight weeks later, when Sam was out for a short constitutional, she wandered by Elkanah and Hannah's flower garden. Gazing over their fence, she noticed how Hannah, lounging in a deckchair, appearing devoid from her usual heavy make-up, totally washed out. 'Are you not feeling well, Hannah?' she asked.

Hannah shook her head before squeezing her eyes shut; she managed to whisper out a 'shocking.'

'What's wrong?'

'Don't ask.' Hannah declared she reckoned she was beyond medical help. 'Ooh, Samantha, every single morning I am throwing up. I think I may be dying.' She prayed for angelic assistance.

Sam quietly offered a knowing smile.

The next day, after the siesta, Sam called in at Elkanah's, to ask if she may examine Hannah.

He hung his head, appearing washed out; there and then, Elkanah would have agreed to simply anything, just for a bit of peace and quiet.

' You're not dying, Hannah ...' Sam started.

'Are you absolutely sure, Samantha?'

Sam's face lit up with a happiness. 'You're obviously pregnant ...'

'Really? Is this what it's like to be pregnant?'

She nodded. 'I reckon so.'

Hannah's chocolate brown eyes swam with happy tears, they freely flowing down the cheeks of her face.

The pregnancy was, to Hannah, apparently like a major miracle. The first time she felt the baby move inside her, something of primal importance happened throughout her inner-most self. She, with all women, with all time, felt utterly irrevocably female. She experienced many feelings of invasion. Another living being was temporarily inhabiting her and she loved it. Even so, she was a bit frightened of all the unknown. Sam did her utmost to reassure her regarding the labour, along with the discomfort which would probably accompany it. All such turmoil was happening, of course, at the same time she was growing smugly proud of herself for finally being pregnant.

Towards the latter end of the woman's pregnancy, Sam regularly called in for a domiciliary visit, palpating Hannah's abdomen and listening to the fast lub-dub sounds from the baby's heart; the infant was in the correct position for a normal delivery. Despite being a good midwife, she was a long way from a London Midwifery Hospital where every eventuality may be discovered and, hopefully, corrected. Here, way beyond the mirage, she, hoped upon hope, this first time mum would deliver spontaneously, to go to full term without any active assistance, without any abnormalities to the foetus. Hearing about a young Shiloh woman, a distant relative of Elkanah who died in childbirth, it did not inspire confidence in Hannah's hopes. 'I don't want to die,' she bemoaned to Sam.

One Friday morning in August, around the time as the cockerel crowed, Elkanah tried his door key into the guest annexe; wisely, Sam bolted the place from the inside. Frustrated, he kicked the door, but, in doing so, stubbed his big toe, making him angry; he banged the side of his fist on the door. 'Sammy. Samantha Anne Webb! Will you open up this blessed door?' he yelled at the top of his voice. 'It's an emergency!'

Reaching for her white towelling robe, to wrap it around herself, Sam quickly walked across her bedroom and through as far as the front door, beyond where he was still yelling. She drew back the rusting bolt, opening the door to see a scantily clad, breathless Elkanah. Before she could utter a solitary word, he pushed, elbowing his way inside.

'Oh, do come in, won't you?' she began with a sarcasm in her tone. 'Don't you ever wait to be invited?'

'No.' Turning squarely to face her, he gently shook her by the shoulders. 'Are you flaming well deaf, or something?'

'Not a bit. And neither is the rest of the town!' Sam rubbed her sleepy eyes. 'What ever do you want, Elkanah?'

'I told you, it's an emergency.'

'Okay. Well, having woken me up, what sort of an emergency are we talking about?' She stared down at his foot. 'Did you know your big toe's bleeding?'

He gulped to regain his breath. 'It's Hannah! She's about to have the baby.'

'Already? Surely not.'

'Yes. Absolutely. Her interfering mother wanted to call out the local women, but I told her to darn well sling her hook; I said it has to be you. So they've gone; come on, then, Sammy! Don't simply stand there looking like a lemon.'

'Elkanah, I have to get dressed. I'll be along in a bit.'

He slightly ginned: 'I can wait ...'

'Oh, no you don't.' Sam scowled and shook her head. 'Now, look away.' Having dressed, she stepped into some new leather sandals, recently purchased from a market trader and, following Elkanah along to his big house, walked straight through into the family room where his young wife was on their chaise-lounge, seeming anxious.

Sam checked Hannah. 'You are, in my opinion, definitely a very long way off labour.'

'But no, Samantha. I can't be, for I definitely felt some contractions ...'

Sam grinned, sitting by her side; taking her hand in hers, she quietly explaining they were nothing but only Braxton Hicks contractions.'

'What? I don't even know anyone by that name ...'

Samantha tried hard not to laugh. 'Those contractions are only where your muscles become tightened and toned. Forget it.' Sam failed to stop a yawn; she glanced down at her wristwatch. 'We'll all go back to sleep, eh?'

'Hmm. Only if you're really sure?'

'Positive.' Sam stated before peering down at Elkanah's big toe. 'Do you want me to see to it before I go back to sleep?'

He looked down towards his foot, shaking his head. 'Don't fuss. It'll be all right.'

One week to the day, again in the early wee hours and long before the cockerel even thought about waking up the area, Elkanah began hammering on the guest annexe's door.

She rubbed the sleep from her eyes. 'Whatever is it now?' Sam complained.

'Sammy!' She was not over keen at hearing him naming her "Sammy", but she fell from her comfy bed to unlock the door. 'What the blazes?'

'Hannah says it's very painful. Come quickly ...'

Within less than ten minutes she made it over to Hannah who was in well established labour, yet, being a first baby, it was quite a while before she became ready to push.

'Elkanah, make me a cup of tea,' Sam asked, informing him how she felt parched.

His brown eyes opened wide.'Me? Make tea? Why do you think I pay for servants, eh?' He waved for the attention of a nearby one, to say that Miss Samantha needed tea. 'Get on with it!'

Hannah interrupted: 'Samantha, ooh, I really do feel I need to push!'

'Okay. Listen carefully to me. Focus only upon what I shall tell you, Hannah.'

'Are you actually listening to Sammy, Hannah?' Elkanah queried, leaning across to his wife, to mop her brow, to stroke her long black hair.

She promised how she really was listening, trying hard to concentrate, but, 'Ooh, it hurts!' ; she soon became getting too tired and so, maybe, was the baby?

Sam was anxious to get the baby out; she firmly instructed: 'All right, Hannah. Hands gripping behind your thighs and take a big breath in. Put your chin on your chest and bear right down with all your strength, with all your might. No! Not with that dreadful noise in the back of your throat. And again, come on ... push really hard! Stop it. Now, no pushing ... pant, pant ... one small, little push. Okay, now the head is out ... your baby has lots of hair, as black as ravens' wings ... And oh, wow ... here we are ... it's a boy!'

'A boy ... a boy!' shouted Elkanah before he kissed his wife.

'Now,' Sam stated, 'I am about to cut the cord, but, when I clamp it, would you like to cut it instead of me, Elkanah?'

'What, me ... cut the cord?'

'Yes. You. Go on. Cut it exactly there ... there. That's it!'

A very proud Elkanah, as he had taken hold of the scissors and severed the umbilical cord, beamed from ear to ear; his dark eyes almost danced with merriment at the sight of his beautiful new son.

He closely stood, watching Sam checking, measuring and weighing the baby before she wrapped the little lad into a big white fluffy towel. Handing him to Hannah, Sam declared: 'Congratulations! You have a fine, healthy son … both of you, very well done.'

Elkanah continued to beam at the sight of their new arrival; salty tears ran, escaping down his sun tanned face as he showered his wife's forehead with kisses. Had the child been a girl, the couple planned to name the baby 'Samantha' after their British midwife. 'Anyway, we'll name our boy Samuel which means "Name of God",' he stated, saying: 'Hannah and I asked for him from the Lord.' He prophesied: 'And he shall grow up to be a very great man.'

Many Samaritan friends and relatives gathered outside, waiting to hear the great news. A great cheer went up as Elkanah announced: 'It's a boy!' Therefore, Hannah's mother became a doting granny, Eable was an uncle, but old Elihu joyfully declared: 'I'm a great granddaddy … wow!'

Samuel was indeed gorgeous, twenty-two inches long and weighing in at eight pounds, two ounces; he was born in the year 1105 BC

Hannah, after the time of ritual cleansing, within her own inner closet, declared: 'I am the woman, God, who stood before you praying. I prayed for this boy child, and you have granted me my desires. My mouth boasts over my enemy … over that nasty Peninnah … I delight, oh, Lord, in your deliverance.'

About six weeks later, Hannah informed Sam how she decided to remain to be as a stay-at-home mum so she could personally care for Samuel.

Elkanah was off again to the Temple in Shiloh. As one of the ancient family of priests, he needed to go every year, to sacrifice an animal. He informed Hannah he would miss her.

'But I definitely shall not go with him,' she stated.

'Why ever not?' Sam quizzed. 'If he so needs you – why not go with him, eh?'

Hannah deeply scowled at Sam, flatly refusing. 'When baby Samuel is fully weaned, then I'll go to Shiloh; definitely not before. Samuel is only a tiny baby and I believe he's too young to travel right now.'

Elkanah was quite annoyed with Hannah, to say the least. He told her so in no uncertain terms. 'He snapped at me and told me to do whatever I pleased; he said he'd do precisely the same.'

Sam could see how Hannah was so doting upon only Samuel, how he had become the light of her life; after all the pre-pregnancy love with Elkanah, her husband, was suddenly feeling pushed aside, as if two's company, but three became a crowd. 'If you're not very careful, Hannah, you shall again lose him to Peninnah. You won't like that, my friend,' Sam added. 'I would strongly advise you to still keep on giving him plenty of attention.'

'With respect, Samantha, you aren't a married woman, with any children of your own, so what do you know about such domestic matters, eh?' She continued to remind Sam: 'All your knowledge comes only from "book learning", whereas with me … well, I am not going to turn into an old spinster, am I?'

Sam shrugged, she hardly knowing either what to say or how to react.

Hannah shook her head, standing her ground, expressing what proceeds behind closed doors was nothing to do with nosey outsiders; Sam should, as far as Hannah was considering, keep her nose out of a married woman's private business. She was implicating how Elkanah had done his bit by giving her a son; for her, that was quite enough.

As soon as the young Samuel was able to alone eat solids, Hannah began to pack up all her and Samuel's belongings. A shocked to the core Elkanah, choking back his welling tears, pleaded, begging on his knees for her to remain in ancient Ramah, but she ignored all his reasoning. With the help from her own parents, a resident nanny and a whole host of her servants, Hannah removed lock, stock and barrel, to settle in old Shiloh. In addition to her usual personal possessions she took a three-year old bull, ten kilograms of flour and some very good vintage wines from her husband's wine cellar. The bull was tethered and sacrificed by Eli, the old Temple's senior priest. Throughout all the journey, Hannah intermittently laughed aloud for she had previously given birth to a baby son; no more could Elkanah's Peninnah, with her cruel and scurrilous tongue, mock her for being barren.

Chapter 6

Samantha, slightly homesick, sighed, she longing to again be able to inhale the tempting aroma of coffee. Her face changed into a slight smile; it would shortly become her twenty-sixth birthday. She relished birthdays, whether it be either hers or those of others. It was probably synonymous with her mother, she making a big fuss of birthdays; Sam, no doubt, inherited it from her. Despite being worlds away from them, Sam became convinced the parents would not forget her special day. She wondered if, due to her being absent so long, they bought some flowers in memory of her; naturally, she would not be home to receive the usual pretty-in-pink card, along with a hip-sticking iced cake complete with birthday candles. As she would blow them out, she would be called upon to make a wish; friend Paula, in recent years, always reminded Sam how, if she breathed the content of the secret expectation, it would not become bona fide. She, walking to the window, to mindlessly peering out, knew her parents and Paula must be desperately worried for her, yet there were no means of communications, to inform them she was safe and well.

Sam, one afternoon, paced the floor of the guest annexe, she needing to seriously think her future; she decided to stop, calling a halt to her meditations, to turn to sit beside Eable, she reminiscing about some of her more memorable birthdays. 'Although my parents own a large, wrap around garden, my mum usually treated a few of my friends and me for a birthday picnic tea; we'd pack up the goodies and walk to Wimbledon's Trinity Gardens.' Sam smiled, adding: 'We young kids ate until we were stuffed.' She told on: 'There, in the Gardens, was a central bandstand.'

'A bandstand?'

'That's right. The brass band, all in their uniforms, played many of the old time favourites, including: "We'll gather lilacs in the spring again …" Sam told him how it never seemed to rain during those May days.'

'What? Never?'

She stopped to think. 'You know, Eable, I actually don't remembering any bad weather.'

Filled with thoughts, he wanted to know why the Webb family did not use their own garden for the birthday party.

Sam wrinkled up her freckled nose, thinking for a moment; she wondered if it was because her dad did not relish a whole group of excitable little kids racing around, ruining his striped lawns, breaking panes of glass belonging in the nearby greenhouse where he grew his prize tomatoes. 'However, maybe my most memorable birthday was naturally my twenty-first, my then coming of age, when there was a large surprise party in a local hall.'

'You were a lucky young woman.'

She agreed, indicating to the small white pearls in her pierced ears. 'They were a present from my parents.' Henry and Daisy Webb purchased them from an old

Jewish jeweller in Wimbledon Broadway; old Mr Abram, the proprietor, had, four years' previously, pierced her ears.

'Did you know that Mick fellow then?'

She could not even bring herself to repeat the guy's name without welling tears; shaking her head, she declared: 'Fancy your remembering him?'

He raised his dark eyes heavenwards, raggedly sighing long and hard, coming right out to inform her how, he and his brother, had heard more than enough concerning the enigmatic Irish figure from Balygar.

Were he and Elkanah a little jealous? she wondered. Or simply bored to tears by the name of Mick?

Whatever, Eable also wished to give Sam a memorable birthday gift. He was well known throughout ancient Ramah for his stunningly fine art; even as far as Jerusalem many connoisseurs commissioned his work. In both ancient Shiloh and Ramah Sam previously helped him launch six successful art exhibitions. Drawing portraits definitely became his forte; future brides were more than happy to sit for him, they wearing all their extravagant finery, to commemorate their special wedding day. When Sam opened his portfolio and leafed through his many drawings, especially those of his beloved Hunter, for a birthday gift she asked if he might sketch her ... a drawing she may cherish forever. Flattered, he became delighted she asked; only within the seclusion of the guest annexe's bedroom, it should soon become arranged, to be completed in time for her birthday.

Days later, when sitting for him, she soon became bored stiff from doing next to nothing. While she propped comfortably against a whole pile of pillows and cushions, she asked if she could be rearranged, to be seen to be reading a book, or something or other?

'I don't agree.'

Sam, upon the only sofa, tried to relax with big breaths, to meditate about other stuffs, such as the black, sugar free coffee she could not have, about her British friends and Irish Catholic family. It became difficult to cease thinking about them who must surely be missing her, as she them.

A dejected looking Elkanah, without a bye your leave, located his own door key, he letting himself into the guest annexe; promptly, he strode through into where he heard their voices, he throwing himself into a nearby armchair. In a flash, his black mood lifted, he seeing her bright auburn hair, long and flowing loose over her shoulders. Normally, she would shoo him from the guest annexe, yet, during that particular time, she informed him she dare not move as his young brother was sketching her.

Slowly, he rose from his seat and hovering as close as he dare, he cocked his head to one side; he first stared at her. His fingers twitched, desperate to caress the silky smoothness of her auburn hair, but, as he faced her, she deeply scowled, declaring: 'Don't you dare touch, Elkanah!'

His ebony dark eyes began to feast his sights upon her; he quickened his short strides to glance over Eable's shoulder, down at the drawing, then back up at Sam, to compare the uncanny likeness. Doling out compliments, at the sight of the fine portraiture, he informing his brother he would buy the work once complete ... how, in that particular case, shekels would definitely become no object.

'This sketch, Elkanah, is all for me, for my birthday.'

'But, Sammy,' he protested with a whine, 'I'd adore seeing you all day and every day. In fact, it would be just as if I was actually with you.' He turned back to his brother. 'Eable, how can you stand at your easel, drawing this vision of pure loveliness and not be affected by her? Now, if I was drawing her ... phew!'

'Stop acting the fool. Elkanah; would you mind telling us why you called in here in the first place? You surely haven't come to pass the time of the day, I bet.'

Tall Eable, rolling again his eyes under dark brows, stated how his big brother came simply to be an irritant. Nothing more, nothing less.

'You, as per usual, wrongly judge me.' Elkanah shook his head. 'Listen up! I came to tell you both how my Hannah's gone for good and, worse of all, she's taken our Samuel with her.'

Samantha questioned: 'She's done what?'

He deeply frowned.

'Oh, Elkanah! Didn't you think to go after them?'

'Yeah.' He nodded. 'Of course. I took my own stallion, trying hard to race after her, but she yelled, instructing her male servants to stop me.'

Sam became almost horror struck.

'No fool, just as with Peninnah's two older brothers, I wasn't going to argue with those stinkingly big bodyguards of Hannah's.' However, upon his return, Huntsman became a little lame, hence he needed to walk the stallion back to the stables. 'My own stable lad's now caring for my horse.'

'I think, Eable, we'd better call it a day,' Sam stated, tidying up the cushions and pillows before brushing through her hair.

Eable nodded and took hold of Sam's wrist, to glance at her watch. Realising the hour, it was almost time for him to nip across to the stables, to check upon his own Hunter's apparent well being. 'Are you staying on, brother?' he asked. 'Shall you be here later, when I come back?'

Elkanah stopped, his tone faltering, he giving the real reason as to why he was there. Mindlessly, he felt the dark stubble around his chin and shrugged. 'Oh, I really don't think so. I simply came across here to tell the two of you I'm soon moving out of my big house, so, if you'd like to have it ...'

Sam promptly interrupted. 'So, where are you planning to live?' She also knew he slept with Peninnah over the years, which rarely bothered him much. He appeared to enjoy a 'live today and forget tomorrow' policy, half giving his own eternity much of a fleeting thought.

'Me? Oh, I had a long chat with Peninnah; eventually, she agreed I can move back in with her and the kids.'

'Is it what you really want?'

He half closed his dark brown eyes and again shook his head. 'No. Of course not, although it'll be grand to be with the six children, helping them with all their growing up times, doing nice things for them, particularly with the boys.'

With Eable leaving for the stables, Elkanah seated close to Sam, his head in his cupped hands, with his elbows on his knees, to looking sad.

She placed an arm close around him, her thigh inadvertently touching his, she feeling a tug, remembering the brief time they spent together. 'Tell me. I thought everything between Hannah and you was okay, but obviously it wasn't?' She presumed everything was going swimmingly. 'I mean, especially when Hannah was trying to get pregnant ...'

'Getting pregnant!' It was then his turn to interrupt her. 'That's all she actually needed me for – to be nothing but a stud. She stated she never really loved me at all; as soon as she'd had the baby she doted upon Samuel so much, it was as if I no longer mattered.'

'I did wonder if ...'

Elkanah nodded. 'During all the time she was pregnant, I never once strayed anywhere near Peninnah – I swear.' He sucked in a breath. 'I didn't touch you either, did I?'

Glazed with a secret passion and still with the desire, Sam cleared her throat: 'You certainly didn't.'

'Honestly, I then only needed Hannah, Samuel and me to become a nice little family together.' He was a man then stating his inner feelings. 'Once Hannah gave birth to Samuel, I thought she'd also have more babies by me, but she has simply packed up all her necessary belongings and cleared off to Shiloh. It's a sad day, isn't it, Sammy?' He tried to conceal the tears as they came. 'I don't suppose you know, sweetheart, but my Peninnah recently lost one of our baby sons, which was plain awful.'

'Goodness! I can only imagine. It must have been truly shocking, but the little one shall be in the arms of the angels, eh?'

Elkanah half agreed. 'It was a terrible day, to bury our precious little bundle, but Hannah clapped, and danced and rejoiced at its death.'

'Hannah actually did that? No. Are you truly sure?'

'She most certainly did.' He added how she even made up a long and happy song. 'Is she totally nuts, do you think?'

Sam felt unbelievably sorrowful for Elkanah; he seemed inwardly dejected. She clasped his strong hands in hers, but he, pulling away, wiped his wet eyes on the back of his hand, begging her to tell no-one he wept.

Sam smiled, responding with a promise.

He remained silent for a long moment or two before he continued: 'Heavens! I've made a great big mess of things, haven't I?'

'You, Elkanah? Shouldn't think so.' Holding him again tighter in her arms, Sam's then gentle heart turned over for his sad situation. Ramah, where she remained living, became, on the whole, full of extraordinary folk; he was one. She gave him a big squeeze of a hug, her words softly whispering, wishing she could always keep him close.

For once only, he yanked himself from her, turning his back and promptly left the guest annexe; on his way out, he slammed the door so hard behind him, the volume made her jump.

Wounded, dark and lonely, he vowed within himself that, for the remainder of his days, he would live in that ancient city of old Ramah, claiming to be the master of his own destiny.

Around the next day's sunrise, Eable threw on an old shirt and headed towards the stables; he bumped into Elkanah who was loudly snapping at his stable boys, lads who were carrying fodder for the horses and other livestock. He shouted how his own stallion ought to be watered first. Eable, peering down his nose, to interrupt the yelling, reminded his grumpy brother about Sam's birthday, saying how he thought they should arrange to give her a birthday party, to make it as memorable as her twenty-first. Oh, sure, Eable was giving her the portrait he sketched, yet he knew, from all she told him, she invariably enjoyed a birthday party. Elkanah still did not feel much like celebrating anything, but Eable reminded him how it was all about Sam; not him.

'They sing a song, too, Elkanah, which goes like this …' Eable sang, he trying to remember the tune: "Happy birthday to you", and so on. 'We cannot let her birthday to pass, simply because of your black mood?'

'Yeah, all right. As it's for our Sammy, I'll do my best to cheer myself up.'

'Okay then.'

'The party must be a whopper of a surprise from us both, eh?' Elkanah added: 'All the guests must be told to keep it a big secret.'

With all the folk who came to know Samantha Anne Webb, along with those in ancient Ramah who were simply curious to join in the unusual celebration, the brothers tried to purchase a spring lamb from the kosher butcher, although, when he knew it was for Sam, he made no charge; the local doctor organised the smoky bar-b-que when he tried not burn anything. The aroma of him previously roasting lamb and the baker's newly baked birthday cake filled the air as everyone congregated in the still manicured garden belonging to Elkanah's big house. Someone or other even made a happy birthday banner in girlie pink. No-one arrived late.

Sam knew absolutely nothing concerning the huge bash. Elkanah would egg her along by asking her to identify some of the plants in his garden before he left them behind.

She thought it more than a bit odd, but she planned to oblige, presuming it may cheer him up in some odd sort of a way.

Sam was quietly resting, but, with his own door key, he simply let himself in, giving a gentle prod in her ribs. She rubbed the sleep from her tired eyes. 'Yeah. I'll nip over tomorrow, Elkanah. All right? Now, just shoot off and leave me be.'

He shook his head, giving her a kiss, his moist mouth tasting from a sweetness. 'No, Sammy. Now.' He persisted, trying to pull up her by the hand. 'Come on and hurry up or the plants may wilt.'

'Have you been sampling your wine, or what?'

His smile became instantaneous before he began to loudly chuckle: 'Only a weeny bit, just as a taster. Now, hurry up ...'

'Well, okay then.' She thought it was all a little weird. She wondered if he was as crazy as Hannah?

'Sammy ...' He frowned, eyeing her up and down. 'Do you have a much prettier top you could wear?'

'What? I need to be smartened up, just to walk along a dirt track to see your unusual plants? Are you totally nuts?' She suddenly noticed how he was in his finest knee-length posh shirt, the one with the colourful stripes. 'What's going on?' Whatever, Sam told him she first needed a shower, to also clean her teeth. He remained away from the bathroom, sitting on the edge of the bed.

'I've already had a shower and a shave,' he called.

'Why, to be smart while we watch your plants wilting?'

'Absolutely.' He giggled.

Sam smiled, noticing the lift in his previously black mood. She stepped out and away from all her usual togs before hurrying under the spray of warm water, soaping her skin, shampooing her hair, while she hearing him still laughing to himself.

Drying her hair, Sam suddenly twigged; she thought she was to dress up, to receive Eable's portrait of her, for her birthday gift, yet it never crossed her mind there was virtually half of the town waiting for her.

Dressed in her finest, in her ivory linen trouser suit, she completed the elegance by the small pearl earrings; performing for him a little twirl, Sam asked: 'Will I do, Elkanah?'

He smelled her divine perfume. 'Gosh! You are so very beautiful, Sammy.' He, wiping away the tears which sprang up in his eyes, reminded her how much he loved her, and he, no idiot, knew she felt precisely the same concerning him. 'You, Sammy, are my everything, you know?'

She did. Blushing a little at his compliment, she, to the detriment of the wild flowers in the hedgerows, brushed her hand over them as they walked, as they passed by. Kissing quickly under the cloudless sky, they continued along, stepping into his large garden, where a very noisy bunch of Ramah folk, all clapped and cheered, handing her a glass of an extraordinary wine, bringing her right up to where baritone Eable loudly sang, mostly in tune:

'Happy birthday, to you,
happy birthday, to you,
happy birthday, dear Samantha,
happy birthday to you!'

More clapping and cheering carried on as many sang: 'She's a jolly good fellow', even though a few did not know her too well; the local mayor, a white haired overweight guy with a fancy gold chain around his neck, loudly called for Sam to make a speech, yet she was so overcome, lost for words; she choked out a quietly tearful thank you.

It was almost sunset by the time the successful do began to wind down, when everyone, full of Elkanah's very best wine, picked their way home, he leaving the gardener and the usual servants to clear up.

So much took place following her first full day in ancient Ramah, when she left the big house where a domineering Hannah clapped her hands, causing almost everyone jumping to attention, they obeying all her house rules. It was in there Sam discovered coffee and sugar remained enigmatic. Accompanied by Elkanah, she remembered walking the quarter of a mile, or so, to the guest annexe, never believing for a moment, she would become energised way beyond the mirage; surely not her? This was one journey she never thought of taking, she having been quietly living for almost a quarter of a century in one of the smarter areas of London, in the south of England. Her caring parents, she imagined, would more than likely be beside themselves with worry, wondering wherever she could be.

The parents raised Samantha in the self-contained distinctiveness of the well known town of Wimbledon, upon the edge of the Common, there with a measure of rural peace. Henry and Daisy Webb began their married life during the second World War; they were separated for quite a few years while he fought for King and country, times when Sam was not even thought of, not until 1946.

Henry married Daisy, his sweet Irish girl. Dublin was their first home, but then, next to Liverpool and beyond, to the delights of Wimbledon where Sam was born. Sam's maternal grandfather moved in with them after his own wife died; when he also passed away, he left Sam a goodly sum of money. She, having been brought up in the claustrophobic, overprotected world of an only child, she grew to become professionally successful, yet hoping always for her own future to become as a loving wife and mother. Sure enough, she loved her own profession, but Sam tentatively hoped for more, for a modern semi-detached bungalow with a large garden, to settle down with her Irish born Mick, until listening to an older spinster; she caused Sam to almost emotionally collapse.

Her normal routine left behind the life of coffee and the coffee houses, with its freshness, the first giant each morning. Since, she made yet another journey, one way into the unknown, a place her father may well investigated if his Daisy travelled with him to peace time Egypt. Who knows? Whatever, her parents who are only living upon an army pension or two, must be doing their utmost to pay, to discover her whereabouts; but, knowing nothing, they must be homing in upon the intolerable. Even though she was an independent adult, they loved her, their only child. Reassuring themselves, perhaps over their evening meals, they must have over turned every hypothetical stone, unable to bear the thought of her disappearance, the thought of their apparent loss. Becoming like the sluggish fallen leaves, Daisy inwardly complained regarding the sameness of their years, of boring love-making, nearly always in the dark, with him taking her until it was all over and done with for another week. She half wished he would find something else to do, to not get under her feet during the long days. All they both desired was that their beloved Samantha should return, safe and sound. That's how Sam imagined it surely to be, so it ought to become: "Home, James, and don't spare the horses!", as it were. She cast a critical eye over the annexe's bedroom, the large bed where, about as good as it gets, the exciting and athletic love-making took place, where there was always a fizz of new excitements racing through her veins, yet, enjoying them, it was an uncomfortable thought she needed to return to Paula, to her parents, to ease their supposedly anxious minds.

Samantha considered her mission as a midwife complete. Yes, she knew it was definitely time to go home, yet it would be tough to relocate, to leave behind her settled life in ancient Ramah, to return to her Western way of living. She believed she no longer had a choice. How, though, she wondered, might she break the news to Eable, the guy who loved her with a passion? As for Elkanah? Sam believed she would need to gently let him down, not leaving him wounded, dark and lonely without her, too.

Chapter 7

Relieving her servant from cleaning, from working as hard as if she were two, Sam requested the woman to switch chores, for her to instead prepare food, particularly before the goats' milk and cheese, with its heavy seal, turned rancid. Without sophisticated refrigeration, it became a distinct possibility. She informed the woman how Eable should be visiting the guest annexe. 'He'll be staying on here yet once again, for something to eat.'

Her bidding instructions to her servant dumbfounded Eable. He scratched his head. 'Why ever did you tell her I'm only visiting here?' he, but in a whisper, queried.

Wearing a false smile, Sam turned to face him. 'Well, that's right, isn't it?'

'What ... whatever do you mean?'

She shrugged. 'I just presumed you'd be here again, to eat my rations once more?'

Eable appeared a little confused. 'But, Sam ...' he started up.

Sam's fake smile altered to a dead pan expression; she frowned, exclaiming: '"But, Sam", nothing! Elihu depends upon you, for all your help as his carer, yet ... yet, I've heard, through the grapevine, you're eating there, too.'

He quickly interrupted. 'So what? '

'So what?' She leaned forward, refusing to allow him to stammer out his words until she finished her say; she angled her head to continue: 'This guest annexe, with all its food and drink, is meant for me.' She, mounting her own mini rebellion, added how, in her opinion, he was becoming a little like a leach, taking advantage of her and Elihu's generous natures. 'You presume all the goodies are also yours, just for the taking.'

Eable contributed not a shekel towards the house-keeping. The previous week he even left his used clothing for her to wash, stating all over again: 'Well, you are only a woman. It's a chore which women do.' He was walking on thin ice.

Although Sam held an affection for him, it irritated her beyond reason how, from her accompanying him to the street party way beyond the mirage, tight-fisted Eable did his uttermost to 'get his feet under her table', as it were; had he not learned his lesson when he foolishly saw it as his good given right to demand to have his breakfast served up by Samantha, to have it prepared the moment he returned from the stables? She wondered if he saw himself as her master in the guest annexe, he possessing his own door key, enabling himself to come and go as was his want. Even Elkanah began seeing Sam and his brother as an item, when all the time she was secretly loving him, yet the guy was not a free man.

Rarely one for an argument in front of a servant, Sam let the issue with Eable drop ... only for a while.

Two large platters of freshly baked bread and a small roasted chicken were set before Sam and Eable, he who, usually working up in his own vineyards, never contributed even a bottle of wine. The servant sliced up breasts from the bird, cutting away the remainder from the carcass into thin pieces. With wafer thin, refreshing cucumber, she made up two rounds of sandwiches.'You always like black pepper in your sandwiches, don't you, Miss Samantha?'

She did.

The woman was about to peel some juicy Jaffa oranges when Sam piped up: 'Are they your youngsters I can hear out on my veranda?'

The servant became anxious, thinking she may be in trouble; she did not wish her kids to interrupt Sam. 'Ooh, Miss Samantha, I'm really very sorry if they're being disruptive; I told them not to make a noise.'

'No.' She smiled: 'Frankly, it's simply lovely to hear little ones playing; they're sounding so happy.'

'They aren't bad kids.'

The thought struck Sam: 'Listen. Why don't you bring them inside? Get them in, well away from that sun's strong heat.'

'Well, miss, if you're absolutely sure?'

'Positive.' Sam glanced towards the large wooden fruit bowl. 'As you can see, I have more oranges than I can cope with; do give them some ...'

Filled with a gratitude, she remarked how Sam was always kind. 'My older two youngsters were supposed to be keeping an eye on the baby boy while I work.'

Sam clapped. 'Ooh, wow ... a baby? How old is he?' Sam's expression changed to shock, to discover the woman doing chores, despite recovering from a birth only ten days previously. 'Hey, I honestly don't think you should be even considering working; not yet.' She restrained herself from picking up the new born, from hugging the older kids, but, instead, she smiled down at the pretty young girl, then quiet and not a little shy; the tiny scrap, it beginning to whimper, trying to find his fist to suck. 'Go off home now,' Sam told her servant and rest up. I'm more than capable to finish up all the chores.'

'You? You finish the chores?' The woman was genuinely surprised.

'Sure. Neither Eable nor I are not completely incapable, you know?' Sam smiled, noticing the children nudging each other, they eyeing the large bowl of fresh fruit. 'Hey, there, kiddies; you want some?'

Of course they did.

Sam's mouth curved into a quick smile, telling the girl to hold out her skirt; she filled it with the largest oranges. With one too many, she instructed the boy: 'Here, catch!'

The lad beamed as he caught his own piece of fruit. He said would enjoy eating it.

'I'm really forced to work here, miss,' the servant woman explained to Sam; the thought of threatening to become unemployed overwhelmed her near to tears. 'With three young mouths to feed, we really need all the shekels I can get.'

'I understand; but, if you overdo it and become too tired, you'll probably lose your milk.'

'I dunno about my milk; I'm certainly losing my sleep.'

'I bet. You'll still be having night feeds, eh?'

'Also, life's not helped by a nearby neighbour, a widower; he has a large barking dog which wakes us more than my baby might.'

'What about your husband, then? Surely, he's working?'

She shook her head. 'My Joseph was recently kicked by a mule, so he's still recovering from a bit of a back injury.'

'Even so, he could surely pull his weight, especially when it comes to helping with the two older kids ... he could at least keep an eye on them?'

She shrugged, not knowing to dare answer in front of the kids.

'Ah, well. You know what's best concerning your own situation ... I really shouldn't interfere.' She remembered when Elkanah's Hannah reminded her how she, Sam, an unmarried, should mind her own business when it came to families.

After the servant woman rounded up her little ones, eventually leaving for her home, Eable took a sip from his own lemon tea before briefly frowning. 'You, Sam, need to take a leaf out of your own book,' he scolded. 'You need to eat more.'

'I do eat.'

'Not near enough.' Seeing her auburn hair and pale ivory skin, his deep voice added: 'You're also looking as white as a sheet, too. These days, you are seeming more tired than your down-at-heel servant woman.'

They sat and ate the sandwiches together, she licking her own fingers clean. She expressed her worries concerning the servant with her young off spring.

Eable half ticked her off: 'You're much too soft, you know? If that servant was employed by someone like Hannah, she'd have worked the woman's socks off, no matter what.'

'That doesn't mean to say I had to take a leaf out of Hannah's books? Anyway, my fruit made those kiddies happy. Didn't you see their sweet little faces?'

'Yeah, but they are only servant's kids.'

Sam deeply scowled. 'What a shocking to say? You rotten snob!' For the remainder of the meal, she stayed silent, but, eventually she stared him straight in the eye, expressing a sadness. 'Listen ...'

'To what?' he asked with a glint into his dark eyes.

'Hey, don't you start that stupid nonsense again. I've no time, right now, for your bit of tomfoolery.' She bristling, well remembering the day of her arrival, way beyond the mirage, when he glanced around at he knew not.

'Gosh, Sam, you really are in a mood, aren't you?' He, not seeing her as serene, told her he felt as if he was walking upon eggshells. 'I cannot put a foot right with you, it seems?'

'Never mind. It's just I have ... I have something quite important to tell you.'

'What is it?'

She swallowed. 'We'll both need to be very strong, you know?'

He found it difficult to read the expression upon her face.

Samantha indicated towards the two seater couch. 'Come across here and sit with me.' She remembered how her arrival caused quite a stir, some excitement, yet now she was trying to catch her breath; she would need to give a whole load of explaining, conscious how Eable may well change in a heartbeat. 'It's very important.'

With his sculpted features not unlike Elkanah's, he stared, presuming she was still needing the guest annexe as her own abode, to again live alone.

Sam looked down, gripping his hands before half playing with his long fingers; she exhaled a long drawn out sigh: 'I've some news; dear life, this isn't going to be at all easy, yet it really needs to be said.'

'No. I need to explain.'

'Okay.' Pausing, he then declare I think I can probably guess what you're about to tell me ...'

Sam sat back, shaking her head. 'I betcha can't, not for a single moment. In fact, I think it's going to come as quite a shock.'

He narrowed his dark eyes and challenged: 'You're pregnant?'

'What?' Sam almost bellowed out the question.

'That's why you look so pale, isn't it?'

She attempted to interrupt yet he let go of her hands, to have raised an index finger for her to shush, allowing him to finally speak: 'But, hey, I thought we were always so careful when we made love -.'

Sam pursed her lips, mindlessly curling a strand of her auburn hair around a finger into a single ringlet. Before she could get a word in edgeways, someone was hammering their fists on the guest annexe's door, yelling in a local dialect something or other through the letterbox.

She, snapping in disbelief, remarked: 'There's always someone or other coming here to disturb me.'

He nodded and, under his own breath, he hissed: 'I'd better go to see who it is.'

'You had? Why you?' It was her home, yet he seemed to see it as his masculine role to answer her front door.

Sam rolled her eyes heavenwards and sighed: 'Oh, yeah. You go on, then. Never mind me, eh?'

The young stable boy, presuming Eable to be living at that particular address, was on Sam's doorstep, hopping from one foot to the other, recounted how Hunter seemed to have a bad abdominal pain; the anxious lad was loudly urging Eable: 'Come quickly, Master Eable, before your horse dies!'

By the time Eable returned to the annexe, it was late; he seemed physically zonked out. He could hardly keep his eyes open. Before he knew it, he yawned and his head was sinking deep into one of Sam's feather pillows. Looking down at him while he slept, Sam removed most of her clothing before quietly slipping between the sheets next to him; she pulled his body closer to her own, holding him tight. The times they shared on that bed became frankly idyllic.

Soon, Samantha thought, you really shall be residing here, but all alone.

When they both awoke, it was early; yet, sleep seemed to have refreshed her. Feeling an emotional surge of strength within her own psyche, she considered she really could not put off the 'evil day', as it were, any longer. She needed to inform him of her decision.

After breakfast Sam, seizing the moment, sat with him. She heard herself blurting out: 'It's time for me to leave here … to go home to my family and friends, perhaps still even to my midwifery job as a Sister, back to my 1970's life.' Tears welled in her green eyes ; one salty tear-drop escaped, it trickling down her pale cheek, falling from her chin.

He lamented: 'Can't you forget your job? Stay on here for good? Please, Sam, don't leave me.'

It became an ultimatum. 'I've been away for, well, absolutely ages. You surely knew our separation may be in sight? You knew it would happen sooner or later, didn't you?'

He nodded. 'But I love you far too much.' He shivered an ache when they were apart. 'Despite all my clumsy wrongs, all the daft mistakes I've made, I actually adore you, Sam.'

Samantha realized her worried parents must also be pining for her, they, devout, lighting candles, praying regularly in the Catholic Church, for one full day to Our Lady of Sorrows, for her safe return.

'So, my pet, say you'll stay?'

'No. I definitely won't. I've seriously thought it all through; I really must go home.'

'Won't you regret it in the same way as you did with that Mick bloke?'

She half grinned, thinking Eable no longer wished to ever mention his name again.

'Even if you don't bother much about me, hey, think about Elkanah? You surely know, Sam, he loves the air you breath? In fact, everyone in Ramah is bonkers about you.' He reminded her how virtually every adult, including even the mayor of Ramah, turned out for her surprise birthday party.

Sam smiled, telling him not quite everyone, for she remembered the rotund landlady, upon her first night in old Ramah, who told her to either take the vacant room or to clear off, who did not care a rat's tail what she did. 'And that, Eable, was the night when you disappeared?'

He nodded.

Sam raised her eyebrows. 'You never did say where you were?'

'That's right. I didn't, did I?'

A few days later when the dawn began as a bright morning, Sam, all packed up, was preparing to say her goodbyes to the majority of those she came to know and love in the ancient area. She gave Elihu, the shuffling, overweight old grandfather a big bear hug, reminding him to try to lose some heavy significance from around his middle. He patted his own abdomen, remarking how his body was once like a Temple, but Sam quietly chuckled; she over heard a quick witted soul remark how it was then more like a pavilion.

Elkanah visited the guest annexe to sob his Sammy an affectionate farewell; well away from both Eable and Peninnah's prying eyes and listening ears, he whispered to her how he loved her from the bottom of his very being; she, with a heart aching passion, too, adored him, how she would miss him with a gut wrenching pain. She granted him a long, lingering kiss; zero, nothing more.

She and Eable hugged; he grasped her so close she perceived it hard to breath.

Glancing down at her wristwatch, it became time to leave; the entrepreneurial teenager with the overladen donkey yelled for her: 'It's time we were off, pretty lady!' Sam nodded, she stroking the donkey's long ears of grey and brown before patting its neck, knowing how it would awkwardly carry her, her feet sometimes touching the ground; the chatty lad made a double clicking sound, urging the beast to trail to a part of her destination.

Signalling waves until Samantha was well away from everyone, she was soon swishing away the annoying flies, she, having made a beeline through the ancient

Needle's Eye where she found the agreeable cameleer whose equally laden beast took her on its back to the enigmatic, ever serving, white Mercedes' cabby; he stated he owned the one and only taxi with blacked out windows. He manoeuvred her back to the Egyptian side of the silvery mirage. In almost a withdrawn silence she sat in the passenger seat, yet the driver simply grinned: 'You'll be back again some day soon,' he prophesied, desperately trying to console her by tapping her nearest thigh.

Hitching her backpack more firmly, Sam felt utterly exhausted. The purple dressed man in his toppers and tails was nowhere to be seen. Alone, she sauntered up the four or five marble steps, through around the revolving swing doors and into the hotel's bright, shining foyer. She attempted to check in again at its reception desk. It felt ages since anyone well-known heard from her; the usual receptionist promptly informed both the present owners of the establishment, how Samantha showed up.

'Your previous room with its en suite is all ready for you, Miss Webb.'

Sam was not a little amazed; how could anyone have known she would be arriving?

'Oh, our present owner has kept it available, all the time waiting, knowing one day you'd return.'

Before collecting her thoughts, Sam heard herself saying nothing but: 'Really?'

'Yes,' she said, 'so, welcome back!'

'Well, I confessed I'm a bit surprised, but, anyway, thank you very much.'

'Now, Miss Webb, you must be extremely hungry?'

'Absolutely famished.'

'We'll sort that out in quick sticks.' She tinkled a small hand bell; a young porter boy immediately appeared. 'Take this lady's things to room number seven,' she informed him.

He nodded in an obliged recognition, clarifying how seven became his lucky number.

The self same receptionist offered to arrange, with the kitchen staff, for a roast beef dinner to be sent up to the suite. 'What should you like for a desert, Miss Webb?' she asked.

'Ooh, simply anything as long as it doesn't include a Jaffa orange ...'

After the most satisfying of feeds and a long, luxurious soak in a perfumed bubble bath, Sam slept soundly in between crisp white sheets.

She, after a full eight hours, awoke next morning, completely refreshed, only to be confronted by a full English breakfast. The awesome food was accompanied by regular tea in an actual teapot, along with hot buttered toast and the finest of grapefruit marmalades. After so long away, of not sampling such basics, Sam inwardly felt she was verging upon the south side of heaven.

The hotel's receptionist, back on desk duty, 'phoned through, to inform Sam how the hotelier cancelled all her diary appointments, simply to be with her. 'So, please, Miss Webb, wait around for her visit.'

'Me?' Sam wondered why. 'She wants to come to visit me?'

'Yes, miss.'

'Oh, gosh! Why the mystery? Whatever is she like?'

'Very nice.' Sam heard the receptionist softly chuckling. 'Anyway, you'll see soon enough, miss.'

Perplexed and not a little confused, Sam Webb's sudden arrival caused the present hotelier to almost hyperventilate from the immediate shock.

Having sat for a short while on a beautifully upholstered plush chaise-lounge, not unlike Hannah's, she, seeing the advancing time, rapidly dressed in cream slacks and a floral T-shirt; she remained curious concerning the enigmatic hotelier. She did not have too long to wait.

A gentle tapping on the door, shot Sam to her feet. Waiting for a moment longer, simply to compose herself, she opened up; she stared, gazing in amazement at her, in an astounding disbelief, in an astonishment. Her bright green eyes became wide and she was almost breathless. The woman she knew so well, smart in a pale blue silk dress and three rows of pearls around her neck, no longer had deep chestnut brown hair; it shone as a strawberry blonde. On her feet she wore a pair of flat white sandals. Sam clasped her hands, she laughing out loud towards this lovely woman: 'Good grief? Paula!'

From Samantha's start at Hammersmith Hospital, way back in 1964, she had immediately struck up a firm friendship with Paula Lucy Taylor. Both became women who previously cared concerning their patients, they anxious to become brilliant nurses ... perhaps even the best midwives in the world?

'You think you're amazed? I'm telling you, chum, I am absolutely gob smacked. Oh, Sam! How are you?'

'Me? Ooh, I'm actually fine.'

'Are you honestly, Sam?' Paula shuddered, wondering if "fine" was anywhere near the whole truth, for, to her, Sam's complexion was porcelain pale, her figure more slender. However, happy tears rolled down their cheeks as they hugged with a rocking sensation for seemingly a long time until she asked: 'Where, Sam, have you been?'

Instead of immediately replying, she simply stated: 'I'd really kill for a coffee, Paula. I haven't had a cappuccino in simply ages ...'

'Oh, yes, sure. You can have absolutely anything you want ... just say the word.'

'Join me?'

'No.' Paula shook her head. 'Frankly, I'm off tea and coffee right now; those beverages make me feel quite queasy, but you, darling, have whatever takes your fancy ... 'She reached to pick up the receiver of a nearby 'phone for room service. 'Sam, it's been such a very long time since you went missing. What ... where the Dicken's where you? Folk will ask, you know?'

Sam exhaled, trying to again mentally relax within herself: 'I'm back. Isn't that quite enough?'

'Not at all. I simply asked you if you're okay.'

'Yeah, I reckon I am feeling a whole heap better since I had the bath, and, ah, that lovely long sleep in a comfy bed; just what the doctor ordered, eh? Thanks.'

An older waitress knocked before automatically entering the room; she left a tray containing the said coffee.

Sam, pouring and stirring her own beverage with its unique, rich aroma, she heard Paula who, nevertheless, declared: 'Listen, Sam. As soon as you turned up here yesterday, I immediately 'phoned your parents.' When Samantha, his only daughter, presumably went missing her dad inwardly shivered, as if the very word 'missing' struck a chill down the length of his spine; with a careful avoidance of drama, he groaned. 'Both he and your mother Daisy were almost out of their minds, literally sick with worry about you, Sam.'

Sam's eyes lowered; she appeared sorrowful: 'I've so often thought of them. You, too.'

'But you didn't think to either telephone them or me ... not once, simply to say you were safe?'

'Honestly, I really couldn't,' she declared. 'Where I was living there were no telephones.'

' Oh, come on, Sam; there must have been a telephone somewhere or other?'

Sam shook her head. 'Paula, there really wasn't. There was no electricity. Nothing.'

'Well, what about writing us all a postcard?'

'It wasn't at all possible.'

'Don't tell me, Sam, there were no postal services either?'

'That's dead right.'

Paula stared before shaking her head; she did not know quite what to think. 'Sam, I spent absolutely ages ... about a good two-thirds of our so-called holiday together here in Egypt, frantically trying to find you. I almost had a verbal fight with an Egyptian police officer, for I wanted him to report you, Sam, as a missing person.'

'And did he?'

'Hardly! He simply pooh-poohed the idea, stating how you were a grown woman who'd probably switched your holiday destination to elsewhere. What a load of old cod's-wallop?'

Sam swallowed her coffee, almost choking upon the expression; she giggled: 'Knowing you, Paula, I bet you were none too pleased with him?'

'That's an understatement!' she exclaimed. 'Your parents and I eventually had you down as a missing person, in all the big newspapers ... on the television's newsreel, too. Where? Were you kidnapped?'

'No.' She laughed out loud. 'Nobody kidnapped me.'

'Blimey? What then?' Paula quizzed on: 'Simply say something, Sam. Even if you tell no-one else on the planet, at least confide in me?'

'I really don't know quite what to say.' She proceeded to well up, trying to blink away the frustrating tears. 'Please, Paula, don't bombard me with all these questions. Not quite yet.'

Paula moved to hug Sam close. 'I'm so sorry, darling. I don't mean to upset you, but, after all this time away you strolled in here, as if nothing ever happened.'

'Is that how it actually looks?'

The last her mother heard, Sam was about to have a fifteen-minute camel ride. She, clutching at straws, wondered if Samantha, on the way, became captured. 'Did you manage to escape from those middle-eastern people? Was it something like that, eh?'

Sam laughed but, like Hannah, it was without any humour, for there was nothing strange connected with those she left behind, stating how it was not anything as Paula suggested. 'I'm so very sorry. It's an awfully long story, darling.'

She studied her friend's face. 'Tell me, please?' It suddenly hit Sam, she, wondering why Paula was, after so long, still in the self same hotel and as the one in charge; what happened to her midwifery? She saw Paula flashing a gold wedding band upon a finger on her left hand. 'Ooh, Sam, I'm just about as happy as anyone could possibly be.'

'So, who is the lucky guy?'

' Adjo,' Paula added. 'Adjo used to be the manager here. He now part owns this place with me.' Paula declared they fell head in love during the time they were trying to find her. She said how, at first, they became great friends, yet they soon realized how, when they were apart, even for the shortest time, they missed each other.

'Wow, Paula, that's great! Did you marry here in Egypt?'

'Yes, in Alexandria, but you, my best buddy, missed it.'

'Sorry about that, but at least some good came out of my disappearance, eh?'

'Maybe you can look at it like that.' Paula's brow knitted into a scowl. 'Even so, by disappearing without even a bye your leave, you've really hurt your parents.'

Sam lowered her eyes, looking sorrowful.

'Anyway, this will brighten your day. I've more good news, Sam,' she beamed, patting her own abdomen. 'I am expecting a baby.'

'I did wonder when you said you you're off tea and coffee.'

Paula nodded. 'Yeah. So, don't you dare miss that. Okay?

'When is he or she due?'

'Oh, absolutely ages yet. Never mind me; I really think right now you should also 'phone your mum and dad, although I've already informed them you're safe.' Paula persisted: 'It consoled them to know you're here.'

The receptionist interrupted them in a monotonous tone; there was an unexpected incoming call, for Samantha.

As she lifted the receiver, it was her mother's voice which came through with almost an excited scream, she eventually asking after her welfare; almost, after so long, it was as if Sam became a figment of her imagination. While they chatted, she kept hearing Daisy's voice repeat: 'Oh, Samantha, Samantha, I can hardly believe ...'

When the international telephone conversation was over and Sam replaced the handset into its cradle, Paula piped up, stating: 'Your mum's been so upset to the point of being psychologically ill ... all over your absence.'

Sam deeply frowned.

'They're bound to want to know, Sam, all about you; aren't you going to tell them what happened?'

She shrugged. 'I'll need to arrange a flight home. Perhaps my dad will meet me at London's Heathrow?'

Sam's British passport was stamped and handed back. The official gave her an impersonal glance and held out his hand for the documents of the next person in the queue.

Soon she became airborne; she watched an old film. Finally, she was on her way home. In her head she rehearsed all she might say to her parents, assuming they may ask.

Approaching England, it was as if those way beyond the mirage were melting away from her mind. Sam gazed out of the plane's window; it was raining cats and dogs, just as she imagined. Hitting the tarmac and moving through customs, she stared. Having met the incoming flight from Egypt's Alexandria, Sam's parents became more than relieved to finally see their beloved daughter, pale, but well. The three wept, embracing each other; her tearful mother stood, smothering her daughter's face in an abundant of kisses. 'You look so thin, Samantha, darling.'

Had royalty become visitors to their Wimbledon home, Daisy could not have cleaned more; she pumped up cushions and made her husband, who had grown a small goat-like beard, to remove his outdoor shoes, leaving them by the back door. Finicky, she previously hovered, wanting this and that starched, ironed, all crisp, bright and shining for their beloved Samantha was arriving home.

During the following two weeks, Sam dreamed dreams of her time way beyond the mirage; the old town of Ramah, the guest annexe with its big bed, her Eable, but, above all, Elkanah; she was missing him beyond words. One morning she woke too early; with a loud start, she invariably disturbed her parents' sleep.

It was only a couple of weeks to their festooned Christmas of 1970, and, yet to the parents, she became their finest of gifts.

One morning, around coffee time, she and the parents sat at the kitchen table. Her mother declared, she being the spokesperson, how they were worrying. 'Now, Samantha, in truth, daddy and I actually loathe all this mystery surrounding your strange disappearance. You surely know we love you to bits?'

She did.

' ... so why do you feel you cannot trust us enough to speak of this disappearance of yours, eh?' asked Henry.

'Your dad's right. Tell us, sweetheart. Who was the guy you yelled to? Whatever did he do to you, causing you to have nightmares?'

Henry worried if his daughter accidentally became tangled up in some weird supernatural stuff, the not quite human, but her anxious mother did not know what to think. 'Samantha, my dear child ...' she began.

That did it. 'Mum,' she tried not to snap, yet she began to correct her with frown, 'please, do realise, I'm all grown up; no longer your child?' Sam, noticing raindrops upon the window's pane, switch the subject to the British forecast. 'It is stiflingly hot where Paula is in Egypt.'

'All right, but, what I am trying to say is, daddy and I could arrange for you to see a counsellor, to maybe give you the sort of chat you may need?'

Sam wondered if her mother was speaking from experience, for Paula let it slip Daisy was in psychological bits concerning the disappearance. Whatever, swallowing the dregs of her coffee, she was doing her uttermost not to show any more irritability. 'I have already told Paula, I'm fine; really, I definitely do not need any help.'

'At least stay on with us ... until you are feeling well again, dear?'

Sam shook her head in sheer exasperation and took up the reasoning. 'I've told you a dozen and one times; I am not ill! Look, I honestly appreciate all your concern, but perhaps it's time for me to move out?'

Henry inhaled a breath, stating a firm no before glaring daggers towards his wife, telling her to stop her incessant fussing; it was getting her exactly nowhere. 'By the way, Samantha, I've kept your car nicely ticking over. It still runs beautifully and ...'

'... it's parked here in your garage.' She noticed it. 'I can't thank you enough.'

He switched to flop into his favourite old armchair, adding: 'Oh, yes, and the other thing; your apartment … it's been empty since Paula cleared off to marry that hotelier chap … what's his name now?'

'Adjo.'

'That's the fellow. Anyway, to keep your place spotless Jenkins popped in for two hours every week; under your mother's watchful eyes, it's all now absolutely tickety-boo!' He asked about her popping over to see the pristine Earls Court pad. Sam thought again about removing, but, despite the night terror, Daisy wanted to cosset her one and only adult child, to tuck her down in their home; yet, she was use to being independent.

A junior reporters was sent from the local rag, anxious to discover if there was any more news about Samantha. As Henry opened the front door, the young fellow noticed her walking across the hallway. 'Please, sir, only a few words,' he begged. 'I can see she's with you.'

'Hang fire, son.' Henry swung around to his daughter, requesting her permission to chat with the reporter. Before she could answer one way or the other, he, in a lower voice, stated: 'Samantha. Listen to me; during the time you were missing, we used the media, especially his newspaper, to try to help us. I can't simply shoo him off now. What am I to do? What shall I tell him?'

Again, the young fellow piped up, quizzing: 'Please, sir, only a few words … may I come in?' He declared he would then be the first to have the story. 'It may help my career no end …'

Her father stretched an arm across, keeping the rookie cub on the doorstep.

Sam came to the front door, looping an arm around Henry's ample waist, she agreeing to make the briefest of statements, to the effect how she simply decided to extend her time in the Middle East. 'It's very interesting, as my father will confirm.'

'Why?'

'Well, he was partly there during the last world war. Weren't you, dad?'

Henry nodded.

Sam watched the young fellow scribbling away, nineteen to the dozen; she continued: 'I moved across to old Ramah in ancient Samaria. There I was asked to work, only once, as a midwife to a local dignitary.'

'So, why didn't you contact, to say you were all right?'

She shook her head. 'At that particular place there were no means of any communications; now I am back home, staying with my parents. That's about it.'

'So, Samantha, if that's really the end of your story, why are you still here with your parents, and not living over in your Earl's Court apartment?'

'After Christmas I shall be moving out from here; in the meantime, I'm here until the New Year.'

'And ...'

'And I do wish to thank you for all the help your paper gave my parents.'

'Yeah. All right, but I need to ask you one more thing?'

Sam raised her eyes heavenwards and sighed. 'Which is what?'

'Were you, at any time, actually held as an hostage?'

'A hostage? Good grief! Not at all.' Sam stared face on at him; she shook her head, grinning at the very thought of his words before literally laughing to confirm a most definite no.

'What was ..?' he started up a second query, but Henry promptly intervened, pulling away from Sam and stepping out in front, half eclipsing her slender frame. 'That's quite enough for now, son. My daughter, who is very tired from her long journey, has nothing else to tell any of us right now.'

'So, shall you all be saying more ... at a later stage? May I call again tomorrow?'

'Samantha is dog tired. Leave her be, for the time being.'

'So, when shall she be fit enough to talk?'

'Very soon. I promise.'

After the lunch dishes were cleared away by his wife, Henry again settled back in his favourite armchair, ready to ask Sam if she was honest with the young reporter, if that was truly all which happened.

Evasive to the last, her thoughts remained with Elkanah. 'Not again, daddy, please,' she answered with a lengthy sigh. 'Let's leave it be for the time being, eh?' She reckoned, had she told her father the truth, well, would he believe her?

A couple of days later, Sam drove to see her empty Earls Court apartment. It sounded hollow; no longer was she relishing her own company, but wishing Elkanah was with her. Returning to the home of her parents, she again asked her mother: 'If it's not too much trouble, I should like to be with you for Christmas, please?'

'Too much trouble? Oh, Samantha, just having you here with us will be our best Christmas ever. When you didn't show up for the last two Christmas Days, well ... oh, darling, daddy and I were just about beside our-selves ...'

'Did you think I was never coming back?'

'We never gave up hope. Neither did Paula. Not for a single moment.'

At ten sharp, Miss Maude Moore, the Head of Midwifery Services, agreed to see Sam. Passing by her busily typing secretary, Sam, power-dressed in a navy-blue suit, arrived outside her office in good time; a green light appeared over the woman's heavy oak door, indicating for her to knock and enter. Inside and sidestepping her sleeping mongrel, the green light switched to red, a bit like in a Catholic confessional. Miss Moore, a stiff and starchy woman with a pinched face, probably in her mid-fifties, became seated bolt upright behind a green leather and dark mahogany desk where there was an ink stained blotter; only within her field of work, she was powerful and intense, wearing her long greying hair plaited around in the style of a coronet, it half concealed under a white frilly cap; her piercingly blue bespectacled eyes half managed a weak smile, and, indicating for Sam to be seated. 'May I offer you a coffee, Miss Webb?'

Sam, hands folded in her lap, politely refused.

'So, why have you chosen to see me, Miss Webb?'

'Oh, it's about my returning to work as a midwife.'

The woman sucked a sharp intake of breath before shaking her head. 'When I didn't hear from you, for it's been a very long time, well, I had absolutely no choice but to replace you. What a pity, for you were an outstanding midwife?'

'Is there nothing else for which I could be considered?'

'Not at all.'

'You mean, you have absolutely no vacancies, no posts in midwifery for which I could apply?'

She declared it was exactly correct.

'But, with respect,' Sam intervened, 'I thought you were urgently short of midwives?'

The woman became adamant. 'For you, Miss Webb, I can offer nothing.'

'If a vacancy becomes available ..?'

She falsified a lengthy sigh. 'You don't seem to understand anything I'm trying to convey to you.' She, claiming to be fair, was trying to speak gently.

Sam gazed.

'If I took you on in my employ, how would I know you wouldn't disappear again, Miss Webb? I don't. When I employ professional women, I require reliable staff ... those who are dedicated enough to give our mothers and babies one hundred per cent - nothing less.' She stood to stretch out a hand. 'Now, I sincerely wish you well for the future, wherever it may lay.'

Realising there was nothing Sam could do to remedy the embarrassing situation, she rapidly beat a retreat.

Her parents decided to give their daughter some Christmas money and, with the gift, Sam hoped to purchase an original piece of art, to hang on one of the bare walls in her London apartment; she decided to search the Chelsea galleries.

Chapter 8

Sam missed Elkanah. He was so far from her.

She remembered those early mornings, in the noisy farmers' markets where nothing altered. Servant girls were drawing water from the wells, preparing breakfasts with their freshly baked bread, goats' cheese, along with fruits from the vineyards. Entrepreneurial fat women lugged their heavy black pans to cook delicious soups-of-the-day over an unsafe oil fired blue flame.

During her time in Adjo and Paula's hotel, Sam slept like a baby, yet since, tiredness was still hitting her, causing mornings to remain fatigued; she longed, after a night's sleep, to simply turn over again, but the extra slumber made her to dream of the tall, broad shouldered, dark-haired priestly guy's face, he sensual, warm and friendly. She remembered travelling with his young brother upon his trusty stallion. A type of a worry invaded her as she remembered her down-at-heel servant, with her two kids enjoying their oranges, of the new baby boy, frantically searching for his fist to suck. Mulling over those times, all so different from the rest of the western world, she needed to heal her own psychological wounds, of missing Elkanah; she, lonely, knew she needed to continue retaining her surrounding walls of silence. Whatever, being amidst those ancient people caused her to experience a deep sense of belonging. Had she overburdening both Paula and her parents concerning such far off charismatic lovers, Sam became convinced they may probably either permanently snap closed the subject or insist upon her acquiring either therapy, they believing her to be locked within a delusional state. None would surely accept how she, as a good midwife, helped Elkanah's second wife, Hannah of old, to deliver Samuel, a healthy male child born in the year 1106 BC., an infant to grow into a great Old Testament prophet. No. For her own sanity's sake, Samantha became determined to keep schtum.

With half the excitement of a kid waiting for Christmas morning, waking up in the early hours of the night, Sam became relieved to be in her own apartment. It was one of those self-contained places which was once a gloriously city Victorian Mansion. Charles Dickens may well have known it with its old dark oak furniture.

There were several others renting the adjoining apartments. Two kept themselves to themselves. When she smiled in their direction, they simply blanked her, as if she was invisible. One sitting tenant, originally from the beautiful Ireland of somewhere, seemed, in her lay opinion, seriously insane, as if in a unique world of her own; she often drifted down the twelve carpeted stairs from the attic apartment, carrying a stuffed leprechaun, it wearing green and white striped socks; and Henry and Daisy Webb, Sam's parents, worried concerning their own daughter's mental well being?

Daisy longed for Samantha to settle down; she considered she ought to acquire a good job and maybe, in a serene way, find a handsome 'Mr Right'. She hoped her daughter might live in a suburb of London, forgetting the so-called far away Samaria, along with its puzzled.

Paula, the last occupant in Sam's rented apartment, abandoned working in London as a midwife for a new life in Egypt's Alexandria, with her beloved Adjo, giving him her all at the altar. Daisy hoped for such a happiness in her own offspring, but Sam did not relish the matchmaking.

When Sam and Paula previously shared the London apartment, there was a happiness between them, they taking it in turns to cook, to pull something odd from their temperamental oven, using basic recipes, everything from delicious fruit pies, to shovelfuls of prepared dishes, only known to them. It seemed an age ago; perhaps it was, for some of the place remained empty, needing either a seriously large framed mirror or an extra special picture to be hung in the sparsely furnished dining room.

Upon impulse, Sam, wrapping warm against the temperamental British winter, jumped into her run-about-town car and, amidst the wailing of sirens filling the air, manoeuvred her way through the ghastly bumper to bumper in the Chelsea King's Road's early rush hour. Checking her rear mirror as she backed into a side road, she switched off the ignition, considered she could have walked faster; however, a little exasperated, she picked her way through shoppers, along to one of its art galleries. There were a plethora of similar establishments in and around the area, yet, only one caught her eye. She could not quite understand why, but, in an odd way, she felt somehow drawn to one establishment where everything remained neat, yet inspired.

Light and airy inside, behind a corner counter sat the gallery's lone receptionist; she nevertheless came across as a smartly dressed, slender and clad in a tailored blue trouser suit.   Maybe she is around mum's age? Sam thought.

Immediately setting aside her magazine, the receptionist seemed half relieved to see Sam. With the fussy pretence of a practised, welcoming smile, she asked if she, Sam, needed any help. Before she had a chance to draw a breath in reply, the woman continued to quiz: 'Are you looking for anything in particular?'

Standing behind a red roped enclosure, Sam half shrugged. 'Well, I'm unsure. You see, I've been given some Christmas money from my parents and um ...'

Henry and Daisy Webb thought the cash might come in handy, for her to acquire something or other for the Earls Court apartment. It was, they stated, for her to alone decide.

She turned back with a sigh to face the woman. 'I first thought about getting a big mirror, but, err, on second thoughts,' she hesitated, 'I think I'd prefer to buy a picture ... that is, if I can run to it? Oh, I dunno. I'll have to decide.'

The woman, sitting back down, gave the hint of a nod, saying something to the effect how Sam came to exactly the right place, declaring: 'We do sell some very beautiful antique mirrors, as you can see?' She briefly half rose from her chair, offering with a flick of the wrist, with a sort of a flourish. 'But the sale of original art is really our forte.'

'Well, since my previous flat mate moved out, she taking all her pictures with her, my dining room wall looks pretty bare.'   Sam stated she believed it was definitely crying out for something different, maybe like a painting. 'So …' she began,

'… so,' the woman interrupted, 'you thought you'd come here?'

'Yes.'

'That's good.' Keeping up her staged smile, ready to answer any queries Sam may have had, she advised her to feel free, to browse at her leisure. She returned to mindlessly flicking through the pages of her reading matter, yet half keeping an eye out for Sam.

Falsely and loudly, Sam sighed, slowly wandering around the small gallery, gazing, searching through most of the sizeable pictures, yet there was nothing she really fancied. Either it was the wrong size or way out of her price bracket. When she previously mentioned to her parents how she would like to use the Christmas money to purchase a piece of original art, her mother suggested she should nip into Wimbledon College of Art and Design, to buy from a hard up student, yet she suddenly twigged the College would be closed for the Christmas holidays. So, that finished that.

Sam wandered, retracing her steps, back and forth, noticing how there were many oils on canvases, depicting mostly various African wild animals, particularly of endangered elephants. Apart from those, there were a few of a stallion. Before Sam could question the prices, a woman hurried in to buy some last minute Christmas cards; as she paid for them, she half glanced in Sam's direction, half as if she knew her, yet she did not. Handing over the correct cash, she wished the receptionist a happy holiday before leaving in a mad rush with the farewell of a 'toodle-oo'.

From a studio-cum-workroom, obviously based in the rear of the gallery, a tall fellow, made an appearance. In stark contrast to the smartly dressed receptionist, he wore a sloppy taupe coloured knitted sweater and paint covered stone washed jeans; he asked the woman if she also might cast an eye over his piece of work. Sam heard how she would; he nipped off, to returned with his new painting, advising her not to touch. Some of the varnish remained tacky, although he thought it was probably all right.

'Excuse me, please?' Sam piped up. 'May I also have a look at your art work, too?'

Six inches taller than her, it was his deep chocolate brown eyes which, for a moment, held Sam's gaze, as if there became an immediate connection, not unlike some sort of a chemistry between them; for a split second she experienced a strange experience of deja vu, half as if they met before; yet, she reckoned it was quite out of the question. He turned around his painting, holding it up in front of himself, for her to see.

'Don't touch. It's still a little ...'

'... tacky. I heard you.'

'Yeah.'

The woman behind the counter volunteered how, any person who may bought the work, should be delighted. 'Just one thing, my darling ...'

He rolled his dark eyes heavenwards before deeply scowling, presumably not being an artist who cherished a critic, yet he had asked.

Sam listened on how the woman had wondered about the background, as if it perhaps detracted from the central subject. He, turned to Sam, asking what she thought.

'It's beautiful.' Sam did not wish to come between him and the one who named him 'darling', she adding how she had noticed there were a few pieces of horses. Pointing, she asked if they were his work, too.

They were.

'My word! I confessed I am amazed.'

'So, are you an artist, too?'

She stated no, yet she knew what she liked. 'You're also a very gifted equestrian artist.'

'So? Do you think this work is okay, then?'

Sam, without answering, told him how, several years ago, one rainy day she went into the National Gallery. 'It was in there I saw George Stubbs' masterpieces, where it showed his horses.'

The guy in the taupe top first grinned before laughing with a false modesty: 'George Stubbs was probably the greatest horse painter of all time.'

'Perhaps you ought to be taking a fresh look at your own work; maybe you are another George Stubbs?'

He beamed at Sam's compliment, although he reckoned her words were simply flannel. Placing his fresh oil painting aside, he stood, arms folded, telling her how he owned his own stallion, it being stabled in Wimbledon.

'Ooh, when I was a little girl, I kept my own pony at the Dog and Fox stables.'

'You obviously know Wimbledon?'

'Of course.' Sam smiled, telling him how she was raised near the Common, just over on Parkside.

'Fancy that?'

'James.' The woman interrupted: 'Why don't you show this young lady the painting you did of your own stallion, huh?'

He nodded. 'It's in my studio, here, in the back room.'

Sam glanced at her wristwatch. 'Well …'

'I'll only be a tick.' He was as good as his word.

Sam became taken aback; she experienced a shudder slithering down the full length of her spine. 'Oh, my?' she gasped, bringing a hand momentarily to cover her mouth with a smack. 'You … you painted this?' For a brief moment her heart seemed to race, thudding within her chest, up into her throat; stealing a breath, she swayed a little. All she heard seemed to echo, as if out of ear shot. For Sam, it was suddenly too difficult to remain upright; her legs felt like jelly, as if they would no longer support her. Momentarily, she wondered if she may flake out. She never fainted before, not that she could remember, but, if this was how it felt, she hated it; all was way out of her control. The surprise, no, the immediate emotional shock of seeing his painting also felt as if all those way beyond the mirage returned into her western way of life; any colour appeared to drain from her already porcelain skin.

'Oh! Whatever is wrong, my dear?' Sam could hear the woman quiz, she hurrying around to support her. She frowned, firmly instructing the artist fellow to set aside his painting, to promptly bring over the chair; slowly, Sam was gently eased onto the seat, her head flopped down between her knees until she was able to regain an upright position. 'There now; would you like me to get you a drink of water?' she heard.

Another prospective client stepped halfway through the shop door, saw a little of the happenings and thought better of becoming involved with any form of first aid;

he skedaddled before the receptionist could offer him a practised word of welcome.

Feeling vulnerable and trying to obliterate the memory, Sam refused the water. 'I'm honestly fine now … absolutely all right.'

'Are you really sure? Should I call for a doctor?'

'Definitely not.'

The woman became persistent. 'The G.P.'s surgery is only around the corner. Our own doctor is very nice; she'd visit at the drop of a hat, if I asked.'

Sam shook her head. 'No, thank you. I'm really okay. In fact, I'm feeling a bit of a twit, right now.'

'Is there someone else I could call for you?'

She didn't want to concern her parents.

'Did you come here on an empty stomach, without any breakfast?'

'No. I ate.'

'Really?'

'Absolutely. I actually had a bowl of porridge …' Sam remembered how her servant, way beyond the mirage, made it from grinding dried ingredients, mixing it with twice boiled water, adding fruits and berries from the nearby hedgerows.

She took Sam's hand, patting the back of it. 'You still look deathly white … so pale, my dear, almost as though you'd seen a ghost.' She smiled: 'You haven't, have you?'

Sam withdrew her hand, considering it to be a silly question.

'I wonder what on earth made you feel faint?'

'Well,' Sam sighed, 'it all sounds a bit far fetched, but I reckon it was the immediate shock of my seeing the painting by that young man. I just didn't expect it!'

Inwardly, she wondered why should she have bothered so much.

Before Sam had a chance to say any more, the woman interrupted: 'This, by the way, is my son James ... may I introduce you?'

He narrowed his dark eyes and, angling his head, smiled, wondering about offering a friendly handshake, yet he thought better of it.

'He's obviously our young artist,' she persisted. 'We, with my husband who teaches art, own this gallery -.'

Sam smiled politely, as if who owned what, was anything to do with her; positive, she was convinced she saw James some other place, but where? she wondered. His face, familiar, she could not quite place him. 'The painting ... tell me, it's obviously all your own work?'

'Yes. It is a painting of my grey stallion – he's the one I was telling you is ...'

'... in Wimbledon?' Sam was keen to know if the painting was up for sale.

James nodded with a lengthy sigh. 'I suppose it has to be.' He sounded somewhat reluctant to flog it, as if too precious for him to release.

His mother told Sam: 'My son seems to be either photographing or painting his beloved horse's portrait; old Hunter is, right now, the light of his life.'

'You've called your horse what?'

'Hunter. Why?'

Sam, despite the time of day, felt she may be half dreaming; whatever, she wondered, was happening to her? 'Hunter, huh? What an amazing coincidence?'

'Coincidence? How do you mean?'

'It has to be, for I once knew someone who owned an identical stallion … ah, never mind, for it was actually ages ago.'

'If you really wish to purchase this piece of my work … 'he started, totally unaware of memories which were not his.

Sam butted in. 'It half depends upon how much you're asking; although, I would love to own it.' She explained: 'You see, as I already told your mother, I've a bit of Christmas money and I thought I might blow it on a picture, so …'

The fellow informed her how much he expected.

Sam frowned, thinking for a moment or two before the price became agreed by the shaking of their hands, although Sam reckoned he may well have held hers longer.

'Then, I'll need to finish off the back of the frame … if you give mum your home address, we'll have it sent to your home.'

She smiled. 'I only live along the Earls Court Road – it's obviously not far.'

'Right ho. I reckon then I could personally deliver it.' He glanced under the counter in a desk diary, while mindlessly jingling his keys in his pocket, he stopping to think. 'Yes. I'll be free tomorrow around five? Would teatime be agreeable?'

'Thanks. That'd be ideal.'

James' mother, Hannah Samuels, as she introduced herself, remained overly concerned for Sam's personal welfare. 'You're still very pale, dear,' she stated with a frown.

'I'm always pale.'

'Did you drive here?'

Sam said her car was near by.

'How about a drink before you leave? I really think you should have a cup of something hot before you again drive?'

'All right then, a quick cup of coffee would be lovely.'

'I'm afraid I only have tea.' she said. 'I can offer a regular blend, unless of course you want lemon tea?'

'Ordinary tea, please?' Sam screwed up her nose at the thought of lemon tea. 'I've recently had my fill of it.'

The woman gave a knowing smile. 'I'm sure.'

Sam raised her eyebrows, wondering why she offered such a remark.

The following day, dead on the dot of five, James delivered his oil painting of Hunter. Sam reminded him all over again it became a Christmas gift from her parents, to which he replied: 'Yes. You said so yesterday. Lucky you, eh? 'He removed his leather gloves, to unwrap the painting, asking if he may hang it for her, but she informed him how she was far from incapable.

All through the following night, Sam tossed and turned, finding it difficult to sleep, with her mind again in turmoil as she considered the previous day's strange happenings. Alone, her memories were of those she knew, those who resided in the year of 1105 BC. She somehow became psychologically transported back to their time, into their lives; whatever anyone else may either think or say, she was neither fooled nor day dreaming. She had not screwed up almost a couple of years of her life, she unnerving herself, with everything topsy-turvy. Sam remembered occasions she and Eable spent together, when their lives became forever exciting, yet never predictable. Sam loved Elkanah, he desiring her more than once when she later declared herself as his forbidden fruit.

The following day, Sam was baking. During the time she was making flaky pastry, James Samuels 'phoned. With the receiver propped between her ear and shoulder, she wiped the flour from her hands on the corner of her apron.

'I'm very sorry to trouble you, Miss Webb, but I think I left my gloves behind in your apartment … brown leather,' he stated. 'I would have taken them off to unwrap the painting …'

'Oh, they are yours, are they?' she asked. 'I thought they may have been dad's.'

He interrupted. 'As you are so near, may I pop across, to fetch them, please?'

'What? Now?' She added how she was expecting a visitor.

He informed her how he did have other pairs, but those particular ones were an early Christmas present from his father. 'I promise I won't even come in, especially as you're guest is on their way …'

'No problem. I'll have them ready for you. Okay?'

James arrived thirty minutes later. 'I guess you like roses,' he declared with a sparkle in his dark brown eyes. He pressed six white blooms into her arms, swapping them for his posh leather gloves. 'I reckon all women like flowers. I bet you're no exception?'

Sam's face shone, bringing them to her nose, she drawing a deep breath, telling him they smelled heavenly; he desired to inform her how she did, too, yet he kept silent. Sam asked: 'They are very lovely, but …'

On his way he deliberately called at a florist. 'For your inconvenience regarding the gloves.'

She was hardly inconvenienced; she so wanted to stroke the side of his face, just as she would with Eable. 'I'll get them into water straight away,' she reassured him, giving him a brief peck on the side of his cheek.

He lifted his long fingers to feel where her lips touched . 'Ah, well. Happy Christmas anyway and, oh, yes ... you now feeling better? My mother was quite worried about you. Me, too. '

'You, too?'

'Naturally.'

'Thank your mother for her kindness. I'm absolutely fine.'

'Good. By the way,' he grinned, tapping his own nose, 'you have flour on the tip of your nose!'

Sam set aside the roses upon a near table and smiled, brushing it away with the back of her hand. 'I've been baking a chicken and mushroom pie.'

He could smell the delicious aroma, wafting through some of the apartment.

'Would you like some?' She told him she could put a serving into a small bowl, covering it with baking foil. 'All you'd need to do, is to warm it through once you get home.'

He blushed. 'Thank you, but I'd hate to intrude, so maybe some other time, eh?' As he was leaving with his gloves, he almost came face to face with Paula, she arriving in the doorway, as he was hurrying away.

'Come on in ... come on in out of the cold. Ooh, it's simply great to see you, Paula!' Sam exclaimed, hugging her friend.

'Hey, never mind me, Samantha Webb, who was that gorgeous bloke I saw leaving from here? Got a delicious man friend, have you?'

Sam smiled, shaking her head.

'My? You kept him jolly quiet, you dark horse!'

'He's not a friend. I hardly know the guy.' Sam pointed: 'He brought me those roses ...'

'Really?' she teased.

Sam's normally pale cheeks blushed. 'Never mind him, Paula. What time did your 'plane land? You must be absolutely dog tired?'

Not having an answer regarding the artist fellow, she persisted: 'Do men often call with flowers?'

'I'm telling you, I hardly know the fellow?'

'That's even worse, you shocking hussy!'

'Stop it, you. Anyway, how long are you here for? '

Paula removed her coat and scarf. 'I've already been in England for several days.'

Sam became surprised.

'Yeah. I was visiting my parents, delivering their Christmas presents, before making sure they gave me something shockingly expensive!'

'And did they?'

'What?'

'Fork out for something pricey?'

'I haven't unwrapped it yet.'

Sam betted Paula had.

'Whatever, I figured I couldn't return to Egypt without calling to see you, too. Right?' She made herself as comfortable as she could upon which was originally her couch.

'How come Adjo isn't with you?'

'It's a frantically busy time for the hotel trade; he honestly couldn't get away.'

'Nothing wrong between the two of you?'

'Us? Blimey! No.' Paula stated how she and Adjo could not be happier. 'What with the baby on the way, life is about as good as it gets; talking about babies, I suppose you'll soon be returning to midwifery, eh?'

'Nope. I now have no job. I've recently joined the ranks of the great unemployed.'

'What? There's a great shortage of good midwives. Everyone from here to eternity knows it's so.'

'Miss Moore decided to make me into being a lady of leisure.' Sam explained how the Head of Midwifery Services wanted reliability in her staff. 'I can understand her way of thinking, but I was a little shocked when she gave me the elbow. In fact, I felt quite a twit by even contacting her in the first place.'

Paula asked how Sam would cope financially. 'Living in this part of London does not come cheap, does it? And now I am no longer sharing with you, what shall you do about keeping up with that exorbitant rent?'

'One of my grandfathers left me a tidy sum in his will. Dad knew an accountant who invested the money for me; I can, for maybe quite a while, live off the interest; so, I'm more than all right for a bit.'

'You're jolly lucky. Whatever would you have done otherwise?'

'Doesn't bear thinking about.'

'What like a rich husband for you?'

She laughed.

'Perhaps that dish of a guy, who gave you those roses is loaded?'

'It's usually your husband who is the tease; not you.'

Paula quietly chuckled before offering: 'Listen, Sam. Come back to Egypt with me; come and keep me company? When you came before, well, you didn't really see much of Alexandria, did you? '

'What? And play gooseberry to you and Adjo? Phew! I don't think so.'

'So then, make it a foursome; bring your new man who brought you those roses?'

She sighed, raising her eyes heavenwards. 'He's definitely not my man, for goodness sake?' Becoming more serious, Sam declared: 'No, Paula, I have promised I'd be with mum and dad this Christmas.' She stated how she had no intention of disappointing them. 'Sorry, but I cannot even think about being away from them.'

Paula understood. Even so, she added: 'Sam, it's almost a couple of weeks yet before the twenty-fifth. Why not fly out with me, to spend a week with us?' She continued on: 'You'd be back in good time to help Henry and Daisy consume their over sized Christmas turkey.'

Arriving in Alexandria in time for dinner, Sam knew, in her heart of hearts, she had not flown all that distance without having a rather special camel ride, when the wide lumbering beast could not quite make it through the ancient Needle's Eye.

Chapter 9

After an early continental breakfast, Sam nipped back to her room, to grab a few overnight essentials, they meticulously folded into a backpack. Anything else remained just as she left them.

Away from the frigid cold of London, she welcomed the Egyptian warmth. Over the street, a couple of hours before she awoke, bakers and sellers of Jaffa oranges, figs and peppers were out in force. Men yelled to attract her attention, to flog their colourfully woven carpets, but she hitched her luggage firmly upon her back, ignoring them. Hearing her own footsteps as she hastened away from the hotel's marble frontage, she stood upon the edge of the curb, glancing both ways and, almost before she could say 'Jack Robinson', a white Mercedes taxi with its blacked out windows pulled up; its tyres screeched along the black tarmac.

Sam glanced at her wristwatch. It showed a little before nine. 'Hi, there!' she exclaimed with a yell, frantically waving with both hands, to attract the cab driver.

Recognising her, his broad grin showed little surprise. 'So, where do you need to go today, my pet?' he questioned; reaching across, he opening the passenger door, he alleging how he just drove all the way from ancient Cairo. 'These days, motoring fatigues me, you know?'

Eager to get on her way, Sam nevertheless scowled, loathing being referred to as his 'pet', yet she said nothing. To be fair, he neither knew her name, nor she his.

Before attempting to climb into the passenger seat, from one of her jeans' deeper pockets she fished out her small money purse, making sure she brought enough local currency to pay. 'I'd like to take one of those fifteen-minute camel rides,' Sam stated. 'I can see from your dark eyes, you're looking tired, but would you, please, be able to take me to wherever it happens?'

Alighting, he folded his manly arms, he half leaned against his steering wheel. He first switched, speaking with his native tongue, which, seeing the blank expression across her face, he realised it became lost upon her; he reverted to speaking pigeon English, persisting: 'Camels? Oh, don't you remember, this happens to be ancient Egypt? There are lumbering camels to ride, spitting camels to purchase and caramel-coloured camels to spare, pretty lady,' he remarked, a smile in his eyes.

Sam nodded, she asking him not to tease. 'Whatever, do you happen to remember the exact place where one caramel- coloured camel separates from others, where it tries to squeeze through the ancient Needle's Eye, yet it can't make it?'

He did. 'Hey, lovely lady, it's one heck of a ride from here, you know?'

She jumped in the front seat, but, before buckling up, she threw her small luggage upon the back seat; after quite a few moments, he broke the silence, chatting, questioning how long she planned to remain way beyond the mirage.

'Ooh, I'm returning back tomorrow, first thing. As soon as I'm ready to return to the hotel, I'll contact you.'

'Yeah. You do that.' She became astonished for, as he spoke, he patted her right knee before resting his hand upon her thigh. Acquiring no resistance, he kept it there until he needed to change gear. 'I'm usually around somewhere or other ... always available for the likes of you,' he declared, squeezing her leg to make his point.

'Thanks. It's good to know.'

He, letting go of her, gripped the steering wheel, occasionally glancing sideways in her direction. 'Why are you going, yet again, way beyond the mirage?'

'Well, the truth is, I'm planning upon visiting someone special to me.'

'Who is he, then?'

'He lives over in ancient Ramah.'

'My! That's way over into old Samaria.'

Sam knew it.

'Hey, listen to me,' he began, restoring his hand to her nearest thigh. Sam knew his large hand was doing her no harm; 'I'm urging you, in a fatherly sort of a way, to be ultra careful, pretty lady. Some of the folk, especially those young soldiers from the Rifle Brigade during the last World War who'd travelled way beyond the mirage, well, they never returned, did you know?'

She shrugged.

'If you're sick, whose strong enough to carry you out, huh? There was no-one tough enough to help those poor blokes; they became forever lost.'

Momentarily anxious, she remembered how her father, a once serving Army officer, reminisced, he seeing the mirage. It was thought, at the time, those soldiers went AWOL ... absent without leave?

Sam began feeling somewhat apprehensive, yet she quickly calmed herself, shrugging nonchalantly: 'This isn't my first trip to way beyond the mirage. I was always okay then,' she stated, 'for I returned home when I wanted to.'

Before she could justifying herself, he quizzed concerning her young man living in old Ramah, about their close relationship, but, pink through an embarrassment, Sam offered few words; a smile crept across her mouth regarding all the happenings between her and Eable, but, hopefully, she would be with Elkanah. 'I suppose you're not going there, simply to shake hands with the guy, huh?' The driver was spot on. 'Tell me all about it afterwards, eh?'

Sam, astonished, giggled: 'I shouldn't think so.'

Although he was next to a sometimes feisty woman, yet, to him, Sam showed herself as a stunning female; the driver wondered why she did not correct him when it came to his touching her thigh. He nevertheless remained courteous, yet, once in the middle of nowhere, he looked down, half wishing he could have dealt with both his own frustration and hers, but not without her permission. 'Did you mind my hand being on your thigh?'

Before she could reply one way or the other, the cab started to slow down; she was not a little relieved they reached the camels so soon.

Eventually about to leave the lone driver, he reached aside for her, bringing her face to his, he giving Sam a kiss upon both her cheeks before slowly pressing his mouth to hers. His lips upon hers, she cherished the sensations he began to create.

'Thanks for … for a very interesting journey,' she added, not knowing quite what else to say.

He grinned, tapping the tip of her nose. 'I think you'd better be on your way, sweet lady.'

'Yeah. Perhaps?'

'Perhaps? Only perhaps or shall you save yourself for your Elkanah, eh? Tell me, huh?'

Sam shrugged, nodding with a smile, yet it was then they spoke in unison, as together they both stated: 'I'll see you tomorrow?'

He held her face in his cupped hands, kissing her again with what she believed was a heart-warming cheerio, he easing back from the sweet, delectable taste of her mouth; as Sam climbed from the Mercedes and, before she closed the passenger door, she heard him calling her to take care.

In quick sticks, Sam discovered herself in the presence of an ageing cameleer; he helped her ride his caramel-coloured camel; he stated it was able to lead her on as far as the ancient Needle's Eye. During the few friendly words he spoke in broken English, he informing her how there was an earth tremor in and around the ancient town of Ramah; many of the male residents were still clearing away and hunting through rubble. Sam asked him about casualties, wondering if those she knew were safe. He shrugged, seemingly to have no idea.

Before she left him, Sam asked if she might take his and the camel's photograph. Delighted, the cameleer briefly removed his own headgear, he posing, holding next to the neck of the rowdy beast. With a broad, toothless grin, the guy nevertheless wanted to keep one of the pictures, it taken with a Polaroid camera on loan from Henry Webb.

Having finally located the unusual stone Needle's Eye where only sheep and unrepentant bandits pass through, Sam mounted an already laden grey and brown donkey; its teenage boy owner led her safely along the narrow cobbled streets heading up to the guest annexe in ancient Ramah. The year was approaching 1104 BC. Sam thought how, for Paula and Adjo, it would be soon be 1970. They were frantically busy couple, so distracted, preparing for the Christmas and New Year's Eve festivities. She knew they would not be worried about her; she left a hurried note for Paula, stating how she, Sam, nipped off to visit an old friend; she promised to be back, joining them the following day.

Sam first knocked on the guest annexe door, yet, with silence, it seemed no-one was home. The iron door key, usually kept under a nearby stone slab, was missing. She briefly wondered if Eable kept it before removing into the big house? Walking back along the dirt road, she could see the house, previously belonging to both Elkanah and Hannah; it was almost as they left it, except the windows were boarded up and the once beautifully manicured flower garden became overgrown by thorns, thistles and weeds. Travelling such a distance, way beyond the mirage, to see him, she wondered where he might be? She did not know which way to turn; where, she thought, may she stay the night? Surely. not under the stars?

Elkanah, kicking up the dust, leapt from his fine grey horse, leaving it for a lad to take it to the stables to be fed and watered; swallowed up by a joy, he gave a whoop as he, red-faced, came running. 'Hi there, Sammy! You've decided to come back to me, then?'

Momentarily startled, she swung around and beamed, ready to be hugged. 'Hi, back to you, too!' she exclaimed to Elkanah with a sigh of relief. 'I tried to get into the guest annexe, but it's locked. Where's Eable? '

'As far as I know, my brother's in Shiloh.'

'Shiloh? What for?'

He reminded her how they, from such an ancient line of priests, were expected to attend the Temple, to sacrifice either a bullock, a goat or two turtle doves. 'We usually go to the Shiloh Temple every year; remember?'

'I'm jolly glad you're here; it's quite providential, but why aren't you in Shiloh, too?'

He hesitated before almost hanging his head. 'Not this time, Sammy.'

'That's not like you to duck out of your responsibilities.'

He gave a sideways look. 'Do you think I don't know it, eh?'

'So, were you sick?'

'No, my pet, I am grand … just grand.'

'Why then?'

'Do you really want the honest truth?'

She quietly chuckled; from him, she did.

He slightly turned his head. 'Well, frankly, I simply didn't want to bump into my estranged wife.'

'Hannah?'

'Yes.' He recalled how she plotted and schemed. 'You'll remember how she bolted lock, stock and barrel, to Shiloh?'

'Yeah. I remember all right. Have you heard how she is?'

He, ever the sceptic and with a grim-faced, nodded. 'Without even bothering to consult me … and my being the young lad's father, she took it upon herself to arrange for Eli to raise Samuel.'

'Eli?'

Elkanah leaned against a wall, to reply: 'Eli's one of the old priests in Shiloh Temple; he normally stations himself by the door of the Tabernacle. A priest! What the heck does he know about raising little kids, huh?'

Sam thought for a moment or two. 'Perhaps Hannah reckoned it was the right thing to do at the time?'

He was not so sure if it was at all an altogether wise move. 'After all, old Eli made a real mess of raising his own two boys; both Hophni and Phinehas have turned out to be a couple of nasty villains.' Elkanah added how he would not wish to encounter those two fellows upon a dark night.

'So, Hannah is all on her own, without her Samuel, too?'

'Yep. Serves her right!'

Sam did not hear Elkanah's remark as very charitable. 'I bet now, with an empty nest, she'll be wishing she'd had more babies, eh?'

Elkanah heard, via the grape-vine, how Hannah wanted more kids. 'After all, she's still a young woman,' he stated. 'If she'd stayed on here, we could have had a nice little family. '

'You and Hannah never divorced, did you?'

He shook his head.

'Hmm. What a shame you didn't travel with Eable?' Sam added: 'If you'd mustered up enough courage, you could have chatted things over with her; she might even have invited you into her bed, to have you father another little Elkanah for her?'

'Are you kidding?' Elkanah reminded Sam how, when Hannah left for Shiloh, she set her body guards on him, preventing him from following her.

Sam also reminded him how that was then; she declared she may have since had a changed heart.

'You reckon she'll still fancy me?'

Sam exaggerated her sigh, raising her eyes heavenwards. 'If I was Hannah, wow, I should jolly well want you.'

'Really?'

She nodded.

'But Hannah may want me to remain in Shiloh?'

'So? Shiloh for you isn't exactly the other end of the world!' Sam exclaimed. 'Go and woo her … take her some roses?'

'What? Peninnah would go nuts if she found out.' He laughed, remembering one of Sammy's expressions, how she would have 'my guts for her garters!'

Sam smiled before frowning, thinking it over for a few moments. 'If you, as a priest, are also going up to the Temple, Peninnah would never suspect about any liaison between you and your wife; anyway, you aren't married to Peninnah now, are you? She doesn't own you any more than I do.'

Thoughtfully, Elkanah stroked his rough chin.

'Anyway, I've not travelled all this way, to be your scribe of an agony aunt; so, in the meantime, are we going to base ourselves out here, roasting under the sun, or shall you let me into the guest annexe?'

Remorseful, he explained: 'I really wasn't thinking …'

'It's just I've travelled such a long way to visit. I'm now absolutely dog tired.' She added how she heard a rumour concerning an earth tremor; yet, she watched him shrug off her worry with a pooh-pooh, trivialising it as nothing much.

As Elkanah unlocked the guest annexe, to let her in, he suddenly remained thoughtful, unusually subdued. 'You know, I half wish now I'd gone to Shiloh, after all?'

Sam was relieved he had not or she would have kipped beneath the stars. She grinned: 'If you do go to Shiloh every year, Hannah will soon have as many kids as Peninnah?'

'Maybe?'

Sam wearily walked through into the the familiar bedroom, throwing her backpack onto one of the chairs. Sitting on the edge of the big bed, she kicked off her brown leather sandals, massaging her painted toes. 'In a bit, I'll go into the kitchen and make some tea. Will you join me?'

He sat across on the sofa, thinking before nodding how he would. 'And by the way, how long are you staying, Sammy? '

'Oh, this is only a flying visit. I'm out of here first thing in the morning. I've a couple of very good friends waiting for me in their Egyptian hotel; my own parents are also expecting me home in England. You, Elkanah, need a shave.'

He felt around the dark stubble.

With a grin, she reminded him of the morning when she shaved him; he, however, baulked at the distant memory.

Sam, sorting through the kitchen's cupboard, made some tea, handing him some of the steaming hot beverage; as she did, she gave him a quick peck on his forehead. 'I actually think you're a pretty terrific guy.'

'We're special to each other, aren't we?'

She no longer tried to hide the passion in her Irish green eyes; the smile which rapidly crept across her mouth as a wide beam gave way to a laugh: 'You surely must know how I feel about you?' She added how she adored him at first sight.

'You didn't believe me when I told you the same ...'

'But I couldn't for you were not a free man. I wasn't out to destroy your marriage to Hannah.'

He gave her a brief nod, sighing for all which may have been.

She kissed him again, yet thinking she ought to tear herself away from him, to become as strong with him as in previous times. She lived without him before, but, she pondered, how long could she now do without him? 'I am famished. It's absolutely ages since I ate,' she told him. 'Is there no food?'

Elkanah swallowed the remainder of his tea before getting to his feet, he searching through another kitchen cupboard where there seemed nothing more than wine. 'I'm not having you going hungry.' He told her to wait: 'I'll be back in next to no time.'

About twenty minutes later, Elkanah returned with provisions where Sam discovered some salt beef slices, half a loaf of freshly baked bread, a portion of cucumber and a large orange; from a draw he handed her a sharp kitchen knife, leaving her to arrange it on a plate.

Sam's eyes widened in amazement, she asking where he acquired such goodies.

'Peninnah won't miss those bits and pieces.'

'And, what if she does?'

He thought for a moment or two. It was he who gave his mistress housekeeping money for the food. 'When, if she finds it missing, well, she'll just think it's my being extra hungry.'

'Before I leave in the morning, I'll go to the farmers' market, to replace it.'

'Sammy, it's honestly not necessary.'

She said she may be going anyway, just so she ate before her long journey home. He watched her sitting at the crude wooden table, consuming every last morsel, licking clean her fingers after peeling the sticky orange.

'Gosh, you were hungry, weren't you?'

'Starving!'

He smiled when he smelled her usual perfume. Those secret feelings they once both shared, all came flooding back in their minds. He watched her pulling the elastic band from her pony tail, shaking her auburn hair to fall free in loose curls; her bright green eyes smiled up at him and, she warming towards him, became not a little inviting. He poked around in her backpack, taking a hairbrush. Sitting extra close, thigh against thigh, he brushed away her tangles, simply copying as he saw her do upon other occasions; it became a joy to have Elkanah so close.

'I love those little pearl studs in your ears,' he whispered. 'I always have.'

Feeling one of them in her earlobe, she stated: 'This pair of earrings were given to me on my twenty-first birthday, but my mother reminded me "pearls are for tears"; a silly old tale, eh? It occurred to her: 'Why don't you buy something like these for Hannah?'

'Ah, maybe? I'll have to think; either that or something special from the vineyard?' He and Eable were hoping for a better harvest during the following year, even though it was quite a long way off. She took from him the brush, to complete the task, he not taking his dark brown eyes from her.

Previously, apart from once or twice, Sam allowed him to get so far with her before she screeched on the breaks, but, only that one time, she longed for him to welcome her back, to amuse themselves.

'Oh, Sammy, this is so difficult for me, you know? I cannot just be a best friend with you any more,' he confessed.

She looked horrified. What was he saying? Was he passing her over for his long time mistress? Was she receiving a sudden rebuff from him, of all people, to receive the similar rejection she gave her previous fiancee? Was it to be a tit for tat? But no. He again stood to shove aside the used crockery and cutlery before pulling her gently across to where he decided to sit on the sofa. For her to be surrounded by his arms as he kissed her, lingering there. He could taste some of the food on her lips, just as she tasted the strong lemon tea on his. Without a moment's hesitation, Sam tightened the hug around his shoulders and half kissed him back.

'Where, Sammy, do I belong, huh? '

'You?' Poetically, Sam answered: 'Perhaps in dangerous waters with me, yet only for a while?'

'Wait. Stay put.' He remembered the kitchen cupboard where there was only white wine, presumably from his own cellar. He returned to ask: 'Want some?' He held it higher, for her to see one of the half flagons.

Sam looked around for another vessel but there did not seem to be a clean one. She, swallowing the last dregs from her tea, held out the used mug. 'I'll only have a tiny one.' She reminded him how she had an early morning start. 'I don't want any hangovers tomorrow morning; I need to travel back to an Egyptian hotel.'

Elkanah's dark eyes smiled. Together, they enjoyed sharing, yet he took more than she, hoping to prevent inhibitions between themselves, making everything easier. His broad smile changed into a serious frown. 'I need you to know how, Sammy, I'm fed up with playing second fiddle to my young brother. Oh, pet! You surely must know …I love even the air you breathe.'

Sam, becoming a little tired from hearing about both Hannah and Peninnah, leaned her head against him, running her fingertips across his chest. She knew he also might feel a pinch of jealousy if she told him about the cab driver's wandering hand upon her thigh. 'He called me his "pet", too.'

'Did he now, the dog?' Tit for tat, Elkanah was showing more than a little jaundiced envy; Sam smiled as she watched him. Her smile switched to laughter as she explained how the taxi driver was absorbed with fondling her thigh. 'He even asked me to describe what I do with Eable and you. He stated he was sure we do more than shaking hands!'

'What, then did you say?'

'Nothing much.' She pulled aside to swallow another sip from her wine. 'Shall I have more to tell him during my return journey?'

'Sammy! You flirt. I hope you are only teasing me?'

'Of course. I'd never discuss what happens between us. Not with anyone.' She lived with the secrets.

'Do you have a boy friend in London?'

'Not any more.'

Elkanah seemed comforted, lightened by her words when she added: 'Right now, you're all I have been dreaming about.'

'Me, too.' To him, in his time frame, way beyond the mirage, she became willing to become more than his ancient fantasy, with no mysteries between them; Elkanah showed no sorrow, yet Sam loved him.

'Tell me, the guest annexe door is locked,' she whispered. 'No-one can get in, can they?'

'No. When I came back with your food, I also slipped across the inner bolt.'

Sam sighed, she half closing her eyes as she felt him kissing her, he reminding her how simply gorgeous she was; she, reciprocating his love, declared: 'You are why I actually came here in the first place.' After all, she grinned, she told him she did not visit old Ramah for its scenery. She switched to becoming deadly serious, stating she was missing him far too much; she loathed her times without him, even yelling out in her sleep.

Elkanah claimed he felt the same. 'I had the most terrible nightmares after you left, even disturbing Peninnah's sleep.' His mistress became so tired from his dreams, she moved him to their sofa.

'I'm here now, though.'

'Hmm, but not permanently?' He explained he wanted her all the time. 'Ah, this lumpy sofa's no good, Sammy ...' He, setting aside the wine, young and strong, lifted her, laying her across the bed, he hearing her inwardly gasping at his every touch. 'You sure you'll allow this?'

She nodded before giggling, reminding him about the cab driver who kept his hand on her thigh: 'I'll need to have something to report back, to tell him; he said he wanted to know all I do with you ...'

'Filthy dog!' he exclaimed. 'But, oh, my darling Sammy …'

'Wait!' she started, half pulling away from him, she sitting up and away.

'Oh, what?' He lifted his head to listen. 'Whatever is the matter now?'

'Shush!' Someone outside was frantically trying the front door handle. Sam and Elkanah ached to call a halt to their movements, to carefully listen.

'Is a servant, trying the door?' she whispered. 'If we're deadly quiet, they'll hopefully go away.'

'No. The servants would have left hours ago. '

'Who then? Kids acting the fool, knocking on the door before running off?'

Elkanah threw a white bed sheet over her and, stepping into his brown leather sandals, pulled down his own long shirt to cover himself. 'It must be Eable, back earlier than expected.' He cursed with an expletive profanity.

Sam swiftly smoothed the bedding while Elkanah, more than unhappy, slowly staggered from the bedroom, across the living area, to unbolt the front door.

'Oh, Eable. I thought it might be you,' he remarked. 'You're back sooner than I expected …'

'Yeah. Never mind all that.' Eable presumed Elkanah should have been at Peninnah's place. 'Whatever are you doing in here?'

'Well, listen. We've had an unexpected visitor.'

'Eh? Who?'

'Sammy came back to see us again,' Elkanah beamed. 'She's in here!'

There was a brief moment of silence as Eable slowly, quietly closed the front door behind himself. 'Sam?' he questioned, arching a dark brow. 'She's back? 'Curiosity overcame him; he elbowed passed by his older brother, hurrying through into the bedroom. Thrilled to bits to see her, he perched himself on the edge of his bed, too, closing the distance between them.

Breathless, she declared: 'I thought, Eable, you weren't returning here until late tomorrow? Elkanah was going to give me your hotel's address in Shiloh, so I would've visited you there.'

He asked if she would see him in Shiloh, it was obvious to him how she had not returned for good. 'Is this just one more of your flying visits, Sam?'

Sam nodded her head, sorrowfully explaining to him, how she needed to get back to Egypt before going on then to her parents' Wimbledon home. 'I just had something to eat and drink. What about you, Eable? Are you hungry, too?'

He was stuffed full. 'I ate a large dish of beef stew just before leaving Shiloh.' He sniffed, saying how he could smell some wine upon her. She giggled, telling him they sampled some of Elkanah's which was in the kitchen's cupboard. 'Why?'

'Ah, never mind all that. Sam, I cannot even begin to tell you how great it is to see you again. I'm more than thrilled.'

'Me, too.'

`What brought you back?'

'Well, you see, I was in Egypt, so I thought I would make you and Elkanah a quick visit. I miss both of you, you know?'

'We miss you, too. Forgive me, for right now I cannot stay.'

'What do you mean? Where are you going?"

Elkanah interrupted, asking him why, but Eable aimed his words still to Sam. 'Oh, Sam, I am so very sorry.' He came into the annexe, only to dump his belongings after his round trip to and from the Shiloh Temple.

'Why? What ... where are you going?'

'I faithfully promised; I need to go to our grandfather's place.'

'For the whole night?'

He told her yes, to settle Elihu down. 'Grandfather plays up no end if I'm not there. Once he is asleep, I'll perhaps try to creep back, but ...' He, under Elkanah's jealous gaze, kissed her before lingering.

After Eable eventually left, Sam promptly turned back to Elkanah and, as their eyes again met, she longed for him. He rose from one of the bedroom chairs, sitting down beside her, to kiss her forehead. 'I'll also need to leave, just for a very brief while.'

'Now?'

'Yeah. With you here, I was so happy, I very nearly forgot. I swear, Sammy, I won't be long. Wait for me?'

Of course she would, but where would he be? Surely not with his granddaddy, too? No.

Elkanah's best friend's wife recently died in child-birth; he, as a local Ramah priest, promised to help his chum, to place two stones of remembrance at the grave. 'You see, Sammy, the official thirty days of mourning haven't come to an end, not as yet.'

He, more hours later than he expected, made his way into the guest annexe where he sat by her side to watch her sleeping body; she, at the previous sundown, closed the wooden shutters prior to her promptly disrobing. He, removing his own attire, whispered: 'You are so beautiful, my Sammy, so different from our own local women; you're hard to resist.' He soon climbed in beside her, snuggling up so close, his quietly deep voice whispering his awesome love for her alone; in the early hours of the morning, she open her eyes: 'You were so late, that I am sorry, but I just had to get some sleep.'

'Don't worry.'

'It's lovely, Elkanah, to wake up, to know you're there.'

He told her how she was really the only woman for him. 'I am sorry; I shouldn't have woken you.'

'And now you have?' Sam grinned.

Elkanah, having hauled her across in his arms, could not relax his hold, unable to let her free, reminding her how he was a man in love; he, tasting her so good, plundered her with kisses, knowing they so in love. With almost a pain, she was as hungry for him, as he for her with an urgency, with an impatience, their hearts bursting until they were overcome by their own powers.

Sam yawned, acknowledging him with a nod; gorgeous, she walked across the room for her bag, reaching in for her two cameras.

'By the way, my friends and family don't believe you exist, so I brought with me a Polaroid camera ... also an ordinary point-and-shoot camera. The camera doesn't lie!' She had already taken a photograph of the toothless cameleer with the Polaroid, but then, with the same, she was anxious to take one of Elkanah.

He happily obliged upon the condition she also joined him. The camera was new to him; he had never seen such a contraption. Balancing it on a nearby three legged stool and setting the timer, there was one of them together. More films showed Elkanah with her, the love of his life. The Polaroid photographs developed almost immediately, the snaps providing them with some amusement. 'These are pictures I shall definitely not be showing my family and friends!' she exclaimed.

He nudged her with a grin: 'What about your cab driver? Didn't he ask to be told about what goes on between us? You could show the old rascal.'

Cameras placed aside, they cuddled. 'I don't ever want to let go of you, Sammy? 'Elkanah declared, gently caressing her.

'So don't.'

'You'll be gone this morning. I may never see you ever again. Just snuggle up, eh? Let me continue to hold you?'

Using his own key, Eable crept in the guest annexe. It was about the time he usually left for the stables but, as he knew Sam was visiting, he left Hunter in the care of the stable lad. He returned to his bedroom, only to see the sleeping pair. She stayed resting tight against Elkanah's still body, a comfort for them until they dropped asleep. Elkanah lifted a heavy eyelid, having slept fitfully, he soon disturbed by the movements of his brother. Eable had spotted the camera, he not knowing what it might be. Elkanah whispered to him the quick explanation; he pointed and pressed the button, taking a photo of Sam. The camera flashed, immediately waking her with a start.

'What's happening?' she asked, lifting her head. 'Whatever are you doing with my camera, huh?'

'Shush, Sammy. It's all right. Eable just took one of you. Okay?' Elkanah whispered. 'Don't move, my pet. He's doing no harm to your camera.'

'Oh, Eable, I didn't know you were here?'

'Yeah. I know!'

That morning Sam, showering, came to ready herself for the off. 'Eable, where's your brother? 'she asked. 'Where's he gone?' Quietly, slowly and carefully, she sat herself down at the kitchen table, the legs of the chair scraping noisily upon the tiled floor, her sore head in her hands, nursing her pounding headache; she reached for her sunglasses, to blot out the morning sunlight, it streaming through the shutters, previously opened by Eable. 'For the first time in my life, I have acquired a dreadful hangover.' She found two paracetamol tablets in her bag, promptly swallowing the pills with some lemon tea Eable brewed for himself. 'I shall never again touch any more of Elkanah's wine … never, ever again. It's lethal. And shush. Please, don't speak so loud.'

He became unaware he was.

Once the analgesics had eventually performed their job and she perked up, Sam informed him: 'I have to leave from here shortly, Eable. Once I have had a bite to eat, I shall have to kiss you goodbye.'

His head dropped, he appearing like a sorrowful, spoilt kid instead of the grown man he was. 'I wish you could stay on.'

Sam made no response to his whining wishes, but rapidly switched the subject, telling him how she had brought with her some goodies.

'For me, Sam?'

'Yeah. Of course it's for you. Wait a sec.' She nipped back to the bedroom where she originally dumped her rucksack. She lugged it back to the kitchen, placing it on the seat of a wooden chair; with Eable leaning over her shoulder, she unzipped a large compartment where she fished out a quality sketch book and a tin box of coloured pencils – pencils with all the colours of the rainbow. 'These should keep you more than busy.'

He, thankful, could hardly believe his eyes. Still fascinated by the camera, he asked: 'Will you, before you leave, take a picture of Hunter, too? He is a big proud horse; he would love it.'

'You figured out how to use the camera, so, while I eat, you quickly go and take it, huh? Incidentally, speaking of Hunter, I have in my London apartment, a large oil painting of a grey stallion; it's the absolute spit image of your horse. It is also named "Hunter". How spooky is that, Eable, huh?'

'Where did you get the picture?'

'It came from a London art gallery – a present from my parents.' As Sam spoke with Eable, as she stared at this big broad man, tall with those dark, chocolate, piercing eyes, she experienced a strange feeling of deja vu. Had she seen his double some place; yet where? Most odd, she thought.

Showered and clean shaven, Elkanah made a timely appearance. 'I have decided, Sammy, to make a visit to Shiloh. Remember about our chat yesterday? I'm taking your advice.'

'My? You don't let the grass grow under your feet, do you, Elkanah?'

Eable was eager to be in on their conversation, but his big brother closed in on him, threatening him with his very life, never to breath a single word to another living soul, especially to Peninnah.

'Sammy, if you are soon going to be ready for the off, I can give you a lift on Huntsman … my big stallion. I can take you as far as the old Needle's Eye. Would that be a help?'

Eable turned to Elkanah: 'Sam had a bad headache,' he chuckled. 'A hangover!'

Elkanah stared at Samantha and grinned.

'I'm all right now.'

Leaving ancient Ramah became always tough for Sam; then became no exception. With mustering an emotional strength, she said her goodbyes to Eable, and, with Elkanah's help, she mounted his beautiful grey horse. Seating herself behind Elkanah, she, with no helmet, held tight on and around his waist. Half way, he pulled the horse to a halt. He explained to Sam how, when they rode the distance to Shiloh, they always stopped, to rest their animals at the water's trough. 'We naturally take great care of our horses, otherwise we become stranded,' he explained. 'Huntsman needs a break. We do, too, or we get saddle sore.'

'And where are we going while your horse is watered and rested?' Sam quizzed with a broad grin. 'What happens to us, as if I didn't know, huh?'

He placed an arm around her shoulders before pointing, smiling. 'Look! See the little cave across the way?'

It was no great tourist attraction, but she did.

'Yes, well, when all my men are with me, the younger ones dodge the hot sun by sheltering in there where it's cool.'

Sam, no fool, knew what happened in the caves. 'When I get home to England it'll be midwinter; my, it's bitterly cold there. Probably snowing? Nothing like here, eh?'

'I bet! Anyway, don't try changing the subject; listen. Only if you want to, Sammy, will you come with me into the cave?'

She, knowing that was coming, exhaled as she thought, half swallowing upon her own saliva, not knowing quite how to react.

Elkanah was anxious for her to agree. 'You know me well enough now; I'd never force you to do anything against your will.' He told her that would be nothing more than terrible. 'You do believe me, don't you?'

She claimed she did.

' You and I should not be seen in there. It's usually deserted ... it'll probably be only you, me and the echo ...' He constantly reassured her in the best way he knew how; he was aware Sammy cherished such moments as utterly private.

'What if someone does come along?' she questioned. 'What if they see us?'

He shook his head. 'They won't. Not today. Remember, when we came back from our annual trip to Shiloh, a whole group of the guys used this cave to have their women. Every few yards around the cave's walls there were groups of men and women; you don't have to be clever to imagine all they did! Anyway, right now, we are quite alone.'

Sam finally nodded in agreement. She quickly removed enough for him, smiling broadly; she was happy as he kissed her, pulling her so close, wanting her, taking her. Aroused, they always had powerful effects upon each other. Completed, they fulfilled, she having rediscovered him all over again, for herself ... yet, for him? She delighted in him, yet she informed him how he should be on his way, to encounter Hannah, to begin to make more babies for her – one every year.

'You don't feel jealous about my going off again to see my Hannah?'

'Well, yeah, to be completely honest, I actually feel quite green with envy.'

'Oh, gosh, my sweetheart! I didn't think you were that sort? By the way, do you still have your Polaroid camera, Sammy?' he asked, a cheeky glint in his dark eyes.

Sam nodded, taking it from a padded pocket in the side of her rucksack. Together they finished the film; he kept a couple of the pictures for himself. He swore he would show absolutely no-one. Sam was still available when some dust fell from the roof, then came a deep rumbling, echoing from within the very depths of the cave; some large stones began to fall by the entrance.

Elkanah raced to rapidly bundle up all their belongings, he booming at the top of his voice, for to her to rapidly get out.

'But, but I ..?'

'Run! Run! Run for your very life! Samantha, quickly … get out or we'll both be trapped?' he yelled. 'It's yet another earth tremor …'

They made it outside, only just in time, to see many more huge boulders filling the entrance of the cave. 'Phew! That was a near thing, Sammy, my pet,' he declared, holding her close to his chest.

He momentarily left her and went straight across to his stallion, to breathe his breath into its nostrils, to calm him down.

As she dressed, the young entrepreneurial fellow with the overladen grey and brown donkey came along the road, avoiding the rubble, for some had fallen half way across the street. 'Take you to the old Needle's Eye, pretty lady?' he called, picking his way over the fallen stones.

'Yes, wait!' she yelled to the teenager. She turned back to then the love of her life: 'Elkanah, I'll go with him. Okay? '

'You are really sure? '

Sam nodded. 'It was very kind of you, but we both know the old Needle's Eye is actually out of your way. You need to be getting off to old Shiloh, to Hannah. Go and father another little Elkanah!' she declared, kissing him as ever.

'You really do love me, don't you, Sammy?'

'When didn't I? From the very first moment I saw you, from the first time we touched, when you sometimes held my hand, I knew it.'

'Why didn't you tell me all these things?'

'How could I? First, you belonged elsewhere. I've needed to wait, to become patient; who knows then of our future together?'

Sam made her way back to Paula and Adjo's hotel where they all wished one and another a happy Christmas. At the airport Sam sat quietly in the club class lounge where she grabbed a black coffee. During the uneventful flight she thought, at first, about her big strong Elkanah before Eable, yet, once home in London, for some unknown reason to her, she began to remember the guy at the gallery. James Samuels seemed nice; inwardly, she smiled to herself, thinking of whether or not she saw him somewhere previously; he seemed familiar. Deja vu? Maybe?

Chapter 10

On the Wednesday morning, two days before the Christmas Day of 1970, a frigid icy wind became forecast. Sam appeared more washed out than usual – what her unqualified mother diagnosed as being a little liverish, maybe from lack of sleep? Without much considerable effort, Sam's complexion, nevertheless, occurred flawlessly healthy; cosseted by her thick winter coat with its faux fir trimmed hood, she briefly left the snug warmth of her London apartment. She climbed into her car which, thanks to her dad, was in great shape, it handling like a dream; battling with the tangle of traffic along the Chelsea's King's Road, within fifteen minutes she was outside the Gallery where she only planned to drop a seasonal card through its letterbox. Sam began wondering the logic of it. Certainly, she thought, traders sent out greeting cards to their clients - rarely the reverse.

Parking, as ever, became a London nightmare; locking her driver's side door, it was impossible to miss how cops and traffic wardens were out in force. There were almost as many as in the Salvation Army band, they playing: 'God rest ye merry gentlemen' and 'Joy to the world' before rattling their money tins, anxious for folks' spare cash.

Catching sight of Samantha through his shop's front window, James Samuels became frantically waving in her direction, he mouthing for her to wait for a moment. Hurrying around to open up the shop door, he welcomed her in with a smile: 'Do come on in from the cold and, oh, by the way, thanks for this.' He slit open its red envelope, discovering the home-made card, promptly reading the seasonal sentiments she scribed within.

'That's very beautiful!' he declared. 'Its calligraphy must have taken you ages?'

She had no choice but to stand, waiting for a moment or two before he gave her a quick hug which, to her, seemed long time coming. Following him deeper inside, she remarked: 'I expect you're snowed under with Christmas cards?'

'Yeah. Just a few, but only by those we couldn't sell!' He quietly chuckled, pointing to a far corner stall where there were a variety of cards, from Christmas to birthdays, along with everything else in between. 'Didn't you notice them when you came before?'

If she did, she forgot. Ah, well, she thought, at least I had those white roses. Can't expect everything.

He, smarter than when she saw him before, asked if she was in a mad rush?

'Me? Yes. Why?'

'So, you've no time to have a coffee with me?'

Sam smelled its deliciously tempting aroma, but her wristwatch told her she really should skedaddle. She did not relish a parking ticket; glancing around at a nearby chair, it seemed to be occupied by a curled up, sleeping cat over presumably some of his comfy stuff; James was about to shoo him off for she did not relish the white cat hairs on her dark clothing; she perched herself up on the counter. 'When I was here before, your mother could only offer tea.'

He half grinned, informing her how that was then. James told Sam how his parents, unlike him, didn't live over the shop. His mother obviously forgot to bring coffee from home. 'You can still have tea, if you want? Say, if you do.'

Sam screwed up her freckled nose, shaking her head. She kept a close eye on the time; it was fast becoming a premium. She sighed: 'I'd love to stay for that coffee, but, I must leave.' She briefly mentioned how her mum was recently given a parking ticket. 'And I don't relish having one ...'

James claimed he understood, but, before offering a rain check, he began thoughtful, as if he was about to say more.

'You have something on your mind?'

' Well, um ... only that I was thinking about getting my mother to cover this lunchtime period,' he added; he planned to eat over at the Swiss Centre's restaurant.

'Today? In all that crazy, Christmas traffic, you're going over there?'

'I suppose it's a bit silly. It's just I quite like their food ...'

'I'm sure, James, but the traffic's madness out there.'

He remarked with a slight grin: 'Yet, you came out only to deliver my beautiful card?'

Giving no voice to her scruples, she stated. 'Your one and also quite a few others.' Sam declared this so he did not consider himself over the top important to her. However, she lectured Elkanah ad infinitum to be honest; she was never in the habit of bending the truth. She should not start then. Sam told him, how it wasn't until she set off, she realised how congested the streets truly were. 'Anyway, I'm glad you're pleased with my little bit of Christmas to you.'

James, having propped the home crafted card up also on the counter, smiling toward it again where it depicted the Holy Family, told her: 'It's just I loathe eating out alone; it makes me feel a bit like a spare part, you know, when everyone else seems in a couple.'

No fool, she had a good idea where the conversation was leading.

'Hey, just as a friend, nothing more, you wouldn't be free to join me, would you?'

Bingo! Sam was absolutely spot on! She frowned, hesitating for a moment or two.

He, with puppy dog eyes, persisted. 'Oh, do, Samantha, say yes,' he stated, slightly raising his voice to stress his point, to acquire his own way.

Sam fleetingly noticed he had the same way of running his long fingers through his dark wavy hair, not unlike Eable. She, through the window, also saw some flurries of snow, they appearing like tiny white feathers fluttering in the air. Having only just returned from the balmy warmth of Egypt, from the blazing heat way beyond the mirage, she became unsure. She knew, though, she could also do with some distractions from her trip, to free her mind from the flashbacks, of her enigmatic lovers. Had she the heart to refuse James who brought her those white roses?

Sam stated, offering him a warm smile. 'I'll need to nip home first, to get changed into something more suitable than these togs.'

James intended picking her up, driving her over to the Swiss Centre, but, oh, that Christmas traffic was, it seemed, worsening by the hour; she suggested it would be wise to house their cars, to travel by public transport.

He agreed, making plans to meet with her in an hour and a half.

As Sam was about to leave The Gallery, the handsome little cat yawned, stretching his furry body into an arch before jumping down; attempting to wind himself around her legs, James scooped him up in his arms. 'See, even my cat likes you, too?'

At the restaurant, Sam, sitting opposite to him and making small talk, asked if he liked London. The lively Soho arose in their conversation; its famous Windmill Theatre, a well-known establishment, never closed, offering non stop reviews.

'How do you know so much about it all, Sam?' James asked, raising his dark eyebrows.

'Oh, one of my then fellow students, sick to the teeth with being flat broke, quit the nursing degree course half way.' Sam added how Katie, as a colleague became known, was one of those semi-nude girls. 'Some of our buddies, including my friend Paula and I were invited to her initiation; there Katie was, no longer in her grey nurses' uniform with its yellow belt and black laced up shoes, but in dazzlingly silver high heels, being christened in Champagne, with plenty of money accumulating in the bank.'

'And you went to see her routine?'

'Some of it; I actually didn't stay, for I was due back on duty …' Sam smiled: 'Then, Katie very nearly married the Windmill's Irish doorman.'

'But she didn't?'

'No,' she giggled, 'My friend Paula heard Katie gave it all up to become a cloistered nun, somewhere in Rome?'

'Seems all a bit far fetched?'

Sam laughed it off, but James deeply scowled; she thought it sensible to quickly change the subject. They chatted more comfortably, briefly about some recent black and white films released up in the West End, some old 1930's music, his previous overseas travel and only a little about his art at The Gallery.

Sitting in the busy Swiss restaurant, the luncheon mostly continued in a more relaxed way; it was a reasonably pleasant affair and they continued to converse easily about his work. 'My dad teaches art to senior students and he's coached me no end.'

Sam listened intently. 'That's good.'

'You'll be getting tired of hearing about me,' he remarked.

She, not exactly quiet, chatted nearly as much as he.

'It's simply I feel comfortable with you, Sam, almost as if we'd known each other for absolutely ages.' He reached across the table to gently touch, to cover her hand. 'Your hand feels icy cold.'

She very nearly placed her other chilly hand on top, to prevent him from withdrawing his own, yet she thought better of it.

He smiled.

'Now,' Sam, towards the end of the delicious sweet course, started, 'at the risk of my sounding sickly corny, would you like to come back to my place for coffee, instead of staying on here?'

James Samuels gave the po-faced stern deep frown again, shaking his head; he, having glanced at his own watch, remarked: 'I'm sorry, but I hadn't realised the time.' He raised his hand, clicking his fingers, indicating to the waiter how he needed the bill.

'Would you like us to go Dutch concerning the bill?' Sam asked. 'I'm more than happy to ...'

'Certainly not,' James stated: 'I was the one who invited you.' He planned to quickly see her home, but she said she could cope alone, to walk the road ahead by herself.

'Regarding my offer of the coffee,' she piped up again, yet with a smile, 'it definitely was not a case of "Come into my parlour," said the spider to the fly". I'm not like that, James.'

James nodded, offering how he only invited her out as a bit of company for himself.

Sam bit her lip, wondering: Was that his way of giving her the brush off?

Alone and lonely, Sam sat in her apartment, curled up on her sofa, staring at the print in a novel, yet little of the story was sinking in. How she wished she was way beyond the mirage, in Elkanah's guest annexe, she swathed in a white towelling robe with her wet hair falling over her shoulders; there were candles illuminating that kitchen, a place with basic cutlery and cookware. In the bedroom the noonday sun would beat down on the roof; regularly, she was beloved by Elkanah instead of her then being in London, listening to Handel on her radio, of being frozen outside. She was beginning to wonder about James, the way he smiled, his gentle touch; forget him, she thought, resuming her novel in the hope her mind would cease from drifting upon a fellow who turned down her simple offer of a coffee. Surely, as she laughed about Katie's opening, James did not tar her with the same brush? Even the craziness of the thought made her smile.

When Daisy knew their daughter would be coming for Christmas eve and onwards, she urged Henry to bring all the decorations from the attic. They were the same ones since Sam was a toddler. Daisy decorated the front door with a prickly holly wreath. With pungent cooking smells, she made a Christmas pudding in which were three sterilised coins ... lucky sixpences; sage and onion stuffing became ready for the plucked turkey, not forgetting the mulled wine. Remembering her own growing up years in Ireland, Daisy baked a seed cake. The oversized fir tree went into its usual corner of the large living room, festooned with umpteen decorations, with the gold star fixed to the top branch. Below, presents were beautifully wrapped in red, green and golden ribbons. She was determined it would be a Christmas to be remembered for their Samantha was home safe and sound. To Henry and Daisy Webb, their daughter became their best gift! Nevertheless, to them, with heaps of her love, she gave her dad a new wristwatch and her mother some disgustingly expensive perfume, both from duty-frees.

Midnight Mass meant sleeping late, through much of the morning, hence Christmas Day with Sam's parents started late. Finally, at about two 0' clock that afternoon they all sat together to eat their Christmas dinner. Each pulled a Christmas cracker, purchased from Harrods; they all wore silly paper hats. Her dad made his annual wisecrack, he saying the best cracker he ever pulled was his wife Daisy; Samantha raised her green eyes to heavenwards and, in unison with her mum, groaned. By then the roast turkey, along with all the trimmings became delicious. Following the grand blow out, her father promised to tackle the washing of all the dishes, but he soon nodded off in his favourite comfy armchair. Sam, listening to his incessant snores, decided to roll up her sleeves and deal with the kitchen's mess.

With the kitchen then resembling tidy, she and her mother sat down together at the breakfast table where they both nursed a well earned mug of refreshing tea.

'This young man, Samantha,' began her mother. 'Did you fall for him, just a wee bit?'

'James?' Sam laughed without humour. 'Of course not. We've only been out once ... just over to the Swiss Centre for lunch. Nothing else.'

'Ah, now. You must fancy him a little?' Daisy quizzed; 'If you didn't, well you wouldn't have spent all that time, making him a special Christmas card?'

Sam did not respond concerning the card; she happened to mention she asked him to her apartment for a coffee following the lunch date. 'He totally misunderstood my motives.'

'Yes, well, he would, wouldn't he?' Daisy laughed. 'But, to be fair, he'd previously brought you a dozen red roses -.'

'No, he did not. He gave me six white ones in exchange for a pair of his brown leather gloves. I am telling you, there's absolutely nothing between us. We're not even friends any more. Nothing.'

'Really?'

'Really and truly. He's a bit of a drag about his art; there's also a sort of love affair with a horse called Hunter ...'

'Well, with the Christmas money daddy and I gave you, you did buy a painting of his stallion.' Her mother, still brimming with old fashioned feminine curiosity, asked if he was very handsome.

Sam, replying as to how he is good looking with brown eyes, secretly like those of her ancient lover, James was charming and professionally, quite successful … the perfect young gentleman, he had impeccably fine manners.

'Do you know, by the time I was about your age, I was married to your father and expecting you? If you don't hurry up, my dear, you will be left on the shelf! Do you really want to remain an old maid, just like your father's sister, poor old Harriet?'

Sam inwardly groaned.

By New Year's Day, Sam, who could tolerate the match-making no longer, planned to return to her Earls Court apartment, but, coughing and sneezing, she began with a heavy winter cold, aching all over in her limbs. She attempted to get up, but failed. Daisy told Henry how Samantha looked like death warmed up, with a sore throat which felt like sand paper. Her mother, worried it could be the start of the dreadful Asian influenza, for there was a lot of it about, touched Sam's forehead; she was burning up, although she claimed she was shivering. Daisy took it upon herself to contact their old family Doctor, she requesting an immediate home visit.

He, within the hour, hurried up the stairs and into Sam's bedroom, sat by her bed; he listened to Sam's chest when no-one spoke, when she took deep breaths. He undid his outer coat, to pull out a fancy gold pocket watch; feeling and timing her pulse, the old family doctor gave her hand a gentle squeeze. 'Open wide,' he instructed, telling her to say: "Ah!" Hmm. That looks nasty.'

'Samantha's temperature is 102, Doctor,' Daisy stated, showing him the thermometer as proof of her honesty. 'I'm very worried about my daughter's health.'

He tucked away his posh watch before replacing his stethoscope back into his deep pocket. 'Ah, Samantha's not a little child, you know, Mrs Webb?' he stated, reminding her how her daughter, the dear girl, a previously good nurse, would know exactly what to do for herself. 'Two Paracetamol every four hours, along with plenty of clear fluids, but she must keep well wrapped up, staying in the warm,' he carried on. 'If she really doesn't improve within five days, then don't hesitate to call me again. Okay?'

Her mother admonished: 'Samantha, dear, you really do need to start taking better care of yourself. All this gallivanting off to both Egypt and then to Samaria, simply at the drop of a hat, along with goodness only knows where else, has naturally had an awful effect upon you.'

She, with tears blurring her eyes, felt too wretched to argue.

'You're obviously thoroughly run down, lass. Living all alone, were you honestly eating properly?'

Sam sighed a long ragged sigh, raising her Irish green eyes upwards, declaring: 'I honestly wish you wouldn't fuss; like the Doctor told you, I'm not a little kid ...'

Nevertheless, Sam did feel exceedingly unwell, having spent most of the New Year tucked up in bed. By the beginning of the second week of January enough was enough; she planned to pack up her belongings, to return to her Earl's Court apartment, assuring both doting parents she was fine. She informed them how she was well over her ghastly infection, performing her utmost to sound cheerful.

'All right. So, now you claim you're well again, what about contacting that handsome young man, Samantha?' Her matchmaking mother pressed. 'Why not give him a 'phone call?'

'What? Are you kidding?' Her heart sank at the thought. 'I'm definitely not running after him.'

'You'll need to gee up, my girl, or he'll find someone else who'll take his roses!'

'I'm beginning to think it was a mistake on my part, by my telling you about those wretched flowers,' Sam remarked, sounding almost curt. 'You're nearly as bad as Paula ... worse, in fact!'

'Well, she wasn't exactly slow in catching a man, was she?'

Sam exaggerated a heavily sounding sigh.

'And now Paula is having a baby.' Daisy wondered if she would ever become a granny.

Back in her Earls Court apartment, there were quite a few messages on the answer machine, three of which were actually from James Samuels, surprisingly asking if they could again meet up; she decided to give him some space, to 'phone him back at her leisure. No rush, she thought.

The weather was threatening to rain, yet, with the current state of her food store, it was out of the question to leave her cupboard bare. Rather than take her car through the crazy, ever honking London traffic, Sam hailed a black cab, to take her to Harrods – her local grocer. She was just making her way through the doors, she engrossed with a grocery list, when her eyes met those of somebody familiar; quickly, Sam glanced away, hurriedly moving into the food hall.

The woman reached out. 'Excuse me. It's … it's Samantha, Samantha Webb, isn't it? '

'Sorry, but do I know you?' Then she twigged: 'Ah, yes. Of course, you're from where I bought the paining?'

The woman smiled, giving a nod.

'Sorry. For a moment, I couldn't quite place you -.'

'Well, we only met briefly, just before Christmas.'

'Is your Gallery closed today?'

She shook her head. 'It's James' turn to work today. ' Sam smiled.

'Anyway, this morning I have the luxury of being at a loose end, so I thought I'd pop in here for morning coffee.'

'It's always lovely here, isn't it?'

She nodded, saying her husband was a teacher of art. 'Hence, the reason why I work in The Gallery. It gets me out of the house, to meet people, which is nice.'

Sam thought, speaking softly: 'Hey, look, give me time to go around, to buy much of the food I need; then why not come back with me to my apartment; help me eat some of it?' She glanced down at her wristwatch. 'I could meet you back here in, err, half an hour?'

'Oh, no thank you. I really shouldn't impose ...'

'I'd be pleased for you to join me.' Sam stated, giving a smile. 'If I really thought you'd become an imposition, I wouldn't have invited you.'

The woman paused for a short moment before beaming with gratitude. 'All right, but while you shop, I'll buy you a bottle of a good wine. Okay?'

Back at the apartment, Sam hurried to switch off the 'phone with its loud machine; she certainly did not want Hannah to overhear James' messages and, after a predictably delicious luncheon, the woman's face lingered upon Sam's, almost as if she was about to express a concern, perhaps needing to converse? Sam was raised by her dad to be one who listens, by Daisy to become gently kind to folk. Nevertheless, she was itching to ask: 'What's playing on your mind?' Although the tone of Sam's voice may have sounded softly kind, maybe it was too soon in their relationship to be frank? Over the fine wine the guest selected, they faced each other with one of those awkward silences, but it was Hannah Samuels who broke the difficult quietness; looking upwards, she remarked: 'I see you've my son's oil painting up on your wall?'

'Uh ... oh, my Christmas gift?'

'Yes. I remember. It looks quite good placed in your home, doesn't it?'

'Yes. Mum and dad have yet to see it.' Sam explained how she'd been away from the flat. 'I was quite ill over the New Year.' Sam added: 'Today is my first day, back here, to be out and about.'

Hannah set aside her glass, to reach forward, softly touching the back of Sam's hand, in the way as her son at the Swiss Centre's restaurant, although their sentiments were dissimilar. 'Right. I must leave you to rest up?' She asked Sam to 'phone for a cab. 'Had I known, I wouldn't have come here today.'

Sam possessed an extension telephone in her bedroom; away from Hannah's ears, Sam was informed how the taxi would be just outside the building within fifteen to twenty minutes.

As Hannah was wrapping up well against the January elements, she told Sam: 'Forgive my mentioning it again, but I think I know why you seemed quite shocked ...'

'Oh, gosh! You mean, when I first saw the painting?'

She did. 'You see, Samantha, I've been where you obviously were, on Eable's Hunter, in Ramah. I'm right, aren't I?'

'It's my secret.'

Hannah stated it was hers, too. 'Hmm. I use to be a history teacher. Did you know?'

Sam shook her head.

'James never said?'

'Nope.'

The woman raced to explained her speciality became Egyptology. With a degree in history, she taught in a girls' public school, yet gave up once James came along. She then became a stay-at-home wife and mother until her son finally became independent. 'Now, as you know, I work as a receptionist in The Gallery ...'

'I returned from Egypt just before Christmas. During the two occasions I went to Egypt, so much seemed to happen to me while there.'

Hannah raised her well plucked eyebrows.

Sam explained how her father was abroad with the Rifle Brigade, with the late actor, David Niven; it was during the last World War. 'Daddy so wished to return to Alexandria, to see the place in peace time. However, all his plans came to nought when my mother refused to fly. They, as a result, gave their holiday to my closest friend and me. Paula, she's my buddy, had a whirlwind holiday romance; she's now happily married to an Egyptian. They're even expecting a baby.'

'Ah, that's all very nice, but you haven't told me what actually happened to you, have you?'

Having previously told no-one all the ins and outs, Sam wondered if she should trust this comparative stranger; for what seemed another embarrassing silence, she eventually offered: 'Dad, quite a while ago, spoke to me of seeing a mirage; that was when he was in the Western Desert, so, always ever the curious one, while I was out there I tried to find it for myself.'

'Go on.'

'Well, sure, I know a mirage is only a strange phenomenon between the heat and the cold, but, oh, never mind. Let's forget it, please. It is all a little odd … your taxi will be here in quick sticks.'

'Tell me, please. What did you find way beyond the mirage, huh?'

Sam was quiet for what seemed a long, awkward moment, not knowing quite what to say, how to respond to this comparative stranger. How would she know this woman would not blab to all and sundry? What if she filled in the press? She thought to take a chance anyway and nodded. 'Yes. I did investigate. However, you used the unusual expression: ''Way beyond the mirage''. How do you know about it? '

Out of the blue, as it were, she stated: 'That's where you saw the grey stallion; it's where you rode Hunter, wasn't it?'

She gulped, coughing as her own saliva seemed to go down the wrong way, causing her normally pale face becoming hot, flushing a high pink. Her usually bright green eyes almost filled with glistening tears; it was tough attempting to choke those back. Trying again to conduct herself with some dignity and decorum, she was almost lost for words; she did not know quite what to say, for how could she have discovered such things? Was she some sort of a psychic? But no.

'Samantha, this is exactly what happened to me, way back in time. I nervously ventured way beyond the mirage prior to my planned marriage; all my immediate family, as well as my then fiancee's family thought I was missing. Some even thought I had deliberately disappeared due to pre-wedding nerves.'

Sam shook her head and gasped. 'Me, too. The first time they reported me missing. I have been way beyond the mirage twice now. That is where I saw ...'

'It's where you saw your Eable's grey stallion – did you also ride bare back together?'

'We did.'

'It is also totally identical to my son's horse; that's why you were shocked to the core when you saw the painting?'

Sam gave a nod in acknowledgement.

'I very nearly didn't return, but a huge wedding was already arranged. I had no choice but to come home.'

She asked if her husband knew all this, to which Hannah's brow knitted together into a scowl; she told her no, for he would think her nuts. 'I guessed about you, Samantha, when you reacted regarding my son's painting ... when you said you'd been to Egypt and Samaria. Sure, it was a long shot, but, please, Samantha, you mustn't ever breath a word. I have kept it a secret all these years. Promise?'

'I swear, while you live and breath, no-one shall hear anything about it from me. No-one at all. And, vice versa, you won't tell about me?'

'Of course not. Never. However, with me, there's more.'

'More?'

'Grief, yes!'

'Like what?'

Hannah hardly knowing how to continue, she half stumbling upon her words: 'Did you notice James' features ... his build? About to drop a bombshell, she told Sam they were father and son. 'Eable told me if I really loved him, I'd have his child. Like a love sick fool, I returned to England already pregnant.'

Sam, shocked, became slightly curious concerning Hannah's husband in all this.

She lowered her dark eyes before staring Sam straight in the face. 'I've never told a living soul this ...' She started, saying how she was far from proud of herself. 'You see, I actually hoodwinked him into believing he'd fathered James; they're actually great buddies and love each other. When James was born Charles was excited he had a son.'

The doorbell thankfully twice rang. 'Hannah, quickly it's your cab.'

The women hugged a farewell; Hannah thanked her for the scrumptious luncheon. 'The apple pie was really lovely.'

'I fear it was Harrod's own. Not home-made this time.'

She did admired Sam's home. 'You must come to us some time, eh?'

'I should enjoy it,' Sam declared, half bending the truth.

'So shall James?'

Chapter 11

She wanted Elkanah to sort out his personal affairs. Throughout a former excursion way beyond the mirage, she cajoled him not to avoid his estranged wife; Sam highly impressed upon him to toughen up regardless, to ride his stallion to the ancient city of Shiloh where his ex settled.

Sam's shoulders sank; she paused, becoming distracted by the distance in her own thoughts, realising the tables, for her turned. Maybe, she thought, it was a mistake to share the past with Hannah Samuel's their odd testimonies. During the subsequent weeks, she reckoned it best to stay right away, even from James, too. In such a metropolitan city as London, it should be simple to avoid them.

Meeting first with her dad in his local watering hole, Sam usually spent Sundays with the parents; they all donned their Sunday best. Daisy preferred to shoo them away from the domain of her kitchen, for her to cook an awesome roasted beef with all its appropriate trimmings; a brisk afternoon walk across the west side of Wimbledon Common, frequently as far as Cannizaro Park, with all its rhododendrons, where she inhaled the heady fragrance of a thousand blooms, invariably helped work off some of those hip sticking calories.

Smooth and sophisticated, Paula telephoned once or twice a week, she blowing the international costs; friends from when they were once practising nurses, she would happily chat nineteen to the dozen, she entertaining Samantha, mostly concerning her modern Egyptian life where they either seldom noticed poverty or gave it much thought.

Nights, tossing and turning, remained lonely for Sam. Breathlessly, she tried not thinking of those ancient men, those who, in her flash backs, would chase away her much needed sleep. In her mind, however, she invariably became overwhelmed by Elkanah's proximity.

She abandoned all such thoughts concerning returning to work; the monetary interest from the welcome inheritance of her late grandfather's estate permitted her independence, for her to remain as a self sufficient woman. She neither needed nor wanted to be tied down by any hospital's rigorous shifts.

Sam still avoided James' incessant 'phoning; by declining to pick up the calls, it caused her answer machine to store the messages. She heard his recorded deep voice declare: 'Since we left each other, just before Christmas, honestly, I've really missed you ... um, do you think, Samantha, we may be able to meet up again? Whatever, yes or no, will you at least RSVP to my most recent messages?'

Why should I? she wondered, for, just before they parted, when he naturally refused her naive offer of coffee, he stated how he only required her as a chum, when he needed to eat out? I dunno. How the heck should I react to him, since also knowing of his mother's long time secret? No, he can jolly well stew in his own juice, for there are plenty more fish in the sea. She, deep within herself, was unsure if she even liked the fellow.

Chewing over many interior worrying issues, Sam swished open the living room's heavy brocade curtains, staring mindlessly through the high Georgian sash window for seeming a longer moment. She watched the curving, busy grey London street across and below where, had there been children, none would be safe either alone or together, they playing out. Had she been way beyond the mirage, young, squealing kids may have played while ever chomping nanny goats were milked. Sam would still be cherished by brown eyed Elkanah, he loving her with a deep passion. She flitted her thoughts back to Hannah Samuels' recent luncheon visit. A chill coursed through Sam as she remembered how winemaker and talented artist Eable became pleased when he thought he made her pregnant; Hannah, chased by such dreams, permitted him to cherish her. He would, with a strange gratitude, had seen it as nothing but a perfection; she, nevertheless, needed to live for a whole generation, harbouring such secret consequences. Even so, without her ancient Eable, Hannah would never have given birth to their beloved James.

Distracted from such personal meditations, Sam's door bell twice chimed. Sighing by the intrusion, she rushed, striding quickly through into the spacious hall, first peeping through the front door's magnifying spy hole; her dad arranged to have the tiny hole placed in place. Henry reminded her: 'Watch out! It could be any old Tom, Dick or Harry out there, Samantha, and, with your living all alone in London, you have to always first check.'

Sam was dreading such a moment. 'Oh, no … James!' With a jaw dropping surprise, she exclaimed the three words; he obviously heard the sound of his name being groaned, of her quick movements. It clearly was not the first time he visited. With little or no choice, Sam needed to unlock, to open the door, yet keeping the chain on. Not expecting any callers, she was in nothing except a short white towelling robe. She smelled from the delicious perfume the far away priestly brothers so cherished in their nostrils. 'I'm sorry. I wasn't exactly expecting anyone, James. It's really not convenient.'

'Are you not alone?'

'Yes. I am. Tell me. What is it you want?'

He leaned his forearm against the door jam. 'Didn't you get my 'phone messages?'

'I did.'

James sighed, telling her how it was very awkward, he speaking through the few inches in the doorway; he asked if he might, at least, be allowed to step inside the hallway? Nothing more. He stood to his full height of six feet while Sam closed up, only to release the chain. With the front door reopened, he quickly entered, but only by a couple of steps before she changed her mind; she stood, blocking his way, preventing him from walking in further.

Barefooted, Sam stood, she having folded her arms. 'Now, is that better … you can speak to me?' She, wearing only one long towelling garment, heard herself asking this man who she reckoned did not possess a dangerous bone in his body: 'Look, you'd better come through into my lounge?'

He hesitated in the doorway, stopping to think for a moment. 'Are you absolutely sure you don't mind?'

Sam looked at James and then back at her appearance before again staring at him; tightening the white towelling belt, she stated she did a bit. 'It's best if you'd go through into into the lounge while I go to get myself dressed? All right?'

He, bolt upright, kept himself quiet, doing precisely as he was told, sitting himself on one half of a settee.

When she, softer within herself and her cheeks a little pink, reappeared, he politely stood, only briefly; she, wearing her favourite denim flares and a floral T-shirt, her auburn hair remained damp from the quickest of showers. Eable, she remembered, loved her hair wet, when it fell in curls, to almost cover her shoulders. She emerged, running her fingers through it as if they were a comb. 'Now then; tell me, James, why are you here this morning?'

James appeared almost like a naughty lad about to be ticked off, instead of the grown man he was. 'Yes. Forgive me, Samantha, but I left you quite a few telephone message; you hadn't responded so ...'

'...so you thought, if the mountain won't go to Mohammed, Mohammed would come to the mountain?'

He shrugged before giving a broad smile. 'Maybe.'

Sam half grinned. 'Anyway, do you fancy that mug of coffee, after all? I reckon it's too early for anything stronger ... unless, of course, you'd like a small wine?'

James missed her snide remark about the coffee, saying he enjoyed it first thing, but he shook his head, fancying a tea. He put his hand up as if he was stopping the traffic. 'I don't take sugar, thanks.'

'By the way. I've only decaffeinated tea. Nothing else in the tea situation.' She noticed how he was about to follow her into the kitchen, to help, 'No need, James. Stay back where you were. I'll bring it through.'

A few moments later Sam, eventually handing him his mug of hot unsweetened tea and, hunting to make small talk, asked about the well being of both his Tom cat and his stallion; it wasn't as if she was riveting to know. She was only searching for something to say, to break any awkward silences between them.

He smiled. 'Hunter's now as fit as a fiddle – quite back again to his old self,' he replied.

'Why? What was wrong?'

'Oh, it was all over Christmas and well into this New Year; he was really under the weather.'

She hesitated, biting her lip, before quizzing concerning his horse's name. 'When Hunter was bought for you, do you remember whose idea it was to name him Hunter?'

He shrugged, saying how it was quite a while ago, but he thought it was his mum's idea. He informed Sam: 'During her much younger days, she knew a man who owned a stallion named Hunter. I forget all the details.'

'Fancy?'

'Yes. Anyway, because of that, we knick-named him Hunter, too.' He placed aside his empty mug. 'Would you like to come for ride with me sometime, Sam?'

With a sip of her own coffee, at one stage Sam may have have experienced an excitement, yet not then. Following her recent 'flu, it had knocked the stuffing from her.

He questioned, his eyes fixed: 'Oh, I never even thought to ask you, if you can ride? Do you?'

Sam nodded.

'Are you a good rider?'

She half smiled an enigmatic smile, remembering herself upon that first excursion with Eable when he became a little too forward. There was also the more recent ride with Elkanah. 'I'm pretty good,' she declared, trying to hide a grin.

Seeing James, tall, broad across his shoulders, he had dark wavy hair which needed a thoroughly good cut; he half smiled with big brown eyes in the same way as his ancient counterpart. She wondered, at first, if it was the living room's light, but, no, he really did possessed the olive skin his mother mentioned; with Charles believing he as his own child, had he simply ignored the difference?

With teeth, so white when he laughed, she could have described Eable to the tee … the absolutely spit image. 'Anyway, Hunter's not the only one who is well again,' he continued.

'What?'

'Me, too.'

Sam removed the mugs aside before flopping back in her own comfy chair, declaring how it made the three of them. Her mother Daisy always swore things went in threes. 'Just after Christmas, James, I had a seriously bad dose of the 'flu.' She raised her eyebrows. 'So, you've also been sick? What's been the matter, or shouldn't I ask?'

'Oh, it's all right. It's just I have some cardiac problems.'

The only heart problem Sam was experiencing was perhaps concerning him, but she discovered herself saying: 'You do, darling? Like what?'

She wondered if he heard the adorable sentiment, yet he did not recoil at being labelled 'darling'. 'Oh, I had rheumatic fever when I was a kid, so I simply have to see a Cardiac Consultant, but only once a year now.'

'And where … which hospital?'

He told her: 'Ah, my annual check up was first thing today. Anyway, they seemed pretty chuffed with me.'

She quickly moved to sit close beside him on the settee, very nearly clasping his hands; she, however, refrained from then any touch. 'What did the cardiologist actually say to you?' she queried. She had, when as a newly qualified staff nurse, encountered patients suffering from similar cardiac issues. 'What did he do for you, James?'

'Um, oh, all the usual, such as an ECG and some other blood tests. I was made to wait until he saw the results. Then he looked ultra-pleased and said: '' See you next year, James." And that was that. So, Samantha, I naturally presumed all is well.'

Attempting to change the subject from his own issues, James invited her out to see an afternoon film. Noel Coward's "Brief Encounter" was showing with Trevor Howard and Celia Johnson, but he saw her face fall; she did not fancy that matinee, not then. She asked him to stay indoors with her and share a brunch. 'I really don't feel up to going out. Not yet, for that 'flu has knocked the stuffing out of me, too.'

James definitely wanted to see it, even if she did not. He took her hand in his, determined to pull her a little closer to himself, but his voice became surprisingly husky. 'Sam, oh, I'd actually come here so I could again take you out.' He told her how he enjoyed her company at the Swiss Centre.

Too much exertion, Sam discovered she had little strength. 'I've been thinking about returning back to my parents' place until I'm stronger. Let's see each other, next week? How does that sound?'

James said he should miss her, yet he fully understood.

TWO WEEKS LATER:

'Now you're feeling a little stronger, Samantha, let's go to see the film this week, to end up eating at one of those country pubs, over in Wimbledon, or perhaps across the Downs?' James asked how she felt about his plans. With all his ideas, it was obvious he had not arrived to scrounge from Sam's store cupboard, just as Eable did. 'We could use the train to go up West, but we could then use my car to go to one of the pubs. It'll save you from driving, eh?'

Sam lifted her chin, her lips curved into a smile and nodded. 'All right. It'll actually be a lovely idea.' She said she could well cope with more than just a quick lunch out, with the whole shebang that week.

As he helped her on with a cream hooded coat, he kissed the palm of her hand as it appeared through the sleeve. Quickly, she buttoned up the front of the coat and, looking up, their lips met, softly to begin with, she easing herself closer to him. For him, she tasted as sweet as candy, so deliciously good. He breathed how very lovely she was before allowing her to open up the heart she locked away for the priestly brothers.

'I believe I am seriously in love with you, Samantha.' Since the time they parted, when he refused her naive offer of coffee, he could not erase her from his mind.

Sam cleared her throat and swallowed with a small gulp. She looked back and up into his dark eyes and breathed: 'Love at first sight?'

'Truly.'

She nodded.

'From the very first moment we met, when I brought you that painting of Hunter, then those white roses, I knew I loved you. You have absolutely no idea. I have never felt such an emotional pain. Oh, Samantha … these last two weeks without you, have felt like a lifetime.'

Sam had absolutely no reason not to believe him, although she heard the self same words from her Elkanah, from Eable forever declaring his love. She slowly pulled away; as she withdrew she stroked the side of James' face, the back of her hand feeling like soft silk against his dark cheek. 'I've missed you, too.'

'Really?'

She gave the hint of a nod.

'Sam, I have brought you a small gift.'

'A present? For me? You already gave me those gorgeous roses … and you treated me when we ate at the Swiss Centre; gosh! You're very generous, aren't you?'

James half smiled, stating how he was in two minds as to whether or not to give it to her; he removed a firm brown envelope from his jacket pocket, inside of which was a head and shoulders sketch of Samantha. 'I drew it from memory. Do you like it?'

'Like it? Wow, I love it!' Sam exclaimed with a whoop, giving him a kiss on his cheek. 'How talented you are? I shall naturally buy a very special frame for it. Oh, wait until my parents see it … they'll no doubt also be over the moon?' She propped it up on the mantelpiece.

'I am so pleased you like it … '

'Pleased? I simply don't know what else to say.'

'Listen. Come on; let's get going out?'

Sam gave the hint of a nod. 'I hadn't really felt much like going out lately, but it'd be good for me, eh?' She told him how another day she may see his horse.

'Hunter's due to visit the blacksmith pretty soon. If you're still up to it, we could drive another day soon, to the stables, to take him across to have him shod.'

Sam thought for a long moment. 'Perhaps there'd be another horse, one I could maybe hire from the stables?' She sighed with a smile: 'I could saddle up and ride by your side, eh?'

'Yes. What a good idea? Although Hunter is seventeen hands high; he is a big strong fellow. He'd easily take the pair of us bareback.'

Bareback! Sam inwardly exclaimed. Bareback with him? She remembered riding with Eable, and what a surprise … no, more of a shock? She also rode another stallion with Elkanah, too, when they rested in a cold cave, with their half expected consequences.

After their chat, she glanced out of the window. Suddenly, it was raining cats and dogs. Neither she nor James wished to get soaked through to their skins, so, after all their plans, they ate first at a nearby pub, the couple decided to remain indoors, just to talk while listening to music; they definitely would make it to the West End the following day, to see the film he mentioned. Sam remembering recently seeing its credits somewhere or other and thought it was a great idea.

They discovered how about anything could happen in London. Just after they left the train a middle-aged woman, shabbily dressed, was hit by an underground train; they saw it happen, they and umpteen other commuters; the poor thing was plummeted beneath the carriage with all its whirring cogs and gears. Apart from the sad story, they did enjoy their time together. On their way home from the luncheon, they first stopped at a new coffee bar and each drank a cappuccino, leaving them both temporarily with a white frothy moustache. They cherished having been together, linking arms on the way home before hugging each other so tight it was as if they would need to synchronise their breathing, the rise and fall of their chest walls, as if their feelings were in a disarray; they were glad to return home to her apartment, but they were again hungry. They removed their coats, along with their wet shoes to prevent her living room's nice carpet from becoming marked. The golfing umbrella belonging to her dad was left open to dry in the hallway.

As the afternoon moved into evening, James declared: 'I'm not here, Samantha, to eat your food.' After a lot of hoo-ha and discussions between Sam and James, he used her telephone to order one of the new Chinese takeaways; unable to cope with the chopsticks provided, with fingers, forks and some hilarity, they ate together at her kitchen table.

By ten 0' clock he stood, holding her in his arms, to kiss her good night. 'I must be on my way now.' He explained: 'I leave home early most mornings.' He declared on how he saddles up his stallion and canters across the bridle ways on Wimbledon Common. 'I leave

all the tack for my horse in the Dog & Fox stables.'
James chuckled: 'I try not to return into The Gallery,
foul smelling!'

'And on the mornings when you cannot, like when
you went to the hospital for your annual check up?
Who sees to Hunter then?'

'Dad pays the folk at the stables, the same ones as those
always in the evenings. Hunter is never neglected. Why?'

Sam shrugged, wondering: 'I've had a thoroughly
great time,' she stated, reassuring him. 'Oh, James, I
think you're, well, more than special to me?'

'You're the one who's incredibly special. Another
time, my sweetheart, I'll wine and dine you properly,' he
told her, making as if to leave. 'Now, I really have to go
home or I shall be wearing out my welcome.'

'No.' Sam frowned: 'Please, don't leave me. Not yet.'

James, being a good man, considered her words,
with masculine emotions swelling in his chest. He challenged: 'Are you absolutely sure?'

She slowly nodded her head. 'Yes, I am.'

'You're aware of what you are implying, what's
coming across from you to a fellow like me, huh?'

Sam hugged around him tight, staring up into his
face, at his strong jaw, she giving him the hint of a nod.
Resting her head warm against his chest, she could hear
the steady beating of his heart. Nothing compared to
the fizz she experienced as he caressed her. Without a
shadow of a doubt, this surely had to be true love, too?

'Just one thing, Samantha ...'

Expelling a long ragged sigh, she murmured: 'What's
that?'

'It's your answer machine, flashing red. Should it be?'

Chapter 12

Trying her uttermost to ignore the disembodied answering machine, Sam half regretted the day she purchased the thing. Its flashing red light, when ignored, flipped across to an irritating bleeping; rapidly, it became an annoying intrusion into their together time. James half grinned, asking if she loathed the apparatus when he previously left messages. With a resigned sigh, Sam had to pull from him, with little choice but to succumb. Amidst junk messages, there came a surprising one from Adjo, the Egyptian hotelier who married Paula. Adjo's usual laid back deep voice sounded earnestly worried, he attempting to make Samantha feel the same; he stated Paula became a patient in the maternity wing of the city's hospital.

'Following a prenatal check up, Paula was admitted for a complete rest; she asked me to tell you she has the risk of pre-eclampsia,' Adjo continued. 'I've strict instructions from her to say she's "bored out of her skull"; she's missing you, her best friend. Hey, Sam, it's a bit of a long shot, but you wouldn't be free to fly out for a bit of a visit, would you? Please, let me know.' There came a brief pause, as if he was almost stuck for something more to say, before he declared: 'Flip, I hate speaking into these awful inanimate objects.'

'Me, too!' added James with a grin, he raising his dark eyes heavenwards.

Sam furrowed her brow, clearly troubled; she tore herself from James, clasping her hands in her lap, to listen to Adjo's message for a second time around.

James stated her friend's diagnosis sounded serious as he gently moved aside, he ready to say his goodbyes. 'Listen, my love. I really think I ought to leave so you can either 'phone Egypt, or to do whatever it is to sort out your arrangements.' Sam was about to object, but he firmly shook his head and, pulling away, declared: 'No. I shall skedaddle and drive off home.'

'But, James ...' she started, half whining with the sound of a protest.

He interrupted. 'I promise, Sam, I shall contact you another day very soon, right?' James wondered who the Dickens Sam really was, a woman who could shoot off to Egypt, to fly out there, first class, at the drop of a hat, simply because a friend became a little bored with her days? Didn't this Paula woman not have either letters to write or a novel to read? It became beyond him. He knew Sam had no job in either nursing or midwifery. Even if she did, neither professions brought in big bucks; she also resided in one of the most expensive areas of London, making Harrods' food hall as her local grocer. As for her father's influence, he was simply a previous army officer who sometimes played a round of golf, he living off a few pensions. Daisy remained as a long time housewife, but, maybe James had missed the whole shebang? Perhaps Sam became an heiress, with her own lot, with a stash of cash hitting her bank account? He wondered how he might financially keep up with such a well to do woman? His own dad, Charles Samuels, was an art teacher, having sacrificed luxuries to provide him with an education; along with his own parents, James was working many hours to help The Gallery become a financial success.

Sam, not caring if she either wore top designer gear or not, frowned, longing for James not to leave.

Blowing out a long sigh, he was trying to ease the situation. 'Look, sweetheart, I only turned up here with both that sketch of you and to take you out, my visiting you on the off chance.' He stated he ought to have simply dropped the portrait through her letterbox. 'It wasn't as if I was invited here, although we've both enjoyed a great time out together, haven't we?'

With the hint of a nod, she agreed.

'I have, anyway … now, what if I have your overseas 'phone number, Samantha? I could maybe call you once you are in Alexandria … in a day or two? How does all that sound?'

'Oh, no. I'd really want you to stay with me.'

James stood as if to walk to the hall, to get his coat. He turned to face her. 'Sam, darling, none of any of this Egyptian stuff has anything to do with me. It's best if I clear off, to leave you to sort out all your plans.' He made yet again to the hall, as if to reach for his top coat, but she gently led him back by the elbow, for them to again sit together on the sofa. 'Oh, no!' she exclaimed. 'Please, I am asking you, don't go right now.'

James, sighing all over again, only to please her, returned, yet he remained sat bolt upright, not leaning back. 'Sam, your Paula and her husband are your special friends. Not mine.'

'But ...'

'Ah, now, don't start any "buts". I couldn't cope.' James, remembering his mother manipulating his dad in similar ways, pulled away; raising and wagging an index finger, he asking Sam to at least shush, to let him get a few words in edgeways. 'Look! I hardly, as yet, even know you, let alone my being plunged in with a group of overseas strangers. You're an intelligent young woman; can't you understand that much about me? I'd feel totally lost, like a fish out of water ... no, Sam. You go off to sort out what is needed from you and I shall see you again once everything is quite settled. I promise.'

Sam paused for a moment. What if, once again in Egypt, she again became lost, way beyond the mirage all over again? She tried to tell him how she did not want to be without him.

He raised his dark eyes heavenwards, before facing her once more. Was she not listening to a single word, he wondered? Hadn't he promised to see her again, so however could she believe otherwise? James frowned, shaking his head. 'You've not a cat in hell's chance of losing me,' although, he thought, she might if she continued to behave pushy.

'In all honesty, tell me, do you really want to go off home right now?'

Cupping her face in both his hands, he continued to smile; he kissed her upon the tip of her nose, stating how, of course, he did not actually want to leave, but stress, adrenaline was bad for his heart condition, as well she should know. Nevertheless, he reminded her how the time they were spending together, was only their second real date.

'I know all that stuff, but … but, at the risk of my sounding a bit too pushy …' Pushy? Samantha rapidly became every inch of it all. 'I'm really and truly desperately sorry if I was acting like a spoilt only kid, but, James, it's simply I honestly want you to stay on with me - .'

'What?' James grinned. 'All night, too, Sam? No. Do you actually know what you're asking of me?' He, a normal, heterosexual male, was surely pleased to oblige, but he confessed he was surprised by her determination. 'I'm not exactly a youngster, you know? Of course I do!'

'Hear me out then, James?'

'Yes. All right.' He loudly sighed again. 'It looks as if I'm going to have no choice, doesn't it?'

Sam gave a weak smile. 'Right then. If I can arrange a flight, I shall fly out to Alexandria first light tomorrow.'

'Whoops!' He grinned into her smiling green eyes. 'I think I can hear another "but" coming my way … so, go on. Say what's on your mind, as if I wouldn't know.'

'Okay. I was going to ask, why don't you come with me, too?'

He again raised his own dark brows, they nearly touching a lock of his untidy hair, he gasping in a surprise. 'All the way to Egypt, eh?'

She nodded.

'Samantha Webb, in my book, that's almost insane!'

Laughing, she opposed him, saying: 'No, it isn't.'

James shook his head and, with another lengthy, faked sigh, remarked: 'You're certainly full of surprises, Sam.' He added: 'If nothing else, I reckon there'll never be a dull moment all the time I'm with you, eh?'

'Well, you did say you missed me when we're apart, so why not be with me?'

'Are you serious?' His dark eyes widened. 'You're not acting the fool, are you?'

'Definitely not.'

He needed every second to gather his thoughts; he again ran his fingers through his dark hair, not unlike Eable might. 'Let's get this straight. You're nipping off to Egypt only because your chum has become a little bored and you actually want me to fly out with you, too?'

'You've hit the nail right on the head.' She persisted, pleading with him to travel with her to Egypt. 'So, would you be able to make all the arrangements ... and at such short notice?'

James became thoughtful, half ready to inform her how it was way out of the question, yet Sam looked up at him with her big eyes; she, as an only child, learned such a doleful expression when she was determined to stamp her own way, usually from her dad. 'Oh, do, please, my love, say you'll come with me?'

Obviously, under normal circumstances he should loved to holiday where there were sunny skies and the warmth from the blue Mediterranean Sea, to have the sand between his toes! He exclaimed: 'I admit it would be great to be away from the grey drizzle of London, only for a bit. Yet, oh my, you've really dropped this one on me?' He, all over again, ran his fingers through his untidy hair, thinking seriously about it, all over again. 'It's so late, I cannot 'phone my parents.' He said if he did, they'd go into a flat spin, thinking something became seriously wrong. James said he would leave a message upon their own answer machine, to ask his mum to step in to run The Gallery for him; 'Knowing her, Sam, she'll be fine.'

'And Hunter? What about him? He can't see to himself.'

'As I previously told you, the owner of the Dog and Fox Riding Stables will exercise him in my absence; my horse is never be neglected.'

A deep groan slipped from her lips. 'Oh, wait up.' Sam was concerned about James, not having been vaccinated. 'Before Paula and I first visited Egypt, we both went through a whole rigmarole of injections, to prevent any tropical diseases invading us ...'

James interrupted, telling her how he had never been to Egypt, but the previous year he visited a remote area of Kenya; 'It was a sort of a mercy dash.' He smiled as Sam offered a wide-eyed wow, she asking what he actually did there. Wistfully, his mind floated back to Africa; he briefly explained how he was only part of a Catholic group, helping orphaned children. 'Anyway, it's a long story. I'll tell you about it another time. Okay?' For Kenya, he was fully vaccinated.

Sam wondered considering his present cardiac issues, if, during his time abroad, he remained well.

'Yeah. Fine. Anyway, if I'm giving in, to coming with you to Egypt, all I'll really need to do is to nip back home and pack a bag,' He smiled as she, hugging him close, declared: 'I confess it'll be great for us to be together, to get to know one and another better, huh? A lovely holiday?'

Sam with a blur of happiness, with nothing short of the miraculous, became satisfied as the two more than embraced for a good night.

Meeting up the following day, in the frantically busy Heathrow, they did all they could to avoid the tourists and families who moved at snails' speeds, she was worried they may miss their flight; she checked her wristwatch. While James, in line behind a business-woman, acquired health insurance, along with the correct foreign currency, Sam had reached her own way, to purchase their club class airline tickets and all was agreed. She was anxious to see Paula. Prior to their flight being called, she left James with their hand luggage while she made a quick international telephone call to Adjo; to put James' mind at rest, Sam promptly confirmed all the necessary hotel arrangements. 'Incidentally, Adjo, I shall this time not be travelling alone.'

He yelled for her to speak up. 'It's a shocking line ...'

Sam swallowed to raise her voice an octave: 'I shall have a friend with me. So, may I make a reservation for both of us to stay in your hotel?'

'Sure. What's her name?'

'Actually, Adjo, my new friend isn't a "she" – .'

'What do you mean? It's an hermaphrodite?' She could hear him laughing at his own joke.

' That's not even funny.'

'So, is the booking for the new honeymoon suite, Sam?'

'Adjo! Please, don't tease ... you may well scare him off -.'

He apologised.

'Anyway, if it is okay with you, we'd really like to share a room.'

'Hey, wait until I tell Paula your bit of news! Ooh, this bit of gossip will definitely perk her up; incidentally, all fooling apart, do both come as our guests. By the way, what's Romeo's name?'

The international line suddenly went dead, leaving a whirling sound.

Other than some brief turbulence, the flight to Egypt became uneventful. Except from when they ate an in flight meal, James dozed. Sam stared mindlessly out of the window, over the top of the clouds until they landed, hitting the runway in Alexandria. She, yet again, glanced at her wristwatch.

He yawned behind his hand. 'It's two 0' clock Egyptian time.'

It was almost an age, locating their bags, to get through customs, finding a vacant cab to take them to the correct hotel. A white Mercedes with blacked out windows came from old Cairo, offering his taxi services; a knowing Sam shook her head and declared: 'Not today, thanks.'

The enigmatic driver became disappointed. 'I could take the two of you to places unknown!' he exclaimed.

'I bet you can.' She told him: 'Another time, eh?'

'What was wrong with using him, Sam?' James asked.

'Oh, I know him of old; we need to use a regular taxi.'

Throughout Sam's first trip to Egypt, Adjo was the hotel's manager, but, when he became engaged to be married to Paula, the property was up for sale.

Sam filled James in: 'As a marriage gift, Adjo's family purchased the property, lock, stock and barrel, presenting it to them on their wedding day.'

'Wow! Some wedding present, eh?'

'Absolutely. Anyway, not to be outdone, Paula's parents paid for the entire establishment to be renovated.' Sam remembered being told: 'Architects and local builders made it into a five star place, luxuriously expensive to the last detail.'

'You've been here before?'

She nodded. 'Both Paula and Adjo … well, it's not only their livelihood, but their home.'

A receptionist, she an Egyptian and probably a similar age to Sam and James, greeted them with a wide, beaming smile. Behind her a sign read: "Beauty is everywhere, so enjoy your stay in this hotel." 'Welcome back to Egypt, Miss Samantha. You won't have heard the news?' she declared. 'We're all thrilled about the baby …'

Sam stared almost in a disbelief at her, before at James and again back to the receptionist.

The woman briefly glanced up at the clock on the wall. 'I think it was at least two hours ago now; Paula needed an emergency caesarean section. It was her blood pressure, you know – it soared much too high; so they had to get the baby out very quickly.'

'How are things now?'

She shrugged. 'All I know is, mother and baby are fine.' The receptionist wrote the address of the hospital.

Sam collected her thoughts for a moment or two. 'Perhaps you would first show us to our room so we can freshen up, please? If it doesn't become passed visiting time, I'll grab a cab to the hospital?'

James gave Sam a little nudge, 'Don't tell me, we've come all this way to Egypt, on a wild goose chase?'

She scowled. 'Not at all.'

A young porter carried their luggage. 'Do follow me,' he instructed, glancing back to make sure they were upon his heels. 'By the way, you do not have a double room.'

'We don't?' Sam queried before wondering why, for she sorted out all the accommodation before they left London.'

Sam heard the porter quietly chuckling.

'Mr Adjo left strict instructions for you to share a suite; it has gorgeous views overlooking the deep blue of the Mediterranean Sea. Very beautiful. You wait 'till you see it, eh? Wow!'

'Ooh, how lovely?' James declared. 'I'm so glad I brought my sketch book.'

'And me ... my dad's camera?'

Two and a bit hours later, having kissed Adjo's both cheeks, congratulating him on being a first time daddy, Sam sat holding Paula's hand. The couple were chuffed they had a gorgeous new baby daughter. They, after months of deliberating, decided to name the six pound, one ounce bundle Amy Rebecca Helen.

'I'd brought you a white baby's shawl,' Sam added. 'I left it with the hotel receptionist; she said she'd pop it through into your private quarters.'

'And I also previously left in your suite some of our finest Champagne; it's for you, Sam, and your mystery man,' Adjo told her with a broad grin. 'What do you think of your accommodation?'

Sam thanked him for his awesome generosity.

'All part of the hotel service for a good friend.'

Paula, although tired, managed a happy smile, asked about James. 'Adjo told me you've met someone.'

The light in Sam's green eyes brightened and her heart fluttered at his name. 'He's the guy who brought me those roses; remember?'

She nodded. 'So, where is James right now?' She asked: 'You've not left him outside, sitting all alone in the corridor, for goodness' sake? It'd be just like you to do such a thing.'

'He remained at the hotel.' Sam explained how he is a little shy. 'James doesn't yet know you.'

Having left the three back in the hospital, she hailed a regular cab, promptly returning to the hotel. Her waiting young man, perfumed by the aftershave Sam purchased for him in duty-free, remarked how Sam appeared elegant; he would shortly discover how, whatever the occasion, she always rose to her utmost to be sophisticated, yet serenely relaxed. He enquired after her friends; she told him how they were fine and the baby was absolutely beautiful. 'Amy has Adjo's dark hair colour. Seeing the tiny little new born, ooh, if I am not careful, I'll be getting broody ...'

James gasped, hesitating for a long moment, he feeling as if he wanted to beat a retreat; his dark eyes lost their lustre, he appearing more than anxious.

Sam turned her face, to giggle, reassuring him she definitely was not serious and not to distress himself. She flopped on the sofa, kicking off her shoes.

'Something to drink?' he asked, pointing to the bubbly. She nodded, looking at one of the suite's printed menus from the hotel's new seafood restaurant; the freshly caught lobster was attracting her taste-buds ... his, too. 'We need a thoroughly good meal now, huh?' She put her head on one side and smiled broadly.

Moving closer, she slowly surrounded her arms around his neck. 'Kiss me, James.'

He beamed admiringly, his masculine passions quickly aroused; he traced his hand along the soft curves of her sensual body. 'Oh, how I wished, Sam, darling, we'd met sooner,' he suggested with a hushed whisper, 'I cannot even begin to tell you how much I love you.'

She smiled. 'Me, too.'

'Do you really mean it when you say you love me, Sam?'

It was a strange sensation regarding a guy she was still getting to know, but when he asked: 'Really, as much as I you? 'Sam thoughtlessly replied: 'Oh, Eable, my darling … you know I do!' As soon as the words left her lips, she flushed a bright pink, her cheeks becoming hot, she not knowing quite how to handle the erroneous faux pas?

James glared at her, he holding her by the shoulders at arms length; he staring full into her anxious face. 'Whatever caused you come out with that, eh?' he quizzed. He let go of her and sat himself back away onto the sofa, staring in a shocked disbelief.

Her breath seemed to catch in her throat. 'Forget I ever said it; anyway, I need to have a shower …' she began, changing the subject.

'Yes. Okay. But, first, tell me honestly why on earth you called me Eable?'

'I can't.'

'What do you mean by "i can't" ? No-one, not even my parents, ever speaks of my odd middle name.'

Sam's thoughts, back in Egypt and this time with James, were subconsciously upon Eable. As James touched her, she felt as if she was somehow transported into the Samaritan guest annexe where they made love. She had opened her mouth. Through her deep and special memories, the wrong name fled from her lips

'I never told you my full names of James Eable Samuels ... but you always simply call me James, never Eable.' He thought for a brief another moment. 'How did you discover my middle name? I'm positive I didn't tell you.'

She again shrugged. How, she thought, was she going to worm her way out of this? 'I think it is a rather unusual name,' she told him. 'It's certainly different from the usual run of the mill?' She suddenly piped up with the stupidity: 'So, what's wrong with my calling you it, but only when we make love, huh?'

He began to wonder if his new girl friend was nuts; frowning, he offered: 'If it's really what you want ... 'He shook his head. 'Even so, I reckon the only way you could've found out is if my mother said ... did she? What did she tell you when you had lunch together? '

Sam shivered, hating the lie: 'Oh, I forget.'

Days into their Egyptian trip, Sam was informed by their room maid how Paula was being discharged from hospital, which many believed it too soon; Adjo was driving to fetch his wife and new baby, to bring them home. A beautifully designed nursery became prepared. Paula's parents, her dad being an international banker, were expected to fly to Alexandria, to see their new granddaughter. Adjo's parents who lived an hour's drive away, already saw the new bundle.

Enjoying the evenings, Sam and James joined Adjo, Paula and her parents for dinner; with Amy sound asleep in her cradle, all but Paula savoured the fine wine; they followed the small feast by sitting on the veranda for coffees and handmade mint chocolates.

Paula, tired out, excused herself. 'Come on, Adjo, we both need some rest,' she said. 'So, let's get some sleep while we can.' Her family followed on.

Before retiring to bed, Samantha and James gazed up a the stars, deciding to have a stroll along the beach, they holding hands, talking softly about all the things young lovers say.

The morning after, both sets of grandparents swooped to coo over Amy, to boast of her beauty, and how they compared with Adjo and Paula when they were babies.

Not use to baby talk at close quarters, enough was enough for James. He took from his luggage, his sketch book. 'Sam, sweetheart, as this is my first trip to Egypt, I really feel I cannot come all this way without seeing the Pyramids ... and I would like to have one of those fifteen-minute camel rides. Coming with me?'

She shook her head, exhaling a deep long sigh. 'Paula isn't the only one who is tired. I'm also feeling zonked out, James; frankly, I'd rather stay around here, only for a little while.'

'Ooh, I hate to leave you behind, but ...'

'Honestly, James, I really don't mind if you go off sightseeing.'

'Really?'

She again sighed. 'Really and truly. So, enjoy yourself; I'll see you later, eh?'

Sam then almost panicked, remembering how she herself became energised, way beyond the mirage. She almost gasped, screaming: 'Stay safe, James!' She yelled louder: 'Please, don't go, darling?' He became out of earshot.

Rapidly, Paula experienced an unbelievable weariness; her desire was to be left alone with their new baby, to become accustomed to Amy. 'Oh, Sam,' Paula bemoaned. 'I am absolutely dog tired.' Tears flowed, rushing down her tired face. Sam hugged her tight, allowing her friend to sob out those post natal baby blues before the upset became out of control.

The time Sam and James spent together became special. It was an occasion when they, too, were able to come to know each other, they confessing how they had rarely been so happy in the whole of their adult lives. The week they shared, however, became, to them, nothing but idyllic. It exceeded, they claimed, every expectation for they were a couple in love. It was, nevertheless, time to go home, back to a reality.

'What time's your flight?' Adjo asked. 'I'll drive you both to the airport.'

Sam grinned, staring straight into his bleary dark eyes. 'Adjo, you look jiggered. Has baby Amy kept you awake all night?'

He rubbed his dark eyes, looking more dead than alive. 'Amy, bless her, slept all day yesterday and she yelled from two 0'clock this morning. Paula, though, is even more zonked than I am!'

'Adjo, we'll grab a taxi. Okay?'

' It might be safer.'

Sam and James sat together in the club class lounge, close, holding hands and sneaking the occasional kiss.

She informed James she did not fancy returning to her pad alone. 'Come back to my place, once we return to London?'

He was delighted she would offer. Before they discussed more, their flight was called. It left on schedule and, on arrival into Heathrow, she suggested they would chat over their future arrangements, but in the following morning. 'After a whole week of living together, I don't fancy my life alone; I love you too much, James.'

Back in her place, she unpacked her belongings, plugged in the coffee pot and, with a yawn behind her hand, flopped onto the big comfy sofa.

That night they slept soundly, comfortably wrapped in each others arms; the following morning they awoke late.

'You want something to eat, James?'

He shook his head.

'You don't? Really? What's wrong?' Sam noticed he took on the pale colour of stone. 'Tell me.'

'I dunno.'

'Seriously, if you're unwell, you have to say; you see, I don't read minds.'

Before she asked another word, he, holding his right side, said he was a little nauseous. 'Perhaps I have eaten something which disagreed with me … it's making me feel quite horrid.'

'Sweetheart, have you ever had your appendix removed?'

He again shook his head. 'Years ago, when I was a little kid, I was told I had a grumbling appendix, but nothing was ever done about it, maybe because I'd had Rheumatic Fever. Why?'

Before anyone might say: 'Jack Robinson', a nurse in the Casualty Department at the Westminster Hospital hurried through, with him, a series of questions before she gave him a consent form. 'Sign this, James,' she instructed him. 'You're going straight down to theatre – and fast!' He did precisely as he was told, although the anaesthetist was informed how James suffered from cardiac issues. Sam, standing alone in the corridor, was told by a doctor in green theatre garb, to go home. 'See him tomorrow morning, Miss Webb. Your man shall be out for the count for the rest of today.'

Sam returned to her apartment, quickly telephoning his parents. It was his mother who answered.

Chapter 13

Samantha's long, manicured hand gracefully waved away any objections from either her family or his. For wholly recovered from his appendectomy, James, although still retaining the apartment above The Gallery, with suitcases, boxes and half filled crates, removed into Sam's rented London apartment. Together, the couple's embracing simply said it all; as if she had just jogged around the early morning streets, she breathlessly reassured him of her love.

He, having left his cosseted Tom cat with his mother, peering beneath his long fringe of dark eyelashes, declared: 'My weeks of convalescence, Sam, was hellish without you.'

'That awful, eh?' She did not minimised the words, but grinned, indicating for him to briefly join her on the settee; Paula, upon emigrating to Egypt, left that item of furniture behind. It was still comfy, although, in Sam's opinion, it could do with being professionally recovered.

'My month without you was atrocious.' James, half attracted by her intelligence, he recognised it as bright as her beaming white smile; she, with sparkling green Irish eyes, and, oh, that little turned up freckled nose, he even cherished the funny little way in which she adjusted those stray auburn curls, they tucked behind her pierced ears; never did she offer anything such as a dramatic pneumatic sigh when he offered his love. She could not even pretend. 'What with my hospitalisation, and then all the recovery time at my parents' home, it really was diabolical, Sam, being without you.'

Various times Sam attempted to visit James while in his parents' Surrey home, where he was virtually forced to convalesce. His over protective mother, Tom cat winding around her legs, would stop her dead by their front door, informing how James was quietly resting. Whatever the weather, come rain or shine, Hannah, as sneaky as the cat itself, kept Sam upon their doorstep, stating he was too unfit for visitors. Never informing she visited, she jealously gave her son the impression Samantha kept away, she not bothering to call. 'Phoning was a waste of time as it was always his mother who lifted the receiver. Letters and cards mysteriously went astray, presumably lost in the post? Hannah, in Sam's lay opinion, sadly possessed a chilly heart.

United again, Sam subconsciously flirted with him, resembling an enticement in her new floral T-shirt, it moulding to her slender figure. In its entirety, everything appeared lovely; even the London apartment was always kept pristine, having been made immaculate, into a comfortable home, a place to simply cherish one and another's company.

Following one passionate moment, Sam propped herself up, she leaning on one elbow and looked into his happy face. 'Incidentally. James,' she started, 'I half forgot to tell you, I heard from Adjo and Paula the other day and ...'

He placed his hands behind his head and softly chucked. 'So, what's new, babe?' He stated it would be a strange time if she did not hear from her friends ... they then being his buddies, too.'

Sam lowered her brows to hesitate, frowning at his interruption.

James wrapped his arms surrounding her, apologising for chiming in, he urging her to continue; she nodded, informing him how Adjo and Paula asked her to be one of Amy's two godmothers. 'I'm in two minds, whether or not to accept, what I should say to them.'

'Oh, but why should you even think of turning down such an honour ?'

Slowly, the deep frown across her brow relaxed. 'Well, you see, James, I'm so far away; I have wondered what sort of an input I should have in Amy's young Egyptian life, in her growing up years?'

'You're surely not going to refuse them?' he asked, placing a finger to her lips. 'You just shouldn't.'

Sam volunteered: 'No, I haven't really had much time to have given it any serious thought, but ...'

'Go on. What then?'

Sam became thoughtful before shaking her head. 'Well, when all said and done, Amy is only a plane journey away.' As she, Sam, was all ready in touch with Paula and Adjo, it was obvious she would keep in touch with Amy, too. 'What do you think, darling?'

'What do I think?' He told her how he thought she'd make an excellent godmother, 'but now, sweetheart, I need some coffee.'

'Hmm, coffee, now that's a jolly good idea?' She smiled, remembering all those times when she was way beyond the mirage, when she longed for even its tempting aroma, let alone a whole mug full, it to be taken for granted in her Earls Court kitchen: 'After Amy's Church baptism, there's going to be quite a big occasion … champagne, fireworks, the whole works!'

Dressing and remaking their king-sized bed, she told him how she would telephone Paula, to tell her how they would both be there. 'Okay?'

With James happily smug and claiming how he was a whiz in the kitchen, Sam followed him into there, where she always kept her diary. She flipped over to the relevant page, to give James the date of the baby's baptism; straight away, he hung his head.

'Oh, Sam, I am so very sorry, my pet, but, on this occasion you'll have to fly out to Egypt without me.'

'What? Oh, no, James. Don't you honestly think we've been separated long enough? What with your extra long convalescence and … and …' She gulped a deep breath, glowering, waiting in anticipation, for an excellently good explanation.

He, with more than a tinge of regret, moved to the lounge and flopped on the nearest settee, she coming beside him, the diary clutched under her arm. Disappointedly, James stated how he would definitely not make the baptismal occasion as it clashed with the launch of his dad's unique wood engraving exhibition, when he, as his only son, would be required to be at the special do; James declared the Egyptian event would sadly clash with the once in a lifetime spectacle, the Academy showing his dad's awesome wood engravings.

Sam remarked with her own two-pennyworth, how Amy's baptism was also a once in a lifetime event, too. 'I knew your dad taught art, but,' she added, her voice almost cracking, 'I didn't know he is also a top notch wood engraver.'

'Yeah. You should see it? His work is truly outstanding.'

'That's great. Anyway, can't your mother take your place?'

'Silly. She'll be going with him, anyway.'

Sam tried not to allow her irritation to get the better of herself; she never cherished being called silly. She was anything but. 'Surely, your dad would understand? I mean if … if we spoke with him about the Egyptian situation?' She suggested being the one to have a quiet word with his father.

'No, Samantha. Don't you dare!' James threatened, tilting his head and deeply frowning towards her. 'I gave my dad a firm promise, for me to be at the Academy. I sure won't let him down. You need to understand how a promise with me, means something.'

Sam pouted, saying she did understand. 'It means I'll need to fly out to Egypt all on my own?'

'I'm sure you've done it all before?' He was doing his best to remain cool and composed, yet he was mindlessly drumming his fingers on the arm of the settee before half forcing into a smile.

She grimaced, determined not to smile with him. 'Not alone, I haven't flown out there by myself.'

'So, flying to and from Egypt, all alone, what's the difference? I'd drive you to Heathrow and Adjo would be at the other end in Alexandria. You'd manage; if anyone can cope with the flights just fine, you can.' She, as if a light suddenly switched on in her thought processes, informed James how she could probably make arrangements to travel with Paula's parents. 'I know the Taylors almost as well as my own mum and dad.'

'See, Sam? Problem solved almost within a heart beat, huh?' James sighed, shook his head while half grinning to himself; he, always famished, padded back off to the kitchen, to make them two rounds of hot buttered toast. Along with the tempting aroma of roasted coffee beans filling the air, he smiled as he eventually handed over her favourite mug, it not quite filled to the brim with coffee, but, too hot, he set the beverage aside on a small coffee table. He, with a slight air of sarcasm, paused: 'Mind it doesn't scald your tongue, Samantha?'

His words hadn't washed over her. James drew a breath, exchanging a look, speaking straight, yet smiling down towards her; she had always just about everything she ever desired. She probably wanted to have him all to herself, too, believing how they could enjoy a bright and lovely future together, but only as long as she saw him as her own. 'Try manipulating me, try owning me and we'll never be anything to each other. You understand?' Otherwise, he thought within himself, they might make a good team.

Chapter 14

Samantha heard James in his morning shower, he singing at the top of his voice. She could just smell his masculine fragrance; he previously claimed he could splash it all over himself. Dried off, from the kitchen where he declared to be quite a whiz, she inhaled the glorious aroma of percolated coffee. Normally cherishing her first of the day, morning coffee, she would too be up with the lark, joining him. Not then. After her returning from way beyond the mirage, Sam desired silence. Even the beastly ticking from her travel-alarm became an irritant; before she knew it, James was leaning across to her side of their bed, to give her bare shoulder a gentle shake. 'Come on, sleepyhead. It's apparently going to be a glorious day today.' She covered herself with the duvet again, but James lifted it to peek beneath. 'Rise and shine, Sam,' he insisted, informing her there was a mug of coffee by the side of her bed, he determined she should move her lazy self.

She reckoned she should not feel miffed with him. After all, it was mostly her idea for them to live together, for they declared their loved for each other; yet, she not so much on that particular morning. 'Oh, why on earth are you disturbing me at this hour ... on a Friday, of all days?' Since being no longer employed by the hospital, it became her want to sleep late on Friday mornings, not surfacing until about nine or ten. Half lifting up her tired head, she barely managed to raise her heavy eyelids, to briefly glance at the small clock on her bedside table; she frowned at the inanimate object, as if the hour became its fault. She flopped back, sinking deep into her feather pillows. 'Oh, grief!' Sam grimly complained: 'Haven't you any idea of either the day or its time?'

He had. 'Samantha ...'

'Whatever is it?' Having heard her full name, she, sombrely, urged: 'You'd think there was something awesome about to happen, the way you're behaving.'

He was doing his uttermost not to become equally frustrated. 'Sam. Simply, to please me, only for this one morning, get up out of your bed?'

'James, I simply cannot; anyway, it's way too soon to get up on a Friday. Listen. I know, why don't you come back to bed with me? We'll simply have a nice long lie in, but only with a bit of a cuddle?' She knew, from having been way beyond the mirage, from being with Adonis Elkanah, along with Abe, too, she became physically spent; until she was properly rested, any more relations became out of the question. As far as James became aware, he simply believed she was suffering from the Baptism party, from Adjo's lavish festivities. She had also experienced a bumpy journey, with the changing of 'planes, the second full of turbulence. Curling back into her favourite foetal position, she tugged at the sumptuous duvet, pulling it up over most of her head, with only a small curl of auburn hair showing from within.

James became no quitter. With a firm, dogged deter-mination, he yanked hold of their quilt's corner, throw-ing it back enough to give her yet another shake. 'Samantha Anne Webb! Are you listening to me?'

She, hearing her full name gruffly declared, rolled onto her back, staring up into his seriously ebony dark eyes, half listening to what she considered to be yet another nag. They were both only children who experi-enced the suffocating up bringing by equally doting parents; they were adult kids who became used to having their own way, with no siblings to share; they learned the art of give and take to be tough life lessons. 'Oh, flip this! What's with the urgency, anyway?'

'I want you up ...'

One did not need to be a Brain of Britain to realise it was blatantly obvious. 'Well, oh, James, I'm done in; if I was working in a hospital, I'd probably have rung in sick, for I am feeling zonked out like rarely before.'

He moved to sit on the edge of her side of the bed, asking if she was hung over, but no.

Sam missed her flight back to Heathrow airport. Having left way beyond the mirage right on time, she being collected by the entrepreneurial teenager who owned the brown and grey ass, before waiting for the too wide camel; the chatty taxi driver of the white Mercedes cab with the blacked out windows became delayed from ancient Cairo. It was one long, around about excursion from the cameleers to Egypt's Alexandria.

During the journey, the cab driver, quiet at first, a gleam in his own dark eyes, broke the silence between them, quizzing Samantha about her recent time and attention in ancient Ramah.

'You've been a few times, haven't you, pretty lady?' He remembered how she possessed ancient relationships in Eable and Elkanah. 'Did you happen to see them again?'

She, informing him of her first name, how it usually became shortened, acknowledged by a slight nod.

He flicked his eyes towards her, half grinning: 'And, hey, they romanced you, did they?'

Was that too much of a request? Most probably. Sam lifted her chin, pushing the question aside, briefly explaining how it was not quite the thing to normally query such private and intimate matters. Nevertheless, she chose to tell him how the younger of the two brothers spent most of the night caring for Elihu.

'Elihu?'

With a weary sigh, Sam explained how poor Elihu was Elkanah and Eable's ailing old grandfather who, with all his cardiac issues, would not live forever; she, in the guest annexe, became free to give most of her time to her beloved Elkanah. 'We met this time outside the guest annexe, although Elkanah and I said our good-byes in a cold cave; we nearly became trapped in there, due to an earth tremor.'

'But, thankfully, you were obviously all right.'

'Only just. It's in that cold cave where all the usual couples get together, all along the rocky walls ...'

'The who? Who are all the usual couples?'

Sam added how, half way between old Shiloh and ancient Ramah, during the time their animals were watered and rested, the men get out of the strong sun; in the chill of the cave, against the dank walls, they cherish their own women.

'And, gosh, you can actually see them?'

Sam did not see herself as their regular spy. 'Well, yes, for they're not exactly a coy lot.' She grinned: 'You'd think they'd stop when they see onlookers, but …'

'But they don't?'

'Not a bit.'

'Don't the women get pregnant?'

'Well, it's their own personal business, isn't it?'

The driver quiet, yet again became content to simply settle his freed hand upon her nearest knee; Sam glanced down at her leg, she remembering how he performed similar once before. 'Were you embarrassed by their love?' he quizzed.

'Grief! I wouldn't exactly see it as "love". More likely as "lust".' Sam half closed her Irish green eyes as she tried to obliterate them all from her mind; she neither saw the women nor the fellows as folk with impeccable characters. Brusque, Sam declared: 'They wouldn't be the type of folk I'd want to see as my buddies.'

The taxi driver's chocolate dark eyes flicked sideways, he detecting a frown knitting across Sam's brow. 'You were somewhat horrified by it all?' he persisted.

'At first, I think I was more surprised than anything, but …'

' … but I reckon that you, being a normal heterosexual woman with all the usual feelings, must have become a bit fascinated?' With a gentle patience, he longed for her to explain the moment, to make them remain within his psyche, but she firmly stated a definite refusal.

Sam confessed she, being with Elkanah, her time, precious though it became, was mostly for him. She, from day one, saw him as beyond handsome; he also confessed he loved her. 'He was thrilled, as ever, to see me, for me to meet with him.'

'How did you get around, Sam, for in Ramah, they don't know about taxis, do they?'

'That's right. We rode his stallion.'

The driver wondered about all the time she gave Elkanah; he gave her more time to think before he threw his head back, loudly chuckling, stating he was positive they did not simply shake hands, asking: '"Hello, how do you do?". Don't you appear shocked, Miss Samantha, for it's love which makes the world go around.'

With Elkanah, Sam knew it was a true love between them. Nevertheless, he was an ancient and she a modern Westerner; he was an ancient Jew and she a cradle Catholic. How different could they be?

The guy grinned at her little pink blushes, they rising from her neck up. He, again, glanced sideways in her direction, watching, waiting for her reaction, reminding her how she, with her long, curly auburn hair and pale complexion like ripe peaches, was so unlike any of the dusky skinned maidens in ancient Samaria. 'Even your type of dress is utterly different ...'

Her eyes met his before she lowered her gaze towards her flared, hipster jeans and skin tight T-shirt. 'Once back in England, I shall be well wrapped up in lots of thick winter togs, for it is very cold; it's not baking hot like here.'

He nodded, for all her items of clothing were very different from the Samaritan women's togs. 'Any women I've known wouldn't know of such garments.' He glanced at her slender, but firm figure. 'I'm not trying to be a cheeky old fellow, but, as soon as we reach Alexandria, would you be so kind as to permit me a little peek?' He told her how, with the car's blacked out windows, no-one but he could glance.

Sam shook her head. 'Ah, I actually wondered why your cab has blacked out windows?'

'Now you know, huh?'

'And you're not embarrassed?'

'No more than you were, when you saw those in the cold cave.' He again chuckled, watching and waiting for her reaction; he faithfully promised Sam he would never do her any harm. 'Think of me as being your beloved Elkanah?'

'Forget Elkanah for the time being!'

The guy deeply frowned, as he shook his head, explaining he tried not to be quite so forward, for he highly respected the fairer sex. 'I only wanted to know out of a sheer curiosity; nothing more.'

Believing all his guff, she dealt with his curiosity, just enough to allow the harmless, but nosey driver to deal with his own wondering.

He, affected by the sudden revelation, gasped, exhaling a long ragged sigh. 'I'm wishing …'

Sam interrupted him. 'I know exactly what you men wish for?'

As claiming to be a heterosexual guy, he did. Reaching the city of Alexandria, he pulled up with the usual screech of his cab's tyres, yet he parked in a secluded back roadway where there was no street lighting; it was behind another Egyptian hotel where they kept their empty beer barrels. 'I swear, pretty lady, upon my dear mother's grave, no-one else but I can see you.'

'All right.' Releasing a shaky sigh, Sam removed her T-shirt before folding it neatly across her lap. 'Now, you know about us westerner women.'

He, showing his Adam's apple as he swallowed a gulp, his dark eyes stared, the black pupils rapidly dilating. His hands, she thought, seemed to tremble in an anticipation.

Sam's full lips, so unsettling, curved into a smile towards the grin spreading across his face, but she heard him state, 'As long as you are a completely consenting adult?'

She was.

With one strong arm placed tight around her, hugging her close enough to himself, she knew he briefly stopped his caressing to stare, to savour the prettiness of her face, she smiling before experiencing the warmth of his breath against her. He released her enough to cup her face in his hands, allowing his mouth to locate hers, to embrace her; from the moment their eyes met, she knew it was as if she needed him as no other, ancient or otherwise; it became almost a compulsion. With a slight croak in her voice, she managed to push him back enough, asking the name from the man who was nothing but gentle, how his name was Abe; he was tantalising her. Abe Jacobs was offering her a time with him upon his cab's back leather seat, for it became urgent.

Sam experienced precisely the same fizz, as if she was with her ancient man, for he appeared to her, hardly different; the only change was he was softer, more gentle. slowly laying her back across the rear seat. Before he joined her, Abe seriously warned how they, as a couple, might be pushing themselves with an intensity, to the edge of no control. Mesmerised, Abe Jacobs' gaze became intense; he watched Sam, her auburn hair falling loose, experienced in all she allowed.

With her again in the front seat, with his hand caressing her nearest knee, he drove off to ancient Cairo, first dropping her at the base of the hotel's marble steps. He remarked how he would definitely see her again: 'You'll be back some day soon, lovely lady, when you need to return again to way beyond the mirage.'

'In the meantime, I'll miss you.'

'And I you, Mazel tov!'

Samantha blew Abe a kiss goodbye, he fading as quickly as he came; she, making it back to the hotel's room, gathering the remainder of her belongings, yet she was unexpectedly waylaid by Paula, they chatting about the Baptism, its awesome festivities, everything and nothing.

When Sam eventually reached Egypt's Alexandrian airport, she alone, discovered how the Taylors decided at the last moment, to stay on with Adjo, Paula and Amy; she arrived only in time to see her prearranged flight taking off. Another flight was later due with a few seats available, yet it was held up for a number of hours due to a foolish bomb hoax. As a result, the flight transferred to Greece. Sam sat in its airport lounge, waiting until the next available flight was called. To top it all, where, she wondered, was her luggage? The carousel went around thrice; nothing. She remained until a thirty-something, English speaking Greek located the belongings.

As she ached to cross the abyss to where her ancient men resided in old Ramah, she, a wanting, had not denied Elkanah his desires; how urgently hungry, how

unrestrained as she permitted herself to be lost in a ful-
filment with him, they melding in unison. He, along
with his brother, became men she missed; they left an
empty void within her. It matter not how often James'
heart would beat as madly as her own, it was Elkanah
who inflamed her, she desiring him more than Eable,
more than Abe.

Sam curled up, retreating under their duvet, pulling it
up to her chin. James had learned to take pity upon her
tiredness, leaving her in peace, yet not on that morning.
He held a dogged determination.

'Come on, Sam; put your glad rags on.'

He heard her mutter back all over again how she was
unbelievably tired, how she had no rags, glad or
otherwise.

His dark brows frowned into a deep scowl. To him,
Sam was as lovely on the inside as she beautiful on the
outside, but, nevertheless, she was inadvertently frustrating his plans.

Samantha was naturally tired following Amy's
baptism, considering the half night of indulgences she,
Sam, gave Elkanah, way beyond the mirage. James,
only aware she missed her home bound flights, was
doing his utmost not to become irritable on the day he
had planned almost a precision. His gaze remained
steady upon her, wanting it to become special, a day
never to be forgotten. 'I believe the two of us should
make a special trip out together.'

'Ooh, nothing to do with Hunter?' she begged, for,
having ridden upon the too wide camel, an overladen
donkey, along with Elkanah's stallion, she remained

saddle sore; it was, with such journeyings, not surprising she was fatigued.

'No, we're not going anywhere near the stables.'

Sam gave in, sitting to stare, demanding where then.

'Hey, before you begin to ask, I need you to trust me. Okay?'

Surely, he did not need her reassurance. She stretched and yawned. 'I just remembered. How can we go anywhere? Isn't it today you're doing your stint in The Gallery?'

'Never mind all that.' He was indeed supposed to be working in The Gallery, yet, with the end of half term, he pleaded with his dad, to cover his shift.

'Much more of all this nipping off, and your parents will soon be seeing you as a sleeping partner!' She half coughed with a chuckle at her own brand of humour.

He opened the curtains wide enough to cause her to squint, to shield her eyes from the sudden daylight. 'Dress up in something smart; no denim jeans and a sloppy sweat shirt. All right?'

She nodded, remembering Elkanah asking a similar request prior to her surprise birthday party. Why, she wondered, should James need the same? It was neither his nor her birthdays. Was it the anniversary of the the day they first met? No. Men, she knew, did not usually bother. Whatever could he up to? Her Irish green eyes, filled with a concern, and her mouth feeling like sandpaper, Sam told him she felt both hungry and thirsty.

'I'll make us some breakfast; then, in a while, I shall 'phone us a cab.'

Why did they need a cab when they each owned a car? Where to? 'A regular black taxi, eh?' She broadly grinned.

'Yeah, okay.' He returned her smile, wondering if he missed some bit of humour. 'Frankly, I don't want to take my car …'

'Why?' Sam paused. 'Where are we going?'

James stated how the London traffic will probably be just crazy around the Hatton Gardens area.

Sam's bright green eyes widened. Her nagging lethargy slowly left her in almost a heartbeat; she staring up at him, asked: 'What did you say?' Although, in truth, she heard James well.

'Hatton Gardens.'

'We are off to the London Jewellery Centre? Why? What for?' Sam queried, wondering if it was someone's birthday or an anniversary. She always enjoyed browsing the area; it was over there she purchased baby Amy's bracelet, a pretty gold baptismal gift. 'Who are we buying for this time? Your mum? Ooh, I'm dying to know; put me out of my suspense.'

He groaned: 'Telling you, I'd ruin my surprise.'

'Surprise?'

'Well, considering how we already live together, I reckon it's high time I chose you a ring, don't you?'

Sam's jaw kind of dropped open. 'A ring? You mean for me?'

He smiled. 'Of course, my pet, it's for you; I wouldn't be buying a ring for anyone else now, would I?' He added how there'd never been any other woman in his life. Never. 'There never shall be anyone besides you.' He shuddered at the thought of ever being without her, just as she knew it was still tough without the memories of her Mick, her playful Eable, her ever loving Elkanah, but she hid her tears, doing her best to anchor the past

She wondered, at first, if it might be either a friendship or an eternity ring, but he shook his head, smiling. 'An engagement ring for you, my sweet. Now, are you going to get ready, or not?'

'Yes. I'm up … I'm up! You mean, we're actually going to become engaged, engaged to be married?' Sam gasped, suddenly reaching out, pulling him so close. 'Oh, James, it's a lovely thought.'

'Yes. Now, please, Sam, hurry up to get yourself ready -.'

Sam smiled broadly, but she asked him to sit down, to be beside her. She reached one of his hands in hers, mindlessly playing with his fingers.

'What's wrong, Sam?'

She shook her head before lowering her eyes. 'Nothing really. It's such a beautiful thought, but, think, James, for we've only just had two real dates, the last one ending up as a week in Egypt before your going into hospital? Instead of convalescing here, you went back with your parents. Now, better, you have only recently moved in here?'

He appeared worried.

'There's heaps you do not know about me.' Sam continued: 'What you don't know, James, is that I was engaged before, to someone I loved. He is called Mick.'

'Really? I had no idea.'

She added how she finished with him. 'If we now suddenly become engaged, folk may see me as being with you on the rebound, especially after so soon?'

'And are you with me?'

'What?'

'On the rebound?'

Sam knitted a frown across her brow. 'No, James. Certainly not. It's just … it's just so soon. Think how it may appear to outsiders.'

He stared towards her. 'Do you love me, Sam? I thought you did?'

'You don't need me to tell you; you surely know I love you.' Nevertheless, she knew there was much concerning about her he needed to yet discover? 'Give it time, eh? No more surprises, James.'

SIX MONTHS LATER:

One Friday morning, James shook out a laugh, asking her: 'Will you still allow me to buy you that engagement ring?'

'This morning? Ooh, James, I'd be chuffed to bits!'

'That's settled then.'

She grabbing a large bath towel from the linen cupboard, she still not dare ever disclose her favours given way beyond the mirage. He still would never understand. 'I need to take a quick shower,' she told him. Dressing, she was meticulous, impeccable in every last detail. She glanced in a long mirror to button the jacket of a peach coloured linen two piece, fine for her auburn colouring, for travelling; it seemed to be the perfect outfit. 'Will I do?' she asked him as she did a quick twirl.

'Fabulous as ever!' he exclaimed. 'You look absolutely gorgeous.'

Arriving in Hatton Gardens, the couple visited several fine jewellers until they discovered an old fashioned family run establishment. In the brightly lit shop window Sam spotted a white gold engagement ring with a small single pink diamond; displayed on a bed of black silk, it was the only one ring which really caught her eye.

'Ooh, James,' she pointed towards it, saying: 'I love that particular one.'

They, walking hand in hand, wandered together into the brightly lit shop, Sam seeming to remember the same elderly gentleman; he sold her Amy's gold christening gift, even offering to wrap the bracelet. She smiled towards him, asking if he remembered her. He half nodded, but, as he did, he glanced up, turning to check with the clock on the far wall; he declared how he closed at around two 0' clock, ready to prepare for his sun down Sabbath.

James interrupted, asking the Jewish Jeweller if Samantha could try on that certain engagement ring.

'Ooh, yet another happy occasion, eh, miss?'

Surprisingly, the ring became a perfect fit. Stepping back a little to admire it at arm's length, she exhaled a long and happy sigh. 'It's so very beautiful, James … it really is quite magnificent.'

'You, too,' he whispered, gently squeezing her arm.

'Now, is this your absolute choice, or shall I show you some other engagement rings?' asked the fellow.

Samantha shook her head and beamed. 'No. I really don't need to see any others. This is definitely the one for me …'

James, pleased as Punch, presumed she wished to keep the ring on her finger, not in its small leather box.

With Sam standing starry-eyed at her magnificent engagement ring, she half watched her beloved James reaching inside his coat's pocket; he, pulling out his cheque book, asked the jeweller if it was all right to pay by a cheque.

'Of course, young sir,' he said, nodding towards the use of a black pen affixed upon the length of a long thin chain, it suctioned to the counter's glass top. 'Please, make your cheque payable to: "Mr A. Jacobs".'

Watching James completing the cheque before scribbling his usual signature, Sam half gasped at the proprietor's name, momentarily looking away from her new ring.

'A . Jacobs?' she quietly asked, for there became an eerily similarity in both his name and appearances to Abe. There came back all those self same inner feelings when she first metaphorically stumbled over Hannah and James Samuels, that first encounter with the oil painting of Hunter.

The guy smiled towards her. As the elderly fellow accepted payment, he peered over his spectacles and, seriously, declared: 'I was married to my dear late wife for a lot of years. Now, as you two youngsters obviously plan to eventually tie the knot, I'd like to tell you marriage is wonderful. Marriage is fantastic, the greatest thing our Maker ever invented; you've both fallen in love, and you plan to spend the rest of your lives together. Being married is everything it is cracked up to be, and it is the best thing which could happen to you. Simply, do not expect perfection! I hope you didn't mind my adding a few thoughtful words?'

'Ooh, not at all,' added Sam, happy tears glistening in her green eyes. 'I confess I am quite touched by your words.'

'Mazel tov! Be lucky,' he offered.

'I actually heard "Mazel tov" being said to me once before ... well, to be totally honest, Mr Jacobs, it was about six months ago.'

He nodded with a broad smile.

'And I shall not forget your words of wisdom, sir,' stated Sam's new fiancee, firmly shaking hands with him.

'May I call you both a taxi? It's looking like rain ...'

Leaving the shop, Sam mentioned to James how it would be nice to have the old jeweller as a guest when they eventually marry, to which he gave a nod, he saying it may be a while as yet; they ate a celebratory lunch at a nearby fish restaurant. 'Do you know, Sam, today you have made me so very happy, probably one of the happiest men on the planet?' he told her, although he wondered if he should have first asked her father for his daughter's hand in marriage, if he should have gone down on one knee and proposed to her.

Sam giggled. 'That's all a bit old fashioned, isn't it? Hey, but you know what's going to happen now?'

'What's that?'

'My mother, as soon as she sees my engagement ring, she'll virtually be hearing wedding bells in her head!'

Ignoring the remark about Daisy, James stated: 'I needed for us to become engaged, Sam, so you'd realise how I'm totally committed to you ... not only for now, but forever. You've now no more doubts, have you, sweetheart?'

She frowned a little, shaking her head.

He beamed a broad smile. 'Sam, let's celebrate our engagement ... we'll later go to Claridge's Bar, sampling some of their finest Champagne. All right? We'll then go off and tell the parents. Your parents must know first, Sam, and then mine.

'Later tonight, much later, we'll have our own private celebration.'

'With all that Champagne, we'll be too legless to do much tonight!' she exclaimed, a little mischievous glint in her eyes, although he had no knowledge of her relationships with ancients Elkanah and Eable. To outsiders, Elkanah, Eable and Abe sounded more like a local firm of lawyers than those who loved her. Sam believed James would never understand, never in a million years, so she considered it was best to keep quiet, to compartmentalise her life; no-one would then become wounded.

Paula was excited to receive a 'phone call from Sam. 'You must honeymoon here in our hotel … in the new suite. It even has a four poster bed.' She giggled. 'Hey, but, listen, Sam, I really must go … so busy. '

That night James flopped back into a bedroom armchair, watching Sam prepare for bed.

'Coming ?' she asked softly. 'Or are you too full of Champagne to crawl that far?'

He shook his head.

Sam became thoughtful, thinking upon many things. James was so frank, so honest, keeping no secrets from her. She tried to be the same, yet she decided to hide away those photographs taken way beyond the mirage, those of her with her ancient men; the snaps were playing on her mind, but she secreted them away in the back of her underwear drawer, convinced he would never look in there. 'It was such a truly wonderful day, James. I am telling you, it couldn't have been better had we been royalty!'

Both sets of families, next evening, over indulged, but everyone knew Charles, his dad, would have, in the morning, a one almighty humdinger of a headache. However, James claimed he, himself, was as sober as a judge. He reached to take her hand in his; he smiled down at the ring.

As far as they were both concerned, everyday life became almost perfect, they within their own private world in which they thrived.

Chapter 15

Sam stood, hanging about outside one of Wimbledon's country pubs, she craning her neck; it still remained too early, yet, nevertheless, she indomitable, watched and waited. Her previously anxious expression broke into a broad smile the moment he arrived; he sped, striding out to join her.

Although speaking softly, she half reprimanded: 'I thought, for one moment, dad, you weren't coming.' She experience the same bizarre phobia when she was a youngster at her boarding school, almost as if she might be left by her parents.

Her father cleared his dry throat before exhaling a lengthy drawn out sigh, raising his hands in a sort of Western surrender; he dropped his arms, slipping one around her shoulders, drawing her close to him; with a father's soft heart, he tried to console her in her so-called predicament, giving yet a second long lingering sigh before gently offering: 'This is all totally nuts; you know it is, Samantha, my darling, I'd never forget you – I've never ever let you down so far, now, have I? Go on, chicken; answer me.'

Sam shook her head, trying to deal again with her regular despair. 'Suppose not, but what delayed you today?'

Henry Webb, with a good nature and conscience, was not late; after the obligatory Sunday Mass when he first stepped on the gas to drop Daisy home, he needed to find a garage open. His motor showed drastically low on fuel, he complaining how the classy red Jaguar guzzled petrol at an alarming rate; the chatty pump attendant urged him to pay for a quick car wash, too, to make it pristine. A retired soldier, Henry shrugged such minor events aside as he kissed his daughter's worried forehead. 'Anyway, my sweet,' he grunted, 'my car is in its garage and I waked across to you here now. All right?'

'It's only just that …' She looked him straight into his Irish eyes.

His head high and his shoulders back, he urged: 'Go on. Spit it out?'

Her heart lurched. Spoiled and pampered as an only adult child, she placed her two pennyworth: 'It's only I don't like having to stand out here all alone, waiting for you outside the pub.'

He pointed: 'There is that wooden seat, you know? You don't need, week by week, to stand by the pub's door.'

Delaying around outside her dad's local watering hole, she heard a wolf whistle from a thirty-something guy just leaving. Sam added how it made her feel a bit like a high class hooker - not that she ever met one one at Wimbledon's Crooked Billet, a busy pub with its rows of prettily hanging baskets, they filled mostly with bright red geraniums.

As they, arm in arm, moved inside and searched for two available spaces at the bar, Henry again sighed, raising his eyes heavenwards, before smiling, doing his utmost to promptly change the subject from her annoy-ance. 'That engagement do, Samantha ... my goodness me! That was really quite some occasion, eh?'

Calmer, she sat, one leg crossed over the other, slowly swinging one over the other while accepting the compli-ment; she, with a broad smile, agreed.

'Yes, it certainly was a happy time. What a great evening? Both mummy and I thoroughly enjoyed our-selves.' He stopped to think for a moment or two before he stated: 'Although I have to confess the news of your engagement to that "what's his name" came straight out of the blue. It certainly became quite a surprise for me.'

She, reminding her father of James' first name, putting her head on one side to ask: 'Really, dad?'

'Well, not exactly.' Henry pursed his lips. 'To be totally frank, babe, it became more of a shock, at least, to me anyway.' He remembered her previous fiancee, Mick. 'You know, I really liked that Irish lad from Balygar?' Her dad reprimanded her how she broke the poor fellow's heart. 'I'll never understand this side of heaven, why you finished with him, but, oh, I suppose it's your life.' Henry's small jug of fresh water arrived with his Scotch; he fished around in his pocket for the change, telling the barman to keep it as a tip. The previ-ous evening Henry saw his only daughter bowled all over again, but by a local artist.

Sam, unlike the previous evening's celebrations, was sticking with tomato juice, she grinned towards Henry. Before she could verbally justify the situation, he informed her: 'You certainly know how to drop a bombshell, don't you?' He continued to chat on how he had absolutely no notion she even became more than serious about the new fellow in her life, let alone getting engaged to be married to him. Looking for a second Irish whisky, romancing, it did not take much for Sam's dad to again start chatting either about his previous wartime experiences or concerning his beloved Daisy, always the light of his married life.

A quiet groan escaped from Sam's lips, but, patient, Sam previously heard it all before! In 1939, when Henry, her father, was barely twenty, he received his call-up papers to serve in the army, to a training unit based in the old historic city of Winchester. He invariably ordered men at the double, marching them up and down Magdalene Hill. Silently, King Alfred, founder of the English nation, stood with sword lifted high, his shield by his side, he looking down upon them, who, like himself eleven hundred years before, was prepared to defend our green and pleasant land from its invading enemies.

Before Henry was posted overseas, Sam's parents became married. 'Your mammy will tell you, Samantha, how our wedding was an awesome triumph.'

'She already has ... several times.'

'Aye. It was, according to all and sundry, the best wartime occasion they'd ever attended.'

'Well, I've heard all your stories, but you surely must have known James and I are just as totally serious concerning each other, for we've been living together for well over six months?'

He shrugged away her words, as he knew she did not exactly practice chastity, how, since being in her twenties, she never became a shrinking violet with Mick, along with whoever else turned up before and now after. 'These days, my darling daughter, a lot of folk, young and older, seem to be shacking up together ...'

'Well, I think our living together is perfectly sensible. To begin with, it has given us both a chance to learn more about each other before making the heavy commitment of a lifelong marriage. We are getting time to see if our relationship is right for us.'

Henry shook his head. 'In my day, when your mother and I were courting, it would have been seen as something shocking, as our "living in sin".'

Sam knew about life-styles then, yet she continued to explain how, for her and James, living together was like a trial marriage; how she thought, residing under the same roof, did not mean shacking up with just any ol' bod. It was not playing house. She knew she would probably be leaving behind her independent life of a single woman, to one day have children.

'Whatever, at first, dad, even I didn't know he was planning for us to become engaged. When I found out, I told James no more surprises, but to wait for a full six months.'

Henry smiled, pleased his daughter at least had her head screwed well on when it came to that. 'I bet you took the wind out of his sails, eh?'

'Well, it's just tough if things don't always go his way; he's not a little kid.' Sam told her dad how it was simply too bad. 'Then, on Friday morning, six months to the day, he woke me up; it was then he arranged for a cab to take us over to Hatton Gardens.' She looked down with a new found pride at her finger, flashing her gorgeous ring. 'I can't even begin to tell you how happy I am, dad. I feel as if I'm still floating on cloud nine!'

'I'll tell you who won't be quite so happy, Samantha,' he stated with the look of devilish amusement.

She raised a quizzical eyebrow.

'Your man's father … Charley.'

Sam shook her head, looking a little puzzled. 'Why do you say that? Charles Samuels is truly delighted for both of us.' Charles told his son James he was a 'lucky dog' to have her, how he envied him to have such a pretty woman in his life.

'Yes. Quite right. James is truly a very fortunate guy. I trust he's fully aware of it. No. I was thinking more how Charley had too much of the Champagne. The bubbly didn't exactly agree with him, did it?'

Sam remembered arranging a black taxi for Charles; she smiled, knowing how he would be well and truly hungover. 'James and I remarked how he'd have one pounding thick head.'

'Awe, a couple of paracetamol and he'll be as right as rain, eh?'

She was surprised her father appeared to have discovered so little about James. 'Mummy already knew all about him. Only before last Christmas, James called at my apartment to give me six white roses.'

'Only six? My life! I'd have thought if he was that crazy about you, he'd forked out for a dozen red ones …'

Sam told Henry they then hardly knew one and another.

'But you do now, huh?'

She nodded with a grin, for it was remarkable the grand way it was going for her. 'Didn't Paula tell you he and I spent a week in their Egyptian hotel, at the time baby Amy was born? Oh, daddy, you surely knew?'

He shook his head. 'Nope. I'm always the last to be told anything.'

Sam was convinced her mother must have informed him all about James, yet, he was a man who rarely listen to his wife's news, saying either: 'Yes, Daisy, dear,' or: 'No, Daisy, dear.' He would try to reply as expected in all the right places, before either reading his daily newspaper or attempting to complete its crossword.

'By the way, where is your new fiancee right now … why isn't he joining us today for one of your mother's late Sunday lunches?' Henry asked. 'Don't tell me he's hungover, too?'

Sam said he was stock taking at The Gallery.

'The Gallery?'

'Dad, you really are the limit!' She gave him a slight, friendly nudge. 'You surely remember? I used the Christmas money you gave me, to buy from there.'

'Um, ah, yes, my sweet. Of course, I remember; it's where you bought the oil painting of the stallion?' Henry held Hunter's image in his mind.

'Yes. It's also where he and I first met …'

The smartly dressed young barman deliberately cleared his throat, giving Sam her second tomato juice and her father his double liquid gold, his always regular Irish whisky, on the rocks. Henry turned again to Samantha: 'Your mother hardly slept last night, she's mentally making lists, planning your wedding; I'm telling you, sweetheart, my money in Daisy's hands will be like water down a drain … just as well we have no more girls!'

'Surely, you don't regret having me?'

Henry's eyes widened, he shaking his head, he wondering if he'd half made a slight blunder. In the blur of those happy times, he stated with a reminisce: 'You, Samantha, already know how we were over the moon when you came along …'

'What then?'

He chuckled. 'It's just I thank Our Blessed Mother I've no more daughters, for it is up to me, the father of the bride, to pay for the wedding, did you know?'

'We only became engaged Friday morning. Gosh! It's a bit too soon, to think about any wedding.'

'Don't you believe it!'

Sam noticed upon the bar, some salted peanuts and cheese nibbles; helping herself before shaking some Worcester sauce into the tomato juice, she laughed, firmly returning the kiss to her father upon his own forehead. 'You only pretend to complain, but I reckon you're also loving it too.'

Henry half grinned, he admitting nothing.

'By the way, Paula and Adjo haven't lost much time, either; already, they have offered James and me a week's honeymoon in Egypt. It's kind of them, but way too soon, eh?'

'Hmm; yes.'

'Where did you and mummy go for your honeymoon?'

He was surprised Daisy never told Sam, how he very nearly lost his commission as a junior ranking officer. Henry had requested special leave for his wedding, but, at the very last moment, all leave was cancelled, so, whoops, he went AWOL from His Majesty's Forces. Neither Daisy nor any of the wedding guests knew of his offence. The shock came later. 'Wartime stopped us from travelling to exotic honeymoon destinations, so we borrowed a distant cousin's apartment for a much shorter time than planned.'

'Oh, gosh, daddy, whatever happened next?'

Henry explained with a deep devilish chuckle how, at four-thirty in the morning, his and Daisy's sleep was disturbed by the thud, thud of heavy army boots marching up the flight of stairs. Unceremoniously, the military police, with their peak caps pulled down low over their eyes, burst through the master bedroom door, loudly ordering a half naked Henry onto his feet. The bewildered young Daisy, clutching the bedclothes to herself, became shocked to the core.

'And I came along a year after the war ended … '

'You did indeed, and what a grand day it was for your mother and me, eh?'

Sam smiled.

'Anyway, Samantha,' he began with a sigh, 'when it comes to your honeymooning, for pity's sake, please don't go disappearing again for almost a couple of years; then, way out of the deep blue yonder, return with some cock and bull story about life where there's no electricity, no telephones, nothing? What a load of old guff?'

'It wasn't nonsense; I swear, it was absolutely true.'

'Yeah, but if you weren't held as a hostage, whatever got into you? You, as far as we were concerned, saw you as so sensible … so level headed.'

Sam's smiles changed into a deep frown, she determined not to say another word in her own defence. 'Nevertheless,' Henry persisted: 'I'm telling you, Samantha, you escaped a ''shrink'' only by the skin of your teeth.'

She, lifting a finger to her lips, for him to shush. Desperate to change the subject, anxious they may become overheard by either the bar staff or any nearby punters, glanced at her wristwatch, comparing the time with the clock on pub wall; Henry was reminded by her how it was time to go home, for her mother would have readied roast beef and three veg, all waiting for them.

'Yes, all right, I'll have one more whisky … just a quick one, Samantha. Okay?' He was about to click his fingers, to summon the young barman.

'No, dad.' Sam held his wrist, stopping him. 'Any more and I swear you'll be in trouble with mum. Okay?'

He shook his head, chuckling at his daughter. 'I'm fine, my darling.'

Samantha drew a deep breath, talking straight. 'You won't be if you make us late for mum's Sunday roast.'

His smile faded.

Chapter 16

With the keys having turned in the ignition, she mindlessly switched on the car's radio; Hannah Samuels hummed out the familiar old tune she heard, tapping out its rhythm on the steering wheel. Finally, with her hands firmly gripping the wheel, she reversed from their shop's crunching gravel drive, straight into the hysteria of Chelsea's rush hour. Having worked at The Gallery for so long, she claimed she made the self same trip more times than she cared to remember. Within a heart beat, with no place to swerve, she became unable to avoid the chilling tragedy; without a nanosecond of warning, her car became hit by a deranged drunk driver.

Previously glancing around The Gallery, she, discontent, reckoned it would be more pleasant to have a couple of silk floral displays, she trying to make it appear a little less masculine. She briefly mentioned to her husband Charles she would drive to their usual florist. With the roads seeming more busy, he advised her to 'phone through her order, to having some pretty floral arrangements delivered. Always a strong minded woman, invariably determined to do her own thing, she debated with him, how the florist was only streets away; therefore, he advised her to walk it, but no, she was determined to have her own way, she taking her own new car, showing it off. Charles even offered to drive her; she refused. She stated she was more than capable to drive herself and, with advice from her chatty florist friend, she would be able to choose exactly all she wanted, to perhaps bring back a silken pink floral display. No-one bargained she would encounter a spaced out fool of a drunk driver. The drunk, believing after a previous night of celebrations, followed by a full champagne breakfast, was fit to motor, smashed into the driver's side of Hannah's vehicle.

Moments later, Hannah was in an ambulance with its siren screeching and the blue light flashing, she being on her way to the Westminster Hospital. Eye witnesses, seeing the tangled wreckage became stunned; the two local police constables did their best, trying to move every interested local on. Hannah's skin became grey; her blood seemed to have splattered much of the wreckage. The top notched ambulance crew performed every task they were able, yet it became too late; she was declared dead upon arrival in the Casualty Department. A senior Consultant, pulling off his latex gloves, went off some place else, shaking his head. A nursing Sister overheard him to coldly exclaim expletives concerning his view of drunk drivers.

Sam, startled by the ghastly news, rarely saw Hannah Samuels as her great buddy, yet she naturally never wished the woman harm; softly and lovingly, she became touched with a compassion for the next of kin, along with many she cherished, for those who claimed they cared. James and his dad deliriously sobbed, simultaneously clinging tight to each other. At one stage Charles Samuels swayed, seeming as if he was going to either faint or throw up. Sam, accompanied by her own parents, held a deep, loving concern for his terrible loss, placing her gentle arms around him, hugging him close. James appeared washed out, with nothing much to say. Sam cuddled him; he held her, too, but it was as if he could not quite feel either anyone or anything. Not Sam. No-one. The horse drawn glass hearse took Hannah's body to the nearest Catholic Church, for the funeral's High Requiem Mass; following the intern-ment, everyone in black, stood around for a while before leaving for a finger buffet; the food, amazing, Sam, served her own plate before discovering a seat next to Charles Samuels. As he turned to face her, she, noticing him more tearful, listened again as he stated how lucky James was to have her. 'Unless you count the groom who's going to shovel up the Church's yard, after that horse, you know,' he half trying to be humorous, 'I've next to no-one now, you know?'

'James told me you have sister?'

'Yeah. She isn't a local.' He shrugged, saying how he almost forgot about her. 'She's in Spain.'

With auburn hair bright and shining, with small pearl studs in her ears, Sam, respectable in a black coat and matching court shoes, lifted a smile from her lips. Despite the sorrowful event, she remained looking incredible. 'Anyway. You don't need to feel quite so alone; there's always my dad. Perhaps he'd like a bit of a bloke's company?' She did not want to either speak for Henry or seem pushy. 'Whatever, I'm always here for you, Charles, a listening ear, a shoulder to cry on; any time, do you hear?' Softly and gently with a smile, yet with a natural warmth, she graciously stated: 'I truly mean it. Okay?'

He thanked her, saying how he did not plan on being overshadowed by the doldrums. Charles soon became distracted by others, they all offering their condolences to him and James.

Weeks later, when quite alone in her London flat, Sam was listening to the background of her radio, she distracted by the contralto, Kathleen Ferrier singing, "Blow the wind southerly". Having curled upon one of the comfy sofas, she was cherishing having her quiet "me-time" when the land-line 'phone rang; sighing at its wretched intrusion, she, grudgingly got to her feet, reaching across for the receiver; she answered upon the third ring, wondering who on earth it might be.

'Samantha?'

Only her parents called her Samantha. Stiffly, she asked who it was; the deep, even voice informed her how it was Charles, James' dad. He ploughed on: 'Are you free to talk?'

'Now?' Sam almost felt trapped as soon as she agreed: 'Yes, I reckon so. Why?'

He, with a strain in his voice, sounded hesitant, yet she considered he surely must have half known she was alone, that James was still over the shop. 'You have no-one else with you, no other visitors? Not your parents?'

'No. What's the matter?' Sam asked, yet half wondering if Charles was in need of a chat, nothing much more, but he told her how he recently sorted through his late wife's personal belongings, reading a few secreted away diaries.

Sam listened until his words assaulted her ears. 'This year's diary mentioned a man named ... Eable; it's the same as James' middle name, as I suppose you'll already know, eh?'

'Ooh, shush; please stop. Do not say another word. I mustn't discuss either him, or any of this over the telephone.' She immediately became worried. 'What if your son walks in, he should want to know who I was speaking to. When I tell him it's you, he'd more than likely want to know why.'

'Oh, no. James is still stock taking. He won't be with you for ages, yet. May we meet up some place?' Charles never mentioned about her driving to his Surrey home. 'Perhaps, in town for a coffee?'

'And become over heard? No fear!'

Both suggestions of his, he heard Sam saying a stale no. Was it really all so secretive about the Eable fellow, so cloak and dagger like, he wondered? 'What then do you suggest?'

'I'll ring you back in a short while. I promise.'

Confused by the whole zany palaver, he had little choice but to wait. Sam heard Charles sigh with an 'Okay then.'

In the meantime she checked with James, he confirming he still had a lot of accounts to complete. 'I hoped I'd be back for bedtime, Sam, but, if you don't mind too much, I think I'll kip down here, up in my apartment over the shop … just for tonight. Sorry, darling, not to be with you.'

Sam told him it was more than an okay, although he was really only a spitting distance away; anyway, it was his choice to remain over The Gallery.

James told her how even hours away from her felt like days. 'I bet it's like that for you, too, huh?'

'I'll see you tomorrow.'

James continued to self justify his night of absence: 'It a bigger task than I first imagined; I'm getting dog tired.'

'No worries.'

'Love you, princess.'

She, his so-called princess, having reciprocated the felicitations, hung up. Ringing Charles, she suggested he should perhaps drive to her place.'You are free to come here, to me?'

He was.

Sam, having switched off the radio, quickly took a shower and redressed in her pale green trouser suit; she soon welcomed Charles, giving him the sort of brief hug she may offer her own dad. He returned to her a fatherly peck upon both her cheeks before handing over a large box of milk chocolates, stating he purchased them at a late night garage where he just topped his motor with oil. She thanked him for the nice thought, stating in a jovial way how she may become fat! She set them aside on the kitchen's counter top, for another time.

Charles glanced at Sam's elegant sylph like figure before smiling back at her remark about her weight; he was shown through into the large, comfy living room. She swished closed the curtains while he lowered himself on a cream leather settee. She asked if he had eaten. He grabbed something at a local cafeteria, although he confessed he disliked all their everything with the chips they called French fries; she offered him a glass of white wine, but he refused, reminding her he was not too good with booze.

'I remember at the evening of our engagement … with the Champagne!'

He informed Sam how he had one awful thick head the next morning. 'It was like a very bad migraine.'

'So, what now? Tea? Coffee?'

He patted his flat stomach, telling her he was full from the greasy food, he needing nothing.

The last time Sam saw him was at the funeral. 'You're appearing brighter, Charles,' which was a somewhat obvious remark, simply to make him feel improved within himself.

Bringing his hands to his feel his own cheeks, Charles stated a: 'Perhaps.' He glanced around; the living room, it spectacularly clean, with the atmosphere being light, without any undue clutter. He asked who did her housework.

'Mostly me,' she informed him with the hint of a sigh. When Sam was way beyond the mirage, her mother's cleaning woman kept it pristine. 'Anyway, I heard from James how you're back working ... so, do you have someone doing for you?' Sam remembered how his Surrey house was no small affair.

She heard him inwardly groan. 'Since Hannah died,' he began, refusing the tears which rushed to his eyes, 'my sister-in-law seems to have taken it over.' He added how he dare not even do his own washing. 'She stocked up my kitchen cupboards, telling me what I should be eating. If I go out anywhere, like coming here this evening, Tilly wants to know where I am off to, who with and why.'

'I'm sure she means well, but I'm not someone who would tolerate her ... no way. '

'Ooh, Samantha, she even has a door key to my place and ...'

Sam interrupted, exclaiming: 'You chose to give it to her?'

'Hannah did, to be used only in cases of emergencies. What would you do if you were in my shoes?'

'Goodness me; either I'd get my key back or change the locks?'

Charles levelled his gaze straight at Sam, continuing: 'I know she also snooped through my personal files.' He noticed private items having been moved.

Sam declared, had it been her, she would have hit the roof. 'However, Charles, don't let's be wasting any more time, bothering upon the likes of your Tilly woman,' Sam stated, settling herself down in the opposite armchair; leaning over one of its arms, she indicated, nodding for him to eventually come straight to the point.

Clasping his own hands tight, with his elbows resting on his knees, he again brought up the whole issues regarding his late wife's diaries. He watched Sam's reaction as he mentioned about one particular diary; for over a week he concealed it in his jacket's inner pocket. 'It's still in here.'

'Go on.'

'Well, as I read, I noticed she'd written about a secret you and she shared concerning being "way beyond the mirage".' Charles searched Sam's bright green eyes, asking: 'Where is that place, Samantha?' He previously searched in the local reference library, to look in their large atlas, but no such place became listed. 'I asked around in the school's staff room, especially when I saw the geography teacher; Toby didn't know what the Dicken's I was talking about. He asked me if I'd been hitting the bottle.' Charles laughed at even the thought. 'You know how bad I am with booze?'

'You've not spoken with James … you know, about all his mum's diaries?'

No. He had not. 'James hasn't a clue.'

Sam exhaled a sigh of relief.

'There's a little more about an "Eable" and his stallion Hunter.' Charles peered up at her with his sad dark eyes, half longing for Samantha to clarify the issue. 'Please, darling, I feel I must know about that Eable man.'

It was tough to offer any quick response. Sam's neat brows knitted together into a frown. 'What you need to understand is, Charles, I gave my solemn promise to your Hannah, how I'd never breathe this stuff to another living soul, but ...' It was as if a fierce battle was raging within her conscience. 'Now she's no longer with us, oh, I don't know quite what I should actually do. Perhaps my promise no longer stands, now she's no longer with us. What do you think? You were her husband.'

He tilted his head, reaching out for her. 'Samantha, I reckon you're probably the only person who can clear up this situation.'

'I know but -.' She did not welcome his touch, but folded her arms. Life was never simple.

'Hannah's gone from me.' The whites of his eyes became reddened. 'The last thing I wish, is to become a bitter old guy, spending the rest of my life, believing she was unfaithful.'

Sam experienced an anxiety, as if she was almost being pushed to break a previous promise; she again blew out a sigh to quieten herself. If anyone asked her previously, she would have stated a firm no, explaining how it became her secret, too. 'Hmm. How do I actually know, Charles, you'll also keep my own secret?' Sam dangled her own promise before him, making him to swear. 'The last thing I need is for you to begin blabbing, especially to my parents - never, ever or they'll see me as some sort of a delusional prize fruit and nut, perhaps needing a shrink.'

He shook his head, patting the vacant seat, asking her to sit at the side of him which, following the briefest of moments, she immediately agreed; he tightened his hands around her own, giving his word as a gentleman. 'If I make a promise, Samantha, I always keep it.' It was something he firmly instilled into his son ... and she surely did know it.

'All right,' she began, 'I shall tell you ... you're the first outsider here to really know. '

'Oh, please, sweetheart, do carry on ...'

Many times Sam steered clear of alcohol, unless it was either with a pleasant dinner or to celebrate a bit of a do, but, with all such odd issues, she felt in a need. 'I will talk after I have got myself a small glass of something. Will you join me? Only a tiny white wine, just to be sociable? Come on, Charles. One won't kill you, you know?'

He shook his head, but he waited, watching for her with a bottle and a clean glass, pouring a small one for herself. 'Okay. You were going to tell me your story?'

Sam swallowed two small sips of the fine wine before setting her glass aside. She moved away from his side, back into her own armchair. Facing him, Sam began: 'When I was in Egypt's Alexandria, I discovered a white Mercedes cab with its blacked out windows; it supposedly came from some old remote place in the historical city of Cairo. The indiscreet taxi driver, Abe, drove me way across for a fifteen-minute camel ride.'

Charles interrupted. 'Why did you say Abe was indiscreet? Whatever did he do?'

Sam stared into space as she half smiled, remembering their close proximity. 'Abe took me as far as a willing, yet toothless cameleer who, in turn, led me to an old stone arch. It was knick-named by the locals as the Needle's Eye.'

Charles wondered, questioning if this was the absolute truth. 'Oh, Samantha, are you kidding me with a lot of old guff?'

'Not a bit, Charles. Listen. That particular camel separated itself from the others, it so wide due to its precarious load, it couldn't quite squeeze through the Needle's Eye.'

Charles shook his head, just as if she was enjoying a bit of humour. 'In your dreams …' He sat bolt upright. 'All this is in your wild imaginations, eh?' He stated how he came for her help, not to be mocked in some way.

Almost an annoyance rushed through her; she swallowed some more of her drink, staring, deeply frowning. 'Do you want to know about this, or not? I'm honestly not obliged to tell you a solitary thing, you know? It's my favour.'

'All right.' He half grinned. 'So, go on then. What happened next?'

'Very well. Having been beckoned by a silvery mirage across the desert's horizon, I was shoved along by a huge tumble-weed; it was then I walked on until I found a brown and grey, over-laden donkey. Its teenage entrepreneur took me to a guest annexe in old Samaria's ancient Ramah which, in turn, is in a place way beyond the mirage. In there is a fellow of around my age, named Eable. He, the younger brother of Elkanah, owns a grey stallion … it's named Hunter.'

'Elkanah?'

'Yes.' Sam nodded, telling Charles how Elkanah was an Old Testament priest, the husband of Hannah; they were the parents of the prophet Samuel: 'You can check him out in the Old Testament. Ah, yes and the year is 1105 BC .'

Charles appeared doubtful, grinning. 'You're kidding me, Sam, with all of this … this fanciful fairy tale – right?'

She took up her glass, she deadly serious. 'Not a bit.' She explained how Eable was once pleased to think he may have made her pregnant, 'but I flatly refused him; yet, apparently your own Hannah, time after time, didn't turn him away … '

He sat back, allowing his weary head to fall on the high back of the settee. 'Samantha, this is all too much to take in, to even half believe.'

'Your wife told me that, when she returned to marry you, she was apparently already expecting James.'

'Hmm. Oh, was she now?' He shook his head. 'What else did she tell you?'

'Are you sure you won't have some wine? I swear it's not a cheap plonk, you know?'

Charles' head already seemed in a flat spin; he listened on as Sam informed him how Hannah loved Eable so much: 'That's why she wanted James to take on the middle name of Eable.'

'And I was married to her all those years and yet … ' There seemed glistening tears welling up in his dark eyes. 'Carry on, Samantha.'

'I cannot. All else I knew was when your son got his stallion in Wimbledon, over at the Dog and Fox riding stables, your wife suggested the name Hunter; she'd ridden bareback Eable's Hunter in 1105 BC.'

'Hunter?'

'That's right. I have also ridden since I visited ... way beyond the mirage, I mean. That's about it.'

'I'm astounded! This is such a crazy lot of stuff to take in.' Charles confided in Sam, he always sensed he was not James' real birth father, although he loved him, just as if he was.

'Samantha. I have little choice but to believe you. In this short meeting of ours, you've cleared up years and years of my worrying, of the strange mystery.'

'What a shame Hannah didn't choose to trust you, of all people, with her strange happenings.'

Charles sat, holding her gaze. 'Is this why James' skin is more olive in colour?'

'James and Eable are like two peas in a pod; they are so alike, I reckon they might even be the same person, yet in different times.' She told him: 'I've no proof. Not yet.' She looked sideways at Charles, noticing, though, he also had hair as dark as James, almost as black as Eable and Elkanah's.

'I'm so sorry to have laughed, to have doubted you, but, you must admit, your tale does sound more than a little strange. When, though, was it you last travelled way beyond the mirage?'

'When I flew to Alexandria, for Amy's baptism.'

'Amy?'

'Amy is my friends' baby girl; they all live in Egypt .'

'Didn't James go with you?'

She explained how he chose not to be with her. 'He attended the Academy, to do with your wood engravings.'

'Ooh, yes ... it was quite an honour for me -.'

278

Sam explained how she felt at a loose end. 'I did happen to see Eable, but I didn't sleep with him. Not then.' She told Charles she was very nearly in a three-some, with Elkanah and his second cousin, Todd. 'But I stopped him. I suppose it was shocking of me to sleep with Elkanah, for I was already in a steady relationship with James, although we weren't then engaged.'

'Why then?'

'The truth is, with a passion, I miss those men, especially Elkanah; they aren't just friends, but ...'

'... but they are more than special?'

'Are you sure you don't want some wine?'

'All right, I give in.' Charles indicated by placing his fore finger and thumb together. 'Just a very small one, only to be socialable, then, Samantha. Okay?'

She nodded, acquiring a fresh glass.

He called through, stating how his own Volvo was parked outside; he did not want much drink if he was to drive home.

Sam, remembering about his late Hannah, understood.

Emerging from the kitchen, she heard him, in a flurry of words, plucking up courage to ask: 'What if I wished to travel way beyond the mirage, Samantha? Could I actually meet that Eable fellow?' He stared at her with a lifted eyebrow, waiting for her long coming answer.

Handing him his half glass of wine, Sam sipped her own. 'I certainly wouldn't recommend it. Not for a single minute.'

'Why is that?'

'I'll tell you why. I heard how some soldiers from the Rifle Brigade, which was my dad's old regiment during the last World War, never returned back into our own time.'

'They died?'

'I heard how they became ill; it seems nobody was strong enough to help them. Those soldiers simply passed away.'

'And yet it doesn't scare you?'

Sam said not. She presumed someone, such as Charles, never set out to desire her, but, as she spoke of the ancient life, she began describing, imagining herself watching those in the cold cave, of her seeing them; he, drinking, had savoured her perfume in his own nostrils. 'Samantha, this Eable ... he really does look so like our James?'

'Hannah's diaries, although I haven't actually seen them, didn't they describe Eable? Weren't they quite enough for you?'

'Whatever happened to my wife before our wedding, I'm beginning, wondering now about you.'

'Me?' Sam slightly turned her head. 'Oh, Charles, you hardly know anything concerning me.' She became thoughtful before relenting with a slight nod: 'You may as well know, I actually do have some photos.'

'Photographs of ...'

'Of Eable.'

He, in one, downed the wine, setting down his empty glass. 'Are you serious?'

'Of course I am. I've actually hidden them well, packed them away in my one of my drawers, in my bedroom.'

Curious, Charles, at first almost became hesitant, but stared: 'May I, um, could I perhaps be allowed to see those photographs?' He was only interested to see the one of Eable. Nothing more.

'Ooh, I don't know. I first had a snap of the cameleer. Eable also photographed his own Hunter, too. Even so, most of the photos of him also includes Todd, Elkanah and of me, too. There are none of Eable just on his own.'

'Whatever, will you still at least show me?'

'I dunno, for, well, I'm not exactly proud ...'

He interrupted: 'You can trust me -.'

'It's nothing to do with trust.' She frowned, still unsure quite what to do, yet, if he only wanted to see Eable -.'

'We are both grown ups ... we're also consenting adults, aren't we?' Charles was also likely to become her future father-in-law, which Sam felt it might complicate further issues. 'All right. I suppose so. Even so, it depicts some of me I'd rather not show you; Charles, are you listening?'

Charles stated he had no worries

'But a few snaps shows me with Elkanah ...any nice feelings you may have had about me, could well turn sour.'

'Listen? Frankly, I couldn't care less; it's only Eable I need to see.'

'Yeah, but if I disclose them to you, swear you'll never breathe a word to another living soul, not to James, no-one. You have to promise me all over again? Say it!'

He did. Charles raised his dark eyes heavenwards, exhaling a long exasperating sigh. 'I have already promised you, haven't I? Wasn't it quite enough for you?'

Instead of waiting in the living room, he rose from his seat, trailing behind her into the bedroom. Sam glanced back towards him; they did not speak. From within a drawer she pulled out a blue envelope, full of the said snaps. She sat on the edge of the bed, she signalling for him to sit beside her.

Charles glanced down at the bed, remembering those far off days when he would make advances to his new bride, yet, in vain; he wondered which side Sam slept. 'Where we are now, is this your side of the bed, Samantha?'

'Yeah. Why?'

'Just wondered.' He tried to imagine how it must be to be with her, yet he offered no other words; she was about to show him the much coveted photographs of Eable, of her with those guys, way beyond the mirage, yet Sam pressed them tight to her chest before whispering: 'Here ...' he heard her quickly say before she might change her mind.

Charles, as soon as he saw the pictures of her, as she began again to secret them away, he begged to at least keep one; yet, she remained adamant, telling him a definite no.

'A torn copy showing only Eable, then? Samantha ...'

'No way. You're asking too much.'

His hands, just as she remembered Abe's, began to tremble slightly. He asked: 'I don't want to be with you in the same way any dad would, Samantha. You understand what I am asking, what I'm wanting?'

'I am.'

' When you told me, after the funeral, you'd always be here for me, well, perhaps I misunderstood your kindness?'

She nodded. 'Maybe you did?'

Charles began to whisper her name as he could no longer resist her, yet he half panicked, for neither could resist the other. Sam, just as she could not help herself with Eable, with Elkanah, with Abe, so she held Charles tightly for a long time, not pulling away. As the length of his fingers threaded through her auburn hair, he becoming anxious for her. Within her whole being, Sam wanted to deny him, yet he experienced so many barren years with his late wife. He held her tight to himself while her arms wrapped around his torso. She knew this was not any romance as with James.

'You're incredible, so beautiful,' he declared, in his gentle arms. 'What now?'

She shook her head, declaring: 'Nothing. '

'I am somewhat scared I may well have disrupted your relationship with my son.'

'Ah, no. Not a chance.'

'All right, but after what has only just happened to us here, where do you and I go from here now?'

'Straight back to where we were at the beginning of the evening, Charles, you know?'

Like as with a little lost kid, he bemoaned: 'You mean, not ever again?'

'That's exactly right.'

'Oh, Samantha, after our time together, you simply cannot deprive me in future.'

'You came here to clear up the mystery regarding Eable and … and, yes, I can deny you.'

Forty-six year old Charles abandoned his post as an art teacher, concentrating upon his wood engravings; he sold up his large Surrey home and removed, without the inquisitive Tilly, into the half vacant pad over The Gallery.

Although a firm date in August became not set, in the light of Hannah's untimely death, Sam considered their wedding should become a quieter affair, but Charles Samuels shook his head; he declared it ought to become, like his, a day to remember.

Chapter 17

With he and Sam engaged, James planned for a settled life in the Earls Court neighbourhood where he presumed they would continue living. He inwardly hoped for them both to reliably live eating wholesome food, occasionally drinking a fine wine, he working as an accomplished artist. Children were never on his agenda.

Sam's mother had other ideas. As soon as her Samantha flashed an engagement ring, Daisy Webb immediately put the matrimonial wheels in motion, imagining her only daughter with a glorious wedding, she organising a guest list as long as an arm. Nevertheless, following the Samuels' tragic loss, whatever the parents' input, however much she tried to manipulate the couple otherwise, Samantha dug her heels in, declaring their once-in-a-lifetime wedding ought to remain a quiet, intimate affair. Instead of a large Catholic ceremony in either an abbey or even in the lofty Westminster Cathedral, Sam opted for a tranquil occasion in London's Mayfair's Claridges with a Church's blessing at a later stage? James, who seemed to have little say in the matrimonial matters, did consider Mayfair to be a good idea. Much of their engagement day became celebrated in Claridges' bar. Their honeymoon to be in Egypt's Alexandria, was again sorted without him – a special wedding gift from Adjo and Paula.

Following the public announcement of James and Samantha's engagement, life, particularly for Daisy Webb, became a whirlwind of plans and preparations. Sam's wedding dress, her going away outfit, a professional photographer, a wedding cake and the whole host of flowers, along with seemingly a hundred and one other issues upon her own mother's 'to do' list.

One grey afternoon, Sam jumped into her run about town car, to drive down to Wimbledon, to call in on her mother in the old family home. 'I'm desperately in need of a nice cup of tea,' she declared with a long sigh. Soon removed from the kitchen to the living room, they flopped together on an old squashy sofa; Sam kicked away her pinching shoes, massaging each of her toes. 'Ooh, I've trailed around two bridal boutiques, shops and even along Regent's Street, yet I don't seem to find the right wedding gown for me.'

'Nothing at all, dear?'

'Um, yes, I did see a long slinky one in pure white; it was so pretty with a lot of glitter and sparkle, particularly around the bodice, but, with my auburn hair colouring, it seemed as if I was wearing a posh shroud.' Her heart shaped face appeared crest fallen, she wishing her mum had gone along with her. 'Honestly, that dress did absolutely nothing for me.'

Her mother frowning, remained unusually quiet for a moment or two. She wondered if her daughter ought to be wearing pure white, anyway. 'It symbolises purity and virginity; the same with a veil over the bride's face ...' Her mother's expression changed to a slight grin.

'I don't quite see you as the blushing bride, do you, Samantha, sweetheart?'

'Living with James, it hardly places me in that category, eh?' Sam's smile switched to a giggle. 'I wouldn't think, though, many bother about all that virginal stuff nowadays.' She inwardly reflected, if only her mother knew the half concerning her time with Mick, before being with those ancient guys way beyond the mirage, Daisy would probably have thrown a blue fit if she ever discovered Sam's one time only with Charles Samuels, it just was not worth the upset.

Her mother hesitated. 'Samantha, listen. Underneath my bed is a large pale blue box there's a gold inscription on the lid; I know you're fairly tired but, please, dear, pop upstairs, to fetch it down here for me?'

Sam nipped through the hall, up the familiar carpeted stairs and into her parents' large bedroom; smelling from lavender, it always did. Her parent's private sanctuary, out of bounds to her once she became an inquisitive teenager; she knelt down by her mother's side of the parents' bed, to peer beneath where she discovered the said box. She slid it out, bringing it carefully down the stairs; blowing a little dust away, she placed it on a coffee table in front of her smiling mother. 'This is obviously what you were after,' Sam stated, desperately itching to know its contents.

Daisy Webb, with an elated nostalgia, stared again at the cover, at its ornate gold initials of H & D flamboyantly intertwined. Slowly, she lifted away the flat lid, gently parting the layers of old cream tissue within. 'Here, look inside, Samantha. This beautiful gown was my very own wedding dress. A niece of mine asked for it, but no. I've actually saved it for you all these years.'

Sam gasped, not having expected quite so much. 'For me?' Her bright green eyes widened in total amazement: 'Ooh, mum, I really don't know quite what to say … it's … it's magnificent.' she exclaimed as the stunningly long garment was gradually lifted, to be held before her.

'I also had a very slim figure when I married your father … 'She continued to inform Sam how the gown was specially designed, fashioned just for her by Norman Hartnell, the fellow who was commissioned to make dresses for royalty.

In the grey of both wartime and post war Britain, with clothes' rationing in force and the cities splattered with bomb sites, the dazzling creations of Sir Norman Hartnell became a vision from a fairytale, unattainable to all but a handful of the wealthiest.

Daisy kept the gown folded away in layers of tissue paper; that elegant dress with its beautiful fabric, combined with its sumptuous embellishments, was made by Hartnell's famous team of embroiderers. They were the women who stitched a tiny blue bow into the lining so the bride would always have something "blue".

'It cost my own father the princely sum of thirty pounds … that was a whole bunch of money in those far off days.'

With the 'father of the bride' being the one who normally forks out for his daughter's wedding, it obviously made Samantha a little curious as to how her maternal granddaddy was able to pay for such an expensive Norman Hartnell bridal gown. Daisy never mentioned what he did for a living; Sam only remembered him as an elderly pensioner. Dare she ask, or may she be told it did not concern the likes of her?

'It's more than a gorgeous dress,' Sam continued.

'Yes, it definitely is outstandingly beautiful. I saved it all these years, hoping one day you'd wear it.'

'Really?' Sam wondered why her mother never mentioned the frock before, when she, Sam, was previously engaged, yet she remained tight lipped.

Daisy smiled.

'May I ask something quite personal?'

Her mother's smile changed into a slight frown. 'Well, there's nothing to stop you asking.'

Sam wanted to know where her granddad acquired his finances.

'Oh, is that all?' Daisy admitted her own beloved father, John William Flowers, Jnr., came from a family who made rich pickings from brewing strong beer, causing them to be able to live in some style. 'Granddad's own aunt was the wealthy Kate Mann; in 1924 Kate joined forces with the strong Crossman brewery, to buy out granddad's "Flowers' Keg Bitter", giving him a small financial fortune for those particular times.'

'I only remember granddad, mum, as a quiet old gentleman, he sitting, staring into the flickering flames of a log fire, saying very little.'

'My dad never really recovered from the sad passing of his own wife, but he loved you to bits, Samantha.'

'You didn't mind my asking about your dad?'

'Of course not. Why should I?' She wondered if her daughter knew how they, her own parents, met.

'In Ireland?'

'Yes. If your old granddad was alive now, he'd tell you it was all to do with Flynn, one of the Leprechauns in a smart green jacket which didn't quite do up around his expanding middle; upon the little guys feet were huckaback shoes, already for dancing, but that was just plain silly folklore!' Daisy laughed at the fictitious nonsense. 'Now, Samantha. It was on the third day of September in 1939, just before the break out of the last war.' She told her daughter how Henry was in a local bakery, purchasing two fresh jam doughnuts, when the confectioner declared they were the very last ones … there were no more doughnuts remaining. 'Seeing the doughnuts, my Henry decided to buy both, but, hearing my disappointment, offered to share his with me.'

'And that was that?'

'Not quite. It was a lovely sunny day. We sat together on a park bench, a seat for two, sharing his doughnuts.'

'So, was that your first date together?'

'It was indeed. Anyway, darling, back to this particular wedding gown …'

Sam could hardly take her eyes away from the fine details of the dress. 'May I try it on, please?' she asked. 'I promise you I'll be most careful.'

'I know you shall.'

Sam promptly stripped off her T-shirt and jeans.

'Don't step into it. You need to pop the frock over your head and pull it down. Here. Let me give you a hand, Samantha; now, what do you honestly think about it? Do you really and truly like the gown?'

Wearing it, Sam bustled through into the large hall, admiring herself in its full length mirror, swishing the long, ivory skirt with a rhythmically whoosh-whoosh one way before another. Daisy watching her adult child, with only a mother's heart, became proud.

'Like it? Ooh, I adore it! It's simply perfect. See? It's fitting me like a glove?'

'It is, isn't it?'

'Yes, I'd love to wear this on my wedding day?'

'I very nearly didn't show you, for I thought you wanted a new frock. It's your dress now, dear. Maybe, who knows, one day, if you have a daughter of your own, she'll wear it, too?'

Henry kept popping in and out from the garden, muttering something or other about the begonias. He, upon one of his excursions, happened to have noticed Samantha wearing Daisy's wedding dress. 'That's a pretty frock,' he remarked. 'Your mother married me in one just like it!'

Sam grinned. 'Fancy you remembering this, daddy?'

'Ah, you know, just because I'm a bloke, doesn't mean I forget such things? Now, where the devil did I leave my new gardening catalogue? It has to be somewhere around, doesn't it?'

When as a young bride, Daisy carried a long bouquet, mostly filled with roses and carnations. Sam thought about choosing the exact same, but an award winning London florist suggested smaller, a more fashionable posy. In Sam's auburn hair, professionally curled up on top, she decided to wear a diamond tiara – a family heirloom left from her late great grandmother who went down with the Titanic. Something old, something new, something borrowed, something blue.

'The 'blue' is that wee bow stitched into the lining of the gown,' Daisy, wiping way her happy tears from her damp cheek, reminded her, stating, lifting the hem of the skirt. 'See, darling?'

Having written their own vows, the day of James and Samantha's wedding arrived. Instead of the Rolls Royce her parents desired for her, Sam opted for a beribboned white Mercedes, yet with windows made from a tinted glass. Its driver arrived to collect Sam and her proudly, puffed up father. The torrential morning rain stopped and the warm August sunshine broke through the fluffy white clouds, turning an unpromising day into a beautiful afternoon.

'The wedding car's waiting outside in the drive, Samantha,' Henry called up. 'Are you now ready, sweetheart?'

She unlocked the door, emerging from which became her previous bedroom. When she was a newborn, the room was originally Sam's pretty nursery before becoming her big bedroom when she emerged a little kid. Developing as a sometimes difficult teenager, she was scolded to become more tidy. Right up until her eighteenth year when she entered nurse training, to reside in the nurses' home, her parents always referred to the large pink room as "Samantha's bedroom". Hence, it seemed quite fitting she should be married from there. The mobile hairdresser and a make-up artists had gone. All the men, including James, were promptly shooed away; Paula declared it was bad luck for the groom to see the bride before the wedding service, so off he went. Her dad was not even allowed into the kitchen, to make himself a big, unhealthy fry up; he surely did not want the wedding gown stinking from the aroma of bacon fat? He nevertheless constantly complained he was absolutely famished. The lovely 'Mother of the Bride' and Sam's best friend Paula, who was the stunning matron-of-honour, left.

Sam stood feeling quite alone at the top of the stairs; she, outstandingly beautiful, took even Henry's breath away. 'Ooh, Samantha, my darling child, you look an absolute dream … a real corker!' He stretched out his hand for her, but she refused him, shaking her head.

'What ever is wrong?' he asked. Surely, he wondered, she was not going to dump James, just as she had poor Mick?

She gulped. 'I'm just about scared witless, daddy,' she confessed as she finally decided to walk slowly down those familiar twelve stairs.

Henry Webb was at least relieved she was down the stairs, he remembering those long ago days when she would have been told not to slide down the banisters; now she was a bride, to be given away to another man. He ran a finger around his tight collar before fiddling again with the white carnation in his buttonhole; he smiled at her: 'Oh, is that all? I heard on the grapevine that almost every bride becomes a bit nervous, but you, Samantha, you'll be just fine; come on, now, for your James shall be wondering where on earth you are. I'll bet he's scared, too?'

Her green eyes widened. 'What if he is as worried as me? What if his best man has lost my wedding ring? What if James also changes his mind and dumps me?'

'Now, pack in all that crazy nonsense, Samantha.'

Sam thought of Mick, how she rejected him, so hurting his and her own feelings, of Eable, too, but above all, of her out-of-the reach Elkanah whom she adored with a passion. 'What if I am really making a frightful blunder by marrying James? What if ... what if ..?' She felt as if her words were fizzling out, as if she could not quite think straight.

He beamed, interrupting: 'It's all your pre-wedding nerves, Samantha. That's all.'

'Were you like it when you married mummy?'

Henry reflected for a moment or two, how his own Daisy confessed to being nervous, all those years before.

'No, but I'll tell you when I was really and truly scared stiff. '

Sam, all agog, became eager to know.

'It was when I was in a troupe ship, being packed off to North Africa, to fight Rommel's lot, not knowing if I'd ever see my new wife, my wonderful Daisy ever again?'

The temperamental driver, for yet a second time, rang the door bell with its annoying chimes. Henry opened up the heavy oak door. 'What is it now?' he demanded.

The guy touched the brim of his cap. 'Sorry to trouble you,' he apologised, 'but, I was simply wondering, shall I need to wait here much longer, sir?'

'Yes, you probably shall.' Henry almost snapped, for had he not paid the guy extra well? 'And you shall wait for just as long as it takes ... 'He added: 'My daughter shall be out in a tick.'

The uniformed fellow shook his head, to sigh, returning to sit back in his driver's seat, he regularly drumming on either the steering wheel or glancing at his own wristwatch.

Sam, holding her small bouquet of mixed roses and carnations, told Henry: 'All right, daddy. I'm ready now.'

'Good girl!'

In the back seat of the wedding car, Henry took hold of Sam's well manicured hand, offering one piece of sound fatherly advice: 'Remember, sweetheart, when you are a married woman, you leave us, your mother and father, and cling to your husband. Okay?' He told her she would then belong to James.

'And he to me, too, dad?'

The official photographer was still waiting; a magnificently slender Samantha, five feet six and glorious in a Norman Hartnell's vintage creation, posed with a beaming smile for the popping flashbulbs. Easily having been groomed to perfection, Samantha Anne Webb moved to stand in the entrance, gripping her dad's arm, followed close on her tail by Paula who quietly declared: 'You're late, Sam ... half thought you'd chosen to do a runner!'

Henry ignored Paula's slight tease; he smiled, briefly glancing down at his lovely daughter, taking again her arm in his. 'Ready, Samantha, darling?' he whispered. 'No doubts?'

'None now.' Sam smiled. 'Just one thing ... '

'Oh, gosh! What now?'

'Thank you for being the best dad ever.'

Sam noticed his Irish eyes a little teary, he wiping away a damp cheek. 'Ah, now, come on before you have me blubbering; here we go ... big breath in ... right foot forward, and ...'

The talented organist, beginning to play Sam's favourite piece by Vivaldi. The small congregation rose as she regally entered, advancing towards the waiting and worried James who evidently seemed grateful she arrived, stepped forward – no more doubts; Samantha was devoted to him, simply as he adored her. Henry left her, he joining to sit with his lovely wife, he holding her hand.

'We are gathered here to witness the marriage of Samantha Anne Webb and James Eable Samuels, to share in their joy. Marriage is not to be entered upon or thought of lightly or selfishly, but responsibly in love ...' The service droned on until it was declared to the groom: 'You may kiss the bride'. A smiling James took her in his masculine arms, gently kissing her; the congregation stood again to clap, although her mother searched for a lace hankie, weeping with joy.

Having signed the Register, Sam, no longer Samantha Anne Webb, emerged on the arm of her husband as Mrs James Samuels. The couple were showered with pink, blue and silver confetti horseshoes. 'I couldn't be happier,' she whispered to him.

'Me, too.'

During their exit, Sam leaned across, asking the driver to make a detour to the Catholic cemetery; he was able to drive through the opened gates. 'Please, wait here for us,' she instructed. 'My husband and I shall be back in next to no time. Okay?'

He gave a nod, hoping he would not be kept quite as long as before the wedding.

She, holding tight James' hand, told him how she needed to call where Hannah's body became laid to rest; located, the new bride slowly placed her own pretty wedding bouquet on his own late mother's grave. 'Rest in sweet peace, Hannah,' Samantha whispered, and, holding up her long bridal skirt just a little, genuflected.

As young newly weds, the couple used every private moment, to simply to be alone. Before their honeymoon in Egypt, they stayed for a couple of days in their Earls Court apartment. Their first whole day was mostly making love with a greater intensity, before talking over their future.

On the day before their planning to fly to Alexandria, they needed to pack enough belongings for the whole week, not as two individuals, but as a married couple; she secretly hoped to see Eable of 1105 BC. Sam, married, she half felt as though she was somewhat cheating upon him, her ancient lover. However, the relationship, once shared with him in the guest annexe, became perhaps a fantasy, a delusion in an odd time warp. They made no real commitment to each other. Her commitment switched to James.

Those photographs taken of the toothless cameleer and of old Hunter hid those of Sam, in the guest annexe, of her in certain poses; one such image, snapped by Eable, did not hide her with Elkanah. The prints became hidden in a small personal drawer; she became convinced James would never bother about them in there. The only local who had sight of them snaps was Charles Samuels; the sight of them caused him to fall into Sam's bed. As the newly weds began to pack for their honeymoon, James asked if they had enough items for the entire week's honeymoon ahead, their dream holiday in Egypt about to come true.

'I know what you women are probably like, always needing more.' He noticed Sam had though very few undies.'Now, let me see, I noticed you keep more in this little drawer by the side of your bed, don't you?'

'Yes, all right. I'll see to it.'

James stated he knew all the extras which needed to go into the main luggage, how he boasted he was good at packing. Beneath her undies, he spotted the large blue envelope containing those particular pictures. Sam breathlessly snatched hold of it, to rapidly stuff it again in her drawer, but James promptly asked to know about that which she rapidly concealed.

'It's nothing much more than some girlie stuff,' she lied, but he managed to gently grab it from her hand.

'Don't, James … you really mustn't see in there!' Sam raced to exclaim: 'Give it back to me.'

Too late, he opened the envelope; thunderstruck, he glared in shocked amazement at the immodest pictures of his new wife, the lovely woman he thought he knew so well; he saw her in compromising poses with men. She, at first, tried to feign an indifference, yet, to say James was shocked became a gross under statement – he went into meltdown with her for retaining such pictures; he claimed he was upset at having made a total commitment to Sam, she suddenly a stranger to him. He declared, had he known of those, he would not have married such a woman. Sam pleaded with him to understand, but he stated how the camera did not lie. Emotionally, he pulled from her, sitting himself on an upright chair, folding his arms across his chest. Still in no mood to be pleasant, he half refused to listen, but, in reverse, stated: 'So, Samantha, how are you going to worm your way out of this one? You were once a practising nurse-cum-midwife. I know nurses aren't all that well paid, but was this how you've supplemented your living expenses, as a cheap tart, huh?'

He seemed to remember how, one of the students from her nursing set, abandoned hospital work to become a dancer, she baptised in Champagne, at the famous Windmill Theatre; he presumed Sam was supplementing her meagre salary with porn, hence the snaps? All the time she must have lied, saying her money was from her late granddad. It was as if James did not know the woman he married.

He watched Sam gulp; why, he wondered, did she offer so few words? 'So, go on. Speak up, Samantha!'

'What … what is it you actually want me to say?' she half stammered out her question.

He deeply scowled. 'Try the truth, for a start. Go on. I thought we'd agreed, no secrets between us, eh? But you … oh, I just don't know any more?'

She lowered her eyes, half remaining silent, not unlike a naughty kid instead of a grown woman.

'How's this so-called marriage relationship going to work when you keep snaps of you and those other guys … you posing like … like nothing more than a cheap nothing in a foreign red light area?'

She ran her fingers through her curly auburn hair where there were tangles. 'Honestly. It wasn't exactly like that, James. Truly. And, anyway, what do you know about foreign red light areas?'

'What? Don't be stupid. Everyone has heard of them.' He offered her an ultimatum, wanting to know who the men were, but she shook her head, telling him no-one. Over and over, with a rush of his incessant questions, he demanded, if she ever remembered, the men's names until she finally blurted out: 'Eable. His name's Eable and the other one is his older brother Elkanah. The third man was Todd. If I remember rightly, he was their second cousin. I only met him once …'

James deeply scowled. 'When was all this?'

'It was after Amy's baptism, I felt at a loose end, so I travelled way beyond the mirage.' Sam stated: 'It's where I again met up with Elkanah. He and I were beginning to become close, hoping Eable would join us, but he was over the other part of old Ramah with Elihu, their sick granddad. We'd already seen Todd in a cave.'

'Is all this crazy, all this weird stuff just in your mind?'

'No. Although it doesn't exactly put me in a very good light as Amy's godmother, does it?'

'No. Not a bit. Does Paula know about all this stuff regarding Eable?'

'Grief, no. I met Eable at the breakfast time, after I'd been to the Ramah's local farmers' market for food. I didn't have enough time with him, as it was the moment for me to return home.'

James became mad when he heard Eable's name on her lips; she sobbed on and off for nearly half an hour, showing her reddened, swollen eyes. He lifted his chin. 'Are you going to lie to me any more?'

'I swear I am definitely not lying to you. Not a single, solitary word. You, if you'll quieten down for a moment, James, if you'd come down from your high horse, to listen to me, I'll do my best to explain thread to needle …'

James shook his head, picked up his clothes and dressed himself before throwing a white towelling robe towards her. 'When you and I make love … when we are together, you invariably call me ''Eable''. So, I'm no fool; instead of thinking about me, is it that ancient bloke you're imagining you are with? In your own strange mind … in your own imagination, it is still as if you're with him, eh?' He snapped at her, yet her nerves felt as if they were pieces of elastic, stretched out at breaking point. 'Who else has seen these pictures? Anyone?'

Sam, plagued by the images, shrugged. 'No-one much really.'

'What do you mean by "no-one much really"? Who? Are you going to tell me exactly who?'

She articulated how she dare not.

'I think you had better dare! Go on, Samantha, explain.'

'The three men in the photos, they saw the pictures and … and Abe …and, and -.'

'Go on! Tell me who else saw them?' He fleetingly wondered if maybe she sold some copies to a city of London firm which specialised in soft porn, but she told him no.

'Who then?'

Sam asked him not to raise his voice. 'Promise me, if I tell you, you'll say nothing to him? Promise me faithfully you won't over react?'

He firmly agreed, but his thick eyebrows raised, almost touching his dark hair as he heard her state: 'Your dad.'

'What's this?' he quizzed. 'Some sort of a strange joke?'

'No. Charles saw them.'

'Are you serious? My father, of all people? How come?'

Sam nodded, telling him how, with his dad, it was as much emotional as it was physical, yet he was affected by seeing her with Elkanah.

' The filthy dog!' He exclaimed, asking in an anger: 'Whatever happened?'

Sam, upset, shrugged.

'Tell me,' he demanded. 'No more of this cock and bull; be straight with me.'

Silent, she reached for a box of tissues, to wipe her eyes, to blow her nose. He, at the same time, glared, loudly again raising his voice, telling her to get on with the ambiguity of the tale.

Softly, Sam quietly asked him not to yell for she was not use to such verbal abuse; nevertheless, she continued:

'It was just after your mum died; Charles was asking me about Eable. You see, Hannah wrote in one of her diaries about her and me, how we both once knew the guy.'

'Eable?'

'Yeah.' Sam softly hesitated. She looked up in James' dark eyes before continuing: 'Your dad was keen to know about the ancient fellow, for he wondered if your mum was unfaithful; he believed only I could tell him. I eventually showed him a photo of Eable and one thing led onto another. Nothing was ever planned. I swear; it only happened once. Finito.'

'But, you took him into our bedroom, of all places?'

Sam choked on more tears. 'Your mum always denied him affection; he needed me.'

She, however, simply cried out, pleading to James: 'Let's stop all this ridiculous nonsense.' Sam's heart pounded within her chest, she longing to sob out how it was James she loved, yet he told her he heard all that guff before; he wanted to know about the night she spent with Charles. If she did not say, he would go and have it out with him, once and for all.

'No. You gave me your word. You promised.'

James claimed he also promised marriage vows, which he then considered were a terrible mistake, he just going along with the flow, with all she and Daisy wanted, instead of he simply remaining as an engaged man.

Her green eyes glistened with more tears. 'You don't mean that?'

'Don't I?'

Sam swallowed hard. 'May we stop all this now?'

'Not yet, Samantha, for you also slept with the guy who was your first fiancee, didn't you?'

How could Sam ever forget the times she spent with her beloved Mick? She still missed him so much, she would sometimes scream out his name when others were with her way beyond the mirage, with Charles, with James, too. Sam told him how, with Mick, it obviously was not a celibate relationship; what had he expected? 'I'm not a nun!'

'You certainly aren't, not by any stretch of the imagination. I reckon I'm just in a long line of lovers, some of whom you probably can't even remember. Oh, no. Our marriage,' he taunted her, saying, 'well, for me, it's all been a shocking mistake.'

Sam wrapped her white robe around herself, tightening it with its matching belt, depressed at spending time arguing, speaking out why she thrice went missing. It was hard explaining about Eable; tensions appeared to worsen at the sound of his name until suddenly, although shocked, he seemed it wise to abandon his mad fury, regaining some sort of an equilibrium, with his elbows resting on his knees, covering his own face, yet he hearing only as much as she dare; at last, she had half unburdened herself. 'So far, I've had to keep way beyond the mirage to myself. I couldn't tell hardly anyone about Elkanah, Eable and the others like Todd and Abe, all way beyond the mirage or I should, at the best, be humiliated. My own parents would have had me, somewhat delusional, booked in with either a psychologist or with hypnotherapy. 'I am not overreacting when I tell you, James, I also believe Eable was you, and you are that man, but in differing time zones.' Sam looked into his dark eyes; he stared back at her.

Gathering up the pictures, she attempting to push them away, but James insisted: 'Show me those once again, Sam.'

She shook her head, refusing. 'No. They really need to be destroyed. I shouldn't have kept them this long. I was very wrong. I've made so many idiotic mistakes, yet, I cannot lose you; please, don't hate me, James.'

'I don't.' Thinking of his own fragile heart condition, he suddenly breathed to quieten himself.

'I should really rip up the photographs, I suppose … it is only, if you first take a close look and very carefully, if you try to ignore the men and me, but look at the backgrounds, there are only silvery mirages instead of exterior walls. Even those of Hunter. See? Look … look at it, for Hunter was also way beyond the mirage.'

James could see all she was driving at. How could he, though, not imagine such issues between his new wife and all those other guys who became strangers to him? And there remained the sensitive matter of her with Charles. It became too much for him to digest. He stood from his chair, searching for his own door keys; he promptly walked from the living room into the darkly panelled oak hall, making for his black top coat.

'What? Where are you going?'

'Out.'

'I gathered that much, but this is London and it's getting late …and …' Before Sam could utter another word, he left.

James, not unlike Henry, seemed to be a man who needed to walk off his upsets, his angry moments; unlike her, he could no longer simply sit and talk.

Remembering the past, Sam worried concerning their future together. Throwing aside her white towelling robe, she rapidly showered before dressing into something suitable, perhaps for travelling; she wondered if James might ever return.

It was late when a relieved Sam heard James' key turn in the front door.

He mindlessly wiped his feet as he unbuttoned his overcoat, finally throwing it across the upholstered seat of a Queen Anne style hall chair, he strolling through into the living room where Sam remained curled up, resting quietly on the sofa.

'Hello, pet,' he said as their gazes met.

She longed to again be held. Sam half smiled up at him through tired tears, even forgiving him for referring to her as his 'pet'.

James, only a breath apart from her, nodded, stroking along the curves of her pale face: 'We'll always deal with everything, of all of our future problems, together, eh?'

She promised.

'Yeah. Okay. Anyway, we're going to miss our flight to Alexandria, if we do not get a move on; we haven't even finished packing, as yet, have we?' He, to patch up the quarrels, kissed her and as passionately as ever.

Her heart, her life was belonging to him.

Chapter 18

Sam, quieter than usual, exhaled a massive sigh; making up after their first quarrel became a rhapsodic moment of victories over defeat. Their time in the hotel's honeymoon suite meant invariably sleeping late.

Obliging hosts, Adjo and Paula affectionately arranged to join the couple for an evening meal. Dinner amidst soft flickering candlelight and gentle background music, became a pleasant affair. Sam appeared sophisticated and chic in a show stopper bottle-green strapless, maxi skirted dress. She cherished James kissing her deliciously bare shoulders, he having brushed aside where her shining auburn hair touched. He felt chuffed to be with her, she, nursing a sparkling Montanez Cava wine; as ever, Sam became a bliss to be in their presence. With soft and easy conversations, she invariably caused Paula to sense a serenity about herself.

It was the third morning when Sam, fresh from the shower, quietly sat on the edge of the bed, towel drying her curly hair, pondering if she was right in keeping silent so long, by not previously informing James concerning her time way beyond the mirage.

She felt irate, permitting Eable to wheedle his way into her life, he becoming their dark shadow across in her marriage; yet, she needed to be open with James. Nevertheless, maybe Eable demanded one last chance? Otherwise, Sam considered she may always be left speculating the two guys – the ancient and the present. She knew her own future stretched out with her husband, but, within a mental turmoil, it may release her secrets? Foolhardy, she, in some way, needed to know if they, Eable and James, were the forever entwined? Making love with James ... making love with Eable ... were they, she dreamt, the same, yet within different times? Dare she risk discovering?

'A penny for your thoughts, Sam?' James offered, with a broad smile. 'You seemed to be miles away in all your thoughts.'

'Maybe.' Noticing the time, her large green eyes opened wide as she gasped, deciding they both had better buck up. 'I think we ought to move ourselves or we'll miss the hotel's breakfast time.'

After her continental and he tucked into a full English breakfast, they moved to sit out on the hotel's patio for about an hour; together, they remained under an oversized white umbrella, to shield themselves from the overhead hot sun. Sam, with her auburn hair piled in curls upon top, she appeared as impeccable as ever, wearing an Irish linen trouser suit in an ivory cream. James beamed; proud, he whispered to her how she looked a million dollars. By coffee time they were again joined by their hosts.

'Hello, you two,' smiled Paula, looking upwards . 'Our Egyptian sun is becoming quite fierce, huh?'

'Yes.' Sam smiled, giving a little nod. 'It is just a bit! Anyway, where's baby Amy? I haven't seen hide nor hair of my little godchild since we arrived.'

Paula's happy dark eyes sparkled at her speaking about Amy, for she so enjoyed motherhood. 'Our little miss is off with her nanny. Having such a fine, living in nanny gives us both a bit of a break now and again, although our daughter is such a good baby ... she really is a joy, so lovely.'

'Give her a big hug from us?'

'Will do.'

'Incidentally, I was wondering if James and I might have a bit of a time out. At such short notice, Adjo, would your kitchen staff mind packing up some food for us, please?'

'No problem!' He told her how they would not need anything unpalatable which may quickly become rancid under the sun. 'Plenty of fresh bread and local fruits, huh?'

Back in their honeymoon suite, it became Sam who began to pack up some overnight belongings, placing them in one of their backpacks.

'I thought, Sam, we were only going out somewhere or other, for a picnic lunch? What's with the back-packs?' James turned to stare, as if a little unsettled by it. He asked: 'Do we really need to take the proverbial kitchen sink, too?'

Sam slightly smiled by the "kitchen sink" remark. She remembered her dad saying something similar to Daisy; she would always say the same: 'It's only just in case ...'

'... just in case of what?'

'Well, I dunno really.' Sam narrowed her green eyes. 'I'm not some sort of a psychic.'

Sam remembered the king-sized bed and the two-seater couch; Eable sat on it, sometimes eating from it, as well as making love across it. There were few words explaining how she felt for him. Oh, she certainly did loved him, yet she always secretly adored Elkanah with the deepest of passions. She, in her London apartment, once experienced a tension migraine, remembering how the late Hannah Samuels told how Eable made her pregnant. Perhaps he had?

Umpteen thoughts buzzed around her head, all following the wedding ceremony, so unexpected. The minister who conducted her and James' wedding read from a service book: 'Such marriage is the foundation of the true family and when blessed with children ...'

Blessed with children? There were occasions during her adult life, especially when she worked as a midwife, when Sam longed for a baby, hardly tolerating the frustration of being without; she, with James, never discussed such issues. She wondered if their honeymoon was a good time?

'No.'

'Hold on!' The bright sparkle from her eyes dulled. 'Don't you remember what was said during our wedding ceremony?'

James became adamant. 'You and I, Sam, are only just setting out in life together, still young and adjusting to one another. A kid would change everything for us.'

Sam, with her lower lip jutting out, pouted; it always happened if she did not immediately get her own way. She also, as an only one, quickly learned the sulk; when she was a small child, she knew how to wind her dad around her little finger.

Sam and James enjoyed being together since way before the day of their engagement, she also with Charles, Elkanah and Abe, too; yet, with them it became different. 'But, how should you feel if I'm already pregnant?'

'How should I feel?' He half closed his dark eyes to think. 'Naturally, Sam, I suppose I'd be quite chuffed, but, gosh, you're not, are you?'

Their conversation rapidly changed, they calling into the hotel's lobby where Sam promptly ordered a cab, she first leaning forward, to scribe a brief message for Paula, to say:

"Hi, Paula,

James and I have left the remainder of our belongings in the honeymoon suite. We'll both   see   you upon our return … perhaps, tomorrow late afternoon? Hope that's okay?

By the way, thanks for the scrumptious food. We'll enjoy it all.

Lots of love from us to you, Adjo and Amy,

Sam xxx "

The receptionist tilted her head and glanced down at the hand written note. 'Are you really sure you both shall return all right, ma'am?' she asked with a slight frown, almost as if she could predict the future. She lifted up her eyes to stare: 'Take care, please, Mrs Samuels!'

It seemed strange to be known by her new married name, she naturally having taken James' last name, to proudly become hers – she felt happy to be a married woman, with a gold wedding band upon her slender ring finger. 'How odd! Why do you ask if we shall both return?' she quizzed, carefully watching for the woman's reaction, but, with a deadpan expression, the receptionist stated nothing more.

James, as they, back in their suite, picked up a few more bits and pieces, asked about the conversation with the receptionist; Samantha shrugged, telling him she had no clue concerning the woman's reaction, but then freed it from her mind.

'Do you know where it is we're actually going, Sam?' he questioned, raising his dark eyebrows. 'As you know, sweetheart, I'm hardly familiar with this area.' He wondered if it maybe a bit of a honeymoon surprise from her. 'So, go on; tell me, my princess.'

She shook her head. 'Just trust me, James. Okay?' An enigmatic smile crept across her mouth.

'Well, yes, fine, of course I'd normally completely trust you, Sam, but will you at least tell me where we are going?'

'Oh, all right. I thought, as a very special treat, maybe, as part of our Egyptian honeymoon, we should take a trip way beyond the mirage.' A tentative smile crept across her face. 'What do you reckon, eh?'

It was as if James' entire body gave an involuntary lurch. He half gulped upon his own saliva, it causing him to slightly cough; taking a step backwards, he recoiled from from her touch, but only briefly. 'Phew! Ooh, no ... I'm somewhat unsure about all such wacky stuff,' James stated. 'Listen, Sam, if you'd like to travel there while we're here, feel free, but definitely count me out. It's not for me ...' He, with sudden beads of perspiration glistening upon his brow, demonstrated great misgivings, with a compulsion to the point of beseeching her to exclude him. 'I shall stay on here, Sam; I will be quite content to remain in and around this hotel. I can take my sketch pad down to the beach; I'll really enjoy it.'

Sam exuded an optimistic attitude, with a hint of mischievousness, a playfulness his mother sorely lacked throughout his upbringing. 'Oh, darling, I thought as we're now husband and wife, to spend this one week together?'

With his arms folded, James was leaning against a wall, but transferred, flopping into a nearby sofa. He deeply frowned, firmly correcting how he was usually no coward, up for most challenges, but, being way beyond the mirage became a serious worry, definitely not his thing.

She shushed him, promising they should be fine. 'Awe, so are we both ready, James?'

He, considering the impulse of the entire strange trip, thought they, despite the heat, should be, metaphorically speaking, skating upon thin ice. James, mindlessly touching his own chest, thought seriously about his own cardiac issues; surely, Sam had not forgotten he suffered from more than simply a passionate heart, but he said nothing to be panicky. He knew he never went anywhere without his prescription medications which always offered a quick response; his GTN remained in one of his pockets, wherever he went. 'And we'll really only be away from here for only one night? You do promise me faithfully?'

Sam, tucking a stray piece of auburn hair behind her ear, gave him her word as she packed a few last minute essentials. 'So, are you coming with me, or not? Make your mind up.'

James suppressed an inward groan, pausing for a brief moment: 'All right.'

On their way out, in next to no time Abe Jacobs, the cab driver in the white Mercedes with its blacked out windows, raced from old Cairo; he, crunching along the gravel drive, pulled up with a screech outside the hotel. He, wearing a crisp white open neck shirt, grey slacks and a pair of designer trainers, greeted her, calling to ask: 'Did you order a taxi, Sam?'

James wondered how on earth he knew Sam's first name.

Sam, remembering Abe's name, too, explained: 'It's for my husband and me. We're on our honeymoon, you know?'

'That's lovely. Ooh, it's a long time since I was on my honeymoon. Anyway, you tell me how far you need to go. Then I'll take you, huh?'

Before she answered, her lips thinned; she mouthed in a low whisper, for Abe not to divulge how, during a previous trip in his cab, they romantically did not disappoint. It was easier for Sam to forget how to inhale her next breath than to obliterate the driver's caress from her mind. Through the softness of his kiss, their embracing became a little more than awesome as he rested her on his back seat: 'I am newly married now, Abe.'

He gave a wink in acknowledgement, he remembering her as his very own desert breeze. 'Mum's the word, huh, Samantha?'

James tightly squeezed Sam's hand, thinking for a moment or two. He whispered: 'Didn't you refuse this particular taxi driver when he turned up at the airport?'

Sam glanced sideways towards him, nodding a maybe; yet, there and then, she was informing the same driver they required to be taken as far as the camels and, agreeing a fair price, he, as per usual, asked which camels, for they were in Egypt with camels to spare!

'Jump in the back,' he told them with a broad grin: 'As you are honeymooners, sit close together on my cab's rear seat; cuddle up, if you so wish, but nothing more. Okay?' He grinned, saying to them both how, with the blacked out windows, no-one outside could see any of which they may cherish; he also remembered his brief relationship with Sam. Seeing her with James, he felt not a little envious. Abe threw his head back and chuckled. 'Now, Sam, you are remembering our past, eh? Hey, so, don't mind my feelings. All sorts happen in my cab, didn't it, Sam? You should jolly well know.' She became anxious the driver was on the brink of letting the cat out of the bag, of describing how he took her in an unlit area behind an hotel.

Sam smiled towards James.

'No, Sam.' James firmly shook his head. 'Not in here, not with him.' He was almost positive this was also the self same cab in which he travelled during his previous trip to Egypt, when he photographed the pyramids. Squeezing tight her hand, James seemed apprehensive, reasonably unsettled. He whispered to her how he was uncomfortable with it; he needed to turn back. 'Oh, Sam, let's stop it here,' he pleaded. 'I'm loathing this.'

Snuggling up close to James, thigh against thigh, Sam smiled, quietly reassuring him everything should be grand, just grand, for she travelled way beyond the mirage three previous times; all became hunkydory.

Abe, not unlike his namesake, the nice old Jew in Hatton Gardens, also offered a Mazel tov. Their bored driver stopped the vehicle with a usual tyre screech; he wearing long Middle Eastern attire, nipped out, opening his cab door, calling: 'This is about as far as you go with me … the camel-coloured camel you need is over there. See ?'

'Whatever happened to his shirt and trousers? How could he have changed his clothes? We never saw him …'

'Ask him.'

'No.' James shook his head. 'What the Dickens does he mean, Sam? He said about ''the camel-coloured camel'', but there are many, all waiting for tourists to take a fifteen-minute ride.'

Sam placed a comforting arm around James' shoulders, constantly still trying to reassure him.

'Which camel do we take? How shall we know which one? '

She smiled knowingly as they both mounted one particularly large camel. Her stomach seemed to lurch up into her throat as the lumbering beast rose to its feet, it briefly glancing at the master for whom it toiled. Gingerly, on the growling camel, the newly weds finally set off, she sitting behind her husband, her arms grabbing around his waist; as soon as he felt her arms around him, he waved aside all his worries, feeling protected and safe. However, they annoyingly made slow progress, finally reaching the ancient Needle's Eye. The cameleer's steady voice sounded weary as he told them how it was as far as they could go with him, too, he waving them a fond goodbye.

James, his eyes locked on hers, began to wonder about various issues: 'What about our passports, Sam?' he asked in a low whisper.

'Don't worry. I have them both with me; they're safe in my bag.' A giggle escaped before she could prevent it. 'There are no passports' controls around in these parts.'

Passing through the ancient Needle's Eye's stone arch, the intense sun almost resembled a burning ball, it floating mysteriously within the mists above the dusty town. From a whole jumble of higgledy-piggledy houses and a pile of building bricks, a teenage entrepreneur emerged with an overladen brown and grey donkey, to carry them along the last legs of their awesome journey.

James stroked, patting the neck of the ass. 'What do you call her?' he asked.

The lad smiled, telling him how the donkey was named Beauty. The teen frowned, he turning to Sam: 'I think I know you, pretty lady, don't I? You've been here before?'

Sam, opening her money purse, gave him the amount of shekels and more he required, replying how she travelled the same route several times.

'Yeah,' he commented. 'I thought so. However, this tall, dark and handsome young man who is with you – he hasn't been through the ancient Needle's Eye before? I don't think I know him ...'

'Oh, yes. He's a very fine artist.'

'Fancy?'

'Absolutely. His older brother is Elkanah.'

The lad frowned, thinking for a moment or two.

'Hey, come on. You surely must know him?'

He thought for a moment or two, wondering if perhaps he may have previously sold him some provisions.

Sam reminded him how Elkanah was back living with his mistress; 'She's Peninnah, the mother of his six kids.'

James' dark eyes widened; he was aghast, totally astounded, all the time declaring he never had a brother.

Nevertheless, he, suddenly unnerved, piped up, telling the lad the truth, stating how, like Samantha, he was an only child.

Shaking her head, she became adamant how it was on her journey to old Ramah they first met. 'His name's Eable; he now owns a stallion called Hunter.'

The weary donkey, in the meantime, tossed its head and whinnied, it being keen to be burden free. The youngster listened to Sam, he ignoring many of James' irritations.

James' jaw appeared to physically drop, an umpteen and one questions racing through his mind. 'Are you completely nuts, Sam? Have you finally taken leave of your senses?'

She half turned around to watch him as he incomprehensibly glared. He, a Londoner, demanded: 'Stop it ... do pack it in now! Only my middle name is Eable, as well you know.' The previously soothed away anxieties returned to startle him; worries dangled before him. The so-called dream honeymoon trip was, for him, fading fast, he feeling a great sorrow how he was not man enough to state a firm no to his Samantha. Watch out, girl, James thought, this worm can turn?

Enigmatically, she kept a silence until they were over the stony road; they passing by trailing vineyards, wild goats and unmade streets until they entered Ramah, an ancient town readily thrown into life. Raucous parakeets, green and long-tailed, swooped from tree to tree, revealing flashes of iridescent blue wings in their frantic flight.

Near the entrance of the guest annexe, she dismounted, although James simply stepped off from the ass; it becoming slightly burden free, was led to happily graze with other chummy donkeys in a nearby lush, green field.

Sam lifted a small, flat paving slab where she discovered the iron door key. Opening the only creaky door, she sighed: 'Here we are, James … at last!'

He, James remained half motionless, yet seeing the one-bedroom guest annexe as quite a pleasant little cottage, it was partly cared for between Elkanah and Eable, but neither lived there permanently. Elkanah, since his separation from his second wife, took up a residence with his nagging mistress. Artistic Eable, however, lived with their granddad Elihu, an old gentleman requiring some residential care. 'Aren't we actually trespassing? Shouldn't we be paying rent to someone, or other?'

Sam stared, virtually shrugging. She never bothered to do so before. 'Well, are you just going to stand there, or are you coming in, huh?' she asked.

'Gosh! I'm more than a bit bothered. Is it really okay to be in here? The way you simply walked in, well, you behaved almost as if this guest annexe actually belongs to us.'

'Well, I suppose it does in a way. Only for a wee while - as and when we need it.'

James, fishing around in the backpack for a small torch, asked about the electricity, he searching the wall for the light switch, to which Sam chortled. 'There are only candles in here.'

'Where are they, then?'

'You'll find them in the kitchenette, behind the curtain affair, under that Belfast sink.'

Sam hated Belfast sinks. They brought back childhood memories. As a kid, it was her task to scrub, to

Vim out the one in the family scullery. Once, when her mother was claiming to be unwell, Sam dodged the task, leaving it with a rim of scum; it was one of the rare times when she was about to be physically punished, over such a job. Her granddad, John-William, rose from his old leather armchair, stretching wide his arms: 'You stand behind me, Samantha girl, and my Daisy can't smack you.'

There, in the guest annexe, was an oblong, sturdy wooden table with two home made chairs, the seats being a little dusty. She, with her wet wipes, was able to clean them while James urged the water supply to run clear. Lighting a few large, fat candles and several t-lights, the kitchen sprang into view. Two small soup bowls, along with half of a dozen crude drinking vessels were available. Moving to the one and only bedroom, they gave sudden gasps of amazement; the wall over the only bed was pasted with a series of Polaroid photographs, taken during one of her previous visits; most were of her with Elkanah, Eable, and Todd. Artistic Eable copied some, drawn on pieces of paper ripped from the sketch book she gave him. Sam gazed at the stone wall as she saw herself, way beyond the mirage.

After the first shock, she declared: 'This is all a little mad, but, do you like those pictures of me? Eable sketched those. So, could they have been you, perhaps when you were a young art student? Maybe you did them?'

'You say Eable did it, but then you ask if … if it was me? You want to know if I pasted them up on the wall, or was it Eable's idea? Sam, the way in which you are thinking, I believe it's more than odd! I'm telling you, other folk, like, for instance, your own parents, would see you as delusional and, frankly, I wouldn't blame them.'

Sam could understand.

'I am no fool,' he lectured, 'no underachiever and I'd hate to be regarded as such.' He twigged he was coerced there because she wondered if that Eable and he were the same people, yet in differing times. 'Sam, is that it? Are you are trying to prove it by bringing me here?' It was strange the way James was speaking, of falsity, with a stronger emotion, but carefully controlled. 'Being here, I don't reckon it's going to worry me any more, sweetheart.' He momentarily left her suffocating embraces to walk across each rooms including the bathroom, to close every wooden shutter for, once the sun set, the place felt chilly; in the living room he bent to light the small log fire, it already left prepared.

'With Eable, I made love in this guest annexe,' Sam was in two minds as to whether or not to tell him.

'He queried: 'What about that Elkanah?'

She, as if a quietly soft music played in her own head, refused a reply. 'Anyway, now we're both here, let's concentrate on us; it's our honeymoon. Okay, James?'

He nodded, exhaling a long ragged sigh, half fascinated; he did love Sam, forever desiring her. He moved; she urged him so close. Breathing with an excitement, an exhilaration, Sam waited as he began to carry her to that only bed, to make love, but she tripped, catching her foot in one of the worn mats; she gasped. He had to prevent her from falling, quickly asking if she was all right.

'Yeah. Fine.'

'Sure?'

'I said so.' Sam felt almost coy as she contemplated the vivid, yet the exciting, of them on the bed. As she lay beside him, he momentarily moved aside, almost as if there became an intrusion; with his love, with his deep passion, he turned back to grip her into his arms.

'Ooh, Sam, this is magnificent. Previously, I was honestly scared witless ...'

'But now?'

'But now I'm okay we're here.'

Sam became delighted.

'You look truly wonderful,' he stated.

Before he again touched her, she felt it right to confess: 'I never really meant to call you "Eable" when we made love? It was honestly an embarrassing slip of the tongue ...'

'Forget it. I always reckoned you'd lied, edging your way out of an awkward corner.' James laughed, relieved to, at last, be told the truth. 'Changing the subject, after being here, it'll be strange to return back to the hotel, won't it?'

'I dropped a note to Paula, just to let her know, we shall be back tomorrow.'

'Whatever, I'm half quite glad we came, sweetheart. This really is some honeymoon, eh?'

It had gone midnight when they slipped beneath the sheet, comfortably sound asleep in each other's arms, in their own private world.

As per usual, when she previously stayed in the guest annexe, Eable, around six in the morning, checked on Hunter's welfare; Sam, however, would shop early in the farmers' market, a place for all groceries and provisions. However, when Sam returned with some essentials, James was still lying in the bed. He called for her to come immediately.

'Hey, not right now, Casanover! Listen, at least give me a chance to prepare us our breakfast,' she grinned, beginning to make some lemon tea for them both; she briefly crouched beside him, handing him his beaker, telling him to be careful as it was boiling hot. 'I am so hungry, James!' She knew he must be starving, too.

He seemed physically uncomfortable. 'I wish you hadn't been quite so long, Sam.' He asked her how long she was in the market.

She opened up the wooden shutters, seeing again the brightness of a lovely morning before thinking for a moment or two. 'Probably a little only over an hour. Why?'

Not fooling, James felt engulfed by the unusual environment.

'What's wrong?'

'Oh, I was suddenly feeling a bit scared to be left alone …' Before he could say any more, she was off into the kitchen, preparing their breakfast.

Sam yelled back through, she swankily broke some eggs into a bowl with one hand. 'Scrambled eggs on toast be all right? The eggs, butter and milk are lovely and fresh. I watched the loaf being taken from the baker's hot oven … hmm, it smelled divine.'

'Fantastic!' he called back, realising he needed to get up. 'I'm so hungry, I can hardly wait.'

As they sat together at the table, he only in shorts, they hungrily ate their food; he sat back in the chair, asking about the day looming ahead, of their plans to return back to the hotel.

'May I ask you something?'

'Sure.' Sam nodded: 'Anything.'

'When you were here before, did you ever get sick?'

Sam stopped to think for a moment or two before shaking her head. 'No. Why?'

James shrugged, grabbing another thick slice of the hot buttered toast before offering to clear the dishes, but Sam smiled, telling him to leave it with her. He agreed, dressing into his own clean shirt and jeans; he felt himself becoming a little tired, flopping on top of the sheet.

She washed up the basically crude dishes, leaving the kitchen spotless, for she was one who, like her parents, loathed an untidy mess of any kind. Opening their backpack, Sam asked: 'Do you want to pack up our belongings, or shall I?'

James looked unbelievably pale, he hugging his arms tightly around himself, as if he was cold, yet it became nicely warm. He usually kept his GTN spray close with him, either in a jacket or in his trouser pocket. 'It was lucky I remembered to bring it,' he remarked.

She watched him use it, feeling luck had nothing to do with it. 'Aren't you feeling so well?'

He smiled how that was the issue of being married to a nurse; he could hide little from her. 'Angel, don't start fussing over me. I only feel a tiny bit off colour, but I'll soon be fine.' He sprayed the GTN once more under his tongue. 'Yuck.' He declared: 'It tastes vile.'

Sam felt like no angel - more like the Angel of Death for bringing him way beyond the mirage. In that guest annexe she experienced a mixture of uselessness, guilt and fear; the remote dwelling was no place to become unwell.

'What, darling, do you think is wrong?' she quizzed. 'Perhaps you simply aren't use to this funny old place, eh? Could that be it?'

Before they left the hotel, James was unsure about being energised way beyond the mirage. He firmly decided, once back in London, he would be checked again by the Consultant, for maybe a round of cardiac tests, to make sure all was as it should be. In the meantime he should do his best to quieten himself.

She, for the first time in probably ages, prayed to God it would not become a serious cardiac issue. 'I thought you said your Consultant told you everything was all right. Gosh! James, is it your heart? You really have to say ...'

'I honestly don't know, Sam. I can't quite explain ... I don't think I ever felt like this before.'

Sam watched him rummaging around in a small pocket the backpack, searching for a second GTN medication; the first was showing empty. She pulled his wrist towards her, feeling his radial pulse, but his skin felt clammy; his lips and fingernails were slightly cyanosed. 'Phew! It's too stuffy in here,' he told her. His pulse felt a little rapid, but she thought it was because, even though he was doing his best to be calm, he was uptight.

She felt alone, so lonely as she watched him. Stating the plain obvious, Sam declared: 'What we need to do, is to get back to the hotel; all right?' She held him close to her, tight in her arms as his whole body tensed. She whispered, trying to encourage him to relax, but his fists clenched so tightly, his fingernails marked the palms of his hands.

'Relax, relax and try to breathe slowly, deeply,' she informed him. 'Oh, how I wished ... oh, I so regret bringing you here. I am so sorry, James. If only we'd remained in Alexandria ... this ... it's all my own stupid fault.'

Swiftly, it came to her mind how she had some aspirin in her bag. Normally, she only carried paracetamol, but, in her hurry to pack, she brought aspirin, plasters and along with basic medical items, too. Remembering how, when she was a third year student nurse, working in the Casualty Department, any patient having, or suspected of having a heart attack, was promptly prescribed two aspirin. It was worth a shot with James.

'Here,' she quickly remade some more lemon tea; blowing on it, she instructed him: 'take these two tablets. Come on and swallow these; I am sorry it's lemon tea, but it is a jolly sight safer than the local tap water … come on and get these down you.' She told him she would need to leave him for no more than a minute or two; she would get help.

She raced as fast as her legs would carry her, hoping to see the lad with the donkey, but he was no place to be found. Outside the heat was almost suffocating. Elkanah was her only chance ; outside, she saw a skinny young servant girl passing by. Sam stopped her in her tracks, grabbing the lass by the shoulders, which scared the youngster more than a little: 'You know Elkanah?'

'I do.'

'Okay, so run! Run as fast as you can up to Peninnah's house and bang hard, like crazy, to get Elkanah. Tell him … say: "Sammy needs you". Tell him it is a big emergency! Quickly! Shout to him at the top of your voice, yell so loudly. You understand?'

The girl nodded, ready to set off like a dog after a rabbit.

'Now. Run like the wind! Go on!' Sam loudly exclaimed before rushing back to James, holding him, rocking him in her arms like a kid who had a bad dream.

Within probably three minutes at the most, a breathless Elkanah exploded into the guest annexe. 'Sammy, my sweet pet! I didn't even know you were in here. Whatever is wrong?' Before she could reply, he glanced down at James, first thinking it was his younger brother. 'They are like two peas in a pod, aren't they?'

She nodded: 'Yeah. Never mind all that. Listen? We need help!'

'Anything for you, my lovely. You know it?'

'I need your horse … I need to get James out of here, to a Western Hospital!' She told him to be quick or her husband could worsen.

Elkanah bent to stare, frowning towards James. 'Taking you, chum, on my stallion could well shake you up a bit ...'

Sam interrupted, stating it was their only chance. 'James is well use to horses,' she told him. 'He also owns his own stallion.'

'Right. Best thing would be if I take you, Jamie, my friend, up on Hunter with me, for the stallion's strong enough to take us both. My own Huntsman is a little lame.' He turned to Samantha. 'Sammy, I now own a new chestnut mare; you can ride her as close to me as you dare, right by the side of us. When I have to leave the two of you, I'll bring back the two horses. I'll go to fetch them; therefore, be ready in five minutes at the most ...give me your wristwatch so I'll know the time.' He would not need to bother with the local sundial. 'Quickly!'

She, having given him more aspirin and he more GTN, carrying their backpacks, tried to get James to lean hard on her, but a giddiness coursed through him; tall, broad shouldered Elkanah was a young man, then as tough as any ox, he almost carrying James, helping him up onto Hunter's strong back.

They galloped west as fast as the two horses' legs would carry the three of them. Elkanah knew a short cut over a local farmer's lavender and poppy fields and he kicked and yelled at the animals to flee faster. 'I cannot come the whole way, for we are thousands of years apart, you'll remember? Try to visit me another time, if you can. Let me know how he gets on. Okay?'

Giving Elkanah her solemn word, the young honey-mooners somehow made it safely back through the ancient Needle's Eye upon a scorchingly hot August day; it was rush hour when the noisy traffic seemed to be coming in all directions. Sam, afraid, sat a tired James upon a nearby wooden seat, the sort of a bench one would usually find in a green and leafy London park.

She searched in vain for a cab, but, suddenly, seeing a cop car coming their way, she stepped off the curb, shouting, frantically waving her arms to flag it down, she pointing, indicating towards a tired James; a blue uniformed policeman in a black bulletproofed vest stopped his vehicle with a familiar screech from his tyres. Alighting, he raced across to ask: 'Everything okay with him, ma'am?'

With a look of despair and a ripple of guilt, Sam peered up at the tall, well made cop and, tears in her sad green eyes, sobbed, begging for his urgent help. 'Please, I desperately need you. My husband here has a heart condition; he is feeling very ill.'

He told Sam it would be faster for him to race them straight through to the hospital, rather than wait for an ambulance to arrive, he trying to give James every chance. They chased through a vast number of bumper to bumper vehicles, the cop car wailing, blue light flashing, he cursing at everyone in his way, drove them down town to the nearest to the nearest Casualty department in Ramah. Through his own walkie-talkie, he informed the hospital staff of his EDA., when to expect a James Eable Samuels. They were waiting for their patient. Belting through the hospital's swing doors, Sam yelled at the top of her voice how her husband was having heart issues.

A top casualty officer, the finest available, was waiting; everything else in the unit was stopped, all ready for James. Within seconds, it seemed, the love of her life was wearing a cotton gown, laying on a trolley behind green screens. One of the doctors immediately set up in James' arm an intravenous infusion and the crash team seemed to come from everywhere, all the seniors barking orders, they closing around him to assess the extensive amount of cardiac damage; tooth and nail, they, top notch, fought for his very life. For a while it seemed the fine team of medics were winning, yet James was persistently ashen grey. The odds for his recovery were shockingly slim – Samantha knew it was touch and go, how his life was hanging by a thin thread.

An attractive young staff nurse with a clip board took Sam aside into a small side room, to write down some personal details concerning James.

'Is my husband going to be all right?' she asked, almost gulping in a strangled voice, with a hundred and one questions pounding through her head, yet she seemed to forget them all.

The nurse gave a nod. 'Everyone is doing their best for your husband; you also did the right thing by giving him those aspirins,' she continued, doing her utmost to reassure Sam, stating how she probably saved his life.

'Perhaps, but those eggs we had for breakfast won't have helped his heart.'

'Who knows? There is no point in beating yourself up.'

Sam inwardly knew their being way beyond the mirage stressed James, yet she considered he would have been all right, even as she asked: 'When may I actually see him?'

'Soon, very soon, but not quite yet. I suggest you go and get something to eat, for you need to keep up your own strength for him.' She pointed, directing Sam to the hospital's cafeteria. 'I know you probably don't fancy anything much right now, but there's honestly absolutely nothing you can do here. Come back in a couple of hours …'

'That long?' Sam quizzed; she attempted to glance down at her wristwatch, but realised Elkanah borrowed it. She felt somewhat guilty even going off to eat, but she had nothing else to do; it might pass the time. She purchased a strong black coffee and a large cellophane wrapped cookie covered in white icing. She was about to search in her money purse for enough cash to pay when she heard a slightly familiar voice.

'Hello, again,' it queried. 'How's your man?'

'Ooh, it's you … you were the kind policeman who helped me to get my husband into this hospital.' She suddenly realised she never thanked him.

'Forget it. You had more than enough on your plate.'

'Even so, I am very grateful to you; I'm sorry, but I didn't catch your name.'

He told Sam he had not given it; he was PC Daniel Wiseman. 'Would you prefer to eat at my home, rather than hospital junk?'

Grim, Sam felt she needed to be very close to her James, but she thanked the cop for his kind offer.

PC Daniel took a paper serviette from the self service bar, to wrote down his personal 'phone number. 'If I can be of any help, let me know, I'd be only too pleased to do so.'

'I have no 'phone.'

'Oh, dear. You are in a bit of a pickle, aren't you?' He added how the hospital would ring for her if she needed help; she promised him she would try to remember.

James, so breathless, with an oxygen mask over his nose and mouth, had an electrocardiogram performed, followed by a portable chest X-ray. Everything seemed hunky-dory, so stable, allowing him to be moved from the Casualty Department into the Coronary Care Unit where he was continually wired up to an electrocardiogram monitor. However, in a short while, he became too breathless, perspiring, immediately taking a turn for the worst. Sam was rapidly instructed to wait outside, which scared her; she wondering whatever was happening. They started CPR. Another in the cardiac team was about to use the defibrillator upon him, he shouting: 'Charging ... clear!' James' limp body jumped due to the electrical shock. This was repeated three times, yet the monitor's screen showed a single solitary green line; there was no cardiac response. The medical staff worked so hard until, finally, shaking their heads, they pulled off their latex gloves, giving up on him, he to them being another statistic?

For the kind staff nurse who was supposed to have finished her eight hour shift two hours before, felt a young James to be more than only another hospital number; she would personally be the one to see the new widow, to explain about the death certificate, and so on.

Sam, spotting the nurse approaching from the full length of the corridor, sat and peered up at her, waiting for the fantastic news of her beloved, but the nurse, shaking her head, declared: 'I am so desperately sorry, Samantha.' She started, ready to hold Sam's hand, yet it was Sam who clutched at the nurse's arm, reading from the expression from her eyes, precisely what she was about to say, how they all did our very best for James, but ... but ...

Sam's sorrowful green eyes rolled heavenwards and then, dead beat, she shivered out a sob: 'No. Not James. It's not possible. He cannot be gone. Not him. Oh, no, no!' Sam choked, salty tears streaming down her tired face, how she really could not bear to even hear the words.

The nurse sympathetically asked if Sam had any friends or relatives nearby, folk who could help her.

Sam shook her head. 'Not locally.'

'What about Daniel?'

'Who?'

'My cousin... PC Daniel Wiseman. He was the policeman with you on James' admission.'

'Oh, yes. I forgot. I briefly met him again in the cafeteria, but actually I don't really know him at all.'

The staff nurse was doing her best, trying hard to say all the right words, yet no-one, nothing could bring James back.

Sam felt every sort of emotion, angry within her own self, believing all over again how she should never have brought him way beyond the mirage, thinking his death was her own idiotic fault. 'We were on our honeymoon, you know? We hadn't been married even a week,' she declared, but there was now nobody readily available to listen to all her woes.

Tears streamed down her tired face as she prayed God would hold him in the hollow of His hand, to allow the love of her life to rest in peace.

Somehow, a weary Samantha Samuels, choked up with a deep sadness, a gut wrenching sorrow, made it back all alone to the guest annexe, to try to clear up, to make sure the candles and the log fire were out, to collect their final belongings, hers and James'. However, Elkanah had already visited the place in advance. She found him quietly seated in the old, over stuffed bedroomed armchair.

'I presume he's still a patient in the hospital; how's he doing, Sammy? All right?'

'James,' she began before she shook her head: 'He … he didn't make it, Elkanah,' she told him. She, like Jesus of old, wept. She loudly sobbed in Elkanah's strong arms until it was as if there were no more tears to shed. 'We were on our honeymoon, you know ?'

'I didn't know you were even married. My word, he looked just like my young Eable; for a split second I thought he was my brother … I thought it was Eable in your arms.'

'I know.'

'Are you staying on here, Sammy?'

'Not this time, Elkanah, for there shall be a lot to do, what with flying his body home, perhaps an inquest and then a Catholic funeral, but you know me; I keep coming back all the time, don't I?'

Back to her solitary life, living in the Earls Court apartment, despair invariably gripped Sam and, for very many nights, she would regularly wake from a fitful sleep, feeling physically weak, until one day in 1972, then tired from travel, weary from the bewildered, sick from her bereavement and personally reaching out to the incomprehensible, she was told she was having James' child, a little one probably conceived during their honeymoon, perhaps on that hotel's four poster bed, but more likely in the guest annexe, as a memory of their love.

In the first few months of her pregnancy, Samantha felt somewhat dizzy, beginning to be sick. She, most mornings, craved either plates of porridge or salad cream sandwiches; like Hannah of old, when she was expecting Samuel and Paula, when she knew she was to have Amy, they were unable to face tea or other beverages, they only drinking either orange juice or cold cocoa. Sam's own pregnancy also seemed like a major miracle the first time she felt James' baby move inside her, a strange feeling of an invasion, another little joy inhabiting her body and she loved it. Lonely and alone, she then had no other half when she could say: 'Hey, come over here and feel this baby move!' Despite all her midwifery experience, Sam became frightened of the future labour, with the pain which might accompany it.

Nevertheless, Sam's pregnancy did not progress quite as easily as she hoped, she needing to spend sixteen long weeks upon bed rest. Eventually, allowed up and about, the Consultant Obstetrician palpated Sam's abdomen, he saying, unless anything unseen went wrong, she would be in line for a normal delivery,

It was a Friday morning, around about 6am in May. With a severe backache, Sam realised her contractions began in earnest; she needed a taxi, to race her to the Queen Charlotte's Maternity Hospital. The driver seemed to catch every red traffic light on the way. Within a few hours following her hospital admission, when she, alone, possessed no birthing partner and the contractions came thick and fast; with yet another hour of serious pushing, a beautiful baby, a precious little bundle yelled; when the large wall clock showed at 3.30pm he was joyfully placed in her welcomed arms.

The midwifery Sister smiled. 'Congratulations, Mrs Samuels, you have a gorgeous baby boy, a son.' Checking him, she declared: 'he is simply perfect!'

Weighing in at eight pounds, one ounce, a very much loved Henry James Samuels, to simply be known as 'Harry', yelled his way into this big old world of ours.

There was no James to give her a kiss, to hold his new baby boy, to rejoice in the joy of being a wee family unit. With salty tears, she was overcome by the whole emotional experience of suddenly being a young single mum.

There was, in the meantime, a soft thud as an aircraft's wheels hit the tarmac, followed by a shrill scream of breaks as the powerful jet decelerated down the runway at London's Heathrow. The long haul flight from hot Egypt's Alexandria was smoothly uneventful; the engines wound down to a muted whine as the plane wheeled off the runway before cruising to its allotted bay. Customary procedures completed, a cab brought Paula straight to the entrance of the maternity hospital, she armed with some duty frees.

'I simply had to come here today, Sam. It isn't any-where near visiting time, but, when I told the Sister how I'd just flown in from Egypt, she kindly let me in.'

'Ooh, Paula, I am more than delighted to see you ... you actually missed the birth, though.'

'Yeah. Sorry about all that.' As a long time nursing friend, she sat on the edge of Sam's hospital bed after they had hugged. 'Here, Sam. I have some duty frees. The shockingly expensive perfume is a gift for you, Sam, and the posh wine is all mine! I presume you are breast feeding, so you don't want booze to make Harry sloshed into a wino before his time, huh?' She laughed.

'I think I said something similar when Amy was born?'

'Probably.' She asked Sam about the labour: 'Terrible, was it?'

Sam shook her head. She watched Paula peeking at the little newborn. 'You'll be getting broody!'

'Never in a million years. I'm telling you, Sam, nothing Adjo says or does, shall ever persuade me to have another. One is enough!'

Sam offered a weak smile, knowing how baby Harry was obviously going to become an only child, too.

Overcome by the whole emotional experience of seeing Samantha, her then lonesome, yet best buddy, with beloved James' love child, Paula was pleased to have managed a visit.

Samantha's usually sparkling green eyes welled up, saying how she so missed James, especially at such a time.

Paula pulled up a nearby chair, took baby Harry in her arms and rocked him. 'Maybe,' she declared with a tearful smile, 'perhaps when your Harry and my Amy are all grown up, they'll fall madly passionately in love, marry and live happily ever after; what do you think about that, huh?'

'Well, it's quite a long shot,' Sam stated. 'But who knows the future? I certainly didn't.'

Chapter 19

The days wore on, each almost identical with the one before. Sam did her best to hide the persistent sorrow. Half lost in her thoughts, she remained baffled by widowhood; at her age, she saw it as meaningless. Daisy inadvertently remarked how few ordeals hit folk without a purpose; she should know, for her twin brother, a previous fighter pilot, became shot down by Hitler's lot. Losing James was a terrible blow to her reality, Sam tried to wish away the time of mourning, needing to become convinced by her mother's words. Left young with Harry to raise, she discovered being a lone parent was tough; in fact, life also seemed arduous. Not unlike Elkanah's Hannah, raising newborn Samuel, she half made up her own mind to remain home until the baby boy ate solid foods; before then, weary, it frequently felt she was trudging through treacle, with little energy to contemplate any removal. Daisy, Harry's doting grandmother, invariably baby sat, until one beautiful Sunday afternoon, that is. As a small family unit, Sam rejoined her parents, they sitting out in their familiar Wimbledon garden, enjoying an alfresco teatime. As Sam was about to top up her own teacup with boiling water, she wondered why her parents became unusually quiet, why they kept nudging, staring at each other; it became her father who chose to seemingly drop the proverbial bombshell. He had long taken early retirement from his old army regiment, yet, for Sam, she had little idea he was hankering to see out his golden days somewhere idyllically warm.

Henry, unless it was to do with his wartime experiences, was invariably a gentleman of few words; nevertheless, it was he who surprisingly began: 'As you may remember, Samantha, we've long thought about selling this old home?'

Sam, hearing baby Harry whimper, she picked him up in her motherly arms, experiencing the gentle warmth of his body against her own, to slowly rock him; she reached for a soft white shawl used for the Catholic baptism, it being the previous Sunday during Mass. 'I am listening, dad. Carry on.' What she was suddenly hearing from her own father, Sam hoped was only a pipe dream, for Wimbledon's Parkside became like an anchor for them all.

He, nevertheless, reckoned it was time to shake off emotional memories and concentrate upon the future. He stated: 'Well, it's obviously now far too large for simply your mother and me. Since poor old Grandpa died and you moved out, we seem to rattle around in the old place and, in another few years, I probably wouldn't be able to manage its upkeep, especially this large garden.' Henry's obsessional garden had long since become his pride and joy.

Sam quizzically asked if her house proud mother might soon then have her own way, of a pretty little two-bedroomed bungalow on the English south coast, a manageable place with constant sea views? Maybe, with a lap dog to pamper?

Her dad tilted his straw-coloured trilby and smiled: 'Well, no, Samantha, my darling daughter.'

'What then?'

' The long and short of it is, sweetheart, we've found ourselves a cash buyer.'

'You have? Already?' Sam narrowed her eyes. 'That was quick.'

'Yes, my girl. Not half. An estate agent visited us about a week ago; he was taking down lots of details and photographing the outside of this place, but, on Friday morning, he rang. The buyer is one of those new wealthy pop stars, a singer, cum, song writer who is living in an LA apartment right now. Now loving Wimbledon Common, she wants us out within six weeks, at the most.'

'Gosh!' Sam lifted her chin, not knowing whether or not to congratulate her parents or simply remain astonished; overwhelmed. she stared directly into the firmness of his Irish eyes. 'That's more than a bit soon, dad, isn't it?'

Shrugging away the indifference, Henry tried to focus more upon another cucumber sandwich; a wasp buzzed around, settling upon his first. 'I suppose it is a bit, yet, in these difficult financial days, I can't afford to look a gift horse in the mouth.'

Daisy and Henry lived together in their Wimbledon home from not long after the post war days.'Well, where shall you both go at such short notice? Not too far away, I hope.'

They had caught the vision of Malta.

Sam blinked. 'Malta.' It seemed absurd. Her green eyes widened, yet there was a stirring of resentment as her face became grim. 'You're kidding me, dad. Right?'

He remained deadly serious.

She turned her head slightly, to challenge: 'Whatever do you want to go there for?'

Before he again opened his mouth to reply, her mother chimed in, telling Sam, as a couple, they were sick to their back teeth of the damp, grey British weather; they desired somewhere gently warmer. 'We popped together, to the local reference library, to do our homework concerning the island; we are hoping the warm Mediterranean sun may also help your father's arthritis.'

Samantha and Paula, during their final student days, holidayed in Malta. 'I think you were sadly misinformed by its tourist board; I remember being told by an old Maltese nun how, during the months of July and August, even the locals couldn't cope with the heat ...' When she and Paula visited, it was a February; it was perishing cold and wet, even with flash floods. 'Paula nipped out to buy us both warm scarves.'

Daisy had pared an apple in half, offering Samantha a piece. 'Malta still cannot be worse than here.' She added how they planned to rent a little place until they could find the right apartment to buy.

'Young Harry and I shall never see you,' she stated, half mounting her protest, for she inwardly knew she would not have their regular help, their usual babysitting on tap.

'From Heathrow, as you know it's only about three and a half hours in the plane, Samantha. Once we've settled, visit us as often as you'd like.'

'Oh, and that's the other thing, mum ...' Sam stated, continuing her mini protest, 'I thought you were scared witless of flying. In the past you'd always refused to even go near an airport, let alone actually flying up in a plane ...'

Henry took upon one of his deep scowls, intervening, telling Sam to hush. 'We'll fly out Club Class and your mother shall be absolutely fine once she's actually up in the air, so shush, my girl, and leave well alone.'

'But, daddy ...' she started.

Her father's fixed gaze met hers, he promptly raising his index finger, demanding her to shush each time she attempted to speak. 'No. I don't wish to hear another peep out of you, for all you'll likely do, is to throw a spanner in the works, stressing your mother. Are you listening to me, young lady?'

Quietened, Sam handed the baby into his arms which he adored, she beginning to clear aside the tea plates, never wishing to upset her mother; despite her adult years, she was hearing her dad's commanding voice loud and clear.

Charles Samuels, her father-in-law, stunned by the loss of his Hannah, became heart broken by the untimely death of James; he would never forget the shocking moment when the local police, upon the say so from the British Embassy, informed him how his son, embalmed and in a zinc-lined coffin, was being flown home from Ramah. It was tough for the lone Sam, to not only wade through a Dickens of a mountain of red tape in a foreign land, but to deal with her lone guilt may remain forever.

After James' Catholic funeral, it was agreed between Charles and her to let The Gallery, to go into the hands of a local estate agent, he placing nearly any unsold art works into storage. Hunter was given away to a responsible horsey teenage girl, to love and care for the old grey stallion. Hardly exchanging two good words with Sam, Charles openly blamed her for his son's untimely death, he deciding to keep well away from both her and his bossy Tilly, the latter being given her marching orders. He, setting aside some packing boxes, came upon the additional decision to remove, lock, stock and barrel, to reside with his maiden sister in the south of Barcelona where he planned to erect his own art studio, he specialising in his wood engravings.

Sam, days later, watching dark clouds pursuing her, fled to shelter in The Gallery, just as the storm broke; she tried to state a fond farewell to her father-in-law, she feigning a smile, asking him: 'Won't you also miss seeing your grandson growing up, Charles?'

He, undaunted, briefly shrugged; with no tender mercy of forgiveness, he begrudgingly gave her the hint of a maybe nod. Nothing more.

Days later, Daisy noticed Sam's sad eyes, they usually bright green, like shards of a beautiful glass; they changed, looking tired. 'Only for tonight, Samantha, would you like to leave baby Harry with me, dear? It'd probably be one of your last chances to use me as a babysitter, that is, before we leave for Malta.'

Taking advantage of her mother's welcome offer, Sam decided to grab the opportunity, to cherish some precious moments of 'me time'. Instead of the usual quick in and out of the shower, she slid like a mermaid, luxuriating in a deep perfumed bubble bath right up to her chin. After a long, indulgence from a body soak, with the day fast fading, she dried herself before wrapping up in a white towelling robe; it was then the doorbell chimed. Not exactly thinking sweet and cheerful thoughts towards it, she disgruntled, wondered with some trepidation who it may be. Walking with bare feet, padding across the carpeted hall, Sam naturally headed for the door, peeping through its tiny spy hole; it magnified, she appeared startled as she saw Charles' face. Faltering between the temptation of either ignoring him or opening up only a fraction, she wondered if he had something to say before completing his packing, prior to leaving London for good, yet he might have first telephoned her.

'Oh, hi, Samantha,' he began with his deep voice. 'Am I actually disturbing you?'

Feeling it was perhaps pay back time, she replied with a curt: 'Yes.' She, disappointed, looked down at exactly as she was, someone fresh from the bath; tightening the belt of her white towelling robe, she ran her fingers through her untidy damp hair. 'Why have you chosen to come? Is something the matter?'

With a deep, but a calm voice, Charles blushed, calling through: 'Would it be all right if I came in, Samantha?' He reckoned it preferable than chatting to her than from outside? 'Do you mind awfully?'

She, with a defiance of reality, exaggerated a long, lingering sigh, deliberately loud enough for him to hear as she unlocked the door. She, dramatically, sighed a second time; stepping aside, he walked straight in. Arching up to his height, she permitted him to give her friendly pecks on her cheeks; he could not fail to noticed her pale porcelain features, her face devoid from make-up.

'You appear quite jaded,' he noted. 'Are you not feeling so well?'

Sam, with baby Harry at her parents' house, was hoping, for a change, for a full night's sleep, yet she wanted to say, 'Fine. Thank you for your concerns,' but, not even giving him a sage nod, no coherent answer, she strode along the hall, ushering him along into the living room. 'Please, do sit yourself down; anywhere, wherever you'll be comfortable.' She sat in a comfy armchair, it directly opposite to the sofa where he spread himself. It was about then her mind wandered, to gaze at the recent changes in him, at him being smooth and sophisticated in his appearance, at his shorter haircut, his flared blue jeans and a nondescript clean white shirt.

Seeing how weary Sam actually was, wearing nothing but flip-flops and a towelling robe, his expression became a mixture between concern and confusion, or that was how he seemed to her, he quizzed: 'Where you just off to bed?'

She, a recent partner by marriage in The Gallery, told him not quite, how she simply desired some lonesome 'me quiet time'; she, having previously, poured herself a small glass of Cava wine, politely asked if he, too, wanted something to drink.

Hesitating before refusing, he boringly reminded her how he was not too good with booze.

With her arms folded, she sighed yet all over again. 'I don't mean to be rude, Charles, but is this simply a social call, or what?'

'Sort of. To be utterly honest, I have actually visited here, to eat a large slice of humble pie,' he stated, 'to try to make my peace with you before I fly off to Spain.' Charles informed her how he thought about writing a letter to her, yet, rather than opting for his coward's way out, he figured it best to visit.

'Really?'

'Yeah. And now I've turned up at an awkward moment, it seems, eh?' He almost groaned as he spoke of his guilt, of their strained relationship. 'I need to say I'm sorry for being such a pig, for being so very horrid to you since our poor James died,' he softly corrected. 'After all, you'd lost him, too, hadn't you?'

His words began to unlocked a dam inside, she trying to stop the flow of tears. It took little to make her tearful; she was struggling not to weep all over again … especially not in front of him, perchance he attempted to console her.

'It's been truly a terrible time, hasn't it? We're both widowed now, eh?'

'Yes, but at least, Charles, I have your grandson, my James' child.'

He clasped his hands together; his mouth narrowed, as if he was half biting his lower lip. He, all in a rush, asked after Harry, if the baby was asleep in the next room; she told him no, how he was staying the night at her parents' place. 'My mother adores having him; the baby seems to love his granny, too.'

Charles, aware it was simply the two of them, became more relaxed before frowning. 'The last thing I wish to do is to upset you even more; please, promise me, for Pete's sake, don't blow a gasket …'

Oh, my! She thought, whatever is coming now?

He hesitated. Before making it abundantly clear how he did not set out to upset her, Charles confessed, sharing his thoughts; he wondered, from time to time, if baby Harry really was his grandson and not his own child.

'What?' Sam, startled by what she saw as an insult, stifled a sharp intake of breath. 'However did you arrive at such a wild conclusion?' Suddenly, enraged, her face was as dark as thunder, she ready to give him a piece of her mind.

'Samantha.' He paused, raising his hands in a mock surrender, his deep tone becoming serious, yet soft. 'Allow me to speak?'

She gestured a slight nod in an agreement.

'It's complicated.' He gulped, his Adam's apple showing up in his thin neck as he did. 'It's simply, oh, remember when we slept together, Samantha?'

Sam did.

'Well, you and I never used any protection, did we?'

'Ah, is that it?'

He nodded, stating how it played upon his mind.

Sam's eyes narrowed as she informed him how she and James also had the same, using no birth control, both before the wedding and during their brief honey-moon. 'Yet, oh, I neither know nor care; whatever, Harry is my beautiful son. I shall always try to do my utmost for him, to be a good mother.'

'Yes, indeed. And, so far, you've done a really fantastic job.' He lowered his dark eyes, quiet for only a moment or two, although the uncomfortable silence felt longer before he blurted out: 'Did you ever regret, Sam, letting me into your bed?'

She blushed. 'I suppose you needed to know about Eable, but you also fancied me, too, didn't you?' She nearly informed him how it caused a whopper of an argument between her and James, but she thought it unwise to dig up the messy past.

Everything for Sam, her whole world seemed to be changing at a reasonable rate. 'I suppose, Charles, you've heard about my parents?'

'How do you mean? What about them?'

She told him about their selling up the Wimbledon home, they removing permanently to the island of Malta.

He knew. 'Did you ever get to tell them about your time way beyond the …'

' … mirage?' Sam explained how her parents may have urged her into therapy, but she flatly refused, saying no, she taking a dim view of it maybe in her life; she had tangled therapy up with the then stigma of mental illness, refusing to unravel her life to a stranger with a college degree. 'I am well able to think things out for myself, you know? And can you imagine if I told them all I'd informed you about Eable, they'd believe I am a delusional fruit and nut case?'

Charles shrugged, staring her straight in the eye. 'Not if they saw some of the photographic evidence, huh?' He reckoned Henry and Daisy would only have needed to see the snaps about the toothless cameleer, about Hunter. Nothing more.

'Never. I shouldn't have kept those wretched photo-graphs, even letting you see them. If you hadn't, Charles perhaps you wouldn't have become so …'

'So fired up? Is that what you were about to say?' His eyebrows knitted together into a frown before pumping: 'I presume you since destroyed the others, eh?'

'I jolly well should have, but … but nope, I still have them.' Then she twigged, as if a light switched on inside her brain. 'Charles, tell me honestly, is that partly why you came here this evening?'

He stared, half beginning to stammer his words. 'How, how do you mean?'

'Ooh, come on; I actually think you know exactly what I'm saying?' She, no fool, leaned forward: 'Why not be up front with me now? Were you really here only to say you're sorry for previously being such a rotter to me, along with wondering about Harry's parentage, with all your so-called goodbyes, or …' Sam believed Charles secretly hoped to see those pictures again? 'Did you long for one more look, knowing where it may lead?'

Before he had any chance to speak up another reply, to half self justify himself, Sam shook her head, exhaling another one of her exaggerated sighs; from her own comfy seat, she lifted an index finger, asking him to stay put as she nipped through into her bedroom where she, framed in a soft light, delved through the neat pile of her various silks and lace undies; pulling out the blue envelope, she returned into the lounge, placing it into his lap. 'These what you're after?' she quizzed.

Looking up at her smiling green eyes, he took the envelope, his own dark eyes narrowing.

Sam flopped, to switch, to sit again yet beside him; her own breath almost shuddered as she watched his long masculine fingers trembling as he lifted the gummed flap, to reopen the envelope. 'Keep all of the pictures, if you wish, Charles? I couldn't care a toss.'

He glanced sideways to her. 'Are you absolutely sure?'

'Yeah. But only if you promise me one thing?'

'Oh, gosh! What's that, Samantha?'

'Promise me faithfully you'll never show another living soul, especially to my Harry when he is much older, particularly if anything untoward happens to me?'

In determination, he gave his solemn word. Like moths to a flame, Charles slowly leafed through each snap, homing in at her where she was with those ancient men, guys she forever loved. 'You, Samantha, are so gorgeous,' he told her, fingering the glossy images. 'So very lovely,' he whispered. 'My, those men were lucky fellows! I wish ... oh, there's no point in wishing, eh?'

Sam leaned forward, giving him a weak smile. 'You're really taken by all those stupid photographs, aren't you?'

He was loving seeing her. 'Now you and I are both free, I'm half hoping I wasn't going off to Spain ... at least, not permanently.'

'You and I maybe adults, now virtually living quite alone,' Samantha started, shaking her head, 'but, for me, it's all changed; I don't see myself as free and I won't live with you.' She explained how there could be no more physical relationships between them; they were in a different set up. 'It's all changed and, for me, it would become quite inappropriate.'

He frowned, ready to protest, telling her she was quite wrong.

Determined to interrupt, she wanted to have her say. 'You, through my marrying James, became my father-in-law; above all, you are also my Harry's granddad.'

Charles protested how James was never his birth son; he was actually told how the fellow's real father was from far off ancient times. Whatever, Sam tried to stick firmly to her guns, not encouraging him into her bedroom. Not again.

'Nevertheless, I could still do with your company, Samantha.'

Sam asked him if he really needed to go off to Spain?

Charles offered the briefest of nods.

After James died from his cardiac condition, she half vowed she would never sleep another man; definitely not Charles. Give him an inch, she thought, and he may take a mile!

He gathered up his precious photographic images, secreting them away inside his jacket's pocket.

Before Charles unexpectedly arrived at her London apartment, Sam poured herself a small glass of a white sparkling wine. She, peering into the glass, told him she wanted to finish it before it became room temperature. 'Let me pour you only a small white wine?' She did not enjoy drinking alone. 'Join me, eh?'

He, having sampled similar on a previous occasion, watched her pouring the nectar into a large glass, agreed as long as it really was only a little wine. She half grinned, emptying the bottle, seeing him raise the glass to his nose before it bursting with a fizz on his tongue; as he conveyed his gratitude, with an innocence of no wrong doing, the sparkling white wine left him unafraid, least of all wishing how he might enjoy her with a playful pleasure.

Clear headed, Sam declared, when she photographed way beyond the mirage, it was primarily to prove how she never simply imagined the ancient world; the glossy pictures were not initially meant there to switch on the likes of somebody like Charles, helped on by his unaccustomed alcohol, with the sensations it was creating. She so needed his arms around her, his lips upon hers, they tasting sweet from the wine; the space between them was minute, yet it felt as an empty annoyance. Sam, full to bursting with a love, he just might make her feel whole again, to becoming her saving grace; yet, with a fresh bout of tears pricking their eyes as they remembered their James, she, offered him a black coffee, causing to say how it was time for him to go home, for him to promptly leave. With his hand gripping upon the door handle, Charles bent to kiss her, thanking her for an unusually celibate evening.

A week later Paula telephoned. Listening to all Samantha's woes, she suggested she and Harry ought to abandon London altogether, taking up a permanent residence with them. She stated it would be good for a lonesome Amy to have another little friend around, but, with all the growing unrest in the Middle East, Adjo seriously considered selling their Alexandrian hotel. With his wife and daughter, he considered fleeing the country of his birth. Nevertheless, Sam did not wish to be an added burden to them. No. She decided to return to where she felt nothing but a very deep sense of a belonging, to spend time way beyond the mirage, at least until Harry became old enough to go of to school ... maybe to follow in Henry Webb's footsteps, to attending the Westminster School.

'Samantha, are you completely nuts?'

'Not at all. Why do you ask that?'

'You mustn't even contemplate such a rash thing,' Paula almost yelled a protest.'You dare not bring up a vulnerable toddler in that heaven forsaken hole ... think, Sam? You lost your James there during your honeymoon. What if baby Harry gets sick, too? It's totally insane. And, anyway, how shall you survive? Wherever you are, you need some sort of an income.'

'I do still have a goodly amount from my own inheritance money. I might also supplement my income by practising as a midwife; there shall also be servants to help me with Harry.'

'That's all well and good, but what if you fall head over heels in love again? What if you marry someone way beyond the mirage?'

Sam shook her head, she being as sorrowful as the days before. 'Marry? Me? No. Never!'

Paula declared: 'Never say: "Never".'

Chapter 20

Samantha resided within the upmarket area of London's Earls Court. When she seemed first missing from her friends and colleagues, but, above all, her parents, to way beyond the mirage, her mother's cleaning woman kept the apartment pristine; in her dad's way of expressing, it became all tickety-boo. Everywhere, with the help of Jenkins' elbow grease, the Victorian built home gleamed; it also had its distinct aroma from lavender furniture polish.

With her parents retiring to the Mediterranean island of Gozo, they ditching their original Maltese plan, Sam, dressed in a faded pair of denims, a T-shirt and a misshapen sloppy white cardigan, wondered if she may ever finish packing up her and Harry's stuff. Her task seemed endless.

The large dining room appeared sparse, with its only oil-on-canvas being James' painting. The art work, depicting Hunter, spoke of her late husband's talent; it previously fitted there. Nevertheless, down it came. Sam, fleetingly, speculated about giving it away to the present owner of the stallion, but no. With that, her Norman Hartnell bridal gown, a cream leather suite and a small telephone table, along with her silver cutlery and a miscellany of porcelain, it voiced not so much of her personal taste, but demonstrated her individuality. Alone, Sam briefly glanced out through the high sash window, it framed by heavy brocade drapes, they being purchased with some of her late granddad's inheritance. She decided to leave them up for the next tenant; to remove them, however, would become yet another job and a half.

Moment's later, her doorbell twice chimed, startling her. Sam, glancing at her wristwatch, thought: Must be the chap about buying my car. She was expecting a salesman, ready to buy from her. More than surprised, she had not expected the smiling Irishman she once knew well.

She had no knowledge he, Mick, was in London; Sam, for trivial small talk, politely asked after his parents. He told her he lost his dad, but, to make light of the sad circumstances, quickly stated his mother, remaining in Ireland's Balygar, was as fit as the proverbial fiddle. 'And yours? Still in Wimbledon, huh?'

'No.' She shook her head, telling him: 'They're in the throws of buying an apartment in Gozo.'

'Good grief!' Mick raised his eyebrows, showing a surprise, he remembering how Daisy dreaded any form of air travel. 'What about you, Sam? Why are you wanting to sell me your fabulous car?' Surely, he thought, someone like her, of all people, was not in a financial fix?

A quiet sigh escaped from her lips. He would be half blind to miss the packing cases. 'I'm moving right away from these parts.'

The big Irishman leaned back against a wall, motioning towards Sam, he keen for her to explain.

She suddenly felt apprehensive, but not for herself. She shifted uneasily before sitting on a nearby packing box. 'Ooh, it's a bit of a hot topic with my family ... with my best friend Paula, too. Even so, it's where I think I'll settle, where my baby boy and I probably belong?'

'Gosh! You're a mummy now, eh?' Mick frowned, thinking for a minute or two; from within his leather money wallet, he pulled out to hand her his impressively glossy business card. 'If you get in a pickle, contact me pronto.'

Thanking him, she glanced at it before popping it into her pocket. 'I truly won't forget.'

'I really do mean what I say. Change your mind about the future, Samantha, and, only if you want, that's where I shall be for you ... and, of course, for your kid, too.' He smiled, asking after her little one.

'Harry's fast asleep.' Sam brought a finger to her lips, to shush him. She led him across the hall and into the blue nursery, pointing to the white cot; gently pulling aside the little one's quilt, she told Mick how the baby definitely had the look of her late husband.

Mick stared, whispering: 'Ah, isn't Harry a little angel?' He remembered when he and Sam were together, but the whole issue of a family was never on the cards.

Sam smiled. 'Harry's no angel at two in the morning. Then, he's more like a fallen one!'

Mick straightened to his full height of six feet before turning to plead: 'Don't forget me, huh, Sam.'

'I won't,' she vowed. 'I cannot.'

He, forever remaining, stunned by Sam, kissed her upon either side of her face before, with all the car's necessary documentation, drove off through the streets of

London. With him still more than important to her, she, full of glassy tears, very nearly called off her trip to way beyond the mirage, but no, not to forsake her Elkanah for she loved her ancient fellow.

Sam retrieved the original bond from the landlord to whom she long paid the rent; Paula declined to keep her share and anything else of fine taste, advising her to place everything into storage, reminding her calmly how she, Sam, was behaving unhinged, how she was, in her view, making a terrible mistake. Paula, however, was not up for a quarrel, not after so many years of a special friendship. Even so, in a quandary, she was unable to understand as to what it was all about; why ever was Sam performing such a crazy task and with a young baby boy in tow, too?

Locking up for the final time, Sam declared it was for an overwhelming reason, to try to become the 'perfect mother' for Harry, to be true to herself, too.

Paula asked: 'You mean, you cannot be a good mum elsewhere?'

With only the very bare essentials she and baby Harry may require for their lengthy journey, they left at ten on a Tuesday morning; babies seem to need a whole heap of belongings, as every parent surely knows. She, carrying both her child and the cumbersome load, followed the usual rigmarole, energising themselves to finally reach the ancient Samaritan town of Ramah, it way beyond the mirage. The teenage owner of the over-laden grey and brown donkey did his uttermost to help Sam, yet, eventually leaving her and the whimpering, tired little one immediately outside the door of the guest annexe. She turned, asking the lad to hold Harry while she was about to squat to look beneath the nearby flag stone for the iron door key; it was then she heard a familiar welcoming voice, calling to her: 'Hello there, Sammy. Here, sweetheart, let me help you!' He took the baby from the youngster's arms.

'I'll be all right now,' Sam stated, turning to the willing teenager; she, opening her money purse, gave him more than enough shekels for his payment, along with a handsome tip. 'Thanks for everything; you really are a star!' Sam smiled: 'I think you must have rocked my baby to sleep.'

The owner of the donkey, he with younger brothers and sisters of his own, declared he had a way with tiny babies; blowing a kiss to Harry, he went on his way, along Ramah's main street, calling out, asking if anyone needed to buy his wares.

Sam turned to smile: 'Elkanah. Oh, wow! Am I pleased to see you. Phew! That was some long journey, all the way from London ... travelling by myself with my baby boy, too, I'm telling you, it was no easy trip.'

Elkanah peered in at the then sleeping child; naturally, realising Harry had to be James' offspring, he cuddled him. 'You don't mind my holding him?'

Sam gave a smiling nod. 'Any time, any where.'

'Oh, Sammy, isn't he a gorgeous little chap; he's going to look just like his late daddy, isn't he? You know, the same olive skin and dark hair ...'

'Yeah. Although, if you look in a mirror, my baby is your colouring, too. See?'

'I can see. Now then, how long are you staying here this time?' Before she had a chance to answer, he pleaded: 'Please, Sammy, don't tell me it's only another flying visit?'

'Not at all. I've actually sold up most of my belongings, for I am planning on being here quite a lot of years; at least, until my Harry is old enough to go away to school ... anyway, something like that.' Sam was anxious to move the little away from the sun's strong heat, to be in the cool.

Inside the guest annexe Harry was changed and settled on the only bed. She stared down at him, declaring: 'He cannot remain there for long; soon he'll be rolling off.' Sam told Elkanah: 'I'll have to rig up some sort of a cot side.'

'Fine, but then, Sammy, where shall you sleep?'

'Oh, don't worry about me? I can kip down in the lounge, to sleep on the couch.'

'Forever? No!' Elkanah deeply frowned, thinking, shaking his head before looking up and around at the old place; he remarked how the guest annexe, being so small, was certainly no place to raise her small boy. He suggested she removed into the big country house he once shared with his second wife Hannah. 'It's in a right old state just now. Shocking! Anyway, just you give me a few weeks and I'll make it into a little palace for you both.'

Sam's tired green eyes widened, she giving a gasp. 'Are you really sure, Elkanah? It'll mean a huge amount of expense ... more than I could afford right now.'

He waved a hand to pooh-pooh it. 'For you, my beloved Sammy, and now for our little Harry, nothing shall ever be too much trouble. Do you understand?'

The following evening Elkanah began to immediately make mental lists, stating how Harry would need only the best of nurseries, with the finest of nannies. 'You can have all the servants you need; we'll make the garden safe for Harry to play in, for, before you can say: "Jack Robinson", he'll be toddling around. Now, how do those arrangements sound to you, my sweetheart?'

Sam closed in on him, hugging him tight to her weary body, thanking him with one friendly kiss on his forehead. 'There's just something else, Elkanah, I really do need.'

He folded his arms. 'Anything for you, my pet. Simply say the word ...'

Any previous smile of hers promptly faded, Sam became unprepared to be pussy-footing around; she reaching to touch the side of his unshaven face. Deeply frowning, she asked: 'Well, the one thing I'd like you to do, is to ditch those wretched pictures of me, those of when I was without a stitch ... they are those Eable pasted on the bedroom wall, you know? I seriously don't want them there; just imagine, if one day our Harry saw them? He would more than loathe me for it.'

Briefly glancing towards the images and half chuckling, he reassured her: 'Don't concern yourself, Sammy. Believe me, it's as good as done. Okay?'

'By the way, speaking of Eable, where's your brother?' She speculated he must be living with Elihu, their old granddad; he often cared for the old man.

Elkanah, bracing himself, turned to slowly sit in a nearby rocking chair, he instantly becoming serious. 'No-one has the foggiest.'

Sitting to face him, she asked: 'Whatever do you mean by it?'

'Eable's definitely not anywhere in ancient Ramah. We local men banded together, searching high and low for him; he hasn't been anywhere near his horse for absolutely ages.'

'Awe, come on; he has to be some where?' She seemed unconvinced. 'He couldn't simply vanish into thin air?'

Before any more could be said, Harry began to murmur a whimper.

Elkanah hearing Sam sigh in a tired exasperation, asked if he may hold him? He leaned towards the babe, took the little one and, nestling him in his gentle arms, pushed back and forth, rocking, bending to give the little one pecks on the forehead. He gently, softly sang over and over:

'Row, row, row your boat

gently down the stream;

merrily, merrily, merrily, merrily!

Life is but a dream.'

Looking up, Elkanah declared: 'You know, with the issues regarding my brother, oh, Sammy, it's such a worrying matter.'

'Absolutely. So, who looks after Hunter?'

Sometimes the job fell to the stable lads, yet, eventually, both Elihu and Elkanah decided it ought to be given over to a horse-crazy teenager. 'The kid's the daughter of one of my top man servants ... she's passionate about Hunter.' He added how he wondered if the stallion, when it reared up, was too big and tough for her, yet they, along with a nanny goat, became a contented threesome.

How odd, Sam thought before asking if Eable might be down in Shiloh, but Elkanah told her no. 'He wasn't even over in Jerusalem.' He, pouring out his fears, sighed: 'This probably sounds more than a little strange, but, since the day your James sadly passed away, Eable seemed no more.'

'Seriously?'

He nodded, informing her how old Elihu had, despite a Kiddish, taken the loss very badly. 'The old guy, for weeks, despite his strong Jewish faith, was inconsolable.'

Gulping in a breath, Sam promised: 'I'll pop to see Elihu in a day, or so; I shall take the baby, to show him, eh?'

'Yeah. Granddad will really love that.'

Sam could not get Eable's name out of her head, invariably believing James and he were the self same, yet in different times. Maybe? She, unable to rapidly shake away her thoughts, became unusually quiet. Her voice almost croaked: 'I swore, after James died, I'd have done with travelling, how I would never visit this place ever again.'

His dark eyes narrowed, he wondering why she volunteered to turn up again in his old Ramah.

With her parents in Gozo, her father-in-law sharing his maiden sister's small apartment in Spain and her best friends in Egypt, Samantha had quite enough of London. She, exhaling a long breath from her lips, informed him with a softness, radiating more than a passion for him: 'I reckon, Elkanah, it's here, with you, my love, I feel a deep sense of belonging.'

'With me?' He felt touched by her words. 'Really?'

Sam braced herself, looking straight into his large eyes, loving him, longing to tell him, from the depths of her heart, all his ears needed to hear. Nodding, she then quizzed: 'As I am planning on staying for a lot of years, perhaps I could do some sort of work here way beyond the mirage … that is, once Harry is cared for by a good nanny?' She remembered how Adjo and Paula employed a nanny for young Amy which worked out simply fine; perhaps for Harry, too?

'Work?' Elkanah slapped his thigh, loudly chuckling. 'You, Sammy, working? Like doing what? Skivvying?'

'No.' Doing her best to keep a straight face, she told him how her working was not so funny. 'Actually, maybe I'd work as a midwife; what do you think then?'

'Ah, now that's a great idea! The one person old Ramah needs, is a fine midwife.' He remembered the day when Samantha helped his second wife deliver Samuel.

Sam frowned, wondering how to go about it.

'I dunno. Speak to our local doctor. Make an appointment with him; go to his office; find out what he thinks?'

'Soon.' Sam, only just having arrived, was desperate to first become settled. However, she thought she remembered the local doctor. 'Didn't he come to my surprise birthday party you and Eable arranged? He was in charge of that barbecue?'

'Yes. Fancy you remembering?'

Remembering? Sam remarked how the party was not so long before.

'Speaking of food, Sammy, you must be absolutely famished? Now, what do you fancy?'

Sam, ready to tuck into any available meal, was not fussy.

'Right. I shall see to it how there's plenty in your kitchen cupboards. I know I am hungry.' He told her Peninnah would soon have his big plate of beef stew on the table. 'I dare not be late or she becomes so cross … phew! What a nag?' He added: 'She's like a dripping tap!'

Elkanah had a great time, with a gargantuan purpose in his time, to resurrect the old country house. It all over again became a magnificent dwelling; its large garden sprang into new life, ideal for them all, especially for the fast growing Harry to enjoy. Elkanah instructed the gardener: 'I want the rose bushes pruned right back. The last thing I want is for Harry to prick himself on the thorns.'

Weeks later, after a siesta, Elkanah grabbed hold of Sam, dragging her by the hand. 'Come and see the lovely garden.' It was rich, being sweetly fragrant. He showed off one special corner where low box hedges were planted. 'I'm making a little maze for Harry. When our boy is old enough, he can have a bit of fun, running around, pretending to be lost in there; but, we'll still be able to keep a close eye on him.' He turned his face to her. 'What do you think about that, Sammy?'

'Ooh, thank you, my darling man. I absolutely love it.'

'Really and truly?'

'Of course.'

He told her it was such a joy.

Sam wondered why Elkanah did not do anything similar for Peninnah's kids, for they were the fruits of his loins; maybe it was advisable for her to keep her inquisitive nose out of it? 'My baby boy thinks of you as his daddy, you know?' She added how her little one loved him, 'just as if you were his father.'

'And you, Sammy, how do you think of me?'

'Me? Ooh, Elkanah, do you really need to ask me all over again?' Sam squeezed his hand as she dropped on a wooden bench, sitting close beside him. Her southern English voice was quietly gentle, like a still pool. She glanced, before smiling to confirm: 'Surely, you, by now, must know I love you, even more than the air I breathe?'

He did.

Sam and Harry removed, happily settling into their beautiful new abode; Elkanah became as proud as Punch, he strutting around, overseeing the workmanship. He would regularly check to see the servants were up to scratch; with him on tap, they were scared not to be up to par.

Harry became the light of Elkanah's life and vice versa. One early evening, nearing to Harry's first birthday, the little fellow was giggling, showing off his baby teeth. Elkanah started to count Harry's eight little milk teeth when Sam heard him shout an: 'Ouch!'

'Elkanah, whatever is the matter now?'

'Harry bit me!'

'Bit you with his milk teeth? Ooh, you're now being the big baby, huh?'

The little one began to mouth sounds like: 'mummy'. Elkanah was sitting, playing pat-a-cake, blowing raspberries and cooing at him; Harry giggled, blew a sloppy kiss, pointed and declared: 'Dadda!' Elkanah became quite choked up; he rapidly walked away, wishing to his God he really was his father.

Dressed in her only suitably smart garment in ivory, Sam walked along the gravel pathway before skirting around by pink hydrangeas, they edging up to the large square building housing the doctor's surgery. She sat, waiting in a sparse anteroom before being called to come through an office. She, he declared, appeared healthy enough. 'What's wrong?'

'Nothing,' she smiled. Without stepping upon any so-called midwifery toes, she requested: 'May I be

permitted to set up a practice as old Ramah's midwife?'
Before he could take a breath, she rattled off her London
qualifications, along with her post graduate
experiences.

He crestfallen, Doctor Eli Moses, told her about a
lifeless little bundle, it soon to lay in a family cut tomb.
He explained the child should have been a healthy kid
to a happy couple, but the umbilical cord was severed
before being twice clamped. 'Hence, the infant did not
make it.'

Sam gasped. 'That's truly awful.'

'Sure is. Anyway, rather than being a hands on
midwife, Mrs Samuels, train up those eager and willing
women who only named themselves "midwives", so
that, if the day comes for you to depart, you leave
behind a legacy of qualified women.' He wisely declared:
'Offer them a certificate, a sort of a carrot.'

Rounding up the local 'midwives', Samantha sometimes wondered what she had taken on; she offered
them an eight weeks' intensive course, providing study
notes, homework projects and practical assignments.
Only one woman dropped from the course as she
became pregnant. The day came when each graduated,
three with honours. The local lady mayoress gave a
lengthy, drawn out speech; the tall, slender doctor provided every woman, then each to be known as a 'Staff
Midwife', with a rolled up certificate, all beautifully
hand written upon parchment. The top three had gold
stars upon theirs. All the adults in the town turned out
for the auspicious occasion; every relative and close
female friend sat in their reserved front seats. Each
graduate was clapped; Sam was as proud as a mother
hen with her chicks. She, with Elkanah's permission,

gave a lavish garden party for the dignitaries, the graduates and their immediate families. Sam became heartily thanked. One midwife was chosen to give Samantha a bouquet of six white roses, which caused a lump in her throat; it reminded her of when James brought the same.

Sam, deciding to start up a small School of Midwifery, it became based in one of the surgery's side rooms. It soon flourished, but, with the wisdom from the doctor, she, finally backing off, handed over the reins to those top graduates, training them to instruct others in the skills of basic midwifery. There was such a well deserved puffed up pride among the Ramah women. The high standard of practical care meant live, clean, healthy babies and happy mothers.

Along with her son, Sam resided almost seven good years in the country house. Harry, with his own chestnut pony, thanks again to Elkanah's generosity, grew also into a healthy and happy lad, full of boyish fun, yet not without the occasional bit of mischief, for which he was disciplined in private; whenever he did well, he received outright praise. Nevertheless, she reckoned it was time to have him educated in England, a Western world yet unknown to him. Elkanah could hardly bear the separation; he fell to his knees, to hug the boy, just as if he was his own flesh and blood, until they needed to be physically prised apart. Sam faithfully promised they should be back one fine day, for way beyond the mirage became their home.

Elkanah escorted the two of them as far as the ancient Needle's Eye, where they were left for the willing cameleer to slowly take them to Abe Jacobs who drove the old white Mercedes cab with the blacked out windows. Sam needed to visit the British Embassy, to sort out a passport for her son. Harry, clasping tight to his mother's hand, pushing hard against her side, had never seen public transport, let alone a 'plane.

Adjo and Paula had, during the time Sam was away, sold up their Egyptian hotel and were delighted to be living near her own Taylor family, in leafy Surrey. Amy had started at a little co-educational prep school, demonstrating how she was exceedingly content. Their rambling Surrey house was no small affair; they welcomed Sam and Harry to live in their two story extension, a sort of a granny type apartment.

'Why don't you try to enrol Harry into the same school, Sam?' Adjo suggested. 'Paula and I are so pleased with Amy's academic progress. The Head Teacher, a firm Catholic, is a very nice family chap; I suggest you make an appointment with him? Give his secretary a phone call.'

Amy, who was earwigging, piped up: 'You, Harry, have to call the Head "sir" or he ticks you off.' She, a precocious child, added: 'If a grown-up walks into the classroom, we have to stand up until he tells us to sit again.'

The following afternoon Sam and Harry, he wearing some new western clothes, were shown around the small but well equipped classrooms, culminating in a semi formal chat in the Head Teacher's office, where they were made comfortable in armchairs; he sat back in his own black leather chair, quizzing the boy as to his reading ability, which was more than pleasing.

Away from the lad, he faced Samantha, adding: 'Just one thing, Mrs Samuels, you've probably discovered from Amy's parents, this is a Catholic run establishment?'

Sam had heard. 'My son and I are also Catholic.'

'Ah, that's grand. Your son was obviously baptised in the faith?'

'Oh, yes. When he was a baby.' Sam added how the boy was baptised in Wimbledon, where her own parents worshipped.

'It's simply that, apart from our morning assemblies, and so on, we have a nice visiting young priest who helps prepare the appropriate children for their first Holy Communion and Confirmation. Would you be all right with this for your boy?'

'Of course.'

'And your husband, too?'

She mindlessly fiddled with a crucifix and chain from around her neck, a small wedding gift from James. 'My husband passed away. It was his heart, you know; it was all before our boy was born.'

'I'm so sorry; I had no idea.' The Head frowned, offering his sincere apologies. 'It must be very difficult for you as a single parent?'

Sam slightly shrugged, explaining how time is a great healer, she trying to get on with the living; although, from time to time, she still carried the heavy weight of grief.

'Now, Henry,' the Head began, but the boy quietly corrected him, telling him he was known as Harry. 'All right, Harry,' he smiled, 'tell me the sort of things you enjoy.'

Harry, swamped by the large armchair and swinging his legs, stared at Sam. She nodded for him to speak up for himself. He thought for a moment before explaining: 'I liked riding my chestnut pony bareback. I can also make my own bow and arrow, to shoot wild rabbits for their skins and white meat, and, um, oh, yes, I could go fishing for wild salmon with my Uncle Elkanah.'

'Your uncle who?'

Sam did not flinch.

'My Uncle Elkanah. He taught me my sums, up to my twelve times tables, which I usually get right.'

'Wow! That's super, Harry?'

Harry giggled how it was. 'So, can I come to your school then, sir?'

Sir was wondering who someone by the name of Elkanah might be. However, loathed to display his ignorance, he stated: 'Well, I do have a place here for your son, Mrs Samuels, although,' he wittingly grinned, 'I shall have no rabbits for Harry to shoot!'

By the time Harry reached thirteen he was boarding at Westminster, he, following in his maternal grandfather's footsteps. During the sixth and upper sixth forms, when girls were allowed, Amy became a star pupil prior to her global gap year. Home again, a little more than a boy cum girl friendship began to blossom between the pair, more so during their three years at an Oxford college, an academic seat of learning where they read history.

It was over a morning coffee, Paula grinned, piping up, asking Sam: 'Do you remember way back, just after your Harry was born?'

' What about it?'

'I said to you, I wondered if our two kids might fall in love? Well?'

The parents' dreams became true when Adjo and Paula sent out wedding invitations to over three hundred guests, folk from Egypt, England and one from Ireland, requesting them to attend the marriage of their only daughter Amy Rebecca Helen, to Henry James Samuels, only son of Samantha Anne Samuels, at 2pm on Saturday, 10th. September, 1994, at Westminster Cathedral, and afterwards at Claridges, Mayfair.

Amy appeared in the majestic Catholic Cathedral as a million dollars; in dazzling virginal white, she also took toppers and tailed Harry's breath away. Adjo, equally proud of his gorgeous wife, the Mother of the bride, he gave away his daughter, yet not without choking back his own paternal tears.

With a sparkling finish of glamour, Samantha Anne Samuels, she being the elegant Mother of the groom, wore a classic floral lace fit and flare dress in navy, sequin embellished with a swirl around the hemline; she carried a matching clutch bag, partly covered by a single white rose. Her shining auburn hair and subtle make-up became impeccable – she, naturally, wore those little pearl studs, a twenty-first gift from her own parents. How she wished James could have physically attended, yet, like Elkanah, it was not to be.

Throughout the no holes barred wedding reception, with the most exquisite of cuisine and Champagne, along with prolonged speeches, the radiant couple took to the floor; the lights dimmed and the enticing music quietened to begin a Viennese waltz. Everyone seemed to be in a pair, except for Sam. She felt like a fish out of water, until a gentle Irishman, handsome in his grey toppers and tails positioned himself before her. A sea-soned friend of Paula, it was not a surprise for Mick to be chosen as one of the ushers. Astonished, Sam heard him; wide-eyed she saw him reaching down for her. Breathlessly, she marvelled, longing to be in his arms, to dance the night away. Not unlike a love-sick teenager might, her heart leapt when she heard him asking: 'Sam, will you do me the great honour? May I have this dance, please?'

'Thank you, kind sir.' She beamed: 'I'd be more than delighted.'

A then fool, Sam was the one who broke their engagement; was it approximately twenty-five years before? Maybe. As with the pretty engagement ring she returned, he treated like a priceless treasure. Now, they were moving, smooching together across the dance floor, she with Mick, being reminded how she, Samantha, was the beautiful image he adored. 'The last time we met, my little darling, I bought your car. Harry was then a sleeping baby in a cot. Remember?'

'I remember just fine. And now he's all grown, a perfectly wonderful young man; and today it is Harry's wedding to his beautiful Amy?' A happy tear escaped, running down Sam's cheek.

Mick, only very slightly greying at the temples of his hair, kissed the happy tear away; he knew from Paula, Sam never remarried. He told her he always remained a single bloke, confessing how he was still waiting for her: 'Sam, without you, my whole world is nothing but a faded image.'

She quietly giggled; 'Now, isn't that a touch of the blarney, eh?'

'Blarney? Not at all!' She detected, as they slowly moved around the dance floor, his making her skin to tingle down to her toes, but, passionately remembering her beloved Elkanah, she felt marooned betwixt the sophisticated and the ancient.

'If ever you change your mind, darling, Paula has my new address.'

Sam, in almost a whisper, spoke the possibility: 'You'll find someone else.'

As the music ceased, every gentleman clapped his partner. Mick stood facing her, shaking his head. 'I won't, you know?'

Sam, constant to her promise, proceeded to ancient Ramah where she perceived an ocean sense of belonging, way beyond the mirage. She, along with Harry throughout his formative years, inhabited the unadulterated luxury of Elkanah's country house, they enjoying the beautifully manicured garden. After the dreadful passing of her beloved James, she half-heartedly vowed not to love another; she was, however, informed by Paula: 'Never say: "Never" !'

The returned journey to way beyond the mirage, for Sam, became arduous.

After flying from London's Heathrow to Egypt's Alexandria, she spied a wearisome and ageing Abe, he seated into his white Mercedes with its blacked out windows, became parked into the taxi rank. Claiming he'd just motored from old Cairo, the guy believed she probably required his services. 'Where, my pet, do you need to go today?' he asked, simply as if he had no idea regarding her excursion.

Passed caring concerning being known as his pet, Sam informed him she needed a fifteen-minute camel ride, being where the one camel separates itself from the others, to which he predictably declared with a lingering sigh escaping from his lips: 'This is Egypt, with camels to spare.'

Sam, ensconced, settled in the passenger seat, she opened her money purse, to give him the shekels he usually required. 'Listen, Sam? I'll only need enough money to cover for my petrol,' he quietly stated. 'Put such a lot of cash away; you may be needing it.'

Throughout the lengthy taxi ride, Sam was amazed Abe kept his hands to himself, surprisingly showing no interest in her nearest thigh. After approximately so many years of abstinence, perhaps neither he nor she were spring chickens? Whatever, it remained a lengthy excursion. At her destination, she was left by him, to hunt out the old toothless cameleer, but it was a younger chap, about Harry's age, who stated behind his small beard, how his father passed away. 'Our time of mourning is now officially over, yet I still miss my dad.'

Shading from the brilliance of the sun, Sam again became mesmerised by the awesome sight of the silvery mirage spreading across its desert horizon. However, she confessed to the new cameleer her deep, dark sorrow concerning his loss, to which he sweetly thanked her.

'Anyway, lady, it's now my task to be a cameleer.' He stated: 'I'll take you on my camel; you still need the Needle's Eye, huh?'

Samantha did.

'Fair enough. Here we go!'

Forever saddle sore, she passed through the Needle's Eye and, being clouted in the back by a large tumble weed which still gave her a sudden fright, it was the time for Sam to search out for the young entrepreneur with the over laden donkey. Where was he, she wondered?

'Hello, pretty lady.' Sam heard a deep, masculine voice. The delightful sixteen year old teenager was all grown up, he having become a bearded thirty-eight year old, happily married, he with a second baby on the way. 'How's your baby boy doing?' he quizzed. 'He was called Harry, huh?'

Sam quietly smiled. 'My baby boy is now twenty-two; he recently married a very lovely young woman. Her name is Amy – she's the only daughter of two of my very best friends.'

'Wow! Time flies, eh?'

'You're telling me!'

He explained how the present donkey was his second. 'How long, lady, have you been away from ancient Ramah?'

Sam, with a contented mind, thought as they travelled on, drifted for a moment or two. 'You know, I actually left old Ramah just over fifteen years ago, but, hey ho, I faithfully promised my Elkanah I'd be back; today, I shall please him, giving him the surprise of his life.' She half closed her Irish green eyes, remembering the tranquil peace of his pretty garden, the little oasis which seemed to kiss heaven.

He, the donkey owner, seemed to be waiting for the right moment to break some news. Any broad smile he previously wore, rapidly disappeared from his olive skinned face. Telling Sam his first name was Noah, he strongly advised: 'You'll need to be staying in the the guest annexe?'

'No.' Sam frowned, shaking her head. 'I shall be visiting Elkanah in his big country house.'

'Forgive my saying so, but, unless you have a door key to the big old house, you'd be better off going straight into the guest annexe.'

Sam, with previously a stirring of joy, wondered why.

Noah briefly tethered the animal near some lush grass, to temporally graze; he gestured, asking her to briefly dismount, to set aside her backpack, to sit herself upon a flat stone by that quiet roadside. 'Whatever is wrong?' Sam's happiness, her joyfulness vanished within a heart beat; she felt unbelievably anxious, desperately needing to know whatever was amiss.

The man, sitting reasonably close, reached to clasp her hands, but as in a parental friendship; yet, she knew his words, gentle or otherwise, might sting her. There was nothing to it; Sam needed the truth.

She and Elkanah, they widowed, acknowledged their undying love for one and another; ecstatic and, more than only friends, Sam, living way beyond the mirage, was deliriously blessed by Elkanah, loving him, cherishing him. Between them became a deep loving bond, a comfy companionship, a beautiful friendship when they enjoyed happy hours together; Elkanah loved the air she and Harry breathed. The once crafty fellow who, then young and lusting after her, remained, throughout his middle years, as simply thoroughly grand, just grand.

She hoped and prayed they should never be parted … never, for she deeply loved him. Samantha planned to remain as a woman, requiring nothing and no-one more than her beloved Elkanah. Now, it remained too late; he was gone.

Sam wept.

She could hardly comprehend young Noah's gentle words, he telling her how, one year previously the life left him; a peaceful Elkanah died. He was, as tradition would demand, placed in his family cut tomb in

Ramathaim Zuphim; his spiced body remained up in the hills, overlooking his old Ramah, where the mourners spoke the last words of the Kaddish: translated into English it declared: 'May He bring peace upon us, and all Israel. Amen.' As if embracing him still, Sam located some stones for him, remembering how it must be. She sang as he gently did when rocking their baby Harry:

> 'Row, row, row your boat
> gently down the stream;
> merrily, merrily, merrily, merrily!
> Life is but a dream.
> Good night, Elkanah. I'll miss you.'

Homesick, weeping softly and kicking her heels, some fifteen months later, Samantha decided to pack up her belongings all over again, to return back to England. After the usual rigmarole to quit herself from way beyond the mirage, she lounged back, looking through the plane's window, viewing the London's lights below. Touching down into Heathrow, she remembered the terrible sadness concerning Elkanah, but, with an excitement, to be seeing Harry, Amy, their new baby girl and along with those she knew and loved.

Back upon British soil, Sam wondered if she would again see Mick? Would she discover that special vacancy in his Irish arms? Had he, after all his years of stipulations, of his promises, waited for her?

THE END

Biography

Janice S Lockwood is the sole author of " Way Beyond The Mirage". As an accomplished writer, this is, however, her first completed novel.

Previous published works by her include:

'When Iron Gates Yield To Freedom', an autobiography'. (Ghost written): published by Grosvenor House Publishing Ltd. 2014

'Costly Roots', an autobiography written under the pseudonym of Sarah Cohen and published by Crossbridge.

Other booklets and commissioned articles, both here in the UK and in the USA were published, not least for EWTN's 'The Journey Home'. For her writings, a special award was given in Florida.

Widowed since 2008, she, also an accomplished artist, has three awesome sons, one of whom is sadly missing following an air disaster; she is now a doting granny to Daniel. Residing in North Wales, Janice S Lockwood is still trying to discover the meaning of 'retirement'.

Acknowledgement

Many thanks to Matthew N Bradley for giving up some of his valuable time and effort in the preparation of this my novel.